SIRED BY STONE

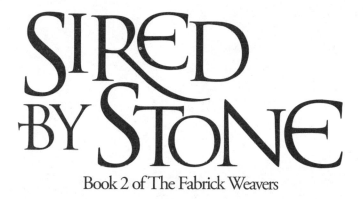

SIRED BY STONE

Book 2 of The Fabrick Weavers

ANDREW POST

MEDALLION
P R E S S

Medallion Press, Inc.
Printed in USA

Dedication

For Traci

Published 2015 by Medallion Press, Inc.

The MEDALLION PRESS LOGO
is a registered trademark of Medallion Press, Inc.

Copyright © 2015 by Andrew Post
Cover design by Patrick Reilly
Edited by Emily Steele

Typeset in Hoefler Text
Printed in the United States of America
ISBN 978-1-60542-606-8

10 9 8 7 6 5 4 3 2 1
First Edition

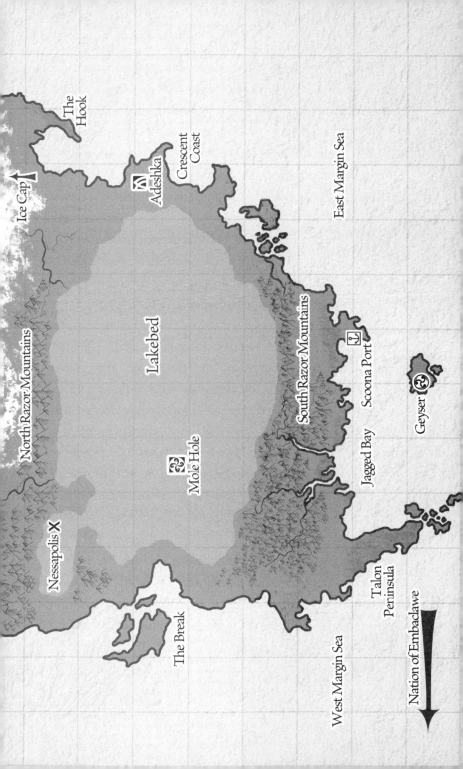

Map of Embaclawe

PROLOGUE

Changing Spots

Adeshka: three hundred square miles of stone and steel kept standing by grime and stink. *Ugh, it just had to be here.*

Before stepping off the curb, Margaret Mallencroix pressed her mask to secure the seals. She couldn't imagine going around without filtration. The air was faintly green, and even with the mask on, the city's reek slithered in. Garbage juice, burning tires.

Autos treated the traffic lights as suggestions. Once in the street, she could go barely more than a step without a vehicle barreling past. She felt invisible, which she wouldn't mind if she weren't bumped so often.

Hasty pedestrians wore a mad kaleidoscope of clothing: spider-silk robes open to reveal deflector vests, taped boiled leather, chainmail hoods paired with slippery satin tracksuits. Some, either brave or daft, walked the rubbish-sprinkled streets barefoot.

Someone jostled her again.

Yes, I do hate this city, Margaret decided.

The bumper of an auto nearly introduced itself to her knees, and her gasp came out of the respirator as a honk. She gave the driver a not-very-nice gesture, which was returned in kind, and splashed on through deceptively deep puddles to the far curb.

She missed Geyser. People were generally pleasant, and the air didn't smell like a stew of exhaust and sickness. Plus you could actually see the sky, not just a basket weave of wires and pipes overhead. All streets in her home city, reaching from the square like spokes of a wheel, offered a view of the horizon: on a clear day, Jagged Bay in its white-capping splendor, the mist-hugged mountains on the mainland. Wondrous. But so far away now.

Finally, she made it. In buzzing neon: The Bejeweled Talon Pub.

Stepping inside, she felt as if that choking churn of Lowtown Adeshka had spat her free. Her ears rang in the sudden quiet, all conversation paused. Unable to discern how many people were actually here within the smoky murk, Margaret forced a confident stride.

When something warm drew a line down her neck, she clapped a hand over it. She wondered for a moment if it was raining here inside but noticed the volume of hunched Cynoscions bellied up to the bar, clutching flagons in their small, nimble pincers. They'd halt drinking on occasion to crane back, eye-stalks angling upward, and breathe deep the misty air. The stuff must've carried vapors of home, just as a salty breeze would've brought Geyser to Margaret right about now.

High on the wall, ethereal blue holodigits displayed the time for every major territory on Gleese. She was pleasantly surprised to see she was early. She'd gotten lost several times since the port. One particular set of digits yelled out to her—those giving the time for the Lakebed. Barely morning there, where Clyde was. *Please be okay* . . .

Continuing, she snapped off her respirator, let it dangle around her neck, and was shocked by the state of its filters. A single hour's walk and the once-white cotton had been stained to muddy brown. *Well, better than your lungs.*

Flinging her cloak over one shoulder, she passed the row of booths set into alcoves along the back. Each had a pinch of privacy. The ghostly-glowing beaded curtains rattled like dry bones as she brushed through them.

She looked in on the cozy little cubby. Lush red leather hooked around a knife-gouged table. Words flicked above in the vacant space. In holoscript: Reserved for Coog McPhearson.

The defector pirate made reservations. Quite the gentleman.

Letting the curtain fall back, she had a seat, removed her engagement ring, and pocketed it. With it, she put away Margaret Mallencroix and became Nevele once more, and waited.

An hour later, Nevele dropped a palm to the grubby tabletop, pinning the plastic coins.

The pirate observed her hand, then trailed his gaze up the rest of her, taking note of her arm. Coog's jaundice-yellow eyes bulged.

She knew how it looked—it being her arm and all—a map of interweaving cuts stitched with twine, string, and dark thread. Odd, sure. She was still getting used to her fabrick. Had been for over twenty years. But to someone who'd never seen her, she looked like she'd been flung into the engine air intake of a starship. If they only knew.

"Fifty spots, as requested," she said.

"Well, I'm not so sure."

"Either you're talking or you're not."

"Aye, but it's of *Geyser* minting," he whined, sitting back. "What'm I suppose to do with that shite?"

"Have it changed," she said, nodding toward the pub's far corner.

While waiting for him to arrive, she'd watched people sulkily approach the Flashcraft with all sorts of things: old clothes, dinnerware, batteries filched from autos. After the machine ran a flickering pulse over the offering, it absorbed it with a *flimp*, and spewed forth its worth in Adeshka coinage, rattling like a machinegun. Or, if you preferred, the instapawn machine could rematerialize something of equal value: interstellar passports, self-cooking meals, clothes, guns. Most preferred the cold, hard coin.

The traitor pirate turned back, trying to contain a smile. No doubt seeing the instapawn, haloed by the fug, was like stumbling upon the end of the rainbow, its golden bounty *so close*. After all, fifty spots of Geyser coin changed to Adeshka currency would fetch a decent haul. Might even come out ahead.

"Sold." Through the bottles he'd accumulated during their haggle, his greasy fingers reached hers, which she kept pressed flat.

With a malignant twinkle in his eye, the same that all creepy men use thinking it makes them charming, Coog stroked her thumb. "Cold feet?"

"Info first."

The waitress clattered through the beaded curtain. Tattoos raced down the sinewy arm that delivered another bottle of Lenny's Pale Ale.

Before she slipped off, Coog grabbed the woman's

wrist. "Hold up. You got chark bars here?"

"Not on hand. Might check that thing over there." She indicated the instapawn with a sidelong nod and, with a shrug, pulled herself free. "And anything else . . . besides the water for you, miss?" She'd hesitated—must've really *looked* at Nevele this time.

Nevele fixed her gaze on Coog. "No."

Despite the shouts for beverages, the waitress lingered. From her periphery, Nevele confirmed she was making that face they always did: dead-eyed gawping as if she were a bad auto wreck.

"Take a picture."

The waitress choked on an apology, mumbled something about good night because her shift was over, and was off.

"Rude lass," Coog said, the curtain swaying. "Personally, I like my beauties with a few dents in the fenders. Truth, I *prefer* them to—"

"Info."

His laugh was like a horse choking on a brick. "You know, I could just lie. Tell you *any* day and time."

"Oh, I have faith in you." Due to the stitches, her smile—even when faked—was a little crooked.

"That's sweet o' you. But why's that, love? Been told I don't possess what you'd call a real trustworthy look." He stroked her hand again.

"Why? Because right now you can feel something crawling up your left trouser leg . . ."

His smile collapsed, thumb stilled. "Eh?"

"You figured it was probably an itch brought on by bone worms or something, but this? This feels different, doesn't it?"

Coog's face fell further.

Nevele's too, except literally—her stitches were gone from her cheek. The skin panels detached as she urged the threads down the tributaries of cuts on her neck, her left shoulder and arm, into her free hand under the table, then out, around the table's legs and up the pirate's.

Each string was a raw crawling nerve, her cartographers mapping by curious touch. His legs were scabby. Here and there, weeping bandages. She stopped only when one of Coog's eyes involuntarily squinted, twitchy.

"So if you fancy leaving with all of yourself intact," she said, "I'd recommend not fibbing. I have an ear for it."

He took his hand off hers. Finally. "They're planning an attack. Got a warhead. From the Mole Hole armory last year." He attempted a nonchalant sip of beer, but the bottle's dregs sloshed in his grasp. He pushed it aside, movements both tight and tremulous.

"What sort of warhead?" She had a slight lisp now with her bottom lip coming unmoored. A sharp nod swung a banner of auburn hair forward.

"A big one."

"And what's their intent?"

"Remodel the guest bathroom. What do you *think* they'd do with a warhead?"

She gave him a warning squeeze.

Coog didn't shout, but his cheeks grew pink. "They're going to topple Geyser," he quickly elaborated. "Not so hard, eh? Those don't grow back, you know."

"Don't you shites ever get bored of killing innocent people?"

"It's not for sport this time. We—they, I mean—have Gorett now. And the good king—wouldn't you know it, the generous wank—promised them the wendal stone. Half the deposit, fifty-fifty."

"It's not his to give. Tell me their plan, or I'll return the money to my bag and be on my merry way—with a set of new additions." Squeeze.

"All right. Bloody hell, all right. They got drills and the rest o' the gear ready, okay? And snapping Geyser off its stem would make it easier to get at. Just go straight down, drag it out. That's what the warhead's for. Like you'd blast-mine, except . . . bigger."

"And after? Can't take a deposit that size anywhere expecting to get it appraised—let alone sold off—without raising the alarm. They'd know precisely where it came from."

He shook his head, sweat dotting the table in small foggy hemispheres. "They're not getting it appraised. Or selling it. They want to *use* it."

"For what? Prop open an enormous door somewhere?"

"To make weavers. Now if you'd just ease up—"

"What?" Just for suggesting such an absurd thing, another squeeze. "Go ahead. Give me your best explanation as to how *your friends* could possibly make weavers using wendal stone."

"Think about it." Coog mopped his brow with a cuff. "Why do so many o' you pop up in Geyser? Something's in the water."

Flam's uncle Greenspire had claimed a similar thing. And it was—according to the old Mouflon—how one Blatta had been able to give live birth. Man and insect spending so much time together in shared proximity to the deposit, living right on top of it for generations. But she'd never really believed it, since this was coming from a Mouflon whose mind had been chewed by cabin fever—or cavern fever, as it were.

But even if it did sound impossible, wendal stone's properties had hardly been studied. It was valuable in its rarity. Never had she heard any other reason to covet it.

"Hypothetically speaking, if the stone does cause the genetic *whatever* to happen," Nevele said, "you can't just get a handful of the stuff and *make* a weaver. I mean, how weavers come about has been documented. It gets passed down on the mother's side. And even then it's not always guaranteed to show."

"Aye, but how does the theoretical weaver mama have that certain something in her to pop out a theoretical weaver knee biter? Gotta do that homework."

"And Dreck has done this? The homework? I'd be floored if the man could even sing the Common alphabet song."

Coog's lips curled. Leftover reverence for his ex-captain? "Well, he seemed pretty confident to me."

"But how? Powder some up each morning, sprinkle it over their morning toast, and see what happens in a few eons?" She snorted. "Plus, it'd require your lot to breed—something I can't imagine any woman being real keen on."

"No breeding required," he said, sad. "A few scientists Dreck had us nab ran some tests. They confirmed it, nodded all the way up until we zilched them."

Nevele suppressed a cringe. "All right. Well, it's pretty plain to me. Pirates are dumb. Fact. And really, it's not going to matter much what their plan is or how many scientists lied to him thinking they'd get out with their lives, because no one's getting the stone—so it's not even worth worrying about." *Why do I sound like I'm trying to convince myself?* "But for fun, hypothetically speaking, how?" Squeeze. "*How?*"

"F-Father Time," he blurted.

Tales about Ernest Höwerglaz ranged from outlandish to ludicrous. One particularly insane one said he traveled to far-flung off-chart planetoids with nothing but a water dropper and a petri dish and, by unloading a few millennia he'd soaked into himself, effectively become a one-man world seeder. Others suggested he was the quantum engineer of the cosmos, patriarch to the great Everything, who, done world making, had settled in Nessapolis. To Nevele, a staunch realist, that was all make-believe, the malarkey prime.

Then again, she was engaged to a man who, for nearly twenty years, had been nothing but a myth himself. *Part* of her must've believed Höwerglaz was real if she'd allowed Clyde to go looking to recruit the mythical weaver. No reason to let Coog know any of that.

"Sorry. I call bunk." And *squeeze.*

"It's *not*," Coog said, a sudden soprano.

A Cynoscion, though a hard-of-hearing species, must've caught that shrill note and angled an eye-stalk over a stony shoulder. Nevele waited until the stalk flipped back, returning its beady gaze to a plankton-whiskey cocktail.

"Even if Höwerglaz is real," Nevele whispered, leaning in, "and that's a big *if*, what use would he be in Dreck's plan?"

"The story goes that Father Time can take and give years, aye? Far as I understand it, let's say you take a bloke and put him alongside a piece of the stone. Then have

Father Time rewind the years out of him and put them back, over and over and over. Forced evolution, skipping the regular, slow kind."

Her scalp went tingly. Whether she believed it'd work or not didn't matter; the prospect was scary enough. Dreck Javelin backed by his own army of weavers?

"So"—she paused to swallow—"when are they going to start looking for Höwerglaz?"

"No *starting* to it," Coog replied, amused. "I've been out of the club for a week now, so who's to say they haven't already found him?"

Something zipped tight in Nevele's mind, like a wire noose. Clyde. He might be inside Nessapolis's city limits by now. Alone. Possibly hurt or worse. She blamed herself; she'd been the one to tell Clyde the Höwerglaz legend.

She raised her chin, ready with her next question, but faltered.

Amid the forest of empty bottles, a gun barrel peeked out. Bottles clinked as the fluted barrel grinded over the tabletop.

Coog's opposite hand returned to cover Nevele's. Again with the dreadful thumb stroking. "Now, if you wouldn't mind removing yourself from my unmentionables, I'll have my pay and be off." He tried prying his filth-rimmed fingernails under her hand. Failing, he clicked back the gun's hammer. "Only got another hour on my ship's parking spot, dearie."

He won't shoot you here. He'd never make it back to the port before the guardsmen got him. Which is exactly why she'd arranged to meet here. "First, when's the attack going to be?"

"Sorry. Be another fifty for that bit."

"And when did we agree on that?"

"You new? Feller with the shooter sets the rules."

With a rattle of beads, a shadow spilled across the table. Waitress again, but a different one, just as thin but less inked. "Hey, guys. Let me clear some of this up." She removed two bottles at a time, depositing them into a tub latched against her hip. She noticed the joined hands on the table. "Date, huh? That's sweet."

Nevele and Coog stared at one another. As each bottle crashed into the tub, the pirate flinched.

The waitress's hand recoiled. "Uh, we have a policy about weapons here, sir."

Eyes on Nevele, the pirate snarled, "Leave us."

"There's a sign," the waitress said shakily, "in all languages spoken in Adeshka: guns are prohibited in this establishment."

"Listen to the nice lady." Nevele batted her eyelashes. "Wouldn't want to spoil our night out, would you, love muffin?"

"Give me my due. I talked."

"When are they going to attack? Date and time." The pirate's hand was warm and moist.

"I won't repeat myself—"

"P-please, if you'll just give it to the bartender, you'll get it b-back once the tab's been—"

"Give me the spots," the pirate said, louder. "And get these bloody strings out from around my—"

"When, Coog? When?"

"The money. Now."

"Date and time, pirate."

"Give me the damn spots." Bottles smashed to the

floor as he hoisted his arm. The gun barrel leveled with her eyes.

Her threads yanked Coog, deflecting his aim.

The bullet discharged with a crack, piercing the back of the leather seat far too close to her head.

Before Coog could get his bearings, the gun already sweeping back, Nevele pulled the waitress aside and swung an uppercut into the air.

Coog blinked, helpless as the threads under the table went tight with a *twang*, sending the table and the pirate airborne.

The pirate sailed, kicking and flailing, among a loose cloud of curtain beads, beer bottles, and Geyser spots.

The waitress, the poor dear, squealed, sent her tub crashing, and rushed for the exit.

Cynoscions, frog-like Gworks, Mouflons, and gin-blossomed humans alike abandoned their drinks and made for the exit, climbing over one another.

The pirate collided with the lazily turning ceiling fan and sprawled onto the bar—things in him cracking wetly—and finally rejoined the floor, gasping and wheezing.

Stepping out of the booth, Nevele retracted her threads, dragging along the twisted mass of trousers. Tossing them aside, she strode over to Coog, who lay moaning in a heap. With a bump of her boot, Nevele sent Coog's gun skidding.

Coog rolled onto his back. His arm was bent at an irregular angle, and his now-bare legs bore a bleeding filigree of thin slices.

"Date and time," said Nevele.

With his arm that wasn't broken, he pawed at the collar of his jacket. A cheap pewter charm flopped onto his chest: a wrench with outstretched feathery wings. "Mechanized Goddess, rewire this one now, free him of malfunctions . . . Tesla the Everlasting Guide, Mage Oppenheimer, *please*."

Nevele hadn't brought any weapons. Getting the go-ahead wave by Adeshka's port security, after enduring the flood of frisk mice poured over her to let them sniff up her sleeves and into the depths of her pockets, had been sufficiently trying without attempting to sneak any artillery in. She glanced at Coog's gun, which had skidded into the crimson glow of the instapawn, and considered picking it up, using it, but thought better.

No one in the Geyser Royal Patrol, not even Clyde, the city's steward, was allowed guns anymore. Flam, head of security, had begged Clyde to permit the guardhouse a cellar cache of rifles. Clyde had reluctantly agreed, but otherwise the city was back to swords and shields as its defense from contemporary weapons. Nevele's own thoughts on it aside, even if she wasn't in Geyser right now, she'd still follow the law as a representative of the city.

Besides, I have my fabrick.

She leveled a palm over Coog's face, sending threads trickling down her fingertips, the ends feeling about his features. He spat and flung his head side to side, trying to finish his prayer to the Mechanized Goddess.

Once in, she could feel his nasal cavity, the back of his throat. His tongue was both slimy and rough. When calling out to his goddess again, a saliva-slickened wad of threads ballooned between his lips instead.

"Unless you want the last thing you ever hear to be squish . . ."

Around the dark mass swelling his jaw wide: "Fruh dahs frum tuh-daw."

"Three days?"

"Yuh, yuh."

"No tricks?" When she gave the strings a small twist, his nose started coming off. Not ripping like flesh but popping free as if it were molded flesh-tone silicone stuck on with wax. Which, apparently, it was.

"Nuh, nuh, I swerr! Fruh dahs, pehse . . ."

She eased the threads back. Coog gagged. His fake nose came free, looped on her strings through the nostril like a barbarian's necklace. She tossed the prosthetic back, and he scrambled to jam it on, embarrassed. She restored herself, the various pale territories of her face creaking as everything tightened into place again.

Stepping over him, mind reeling—*Three days till the attack!*—she picked up the spots scattered among the broken glass and spilled beer. Once she'd pocketed them, she walked toward the exit but stopped in the open doorway.

"Please, I told you everything." Coog attempted to get up using his broken arm. Wailing, he fell back, clutching his Z-shaped limb, gaze flicking to his gun across the room.

Nevele bent to pick it up. "This?"

"No, no, I—I wouldn't've—"

She turned, keeping herself between Coog and the instapawn, and pressed a button. The gun grew lighter and lighter in her hands until—*flimp*—it was gone. She hit another button. Ding.

Transaction complete, she turned back around.

Whimpering, Coog kicked away from her encroaching shadow. "Have mercy, have mercy, have—*wha*—?"

Not doom but chark bars rained down on him. And, lastly, two pence in Adeshka coinage, flipped from Nevele's thumb.

Nevele whirled away, cloak rustling, and snapped her respirator on. As she stepped back into Adeshka's neon stink fog, her voice went out muffled through the filters: "Keep the change."

DAY ONE

CHAPTER 1

The Adventurer, Under Glass

Stuffed into the itchy sea-foam green surcoat and trousers, knees wedged under his too-small desk, the Mouflon tried his best to seem interested. Really, he did.

The rain-capped biddy on the other side rounded out her story, bringing it to a close after providing many, many facts. Throughout, she awaited his estimation of things, wet eyes expectant, spotty hands folded.

Flam took a deep breath so that when he spoke, he wouldn't sound incredibly bored. Which he was. With not only this particular case but all the ones preceding and, likely, following.

Having peace in Geyser was great, sure, but he missed excitement. Once the city had gotten back on its feet and dusted itself off, the natural, finicky, fidgety way of folk, when happy, returned. Appointed as Flam—*Sir* Flam, he kept forgetting—head officer of the Geyser Royal Patrol, he was expecting to kick down doors, saying things like, "It's a long stint in the dungeon for you, bucko." But no. It was all—

"Are you even listening to me?"

"Forgive me, ma'am," he said, sitting up, widening his eyes as if that'd lasso his attention. "If you wouldn't mind, could you repeat—?"

"I *said* what're you going to do about this?"

"We'll find whoever's stealing your newspaper, ma'am." He thumped a fist on his desk. "Rest assured, we'll get to the bottom of this."

"Newspapers? My neighbor is poisoning my—"

"Shite, that's right. You're the one with the plant murderer."

"Not just plants. She's poisoning my *divinnean orchids*, Mr. Flam. And I should *hope* you'd remember; I've told you only a moment ago! I've had my little darlings for forty-three years, and they've bloomed every spring except this, *even* surviving while Ralph and I were sent away with everyone last year, poor things going unwatered that entire time. Which leads me to believe there can be no other explanation. That *wrathful crone* is poisoning them. I just don't understand why. I'm a good neighbor. I wave when I see her out. I *always* make sure when Ralph clips the hedge he doesn't leave any trimmings on her side of the property line. I, I, I don't know what to do. It's positively killing me."

Wanna know what's positively killing me? You, you paranoid old busybody. Flam was *this* close to saying it. Honest. But remembering stilled his lips: *This is my job. Clyde gave it to me because he thought me capable. I shouldn't let him down.*

But—

Flam could hear rain outside. Between the steady trickle, world-shaking thunder boomed. Springtime on Gleese, what a thing. Warm one day, brisk and blustery the next—

"Not even now."

"Sorry, what?"

"Not even now you're listening to me. You call yourself a member of the Royal Patrol?"

"I'm new."

"I remember it from the papers. You were hired nearly a *year* ago!"

Flam propped his chin on a fist. "I thought someone was stealing your newspapers."

She shot to her feet. "That wasn't me!"

As she stamped away, Flam didn't chase her or grovel, just let her go.

For a second, he caught the scent. *Never did Meech send a better gift than the smell of rain.* The door closed, shutting out the sounds and marvelous aroma.

Face mooshed on his palm, Sir Flam sighed.

"That went well." Constable Nula Quartermain sat at her adjacent desk, her uniform the same as his, except flattering.

"I can't focus today." He looked at her hair, the color of caramel; her complexion, suns-kissed. *This day or any other, really, with you sitting there, so perfect.*

"It's pretty dead. Could punch out early," she suggested, grinning.

"Yeah, sure. How do you think that'd look? Me, head officer, playing hooky." He added, "And feet off the desk."

A lot of their friendship, Flam suspected, was forged simply by spending the long hours together. He often wondered if he and Nula would be chums if they weren't coworkers. But since he scarcely saw his other friends anymore, maybe he'd just have to adjust the definition of friendship as he understood it.

Nula dropped her boots back onto the floor but kept her arms clasped behind her head. "You're friends with the steward, right?"

"So?"

"I dunno." Shrug. "Pull some strings."

"Even with permission to do it, if the people saw me shirking my duties, I'd be written off as no better than our most recent king." *Pitka Gorett*: anyone who spoke it would spit out the taste at once. *The traitorous old prick.*

Flam snuck a peek at Nula, suspecting she'd be making puppy eyes.

She was.

He laughed, trying to pretend it didn't affect him much. "All right, all right, we can't cut the *whole* day, but how's about an early lunch?"

Nula raised a fist and took on a deep voice. "The laziness is communicable, indeed!"

They strolled First Circle Street, then up to Second and Third, where there were some bistros Nula liked. She suggested they stop in one because, according to her, if Flam hadn't ever tried their griddle cakes, he hadn't lived.

She was right. The cakes were amazing, especially with the crag-sugar syrup.

She didn't join him with a plate of her own, claiming she'd just eat at her desk and preferred people watching to plate watching. "But go right on ahead. Cheers."

Afterward they went up Fourth Circle, into the artists' ward, agreeing they were just taking the long way back. Down the cobblestone lanes, they toured the elevated city's circular fringe, perusing sediment stone sculptures, knickknacks, and paintings behind leaded storefront windows.

As they sauntered, Nula spoke of her time in the refugee camp, how she'd been scared witless those six months with gangs bullying people out of their rations, how the guardsmen from Adeshka didn't care if you were on your deathbed but only allowed a doc in if you were leaving messy blood trails. "That's why I enlisted the minute I got back. Kind of worked out. There was a whole slew of vacancies after you, Clyde, and Nevele gave Gorett's men the boot."

"Don't forget about Rohm."

"And Rohm, yes, of course." Nula smiled that perfect smile.

"So this marks, what, three months you've been out of training and officially on the job?" He knew precisely how long it'd been since she'd first walked into the station house, how her hand felt in his when they shook.

"Yep, month three as a full-fledged guardswoman—kitted, badged, and everything."

"And how's it going?"

"Well, besides the monotony, which is considerable, and the complaints about how someone's neighbor's lawn has grown to an un*speakable* two inches, I like the guy I sit next to."

"George? Yeah, he is quite the handsome bloke, isn't he?" Flam meant Constable George, who often smelled like onions.

She elbowed him, and they shared a chuckle.

Autos passed them by, seagulls wheeled overhead, the gentle hum of a city at work enveloping them. The gray sky promised more rain. Add the pretty coworker at his side, and Flam was enjoying himself.

They stopped halfway across one of the pedestrian

bridges at the peak of the mossy stone arch, admiring the city's namesake in the town square. You could time it: every fifteen minutes the geyser would give a little puff— and a moment later, the mist dappled. Flam closed his eyes, droplets sprinkling his muzzle. Maybe there wasn't any true adventuring in his future right now, but at least he was outside. Outside, away from desks and uncomfortable, creaky chairs and all that stupid soul-sapping paperwork.

Apparently Nula didn't like the mist as much. She stepped back under the bridge's awning, blinking a lot and frowning. "So what're the others up to now?" Nula said from back there.

"Clyde and Nevele?"

"Yeah. Well, I know Nevele's got that seamstress shop down the way there, but ever since they announced their engagement and had that big party at the palace, it's closed every time I go past."

"Couldn't say. They don't tell me much."

"But aren't they your friends?"

"Aye, but doesn't mean they tell me anything."

"Do I need to remind you what position you hold?"

Wow. Serious. A rare turn for Nula. "What do you mean?"

"You're head of the Geyser Royal Patrol, Flam. *Sir* Flam. No one's been called sir *anything* around here in years. You should be up there, alongside them." She point-ed toward the palace. The sand-colored towers peeked between buildings and the drifting fog. He must've been making a face, because she was quick to add, "I didn't mean anything by it. You do fine at your job."

"Yeah." He leaned on the railing. In the rippling water, he could see his reflection staring up at him hangdog, wobbly and indistinct at the edges. He spat, and the foamy blot struck his mirrored self dead in the eye, scattering him into a chaos of colors: a frail creature. "I'm rather an expert on doing *fine*."

"I'm just trying to encourage you," she said, at his side now. She put a hand on his thick arm, ruffling the tawny fur.

She's just being nice. Don't take it as anything more.

"I didn't mean to upset you."

"You're right, though." His gaze met Nula's eyes, which sparkled when the suns' rays snuck out from the thunderheads, flashing warmly. "You're absolutely right. What're Clyde and Nevele doing that I can't?"

"I thought you said you didn't know what they were doing." Her fingertips still wiggled on his arm, a delicate dance.

"I mean, I do . . . in a way. They don't really fill me in on any details. They probably think I'm too much a git to understand their cloak-and-dagger business."

"Cloak-and-dagger business, as in going after Pitka Gorett and"—she glanced around—"*the Odium?*"

"Well, not going after them, exactly, but . . . how'd Pasty put it?" He snapped his fingers. "'Taking preventative measures.' I mean, he intends to stick to what he told everyone the day you all got back, about not instigating a fight, but they'd try to prevent an attack if possible."

"How?"

He turned to Nula.

"What?" she said, smiling uncomfortably, tucking a strand of hair behind an ear.

"Aiming to take my job?" He was only half teasing.

"No," she said, eyes going wide. "No, no, not at all.

I just find it fascinating since what you and I do is, well, really bloody boring. They're out there, going after the baddies. It's so courageous. Exciting. I mean, you said it yourself: cloak-and-dagger. What phrase in the world is cooler than *that*?"

"Yeah . . ." If not cool, at least enviable.

When thunder shook their bones, they hurried back toward the station house.

"What?" he said. "Don't you think what *we* do is courageous?"

She laughed. It was a good laugh, big and honest. "Oh, you were serious? Well, no, not exactly. Maybe it will be the day we finally get a lead on the despicable turd who's stealing people's morning editions of the *Geyser Gazette*."

"Got that one too, did you?" Flam chortled.

When the downpour started, darkening the town square's flagstones, they sprinted across. Nula's strides were long and exact, clearing puddles effortlessly, silently.

Once back at the door, though, Flam couldn't help but take a second at the top of the steps. It'd been a good break, a nice spell from the tedium, but it'd done little to quell his adventure-starved spirit.

With rain dripping from his horns, he looked out toward Jagged Bay and the sweeping dead landscape of Lakebed on the other side. He'd heard, secondhand from Clyde and Nevele's maid, Miss Selby, that Clyde was heading there. Surprised at the news, he'd gone to play cards by himself that night. Usurp was better with two players, but a solitary game was possible—if markedly less fun.

"Flam, you're going to get soaked," Nula said, halfway inside.

As much as Sir Flam wanted to get on a ferry and barrel toward the mountains and the desert beyond, he returned to his tiny desk and chair.

CHAPTER 2

Sand-Swept Rumors

For a moment the Sequestered Son flew. Beneath his buggy's wheels, the dunes rose and fell. The geography here was rippled as if the Lakebed had been shaped by a giant's sneeze. Clyde Pyne was new to driving but had learned after bottoming out a few times that he had to accelerate, not ease off, before racing up the yellow hills.

With the next, he was ready. When the engine began to struggle, he shifted, and it *roared*. The buggy took to the air for a thrilling, weightless moment. This landing was much better. With a flatter stretch lying ahead, he stomped the gas and held it.

Spotting a rickety lean-to—probably a boathouse when Angler's Lake had water in it—he urged the buggy over, feeling like not its pilot but merely living cargo murmuring pleas.

In the shade, he cut off the engine, vibrations echoing in his hands. He peeled off his gloves, dusty goggles, and the bandanna mask to let the arid breeze touch his alabaster skin.

"This can't possibly be it."

Clyde turned—as much as he could, buckled in as he was—and found Rohm's fiberglass terrarium in the passenger seat coated in layers of dust. "Well, you're the navigator," Clyde said.

Popping open the lid, the frisk mouse inside was poised over the gadget by which they'd been finding their way. "I believe if we start heading more westward, we'll—" Rohm broke off when looking up at Clyde. "My, aren't we a fright?"

Clyde adjusted the rearview mirror. His hair was standing up in every direction. Nevele had been begging him to cut it, preferring his pompadour, but this was another attempt at blending with Geyser's regular citizens—or normaloids, as Nevele sometimes called them, the unwoven. His parchment-white skin and obsidian eyes were things he couldn't help, but letting his jetty hair grow to jaw length like the other men did help him feel slightly more normal—if there was such a thing.

He mashed down the raven mass. "Better?"

Rohm nodded. "Much."

Outside their temporary resting place, Clyde squinted at the suns-scorched landscape and the occasional cactus patch in the bleary heat waves. Even though the Lakebed was absent of grave markers, Clyde couldn't help but think of cemeteries. So quiet.

"So where are we?"

"It keeps changing," Rohm said.

"Changing?"

The frisk mouse used his entire hand to press the navigational buttons. "Yes, the stupid thing's confused. I told you we should've just brought a compass. *Unlike* technology, the magnetosphere doesn't lie."

Rohm slammed a tiny pink fist on the device's screen, latitude and longitude becoming a plane of squiggles. It corrected but still showed them to be—as far as the device was concerned—hopelessly lost, bouncing their dot from here to there as if they were erratically teleporting about the desert.

"Could I try?" Clyde reached into the terrarium.

Rohm slapped him away. Well, more like patted, it being such a small hand.

"Fine, fine," Clyde said. "I'm the driver and you're the navigator. Apologies."

"And don't you forget it."

Clyde had noticed in the intervening year, Rohm had grown somewhat acerbic. When he and all his brothers, sisters, aunts, uncles, and cousins had been together, a sort of neutral amicability had been their standard. But this single member of the Rodents of Hive Mind was all that remained, the entire bloodline of hyperintelligent frisk mice snuffed by Vidurkis Mallencroix. Clyde couldn't much blame him for the bitterness. Whereas Clyde had lost his parents and Mr. Wilkshire—and his siblings, wherever they were—Rohm had lost *hundreds* of immediate family members, right before his eyes.

"Damn it all." Rohm kicked the device across the terrarium, leaving it where it sank halfway into his water bowl. He hopped onto his "intelligence-insulting" running wheel and to the rim of the terrarium, scampered up Clyde's jacket sleeve, and perched on his shoulder. Bracing himself on Clyde's eyebrow, Rohm gazed into the stretching nothingness.

"Glad to provide a lookout tower," Clyde said, trying to estimate where Rohm was looking.

"Nessapolis is that way." Rohm dragged out each word,

giving Clyde no confidence. "I say we head that way and just keep our fingers crossed."

"You're the boss." Clyde started the buggy again. "Okay, back in you go," he said, bobbing his head to the side to drop Rohm into his terrarium.

The mouse hung on, swinging by Clyde's earlobe. "I should stay out here with you. You might get us lost again."

Clyde adjusted the mirror to address Rohm, now on his shoulder. "Me? I'm the driver."

"Fine, all right, but let me make up for my choice of faulty navigational equipment by remaining out here, where I can keep sight on what I assume—and hope—is the right direction; attempt to utilize the natural sense of direction mice are said to have."

Reluctantly, Clyde agreed, waited long enough for Rohm to find purchase among the stitches of his poncho, the one Nevele had made for him, before throwing the buggy into reverse. Sand kicked out ahead of them, almost burying the lean-to.

After squaring up the buggy's grille facing the way Rohm pointed, they tore off, engine bellowing.

And for a while, it's all he could hear—until one sound *did* cut through.

Clyde kept them moving, glancing at the side mirrors, seeing nothing.

Again. A heavy, breathy pop, like . . .

A harpoon impaled the passenger seat, scattering shards of broken terrarium. *If Rohm had been inside* . . .

Keeping on the accelerator, Clyde ducked in the seat. Not that there was any protection in doing so—the buggy had no doors. It was just a cage of metal bars holding the tires, seats, and engine together.

Clyde twisted around to get a peek at their pursuers. Partly masked in a dust cloud, the second buggy kept time with no trouble as if deliberately drawing out the chase, relishing it.

Rohm in his ear: "Look out!"

Ahead, a cactus patch was ready to embrace them with bristling green paws.

Clyde flung the wheel to the left. Barbs scraped down the side of the buggy, a near miss. But the sharp dodge made them lose traction on the slippery sand. The horizon began to tilt. Acting on instinct, Clyde steered into the flip. For a terrifying moment the vehicle, on two wheels, weighed the pros and cons of rolling. Thankfully, it favored returning to all four wheels. The sudden traction made Clyde's head thump the seat back.

Another harpoon sailed over them—sickeningly close.

Clyde fought the wheel. The back end swung out, and he caught a better look at their pursuers' vehicle—twice as big as the buggy, spiked front end, pockmarked steel windshield, monster face on wheels—while the buggy turned a full three-sixty.

Clyde mashed the gas again, but the wheels dug graves for themselves. Something under the bonnet cried. The engine sputtered, fell silent.

Their kicked-up sandstorm drifted over, the entire world yellow.

Coughing, blind, Clyde twisted the ignition again and again. "Come *on* . . ."

The second vehicle's engine noise built to a hellish

crescendo.

"What're they doing?" Rohm squeaked.

Clyde kept trying the ignition. Dead clicks.

A wall of spikes plunged through the swirling sandy murk.

Slapping a hand to pin Rohm against his shoulder, Clyde released his seat straps and threw himself out the other side.

A bone-powdering clash: landing on its grille in the distance, the buggy bounced, spinning and throwing sand as it returned to the air, twisting and flopping. When it landed again, it lay still on its side, hemorrhaging petrol onto the dirt and smoke into the air.

Their pursuers' vehicle didn't even suffer so much as a nick. Clyde confirmed this, lying breathless with the grille mere inches from his face.

"Run," Rohm advised. "*Run.*"

Clyde scrambled to his feet and backpedaled as the vehicle's doors fell open and four men emerged. All four wore bandanna masks and dark-tinted goggles and brandished weapons—swords, a pistol, and a rifle.

Marching toward him, they uttered nothing. Not a cheer, no self-congratulatory whoop of having won the chase. This was a bandit's day at the office. Work.

Clyde took a few strides before he realized how pointless it was. They were in the Lakebed—there was nowhere to hide.

He set his sights on his buggy, willed his legs to pump, fright making every bone feel like gelatin.

A shot rang out, puffing sand near his boots.

Using their wrecked auto as temporary shelter, he found the trunk's latch broken. Squeezing fingers under, he leaned back to drag the trunk door open with his unsubstantial weight. It popped free, supplies raining out. Clyde swatted aside the tent, blankets, a bundle of overpriced firewood, and the cooler box loaded with Rohm's cheese.

For a moment, he panicked. *It's gone.*

"Mr. Clyde, they're coming."

The bandits, clearly used to this terrain, were graceful on the sand. Another shot, this one sparking near Clyde's fumbling hands.

Then he saw it: Commencement, in its sheath, wedged in the bottom. The trunk had been misshapen during the crash and now hugged the sword at either end, greedily pinching it. Wrenching, snarling with the effort, Clyde fell back clumsily when the green sword finally popped free.

Turning on his heel, he sent the sheath aside, the blade singing its liberation.

He held Commencement as taught, recalling the lessons he'd been taking back home from the same man who'd turned the royal revolver into an emerald metal blade: Grigori Gonn, Geyser's most seasoned blacksmith. "It's a dead art, swordplay," the gruff old man had said, rolling his shoulders at the start of their first lesson, "but if you're payin' and got the willin' to learn, I'll teach ya all the same."

The bandits spread themselves wide. Clyde kept hopping back, spinning one way and then the other, fighting to keep them all in front of his goggles at once.

From his left came the telltale click-clack of a rifle bolt. "Ain't you never heard the sayin' 'bout bringin' a knife to a gunfight, boy?"

"I have, and it would apply if this were just a knife."

From the radio clipped to his hip—at quite possibly the worst time—Nevele called out, "Come in, come in. We need to talk, like, immediately."

"Who that—yer momma?" the rifleman said. "Wanna give her a ring back, tell 'er yer busy with yer new friends?"

Misdirection, Grigori Gonn said, was paramount in a fight. While the rifleman was teasing Clyde, a shadow on the ground eclipsed his own. He spun, raised Commencement, and locked onto a curved sword with a crash.

The bandit's face was close, his breath sour with rot. "Shoot, I got 'im."

Rohm, his second set of eyes: "Move!"

Clyde pistoned his boot to push himself away.

A shot shattered the dusty air. The bullet connected—*fwap*.

A sword plopped into the sand, then a set of knees. The bandit bled freely from the hole in his chest, dropped the rest of the way into the grit, and lay still.

"Damn it, Lou," the rifleman groaned, advancing the next round.

Clyde turned to survey the remaining three. One wielding a sword, the apparent ringmaster raising a rifle, and one rattling an antique handgun in an unsteady hand.

From his belt: "Clyde. Come in. I'm getting in line to head home. I won't be able to call you once I'm onboard. Clyde? Are you okay?"

The leader squeezed the rifle stock to his shoulder but lowered it. His expression was impossible to discern behind the mask, but the pause spoke volumes.

"What? What is it?" the shaky one said.

When Clyde glanced behind him, the second

swordsman was charging toward their buggy. "Go. Let's go," he shouted as he ran. "Forget 'im, Emer. Let's get outta here!"

The rifleman—Emer, apparently—remained staring at Clyde for a long moment. "Lemme see yer face. Ain't no way you—if you *is* you—would be way out here."

Clyde, confused, didn't move.

He raised the rifle again. "Yer face. Now!"

Clyde didn't bother throwing back his hood or pulling down his bandanna, just lifted his goggles, his dark eyes and snowy complexion on display.

The rifleman blanched. His aim drifted, and he began backing away, free hand raised. "We ain't done nothin' to ya. Yer fine. Ain't even hurt none. Juss don't . . . eht my soul, awright?"

The rifleman pointed at the bandit with the pistol, whose knees were now knocking. "Eht his. Yeah, here." And without hesitation, he fired upon him, striking him above the knee.

The shaking bandit shrieked, crumpled, clutching his leg.

Deed done, his own safety secured, the rifleman ran for the buggy. The swordsman that'd already bolted slowed long enough to let the second man on.

In short time, the buggy receded into the wind-tossed Lakebed, the roar of its overworked engine fading.

Clyde's pulse rang in his ears, his limbs heavy.

"Please, please don't eht my soul," the man on the ground begged, voice cracking, drawing Clyde's attention.

The sandy earth drank his blood, each drop burrowing as if being chased underground. He'd peeled off his mask. Clyde was stunned. He was no more than a boy. Certainly tall for his age but with a face that wouldn't look out of place on someone half his height. Tears flowed down full cheeks as blood squeezed out between his glove's fingers in thin, steady streams—the wound was tenacious. "Please don't eht my soul. Please."

Clyde had no idea how he, the Sequestered Son no longer a myth, had been treated in the news outside of Geyser. Undoubtedly word had spread, but he didn't pay much mind to the doubters writing the *Geyser Gazette*. Now, given the bandit's reaction, he couldn't help but wonder if some nasty rumors were being tossed around.

Tugging down his bandanna, he crouched in front of the boy. "I'm not going to eat your soul. I don't do that." It felt ridiculous to need to reassure someone of such a thing.

"But how do I know yer not a larr?" Sweat and tears mixed into a sheen, dripping. "They say yer a larr, biggest there is."

"Who says I'm a liar?"

The boy broke eye contact, as if any more would leave him suddenly soulless. "People."

"And do you believe them?"

Rohm flicked Clyde's ear. "Are we conducting a poll? Who cares what people say? Help the little brute."

Rohm was right. Clyde went to their buggy and retrieved the med kit from where the rental agent said it'd be: under the driver's seat. He returned with it and unbuckled the leather case.

Apparently whoever had rented their buggy previously was the accident-prone sort. All that remained were two mushed cotton balls and a spool that once held medical tape.

"I'm dead," the boy said, shaking his head at the barren

med kit. "I always knew I'd die out here, just like Daddy said." He glanced the way the bandits had gone. "I just never thought *he'd* be the—"

"That was your father, the man who shot you?"

The boy nodded, casting his gaze down.

"Blimey," Rohm murmured.

The boy looked up, squinting. "Is that mouse really talkin' or . . . am I . . ." And in an unsettling display, the boy's neck became boneless. He slumped over, arms flopping wide, sand rushing out from under him.

With nothing holding it, the gunshot wound filled and spilled over, blood trickling as if from a faucet. Clyde scrambled for something, anything, to tie it off.

"The strap, Mr. Clyde, the sword strap."

Snatching up Commencement's sheath, Clyde unclipped the leather band from either end of the ornate scabbard and quickly wrapped it around the boy's leg, above the injury, and drew it tight.

The red river slowed, then stopped.

Rohm sighed with relief.

In all the commotion, Clyde had forgotten Nevele had called. He unclipped the clunky radio from his belt, drew out its antennae. "Nevele? I'm here. We just got into a bit of a . . ." No need to worry her. "How'd it go with the informant?"

Static.

"Nevele?"

He double-checked the frequency.

"Nevele, it's Clyde. Come in."

Static.

Something tapped him on a shoulder, then his nose.

He flinched as a blast of thunder heralded the storm's arrival—as if the dark sky hadn't been a sufficient hint. That explained the interference, at least. *Nevele did say she was headed home, right? That much is a good sign.*

Their buggy was well past hope. The engine had broken free, the steaming black fist sagging from the vehicle's underbelly. Dripping, greasy tubes and important-looking wires dangled, torn. Clyde hadn't the foggiest how to repair it.

"So now what?" Rohm said, taking shelter in Clyde's hood.

Lost. Bloody kid on the ground. Dead buggy. And now rain.

"I've no idea."

CHAPTER 3

A Broken King

Rusty bedsprings made their usual morning music. Careful of fragile joints, the skeletal old man sat up, his beard uncoiling from how he wore it when he slept, an organic scarf.

Still alive. Sigh.

After emptying his bladder into the bucket, he moved to the plastic crate where he kept his clothes. He stayed on tiptoes; if he were to lay a bare foot down, he'd likely leave its sole there, peeled off and frozen to the floor.

Even after cocooning himself in long underwear, three sweaters, insulated trousers, and a down coat with a fur-trimmed hood, he shivered. Belting up, he paused, noticing he'd run out of holes in the strip of leather. He rummaged through the heaps of junk for a screwdriver and a hammer. New hole punched in, he buckled, a foot and a half of leather dangling. This used to be a problem for him, but it'd been running short of holes on the *other* end.

Pitka Gorett approached the mirror, pulling his hair free from the shirt so it fell white around his shoulders. Previously it'd been a regal silver, still bearing stripes of nutty brown. But a year in the ice caps had sapped any lingering color from him.

Opening his eyelids wide, he stared into his own

pupils, waiting for any squiggles to show within. He'd been instructed to do this each morning; the eyes were the easiest place to catch an infection's first signs. He stepped back from the mirror, what had once been the rearview for an auto. His eyes were clear. Nothing outside the usual self-contempt.

Gorett stepped out of his storage closet of a chamber, into the hall, wondering what hellishness today held. Whatever it was couldn't have been so bad, since the frosty air was perfumed with whatever they had on the grill . . .

Downright nauseating to him once, grilled slitherer now made Gorett's stomach fidget and mouth flood. He looked forward to Slitherer Day. It was about the only way to tell what day of the week it was, since the transitions between them were indiscernible—the suns, this far north, never set.

With each step, his boots bumped around loosely on twig legs, the air growing more oily and humid. He entered the mess hall, where it was the most powerful, that lovely greasy moistness he could feel almost slicking his skin.

He took up a plate—not caring if it was a hubcap—and approached the counter, behind which they were preparing the breakfast on long charcoal grills.

The two fat cooks, squinting past the fragrant smoke, greeted Gorett with bovine stares. They were the only ones in the Odium who weren't emaciated to husks. And maybe they weren't that plump, Gorett considered, but regular-sized. It'd been some time, after all, since he'd seen anyone with any meat to them.

"Could I possibly request that piece there?" Gorett said, pointing furtively at the fatty neck section of the slitherer.

The cooks, sharing some unspoken inside joke, grinned as a cut from the *other* end of the snow-snake was slapped onto Gorett's waiting plate: a rubbery hank of tail that still wore some corkscrewing black sprigs of singed hair. "Enjoy that."

Bringing the plate up to take a powerful sniff of the portion, Gorett tried to not appear *too* happy, it being the piece he actually desired all along.

He, too, could play their game.

Upon the bearcat rug near the fireplace, he ate with his hands.

Pulling at a sleeve to wipe his mouth, he noticed his tattoo again. Funny, how easy it was to forget it was there. On the inside of his veiny forearm, scrawled while he'd put up a struggle, was *trayter*. They'd done other things too, but this was the most lasting reminder of their abuse, a bruise that would never fade. The Odium, despite being the dregs of humanity, valued loyalty above all, even if it wasn't to them.

Chewing the last squeaky bit of slitherer tail, he examined their handiwork by the light of the fire. They'd used cable wire to punch in the ink. Dot by dot. For hours.

The next stringy tug on the snow-snake, something snapped. Not breaking like a tendon or an elastic artery, but something else. Within the crescent-shaped divot he'd bitten away, a small yellow worm—well, half of one— squiggled in deeper, to hide. A close call. Who knew how many he'd eaten without knowing?

Spitting the mouthful onto the floor, much to the disappointment of the cooks across the room, Pitka Gorett stared at the half-chewed hunk, feeling a lurch in his heart.

Starting small and rising to a roar, declaring he deserved better since, after all, he was technically still a king.

Geyser never had crowns, but he'd considered having one fashioned, perhaps even by the local smithy Grigori Gonn. And he would've worn the thing everywhere he went. Rise in the morning from the lush defarr down from the giant birds in the exotic west, snap his fingers, and his squires would bow and gently rest it upon his brow. What an image he would've cut then. Spiked golden summits raising his height, making him stand straighter, someone nobody would ever defy.

Maybe then, crowned, none of this would've happened. He could've commanded someone to go down there after the deposit and shoo the Blatta. Never would he have had to strike a deal with these heathens at all!

Seated upon the floor, grease on his chin, Gorett received a staggering revelation. *It was all because I had no crown.*

He shot to his feet.

This. Until I can fashion something better, this *will be my crown.*

And then some time passed while the sensible side of Pitka Gorett took a holiday.

When he spilled from his cyclone of momentary insanity, Gorett heard laughing, finding himself standing on the long mess hall table with a hubcap on his head, arms crossed over his bony chest as he stared down all present.

Slitherer grease got in his eye. Springing a hand to rub it away, he knocked off his crown, which went rolling on its edge like a coin. When he dropped off the table to chase it, the laughing exploded to a deafening volume. But right then, Gorett didn't care. He needed his crown, the plate, his crown, so he wouldn't get in trouble with his mother. *This is all we have, Pitka. We have to treat it with care.*

"With care," Gorett murmured, bending to retrieve the plate. But it was still greasy, and every time he tried to hook a fingernail under, he'd just push it across the floor. "With care."

The hubcap parked against a thick-soled boot he immediately recognized.

Dreck Javelin flicked back his neon-green tri-corner hat. "Providing morning entertainment for the boys, are we?"

"I . . . just dropped my plate." Pitka Gorett retrieved it, clutching it to his chest. His eye stung, and his back hurt from all that racing around. "But I have it now."

"That you have. Get your breakfast?"

"Yes."

The men were still laughing. Those with two hands clapped; those with one slapped their knees. Bone-worm infections had robbed them all of one piece or another.

"And did you finish everything on your plate?"

Gorett peeked out from under wild brows, hate in his heart. *They think you're just some funny old man now, dancing about like a feverish monkey one minute, demanding respect the next, nose in the air like some spoiled princess. You're a broken thing now, Pitka.*

Odd. That last bit came to him with his mother's voice. And never once did she say anything like that to him. She hadn't lived to see him become king.

Gorett twitched when Dreck touched his arm.

"I asked you a question."

"Don't treat me like some *fool*," Gorett said, spittle flying.

The laughter filling the room shut off, as if a lever had

been thrown.

Wiping the foamy spatter from his cheek, Dreck said with ominous mildness, "Come along. We need to speak. In private."

With one shove after another, Dreck moved Gorett down the hall. Once out of his men's view, he said, "Good Goddess, man, we need to get you a sign. Something you can wear when you're feeling squirrely."

"I'm *perfectly* coherent—oof—and in full command of my faculties."

They passed through a glass tunnel connecting to Dreck's quarters, which had been the observatory when this place was still a research center.

Once in, under the enormous telescope angled heavenward, Dreck slammed the door behind them. Gorett remained where the last shove had placed him: in the open space of the expansive room. Realizing only now that he'd carried the hubcap all the way here, he set it aside.

Unlike Gorett's chambers, Dreck's didn't store heaps of junk. He had a nicer bed, even an armchair and a chest of drawers. Gorett suspected it was fear that a worm infection would rob him of his skills as a Fractioner that prompted Dreck to make his own meals. He began doing so now by starting a small fire in the corner of the room. A molecule is all it'd take, one pregnant germ. Gorett ran his tongue over his teeth, stomach turning with the memory of his plagued breakfast.

Obscured by soot and frost creeping its surface, a large window of thick glass showed the frozen world in a panoramic display. Just outside and below was a starship, dappled with white. The *Magic Carpet*, the ship they'd picked Gorett up on—painted in the style of a luxurious rug, tassels and all.

Behind it, a field of goods—still shrink-wrapped—that'd been intercepted during delivery. Bales of swiped jewelry bound with large rubber bands. A hundred armories' worth of weaponry both new and ancient: a small mountain of assorted swords, daggers, pole arms, and battle-axes. An overwhelming assembly, the product of many years' diabolism.

But to the pirates, Gorett had learned, it was not theirs directly. Loaned, more like. Because lording over it all, the loot and its dedicated amassers, was a twenty-foot sculpture. A woman. *The* woman. Arms outstretched, face laced with the silver snakes of weld lines, eyes a beaming set of headlights, starship wings hammered into a gown clasped with a string of boat chain. Their Mechanized Goddess.

Every calculated effort of the Odium was in her honor.

Above her, the glacier's fissure. The crack's twin precipices hung agape, a serrated icy maw. Past its sharp teeth, paling the suns to faint white disks, a blizzard blew—the same that'd been pounding the ice caps for centuries, keeping their arctic aerie hidden, to Seddalin Chidester's chagrin, the king of Adeshka's best efforts proving to be a repeated waste of time and money. So maybe the Goddess *did* do more than just give the Odium permission to gather wealth by whatever means they deemed appropriate; maybe she was sheltering them, keeping them invisible. Or maybe the pirates' dogma was infectious and he had spent far too much time here.

"Have they found Father Time?" Gorett remained

standing even though Dreck had taken a seat by his make-shift fire pit, logs crackling in a shallow dent in the steel floor.

Dreck worked a frostbitten piglet from a sack. Gorett had seen Dreck use his inborn talent to dismantle many a metal thing, but whenever it was anything of flesh, his blood chilled.

"They'll figure it out eventually, you know," Dreck said, spreading his fingers over the animal, causing it to gently explode. Bone and flesh tumbled about in a slow tempest of pink cubes.

Watching, Gorett observed the strata of the pig in the sides of the cubes: skin fading into a thick layer of yellow fat, and the white-pink stuff of actual muscle. Sickened but oddly hungry, he remembered Dreck had asked him something. "Um, figure what out?"

With a guiding push of his hand, the meat cubes drifted over the waiting grill as if filled with helium. They touched down upon the metal, sizzling. The rest—those that contained bone and organs—Dreck returned to gravity's mercy, and they flopped to the floor in a loose red heap. "Your act."

"Act? Clearly I'm the victim of a mental disorder," Gorett said, staring at the gore pile. "Brought on, I suspect, by the constant abuse over this past year." Mindlessly, he rubbed his sleeve over the tattoo.

Dreck squinted into the smoke. "Is that all it's been? Huh. Feels longer to me." With a poke of his thumb, he rolled a cube to an uncooked side. "And you might be right, with how you've started to show signs of . . . termi-nal squirrelliness. Or you play it that well. Been checking your eyes?"

"Yes, I have, but . . . playing what well? Why would you think I'm—?"

"You don't like it here," Dreck interrupted, fingering his rust-colored beard. "Can't blame you. If I was so accustomed to the pampered life, I would too, I suspect."

Gorett ignored that. "Again, why would you think I'm acting, Dreck?"

"I can only assume you haven't been to war." And before Gorett could answer: "You must've been, what, thirty or so at the start of the Territorial Skirmish, right?"

"I was twenty-eight, but no, I haven't been to war. What's that got to—?"

"No surprise there. Probably told the draft office you had a bum heart or something."

"I was working in the palace, a page, I—"

"I've been. Last big one."

"The Skirmish? But you would've been a child, a boy—"

"Being a Fractioner has values beyond the obvious." Dreck nodded at the sizzling pig dice. "Locks my bits and bobs when things get creaky. Keeps me spry." He flexed his hands as if they ached. "But we're getting off topic. Suffice it to say I was, hand to the Goddess. And anyone who finds themselves in any war, I reckon, will make it tolerable somehow. Shut off inside"—he poked the chest of his dense coat—"or temporarily wear the face of another man who can weather things the bloke within cannot."

The wind howled, loose powder hissing past in sparkling white waves.

Saying nothing, Gorett watched Dreck press on one of the cubes with the heel of his hand. A spurt of grease made the fire whoosh hungrily.

"But playing a role can be revealing," Dreck said. "Those actions done whilst masked speak more of the man inside than you'd expect." Wiping a rag across his hand, he said, "Peril is a stage upon which we don't wear masks but instead take them off—sometimes have them taken off by no choice of our own."

"But I'm not in peril," Gorett quietly stated. "You said so yourself, when we set our arrangement. I'd be protected, long as I kept my word. Which, I'll add, you haven't entirely held up." He tugged up his sleeve.

"Is that supposed to say *traitor*? We need to nab a tutor sometime, I think." Dreck chuckled. "But you're still alive, aye?"

"In a manner of speaking."

"Oh, cut the melodrama. Could be worse. At any time, in fact."

Gorett pulled his fur collar tighter. Threats were nothing new, but this felt sharper—how casually Dreck had said that. "What're you saying?"

"You're alive only because I bumped the boys' wages up. And I was able to only because of how bountifully we've been blessed as of late." He motioned at the snow-buried loot out the window. "In times any leaner than these . . ." He clicked his tongue. "Well."

"I'm aware of how it works," said Gorett. "And living under such a cloud as that, how *could* I be expected to keep my sanity?" The question was genuine.

Dreck creaked his chair back on two legs. "No, I still think you're pretending. A defense mechanism, like I said." He nodded in agreement with himself and returned his gaze to the grill. "Because you've nothing else to keep you strong, something that makes you want to fight." Dreck dropped his chair onto four legs with a slam, took up a plate—one of actual ceramic, not a hubcap—and scooted two blackened dice on.

"I have nothing to fight for?" Gorett said, offended. "What of my half of the deposit?"

"Aye, true." Dreck flicked open a knife and began sawing into the cube, crunching through the charred exterior. "But I think you heard that the Sequestered Son came out of hiding shortly after we picked you up, when you thought you'd be taking a holiday. Now you letting us take our half of the stone, as agreed, and you getting your city back? Well, neither of those is going to happen." He pushed what he was chewing to one cheek. "Shite's changed, Gorett. You're a wanted man. Not that Geyser would've been much to return to, considering how I've rejiggered the extraction plan."

"It was your plan to take the stone that way all along. You stole that warhead *before* picking me up, remember?" He'd been sitting on that for a while.

"Huh." Dreck's eyebrows rose. "And yet you're not going off on some tirade, calling me a madman?"

"No," Gorett said, looking down at his too-big boots, "I've come to terms with it. The deposit's what's important. There was never any talk of how you'd retrieve it, nor any regarding Geyser's protection. Half the deposit to you and half to me. I'll take mine off-planet, change my name, be the wealthiest man in whatever system I choose to plunk down in, while yours will be going toward . . . strengthening your efforts, as it were."

Dreck speared another cube and popped it in his mouth. "I detect doubt."

"It's not my place to speculate on whether or not it'll work. What you do with your half is your business."

"Colin is excited," Dreck said, swallowed. "Seen him in the halls? That spring in his step? Well, as springy as it can be, down a leg as he is. Still, he's going to be *fearsome*. Like me. He'll be the little weaver brother I always wanted. Two days and some change, Pitka. Champing at the bit? I am."

Gorett said nothing. Colin had been there to hold him down for the tattoo. That braying laugh of his . . .

"Go ahead. Speak your mind. It's just you and I."

Finally, Gorett sat—not in the stained lawn chair near the cook fire but on a corner of the bed, testing its enviable resilience. "Pyne's firstborn didn't really drown because of bleeding lungs like we'd all been told. So imagine my surprise, having worked in that palace for years alongside Francois Pyne, up until he . . . passed away."

Dreck laughed. "Needn't keep that under the rug anymore, Gorett. We all know you'd done it or had it done."

Gorett's cheeks grew hot. To air secrets he'd kept so securely buried felt strange, at once invigorating and unnerving. "Yes, well."

"Ever hear from Vidurkis? Shame, if he's lost. Heard he was *awfully* committed to the Goddess." Dreck took a moment to bask in the amber luster of the statue's all-seeing headlights.

"I assume he's either dead or suffering whatever young Pyne decided was fitting for him." *Either would be fine, long as I needn't deal with that mad dog ever again.*

"Vidurkis had a little sister, right? Worked in the palace?"

"Margaret, yes, the Royal Stitcher."

"Heard it announced on the radio they'd become engaged—the Sequestered Son and her." Setting his plate
aside, Dreck got to his feet, grunting as he straightened
his back. "Your man's little sister is betrothed to the Pyne
who's calling the shots now. Funny how shite works out.
Well," he added, "he named himself steward. Throne's to
remain empty."

"We have plenty of radios here. I'm well aware of current events."

"Yes, but you do know *why* Pyne did that, what that says?"

"He suspects I'm still alive."

"He *knows* you're alive and won't take the throne until
the old king has been retired permanently." With his hand,
Dreck made a gun. "Gotcha in his sights. Ka-bang."

"Best of luck, Little Pyne," Gorett said, chuckling.
He'd meant haughtiness, but it'd come out an anxious titter. "With us way up here, under these constant blizzards,
we're good as off-planet."

"Aye," Dreck said with disinterest, wandering the
room in endless circles. "Sometimes, though—and this is
just me spit-balling here—I can't help but wonder if, given
the chance, you'd trade the wendal stone for the throne.
Or at least a wiped slate."

"We're being honest with one another?" Gorett glanced
at the door. It was closed.

"Just two blokes, chewing the fat."

Gorett let himself say, "In that case, I might, if I could."

Stepping near, Dreck arched an eyebrow. "Oh? *Even* if
it meant breaking trust with your new mates?"

"I wouldn't do that." *You walked right into that one.*

Again, his mother's voice. Why?

"Oh? Come to think of it, your act *can* be pretty convincing. Maybe when you switch from Lord Snooty to the court jester, your loyalty gets just as mixed up."

"You said not a moment ago you think it's an act, that I—"

"See, Gorett?" Dreck said, throwing his arms wide, matching the giant metal woman's pose behind him outside. "Like you, I can also spin my head around." He snapped his fingers, loud, in Gorett's face. "Like *that*. Trust you, then not."

"Dreck, I—"

"We can just as easily take the wendal stone without you, disregard our whole 'You cheat, you bleed' thing, forget I ever said anything about going halfsies. I can cut your throat in your sleep as easily as give you half my plate at every dinner bell. Your life is entirely in these hands right here. Every little second. Consider each a pittance that slipped between my fingers a damn mercy."

"I understand. But . . . w-we had a deal."

Waving him off and hissing, disgusted, Dreck turned away. At the window, leaning with a hand on the thick pane, he peered out, quiet for an uncomfortable length of time.

"All I'm suggesting here," he said at last, fogging the glass, "is that you pray to your god my boys find Father Time. And failing your willingness to do that—since egotistical tossers tend to throw offerings at only their own feet—pray *she* sees something in you that has a purpose." He thunked a knuckle on the glass, toward the staring metal lady. "And if she sends one of those feelings my way suggesting I do something not very nice, I'll do it. My loyalty to her is tempered, incomparably, so you know I will. You've *seen* how much so."

"I have, yes," Gorett softly agreed, fighting to push back the memory of the man who was surely now only a skeleton with a broken back in the desert somewhere. Aksel, whom they'd flung from the back of the *Magic Carpet*. Gorett sometimes saw it replay in dreams, the young man rolling off the ramp, tumbling into the empty sky above the Lakebed. Their glances had met momentarily. Gorett had wanted to help but done nothing.

Nothing, Mother echoed.

CHAPTER 4

A Day in the Life of a Bullet Eater

Aksel Browne's single eye fluttered open. Sitting up, he looked about the rented room, reluctant to return to himself, a prisoner of his flesh and circumstance. At least better than where he'd just been; his nightmares were exclusively about falling from high places.

Luggage—all bearing the Srebrna Academy insignia—was neatly piled into one corner. Since he and Karl were the only ones in need of sleep, unlike the other three, he and the big man alternated using the single lumpy bed in shifts.

The bottom of the closed doorway was lit. Evidently Karl Gonn was already up and watching—or *still* watching since yesterday—in the next room.

After dressing—black slacks, jacket, and tie—Aksel knocked. Karl gave a nasally grunt, and Aksel walked in.

The big man with wise almond eyes sat before a broad accumulation of holomonitors displaying a dizzying mosaic.

"Heading out?" Karl said, gaze never leaving the monitors.

"In a minute, yeah." Aksel leaned on the doorjamb, watching Karl a moment. They'd developed a weird sort of rapport, like two men who didn't think of themselves as their jobs—in their case, uninformed mercenaries for cold-blooded employers—but just two schmoes punching a clock.

The dozens of feeds showed Adeshka's suburban streets, crowded downtown intersections, and endless mega highways. Occasionally a blurt would come from Karl's headset, what Aksel assumed was guardsmen's radio chatter.

"Sleep lately?"

Karl moved a holopanel away with the precise sweep of an enormous hand. "They don't, so neither can I."

"Could always say you dozed off, forgot to scramble a security checkpoint. *Let* them get busted." Aksel was only sort of kidding.

Karl laughed.

"Where are they anyway?" Aksel stepped in closer. Watching the feeds made his head spin. How did Karl manage to sit in here so many hours every day and not have his brain turn to ash?

"Well, Moira's still on recon, and Raziel and Tym were uptown at the port this morning."

"What's at the port?"

"Uh, commercial frigates, starships, tourists?"

"I know that much, smart-arse, but what's there of interest to them?" Karl's gaze shifted, which Aksel knew meant he'd been entrusted with something the Brothers Pyne didn't want shared.

Aksel, the peon here, let it drop.

"Got a lead this morning. Odium defector," Karl supplied instead. "So if you're among the living again, they'd probably like you out there, ready to move."

Adjusting his tie, Aksel stepped near the door. "Soon as I have my coffee." Spurts of rebelliousness helped Aksel remember he was still alive. "Want one?"

"No, just don't forget your suitcase, dear."

Picking up his bag from beside the door, Aksel took one last glance over the room. For murderers, at least they were neat. Aksel was glad, since if they had trashed the place, Vee would have his head. Not that Aksel's sister threatening his life was anything new, but the Chrome Cricket was hers—Adeshka's only combination hotel, pub, apothecary, shipwright, bail bondsman, notary public, auto-body, costume rental, and fireworks outlet.

He locked the door behind him, pocketed the key for room six, and started along the worn carpet.

It was once a brewery, but when the surviving sommeliers left and the building was hosed free of soot, Vee bought the place whole with some friends she'd made while working as a fire dancer on the Originalle carnival circuit. Pooling their savings, she and each of her colorful pals had a slot in the big brick cupboard on Delmark Avenue, while she, voted the most responsible among the circus runaways, assumed the role of landlord.

Bit of a laugh if you were to ask Aksel— his little sister winding up a landlord, of all things. But she did and did it well, really making the Chrome Cricket her own. Rewired the place top to bottom to pass code, put up electric braziers, learning everything she needed in how-to books, no need for any handyman, thank you. Gave all five levels of banisters and hardwood floors so many coats of warm-colored varnish that the place looked like the victim of a honey flood.

It'd been Aksel's stupid idea to suggest he and his "new friends" stay here. For the life of him he couldn't remember why he had. Certainly didn't take long for Raziel to make the connection between Aksel Browne and Vee Browne.

Once he had, he promised if Aksel did anything to betray them, the Chrome Cricket would burn. Again.

Maybe it'd been an involuntary decision. Maybe Aksel, deep down, *wanted* to help Raziel, Tym, and Moira kill their eldest brother but needed a reason to stay in line and do his dirty work obediently, so he'd supplied one himself. Or maybe he wanted some semblance of normalcy while he was a hired gun. And being able to see Vee regularly for the first time in years was a blessing—even if they both had invisible guns trained on them.

She could probably tell her invisible gun was pressing her temple and Aksel had been the thing that'd invited it into her life. Even though he hadn't told her what his "new friends" were up to, he probably didn't really need to. This was Vee. She knew. Just like when he'd lied about his age and joined the Fifty-Eighth militia all those years ago. Minute he came home, one glance across the dinner table and Aksel knew she knew. She was the only one who understood his fences, which knothole to look through to spy the truth within. And now, again, she said nothing—her looks about as torturous as the unspoken lecture.

Turning on the landing, he put on his eye patch, letting the strap fit into the pale indentation crossing his forehead, its home. Hooking his bag on his arm, he slipped on a set of cream-colored gloves to cover the square scar on the palm of his hand—the most important part of his disguise.

On the ground floor, the smells shifted as he strode past the shops. The apothecary's bowel-churning aroma of boiled this and that, the sweetness of drying ink from the notary's, the pleasant industrial tang of the auto-body—heavy oils and new metal.

Ahead, Vee was just opening the doors to the pub. Whenever he saw his little sister, he couldn't help but smile—even if lately it was seldom returned.

Always: cowboy boots, tights or leggings, a miniskirt bearing an animal print of some stripe or another, loose-fitting blouses with billowing sleeves, and hand-blown glass-bead necklaces she made herself. Like him, she was abundantly freckled and blonde, except her mane was struck with bolts of blue.

"Sister. Good morning."

She tapped the wedge under the door and stepped inside, never looking his way. "More like good afternoon. Giving air a chance over alcohol today?"

The place, dark like a good pub should be, held a residual buzz from the night before, matching Aksel's headache: its dark twin, the ghost of good times.

"Mind that." Vee stepped around a crusty puddle, but then she paused to glare back at him. "Or should I be asking you to get the mop?"

Aksel regarded the vom. "Not mine. I don't like carrots. Besides, isn't it the bartender's job to know when to cut a bloke off?"

Vee walked on. "Aye, but that'd be chasing money out the door. What concern is it of mine if they opt to gin themselves into oblivion?" She went behind the bar, clicked on some more lights, which stung Aksel's eye.

He took a seat at the bar in his usual spot at the corner of the ancient hunk of Ciaa hardwood, draping his cheap suit coat onto the next stool. He set his bag on the floor, close, so one leg was touching it.

"Or potato wine themselves into oblivion, in a

particular someone's case," Vee added, filling two earth-enware mugs with coffee.

Aksel shrugged. That was his poison of choice. Indubitably.

"And what've you got going on today?" she said in that Vee way, shaking some crag sugar into her cup but not into his, because she knew not to.

He swallowed self-hate with the first bitter sip, buying a moment to patch a lie together. "This and that." Okay, so not a great one.

"Villi, you'll recall," Vee said, stirring in cream, "got mixed up with a bad lot."

Aksel nodded. Villi, the youngest Browne, had joined a gang. The expected had happened.

"Yes, I recall, but with me, it isn't like that. I'm an adult, for one."

"*Und verdda feri du etta, flawe*," she said, adopting their native language. Adeshka had been their home for most of their lives, but their true home was the scrubby tundra of Kambleburg. Aksel hated it when she used that particular tongue with him since it reminded him too much of their parents, but he knew she used Kamblean only because it blew Common's swears out of the water.

"I know," he said. "I know I'm an idiot. News to no one, that."

"So what're you gonna do to fix it?"

"I think it's a permanent condition."

She rolled her eyes.

"I need the work." *Actually, they'll kill me—and you—if I refuse them.*

She studied his face a moment, for knotholes. "What do they have over you? Money? Do you owe them something, because I could lend you—"

"Stop. I'm fine." He sipped his coffee. "You worry too much."

She scowled so hard her lips paled. "What're they having you do? I see you going out all hours, then coming back all beat up. Taking suitcases all over. That one you have with you now—what's in there?" She stretched an arm toward his bag on the other side of the bar, necklace beads clicking on the clear coat.

"Vee, please," he said, gently pushing her back, "I have a headache."

"And that," she said, straightening her blouse. "You drinking so much. I know you and potato wine were never strangers, but I see you in here every night. It's been grand seeing you so often, really, but I know the difference between a man who drinks to have a good time and one trying to get blinders fitted."

Aksel couldn't help but smirk. "You sounded like Mum just then."

"Why, because I'm asking you to be a good boy? Then I'm glad. Not that it ever seemed to be successful, coming from her—or me."

"I consider you a success, just in a different way. Apart from the puddle over there, this place is amazing. I'm very proud of you."

"Thank you," she said, clipped, "but don't try shifting topics on the sly. I am the queen of evasive maneuvers in conversation. How do you think I keep the bank off my freckled arse? Now, about those four you're staying with up in room six. Are they—?"

An interruption, a second voice in Aksel's head. Karl,

upstairs: "During your time with the Odium, ever meet a Coog McPhearson?"

Aksel stood, picked up his coat and bag. "I have to go. Thanks for the coffee."

"Aksel . . ."

"I'll see you tonight."

Hopefully.

Out on Delmark Avenue, Aksel lugged his heavy bag.

"Coog McPhearson?" he asked Karl. The implant grafted onto his DeadEye didn't have an off switch. Karl, Raziel, Tym, or Moira could join him in his skull anytime they pleased. An ignored call was impossible so long as Aksel remained breathing, Raziel Pyne had promised in that oh-so-cuddly way of his. Off the clock, for Aksel, was an impossible concept.

"Yeah. Remember him?"

"No."

"How about his alias: Proboscis?"

Aksel faltered, flashing back to when he'd been brought aboard the *Magic Carpet*. Specifically to the man who'd chained him to a stationary bike and forced him to keep pedaling. A man with a missing nose: Proboscis. "That's familiar."

"Good. Maybe you'll recognize him," Karl said.

Cutting through the market district, weaving between holey tents, he heard peddlers crying out for his attention, each in a different tongue than the one before. He dodged useless things, little misshapen pots and crates brimming with defunct, cobwebby electronics and cords.

"He's the defector?"

On the other side of the market, Aksel reached the intersection just as the light changed. He sprinted to catch up to the group that'd already started across.

"Apparently. Tym found him on the Adeshka visitor registry. They managed to zero in on his last known location." Aksel could hear Karl abusing a keyboard. "And now I've got eyes on him. Pretty easy to keep him in sight. He's not moving too quick. Whoever he met with must've roughed him up. Explains that call to the City Patrol from that pub in Lowtown this morning."

"Where's he at now?"

Aksel moved aside as a ragged Mouflon lumbered the other way. The look on his—or her—face said, *I'm not about to step aside for any puny human.*

"Twenty-seventh Street. Where're you?"

Aksel chuckled morosely. "Just left, still on Thirty-seventh."

"Quite the hike."

Aksel waited for an opportunity to cross, humid traffic wind riffling his hair. "No shite. So what now? And where the hell are Raziel and Tym?"

"They're following the girl."

"Girl?"

"Just move."

Turning a corner, Aksel started across Thirty-sixth. "So what's the plan, then? Once I get sight of him, take him out?" Aksel was surprised at the callosity he'd heard in his own voice. The bag at his side grew a bit heavier.

"Absolutely not. We need to know whatever he told the girl. Put some speed on it. He's on the move."

"Which way?" Aksel said, ramping up from a stroll to

a genuine run.

"Westbound."

"Still on Twenty-seventh?"

"Yeah, why?"

"Let's use our think meat, Karl. What *else* is on Twenty-seventh Street?"

"The port."

"Uh-huh."

"Can you get to him?"

"It'd certainly be in my best interest to try."

Tearing across just as the light changed got him moving westbound. Pushing through a group of red-robed idiots chanting to someone they called Queen Disease, curses pelting his back, he swung his bag's weight to help pull him along.

"Raziel and Tym might need your assistance once you've got Coog."

Aksel gulped for air, cursing every pinch of mold he'd ever smoked. "Need my help? What would they need my help for? It is just one gal, yeah?"

"Not exactly Mr. Current Events, are we?"

"We don't get many personal days, Karl."

"The girl is Margaret Mallencroix. The fiancée of Clyde Pyne—our mark." Then, suddenly, "Something's spooked him. Get to the port. Now. Go, go."

Aksel charged on. To anyone else, he was just a businessman in a suit and tie bolting to get to the office. No one he passed knew that in his bag was anything but paperwork.

One block, two blocks, three . . .

By the time he arrived, his artificial lung was rattling like an accordion full of metal shavings. But, at long last, the spaceport. The West Lowtown building, one of the first built, with its pompous red-rock pillars allied across a grand staircase. It made anyone marching up feel they were about to meet a god that'd won the lottery. Right now, it was just an obstacle for Aksel, who leaped three steps at a time, tie fluttering.

After bursting through the front doors, he paused and turned away from the checkpoint where people were lined up like cattle in a maze of ropes.

On an elevated platform, Raziel and Tym stood, looking down at him, both in getups that, if you knew how they really looked, would be almost laughable; dab-on foundation that gave them almost *too* even of complexions, those stupid colored contact lenses.

Raziel, the shorter but more malicious of the two, made a small gesture.

Aksel turned, following the man's pointing finger, noticing a chark bar on the floor. Then, a few yards on, another.

"If the brothers were already here at the port, why didn't they go after Coog themselves?" Aksel asked Karl. The Pynes above were too far out of earshot to hear him.

"They're following the girl onto the frigate. Just get Coog. You lose him, it's on both of us."

After sending one last withering glare up at Tym and Raziel, Aksel followed the chark breadcrumb trail and rushed to the stairs that seemed to lead not to the boarding area for commercial frigate flights but the hangar for personal starships below.

Quick-stepping down, he found an expansive, shadowy room, mostly still holding the shape of the original cavern, fitted with a network of catwalks suspended by bulky chains. Among the catwalks, waiting ships varied from the star-cruiser yachts to rust-bucket moon hoppers. The trail ended here.

"Which one?" Aksel said, scanning the catwalks for a man with no nose.

"The *Praise to Her.*"

He charged off again, the hanging catwalks gently rocking under his pounding feet.

He nearly ran right past it. With *Praise to Her* painted on its side in a sweeping, gilt font, the beleaguered starship, crusty with rust, was at least thirty years older than Aksel.

He wanted to jump from the dock onto the wing, but the fact that Adeshka was built next to a canyon gave him pause. The view ahead offered a possible future, one that included a long, screaming tumble to the river below. It was a mile wide but looked like a blue string from up here.

Was Coog even inside?

The starship was completely enclosed with any sort of windshield made unnecessary by electronic eyes set about its flat, featureless snout, like some creature that'd never seen the suns and unloaded sight by traditional means on the road of evolution. Just as Aksel spotted the hatch on its side hidden among the swirly script of the ship's name, the ship's engines kicked on, whirring low.

That answered that.

Aksel swallowed his fear of heights—one he'd developed when Dreck Javelin shoved him out of the *Magic Carpet*. He leaped on, feet clanging on the metal, then walked up the wing toward the hatch.

When he tossed it down, the bag held itself in place by a magnetized bottom. Kneeling, Aksel withdrew the drill.

He set it barking against the hatch's hinge, a golden torrent of sparks stinging his face.

In immediate reply, the ship drifted out of its divot, the catwalk abandoning Aksel. The engines' murmur sharpened into a shriek. It'd be impossible to jump off now. He tried to ignore that fact and pushed the drill harder.

"Have him?"

"Patience, Karl."

With a deafening, one-note *fump* of its forward engines, the ship leaped away from the dock. The soles of Aksel's loafers squealed as he was sent skidding. Netted in the antennae on the ship's cheeks like catfish whiskers, he had an unwanted view of the Déashune River again.

Heart pounding, he dragged himself up and tottered to the hatch. The bag had remained put. Next to it the drill spun on, the handle whipping around, bit still buried.

Aksel snagged the spinning drill, squeezed the trigger, and leaned into it. Its motor struggled, but the hinge finally gave with a snap. He wasted no time in moving up to the second, last hinge.

Cool air rushed around him as the ship puttered toward the hangar door. The midday suns illuminated the canyon's deep ruby stratum, a sight Aksel would've found pleasant any other time.

As the drill sank, liquefied metal pushed up around it. Hitting something disagreeable, it twisted out of his hand. He reached, halting an inch from the wing's edge as the drill somersaulted into the open air—and was sucked into the starboard air intake, banged around a bit, and released in a gray puff.

Aksel blinked. *Well, shite.*

The *Praise to Her* exited the hangar's humid darkness—out over the canyon, suns splashing warmth onto Aksel's back.

The vessel tipped, setting itself for a straight punch toward the upper atmosphere.

Unwilling to take another fall from a starship quite so soon—or ever—he scrambled through the contents of his bag and withdrew a harness. Flopping the round magnet beside his bag, Aksel fed a rope through its hoop. The ship's inclining didn't stop, refusing to wait for Aksel to get his harness around his legs and waist.

The minute his shoes lost traction, he'd just gotten the last clip set. Not a second later the starship barreled toward the sky, engines roaring, the harness biting into his legs. Dangling and deaf, feeling as if his face would be peeled free by the wind, Aksel reached up for his bag.

Coog twisted them up through the clouds.

Dragging his face upward against the mashing force, Aksel reached above his head for the next tool. The bag's magnets surrendered. But before setting off on its long descent, the bag struck Aksel's shoulder in a farewell kiss. Spinning in his harness, he watched it tumble, dispersing its jangling contents. Stuff for every eventuality in the tasks the Pynes sent him on—torture tools, small knives, stun guns—all now rained back toward Adeshka.

He thumbed up his eye patch, and the barrel sprang from the socket, a metal shaft telescoping like a well-oiled spyglass. After chomping down on a bullet, Aksel triggered with a single thought: *Bang.* It hurt to use.

The hinge shattered, and the hatch flopped open. His arms ached with the effort as he pulled himself up the tether inch by inch. The moment he got near enough to the ship's artificial gravity, he was assisted aboard with a vertigo-inducing tug.

Getting to his feet, he noticed all of Coog's stuff that'd been scattered in the breach. Apparently stealing one of his former comrade's starships wasn't enough. There was a month's worth of food and, secured by netting to the bulkhead, bulging potato sacks lumpy with assorted valuables. Not that Coog could really be frowned upon for stealing from the Odium's stolen stash.

Moving quietly, he kept his gaze set on the cockpit door ahead. His DeadEye's barrel remained out, ready, *wumwum-wum* still bouncing around in his wind-blasted ears.

The door flung back wide.

The pirate was framed in the doorway, one arm in a makeshift sling, scattergun in his other hand.

The ship filled with thunder. Aksel contributed some of his own with a quick thought: *Bang.*

Belly burning, Aksel grunted to sit up and pressed a hand over his shredded shirt as the white spider silk slowly shifted to crimson.

Agony doubling him over, Aksel ambled in. The cockpit door hung open, flopping in the turbulence. Coog, trouserless, nose flung off in the fray, lay across the ship's controls, a smoking hole in his chest.

Below the pirate's dead eyes, the black triangle in his face where his nose had been was now a tiny volcano, a river of red running over its edge. Aksel fleetingly remembered why so many of the Odium were missing parts and how each one had been removed so cleanly. He'd experienced it himself, when Dreck Javelin had removed a square of flesh from his palm to mark him ex-Odium.

He took a seat at the helm, noticing a button with a red *M* on it. Hoping it'd do what he assumed, he crushed it under that scarred palm.

A little med-bot, dumped from a ceiling panel, righted itself on spidery legs and scuttled about the cockpit. It estimated Coog, determined he was well past help, and turned to Aksel. Lifting his shirt helpfully, Aksel pointed out the chewed mess of his belly. Chiming its comprehension, the bot sprouted a syringe and jabbed him without warning. Aksel sighed as pain bled away. He felt nil as the bot tweezed out pellets. He didn't dare watch.

Arrayed around the dead pirate's body were vidscreens offering multiple viewpoints of the ship's surroundings. Aksel wiped blood away from one. Cement cubes arranged under the hazy atmo-bubble fell away, and Adeshka withdrew behind them. The autopilot dutifully pushed them in the direction it'd been tasked to. But where?

"Tell me you at least got something out of him before you killed him," Karl said. Aksel could practically hear the big man rolling his eyes.

Aksel glanced at his copilot, who gazed vacantly at the ceiling; then he turned away so that Coog was again on his blind side. "We didn't exactly have tea and catch up." He retracted his DeadEye and closed his lid over it. "Too busy, you know, shooting at each other and whatnot."

Karl sighed. "Raziel's not gonna be happy."

The twin joysticks danced, tweaking the yaw and pitch with the gracefulness only a computer could execute. "Have you heard from the brothers?"

"Last update from Tym, he said they were currently boarding," Karl said grimly, clearly still stuck on the arse-chewing they could expect.

The ship pushed through one bank of clouds into blue skies only to be enveloped by the next cottony swell.

"I'm going to guess they're planning to set a ransom with her."

"Well, they wouldn't have to take that risk if you'd gotten something out of Coog, learned what she already has."

Aksel doubted Raziel would allow someone dear to Clyde to slip away when already so close—like trapped on a frigate with him, for instance, as that girl was now.

"What was I supposed to do, let him shoot me? Wait. What're you talking about? What risk?" His throat dried. "Oh, shite. They were at the port this morning. Did they do something to one of those frigates? Interrogating pirates is one thing . . ."

"What interrogating? You shot him. I heard the whole thing."

"What are they going to do?"

"Where are you now?" was all Karl said.

"Still on Coog's ship." A smaller vidscreen displayed the various programmed destinations, waypoints scattered on the horizon, marking cities and towns near and far. Among them, one, the farthest away, blinked in the ice caps. The Odium's home base? Aksel repeated the coordinates to remember them: negative nine-nine-one; positive one-two-one. *Could prove valuable.*

"Turn back. They want to get the girl before they reach Geyser. You should follow. Might get messy."

"What do you mean, messy? Did they do something to that frigate? Did they know she was going to be getting on that thing, or . . . the hell's going on, Karl?"

"All they said is they need you to follow because they might need to get off early."

Aksel drew a deep sigh, freed it. He made his hand reach over to disengage the autopilot and quickly grab the joysticks before gravity did something spiteful. Grumbling, Aksel brought the ship around in a wide one-eighty. During the hard banking turn, Coog slipped, his head clonking against the floor.

"Apologies, mate."

CHAPTER 5

Tour Guide

The tent was up and had automatically camouflaged itself to appear like any another Lakebed boulder. Inside, Clyde waited out the rain. As he would nighttime. All his life, the involuntary watchman. He observed the sleeping young man, whom he'd begun thinking of as Bandit Boy, just as he'd sometimes watched Mr. Wilkshire and, more recently, Nevele. Never having done so himself, he often wondered what it was like to sleep. Or dream.

Even Rohm, inside Clyde's pocket, had fallen asleep. Getting up carefully to not disturb either of them, Clyde unzipped the tent door and stepped out under the suns, which were now starting to shine again, just in time for dusk.

He salvaged what he could from the wrecked buggy. In the first-aid kit, he found a snakebite info pamphlet, which he used for kindling for a fire. There was no food other than Rohm's cheese, so Clyde got a handful out for Bandit Boy, arranging wedges of it on a rock near the small blaze.

Once confident the fire wouldn't go out on him if he left it alone a moment, Clyde returned to the tent.

There was a shuffling within. When he unzipped the door, Bandit Boy was awake, saucer-eyed, gaze flicking between Clyde and the dead man in the far corner. Clyde thought something like this might happen and had rolled the body over so the man was facing the tent wall. Clyde couldn't be certain but felt confident that waking up with a dead person staring at you wouldn't be pleasant.

"I brought him in only to get him out of the rain. Out of respect," he said.

"Ya dinnit need to do that." Bandit Boy withdrew from the body an inch, wincing as he pushed off with his injured leg. "Wicked sumbitch dinnit deserve it none."

"How's your leg?"

"Well, I got shot. So I reckon it hurts."

"Sorry. I've—"

"Never been shot before? Well, take it from me, mister, it sucks." He kept shifting his weight, unable to find a comfortable way to sit. "Think I could get out now?"

"Certainly." Clyde offered a hand.

Bandit Boy waved it off. "Juss lemme. Move."

Clyde stepped back.

With some difficulty and a lot of cursing, Bandit Boy stood, balancing on one foot, and hobbled from the tent. "What time is it?"

The sand was steaming, the late-afternoon suns cooking the water from it.

"Not sure." Clyde was glad for the ebbing heat, but soon they'd have another problem, the desert's notoriously cold nights. "I've got some food for you here," he said, indicating the cheese wedges.

Rohm popped his head out of Clyde's pocket. Apparently his nose worked even while he was dreaming. "Hey, that's mine!"

"We need to share."

"*We* nothing. You don't eat, which means *I* have to share."

Chin to chest, Clyde shouted at the critter in his pocket, "He's our guest!"

"Quick refresher: he tried to *kill us*."

Clyde had no argument against Rohm's last point, but he apologized to the boy for their unpleasant behavior and offered him a hunk of Asthwadla-azu cheddar.

Accepting it, thanking him, Bandit Boy gave it a sniff, then a hesitant nibble.

Rohm grumbled something about an unrefined palate.

"Yer dumb as hell if yer thinkin' of kidnappin' me. My daddy's mah only kin, and he's already done demonstrated how much he cares for me."

"Kidnap you? Why would you think we'd kidnap you?"

Turning the orange wedge of cheese, he studied where he wanted to bite next. "Juss what folks be sayin' of you." Shrug. "That's all."

"*Who's* saying these things?"

Bandit Boy said around a mouthful, "I dunno. It's everywhere out here. Juss what's bein' said. Had no reason not to believe it, I guess."

Remembering there were more important things to tend to, Clyde ducked into the tent, took the dead swordsman under his arms, and dragged him out. His face was washed of color, and his jaw hung loose—flash-frozen mid-yawn, it seemed.

Lips twisting, Bandit Boy set aside the cheese without taking another bite.

"Sorry." After letting the man down gently, Clyde returned to the overturned buggy to retrieve the collapsible shovel.

As he fumbled around inside the buggy's trunk, Bandit Boy asked if Clyde had any smoking mold.

"No," he said, struggling with the shovel that refused to spring open, "I don't have any smoking mold." With a metallic *shrick*, the tool became a standard-sized shovel in his hands, surprising him. "Besides, how old are you?"

"Eleven. Not that it matters none. I been smokin' since I was in diapers. What, you some kinda goody-goody? You eht folks' souls, and yet yer gonna gimme some daggone talk about *smokin'*?"

"I'm not a goody-goody, and I don't eat people's souls." Clyde walked off a few paces, decided here would be sufficient for a bandit's grave, and drove the shovel into the wet sand.

From his pocket, quietly enough that Bandit Boy couldn't hear, Rohm suggested Clyde leave the bumpkin out here to learn some manners.

"I can't do that," he whispered as he dug.

"You know what they say about Lakebed people, don't you, Mr. Clyde?"

"I do, yes," Clyde grumped, tossing a shovelful aside, then another.

"While they may hold a certain revulsion toward anyone who eats *souls*, as far as their fellow man—"

Clyde jammed the shovel in hard. "Rohm. I said I remember."

"Then maybe you should keep an eye on him. Not have your back to him." Rohm turned around on Clyde's shoulder. "You're lucky to have me for a second set of eyes."

Over his shoulder, Clyde peeked at Bandit Boy sitting by the fire, transfixed by the flames.

"Maybe I'm not the only one who's had lies spread about him," Clyde said.

With narrowed eyes, Rohm swayed each time Clyde bent to shovel again. "Yeah, well, just wait until the cheese runs out . . ."

Twisting side to side, Clyde finally freed the second of the harpoons spearing the dead vehicle. It was a gruesome thing—with a bifurcated tip accounting for half of the six-foot harpoon's length. Hopping down, he staked it at the head of the mound, an impromptu grave marker. After offering the second harpoon for Bandit Boy to use as a crutch, Clyde asked if he wanted to say anything for the man.

"Sure. Here lies Uncle Lou. Good riddance."

Clyde turned. "He was your uncle?"

Testing his crutch with a few exploratory stabs, Bandit Boy shrugged. "So. Where to, mister?"

"Somewhere to get you medical attention. You'll need to be our guide, though."

"Well, there's towns thataway." He pointed what Clyde assumed was east—with setting suns burning the horizon on that side of the sky. "But I doubt *you'll* be wantin' to go anywhere near 'em."

"Why?"

"Recall how my daddy and uncle when they saw yer face? Folks in any town out here are like to act the same. Some braver might even try an' kill you if they believe there's reward in it."

Clyde drew a deep breath. "Regardless, we can't exactly have you *not* see a doctor. Perhaps we can get you near a town and part company at the outskirts."

Bandit Boy squinted at him, a hand up to shield his eyes against the suns. "Why you care so damn much?"

"Because I do."

Bandit Boy chuckled. "Hardly an answer, I reckon."

"I can't not," Clyde said. "Satisfactory?"

Bandit Boy eyed Clyde's belt where he'd tucked the boy's rust-eaten handgun. "Think I might have that back?"

Clyde lifted Commencement, which he was carrying around in his hand since the strap was keeping Bandit Boy's wound staunched. He smiled reassuringly. "We'll be fine."

Bandit Boy laughed. "Gonna need more than a fancy pokey stick! Some nasty critters out here—an' we're like to run into some seein' how yer wantin' to start out so close to sunsdown. Ever *seen* a rocky crawler before?"

"No." But Clyde could imagine.

"Then you ain't never seen a pissed-off one neither. I have. Lucky to be standin' here."

"I'll keep an eye out. You just lead us to the nearest town."

"Hopefully," Rohm put in, "he'll do a better job than the driver we had."

Clyde flicked the lump in his pocket.

"Hey, ow."

Bandit Boy laughed. "I think I like him."

"And I'm sure he likes you too." And before Rohm could voice his disagreement, he said, "So when you're ready, lead on. We'll follow."

"Awright," Bandit Boy said with no shortage of uncertainty, "off we go." He poked the harpoon tip into the sand a step ahead, shuffled up to it, then did it again.

Clyde marveled that he didn't even need to consult a compass.

"But if we get ourselves eht, caint say I dinnit warn ya none."

CHAPTER 6

Slight Turbulence

When her section was called, Nevele stuffed the radio back into her bag, a sourness polluting her. She still hadn't gotten in contact with Clyde. And once on the frigate, there'd be no way to try again—using radios was a serious no-no. She'd have to wait until she was back home in Geyser. She hoped Clyde was just busy or springtime storms had caused interference.

Nevele gave her ticket to be punched by the uniformed Adeshkan guardsman, stepped into the glass tank, and accepted the avalanche of frisk mice poured over her again. As before, it made her miss Rohm. The mice, finding nothing suspicious upon her person, filed into a slot in the floor and the doors opened. From there, Nevele took the elevator down, crossed the walkway to the frigate—the enormous ex-military ship, a horizontal skyscraper with wings—bobbing in the green water of the great Déashune.

Walking up the center aisle, Nevele ignored the scrutinizing first-class passengers the best she could. Before the couple seated next to her could ask why she looked the way she did, Nevele pulled up her hood and feigned sleep.

Ten minutes later, the frigate hammered down the Déashune, using it as a runway, and took wing. After it'd safely hoisted its bulk skyward, a palpable fear lifted from the thousands of passengers around her.

Outside her triangular window, Gleese dropped beneath them. Then, once they were at cruising altitude, the groves looked more like clumps of moss and the geography blended bit by bit into the lush red of the Lakebed's borderlands.

She'd always liked traveling. Especially back when she'd joined her parents, owners of the Mallencroix Delivery Company, on their many interplanetary jaunts. Except when her brother insisted he come too. But this, now, not knowing where Clyde was or if he was okay, was worse than any of Vidurkis's harassments. And worse than even that was knowing what awaited Geyser in three days.

Still not interested in a chat with the couple next to her—who, she'd inferred through their prattle, were on their honeymoon, bless 'em—Nevele slipped on her headphones.

The Skullduggerists. Punk act out of Adeshka. Probably not commonly considered serene with the all-female group forsaking harmony in favor of volume, but it held an almost magically soothing effect on Nevele. "Glitter + Glue" in particular.

> *I wanna be with you*
> *Bad as glitter wants on glue*
> *(Shik, shik, shik)*
> *Shake me some*
> *Love me some*
> *An' say you're through?*
> *Glue-boy glue*
> *An' glitter-girl blue*
> *Shook over you*
> *(Shik, shik, shik)*
> *Stuck on you*

Not exactly highbrow, no, but Nevele could finally take a deep breath without it catching in her throat. She set the song to repeat and sank comfortably into her seat.

With a smile that seemed die-cast, the frigate's flight attendant rolled a tiny cart up the aisle, dispensing drinks and bags of crisps. Her hair was perfect, in these two swoops that nestled twin points at the corners of her mouth. Adeshka fashion could be so odd at times. "Glitter + Glue" began again.

But for all the irritation going on around her—Mr. and Mrs. Normalid next to her and the flight attendant's superfake ways—Nevele couldn't help but smile when thinking about Clyde, the happier times. Before they'd taken on this whole impede-the-Odium thing—during Geyser's restoration, when hope was not plentiful but mandatory.

It'd been when he'd asked her to marry him.

She remembered every detail, helped by the Skullduggerists since she'd been listening to them then, too. She'd been at her shop, in the back patching up something for Miss Selby, when the string of bells on the front door chimed.

Clyde found her at her worktable and, without hesitation, dropped to one knee. Through happy tears, she accepted emphatically. Later that night they set a date and planned to have the wedding at the base of the geyser in the town square.

But not long after, rumors rammed into Geyser. With them, Nevele's fluorescent-pink wedding-day goggles started getting tugged off. It didn't help how each night Clyde began returning to their home on Wilkshire Lane from the palace with worry clouding his face. Refusing to talk it over with her, saying she should concentrate on wedding plans with Miss Selby, he'd head upstairs to the study. Never needing to sleep, he'd spend every minute with his worries. Eventually she demanded to know, sick of essentially living alone in a big, empty house, the only evidence she had a fiancé at all being hollow thumps of ceaseless pacing above.

Oh, how they'd fought.

But in the end, they decided to strike out separately. Not with a nod and a handshake all peaceful and amicable, either. Neither one wanted the other in danger, but the threat of losing the city was so much greater. They lingered during that farewell kiss, both afraid it could be their last.

Heart pounding, Nevele raised the volume on her headphones, frantic to gather the inexplicable peace it gave her, trying to soak in as much of it as possible.

Three days. They had only three days to stop the Odium. She imagined Pitka Gorett, wherever he'd denned himself, fingers steepled, cackling with his plan close to fruition.

Worse, she realized with a start, she was alone, as far as she knew, in knowing their plan. The contents of her head were very valuable.

Faintly: "Miss?"

Nevele drew back her hood.

The flight attendant, who seemed to try not to recoil, quickly turned her smile up from bright to *nuclear*. "Would you care for some crisped ardimires?"

"No, thank you."

"Are you sure? They're complimentary."

The couple beside her tore into theirs. Apparently

they'd been too busy with other activities during their honeymoon to remember to feed themselves. Jealousy ground at Nevele, making her jaw ache.

"I'm fine," she said and tugged her hood back up.

After a few minutes of manically circling thoughts, a neck-jamming turbulence hit. Nevele shot up in her seat, even though no one else reacted. *I'm so jumpy*.

"Miss?"

"No refreshments, thank you, still fine."

"Please come with me."

In the aisle a thin, dark-haired man stared down at her. Not in a flight attendant's or even a pilot's uniform but a plain black suit tailored for a much beefier frame than his.

"Something wrong?" She glanced around. A few people in adjoining aisles—and Mr. and Mrs. Normaloid—all stared at the man and Nevele.

"We need to speak," he said, voice dull. "So if you'd please . . ." He indicated aft with a sidelong nod and stepped aside so she could get out of her seat. She watched his hand return to his pocket and move something around.

Nevele, unbuckling, considered lashing him with her threads. She had keen aim but not good enough to be certain she'd avoid catching someone else by accident.

She stepped into the aisle, mind racing, the man close behind. They passed into the cramped section where flight attendants prepared meals and reloaded refreshment carts.

The man pointed left at a narrow stairwell. "Up."

When she didn't heed him, he shifted a gun-shaped thing in his pocket. "Go."

Reluctantly, she clunked up the stairs. *How the blazes am I going to get out of this one? We're on a bloody frigate. Where can I even run?*

Another patch of turbulence rocked them, making Nevele fleetingly think they'd scraped a mountaintop. Snagging the handrail, she turned herself on the step to look back at him, considering again, threads ready.

"You one of them?" she said, holding her ground on the step above him. "Gave you a shave and a new suit so you wouldn't look so piratey?"

He produced the gun from his pocket. "Go."

She groaned, "Fine," and continued up.

The dining room. Every one of the booths, set upon the luxuriant blue carpet, was empty.

Another quake hit. A few lights flickered, the chandeliers' crystals breaking into a discordant song. Bottles secured in brass shelves behind the bar rattled in time with the electric braziers' nauseating sways. Nevele grabbed onto the edge of the lacquered bar to keep from tumbling over. Something cold poked her lower back.

"Over there."

Taking a seat, Nevele kept her face set, not wanting to give him even the smallest win of seeing her afraid. All the while, her heart threw itself against her rib cage again and again.

Sitting across from him, she finally got a good look. His skin was uniformly the same shade, as if he'd slathered himself in that cakey mud-in-a-tube stuff used to patch fenders. His eyes—blinking often, as if they burned—seemed off somehow. Glassy. Whites too white.

With a glance, she took stock of the empty dining room. There was nothing that could be harmed if she used her threads. But at the same time, he had a gun. She'd need to catch him off guard. Tough, since he never seemed to look anywhere but at her.

"So we're here," she said. "What do you wish to discuss?"

"You spoke to a man by the name of Coog McPhearson earlier today. What did he tell you?"

"Who are you?"

"You *spoke* to a *man* earlier *today*—"

"I heard you the first time."

"Then tell me what he said."

"I think, at this particular juncture, I'm going to respectfully decline. Instead I'll suggest you take that gun of yours, bend over, and—"

"If you don't accommodate, I will give a signal to my associate waiting in the holds, who will trigger an explosive. It will rupture the fuel cells, down the frigate, and kill everyone on board."

Her spine became ice.

"I had no plans to be on this flight today," he said. "I had plans *for* it, unquestionably, but none that involved me being a passenger. But as it's said, best laid plans." He smiled thinly. "So if you want to leave with me and my associate, I'd recommend speaking up." His weird eyes peeked down at his watch. "We've only a while."

"Okay, okay, fine. Coog said . . . he said that I'd be approached by a man to whom I should immediately recommend firing his tailor. I mean, look at that thing you got on. Could fit three of you in there."

Recoiling an arm, movements graceful and measured, he tucked a hand into his baggy suit coat. He set down a walkie-talkie between them. "Thin ice."

A thread lacing Nevele's right arm begged to be freed. She forbade it. "What information could be so valuable? None of these people have anything to do with this. Besides, if you blow up the frigate, you'll die too."

"Another will follow through."

"Follow through with *what*? Getting information out of me? Fat lot that'll get you. I don't think I'm likely to be a talkative corpse."

"You are betrothed to the Sequestered Son, are you not?"

"This is about Clyde?" Things latched into place. She *had* seen this man before, but something was different. It'd been in Geyser. Of that much she could be certain, but in what capacity and when?

His left hand knotted into a fist. When he opened it, she noticed that in the creases between his fingers, something white had been smudged in. Like he'd stuffed his hand inside a jar of flour, wiping it off, but some had remained in the valleys of his skin's texture.

No. It was the opposite. The white wasn't *on* him; that *was* him.

"You're Raziel Pyne."

His cheek cratered over a clenching jaw. "Tell me what the pirate told you."

"Raziel, why are you doing this?" All sassiness was gone now, bewilderment replacing it. "He's been looking for you. He wants you and Tym and Moira to come back to Geyser. He wants to meet you."

"He's *already* met me," he said, volume rising. "He just doesn't *remember* because Father made him tell me that he—" He swallowed. "Doesn't matter. Any love I ever had for him in return is just as gone. Same for Father."

"Maybe . . . if we just talked about this . . ."

"I thought he was dead. For years," Raziel shouted. "Father told us he was dead before he even announced it publicly, to the world, *lying* to *everyone*. And . . . I thought then that *I* had to become the man suitable for the job, prepared for the Commencement. And that's precisely what I was doing when Pitka Gorett usurped Father. At the academy, studying my eyes out, dealing with all the comments that I never have to sleep or eat and that gave me an unfair advantage . . ." He reduced the rest of the statement to a snarl.

"None of that is Clyde's fault. Nor is anyone on this frigate to blame. You kill all these people, and I don't need to tell you . . . Clyde's a forgiving man, but something like *that?*"

"I don't want his *forgiveness*," Raziel spoke to the table's grain. "I don't want a thing from him except his death. And I know if any of Father's stubbornness is in him, he won't be willing to give up the throne even though it's mine. He *got sent away*. He forfeits. And now it's up to me to save the city he's throwing away. He's ruining what I've worked so hard to become."

"So you have a degree you can't use anymore and you think that's *Clyde's* fault? Reason enough to kill him?"

"He should've just stayed away. He should've remained buried wherever Father put him, hiding like the pitiful nothing he always was. What sort of weaver like him could *ever* be of consequence?"

Raziel lifted his gaze, and Nevele saw one of his eyes . . . drift, as if it'd suddenly become lazy. At the edge of its white, she could see blackness behind it. Just like Clyde's. He blinked, and the lens popped back where it belonged.

"He helps people feel better," Nevele said. "That's huge, if you ask me."

"Oh? But can he do this?"

She had to draw a breath—something sharp was inside her, like a long knife with a jointed blade that twisted and swam as it cut, swishing in a serpentine way.

"He scrubs black motes of people's guilt away," Raziel went on, his voice muted by Nevele's speeding pulse. "Hardly fabrick. His is a stillborn gift."

Nevele's vision clouded. Her face felt full, hot. She fell from her seat, squirming on the floor, overwhelmed by the pain.

"I, as you are now discovering, received a great generosity from the stone." Raziel knelt beside her. "One befitting a king."

Her threads reached and lashed, aimless, sporadic.

Raziel pulled at a loose strand. "Would you unravel like a sweater? Every bit of pain you've ever inflicted on anyone." He looped her threads around his fingers as they squeezed him harmlessly in uncontrollable, soft pulses. "Physical, emotional, psychological. Given back. And by your rather dramatic response, it seems you haven't exactly been kind to your fellow man."

"Stop," Nevele managed. "Please."

"I don't know what you can do with these strings of yours, but it'd be wise to not try and harm me. Will you be good?"

"Yes. Just . . . *please. Please.*"

"All right, then." The cutting, white-hot agony withdrew.

Nevele, gasping, sat up and pawed her chest. She glared at him as her threads wound themselves back into her, lacing the skin panels. "There's no way," she croaked, "you're a Pyne."

"How can you be so sure? You've only the one for an example, and he's not much to write home about."

"I knew your dad. He was—"

"A fool who thought Gleese could be changed if he only lived by example, his benevolence becoming contagious. But you saw, if you really *did* know him, that eventually he succumbed, even finally trading in that stupid sword for a weapon suitable for the times."

Nevele remembered now. A party at the palace, back when she was newly the Royal Stitcher. It'd been a lavish affair celebrating some dignitary's birthday. Raziel, Tym, and Moira were in attendance, gloomily occupying the back corner of the reception hall, watching the others have fun. She never suspected their pale faces as anything abnormal; it'd been a masquerade ball, and below domino masks decorated with feathers and gems, she took the unmoving lips as bone-white unpainted porcelain. Not flesh.

Leaving Nevele on the floor, Raziel sauntered to the bar, pulled out a stool, and gingerly had a seat. Unmasking—if only in word—seemed to loosen him greatly. With the gun, he motioned a *Please continue* roll of the wrist. "What'd Coog say, then?"

"What's it matter to you?" She rubbed her chest, the ache lingering. "If they blow up Geyser, wouldn't you win?"

"I can't be a *king* without a *kingdom*, idiot."

Nevele returned to her chair, dropping into it. "Just so you know, I'm through talking to you."

"Hurt your feelings, did I?" He tipped his head to the side, pouting. He thumbed back the gun's hammer.

"Boohoo. Talk."

"All right, fine." Nevele balled a fist at her side. "You got me. You win. Here. Your *prize*." Pitching her hand forward, she sent a spiraling surge of threads.

He flung himself from the bar stool.

Target missed, the column of threads collided and tangled with the liquors shelved behind the bar, breaking bottles with the impact.

At this, Raziel smiled winningly and raised the gun to take aim at her.

Without hesitation, Nevele made her stitches latch onto the shelf and yanked. It snapped free of the wall, crashing over the bar and into Raziel's back, swatting him to the floor like a fly.

Under the crushing weight, Raziel struggled to his hands and knees, lifting the destroyed shelf with him, a multicolored flood of spirits and glass shards raining onto him. With effort, he shouldered it aside.

A majority of his makeup had been washed away. His left eye had lost its contact, leaving it completely black while the other was still its artificial blue-green, its incongruity mirroring the damaged mind behind.

But uneven as his eyes were, from them came a unanimous thing: fury.

CHAPTER 7

And How Did You Two Meet?

The second voice in the Bullet Eater's head informed him, "It's getting dodgy in there. Get ready to move in."

"Let the frigate hail Adeshka."

"What?"

"Let Raziel and Tym get what's coming to them. King Chidester can be the hero. We can be done with them today."

"As nice as that sounds, you know they'd find some way to get even with us, even from prison."

Aksel didn't doubt it. "Fine, aye-aye, portside emergency hatch. On it."

Giving the sticks a sideways shove, he dropped his stolen starship free of the white contrails and tore up alongside the long flank of the frigate. His hands shook, both from the feedback in the sticks with the thrusters being put through their paces and from his fraying nerves.

Try to understand, gods, he begged the ether, *I'm just following orders*. He pushed in near the hatch, which was striped a cautionary red and white. Getting too close set off some kind of automatic security system. Turrets popped from hidey-holes along the second ship's flank and immediately opened fire. With deft shimmying of the sticks, erratically weaving the *Praise to Her*, Aksel managed to dodge a majority of the blasts. He believed one had found its mark. The *Praise to Her* gave a painful whine, and the control panel lit up in ways no pilot ever wants to see.

Plunging and dodging, he kept peeking over, hoping to see the door open. What was taking them so long? Aksel continued barrel rolling and twisting to busy the turrets, all the while wishing they'd just run out of damn bullets already.

"I can't stay here all day. I'm taking fire, a shiteload of it."

"Get ready. They're coming out."

Aksel smacked the autopilot button and undid his harness. As he stumbled through the holds of the ship, the artificial-gravity generator became confused. Aksel used the dangling stowage straps like a ladder.

Reaching the cargo door, he threw the lock and let the wind drag it aside. The bare world stretched before him, the setting suns blinding him. And such a long drop from here . . .

His arm hooked into the handle flanking the door. As the starship bounced, a few times his feet left the floor. Once he nearly spun on the axis of the handle and out.

Through the chaos, a small thought passed: *Redemption's never out of reach if you're willing to stretch some.* But how? And when?

He watched the glass panel in the frigate hatch and waited for shadows. What would he do when he saw Raziel and Tym appear there, wanting to board? Help them or defy them? Flip of a coin, really. He'd likely end up dead either way.

Under the barrage of gunfire, Nevele dove beneath the table. She crawled to the next aisle of the unoccupied dining room. She could see the green glowing exit sign across the room, but right now it may as well have been miles off.

The passengers, clearly having heard the shots, screamed in the decks below. Nevele stole a second to retract the trailing threads and free them in a cracking snap as Raziel stepped out to fire.

He drew up an arm, letting them coil around his wrist, and pulled. Effectively on a lead, Nevele struggled to move, but every time she attempted to jink left or right he'd give her another tug—keeping her in his wavering sights.

Just as she flipped the dessert cart up between them, the bullet pierced it. She gave her threads a pull, and Raziel screamed as they ripped free of his arm. She was about to take aim and thrash him again when the dagger of pain plunged into her chest again.

Clawing at herself, unable to stop, she snapped stitches, and panels of skin fell away. Jumping red veins framed the world above, and Raziel stepped in.

"I wonder how much you've told him. He must suspect something. Only so much can fit under one rug. Ever give my big brother a peek at what you swept under?"

Nevele fought the pain. "You know who Gorett had kill your father, right?"

His face twisted up.

"I take that as a no." To let Raziel see, she let herself think of her brother and the hurts she'd given him.

Apparently he pieced together that Pitka Gorett had assigned Vidurkis Mallencroix to kill his father. Raziel's lips peeled back. He spread his open hand wide and crushed it into a fist.

Another salvo of soul-rending misery came. Blackness crept in, and Nevele sank into it, drawn deeper and deeper.

"It doesn't matter," Raziel said, from somewhere outside the void. "I'll get Gorett's head once I'm on the throne. Dry the banks to their foundations, putting every bounty hunter in the world on the job. But before we can do that, we need to save the city. Now what did the pirate tell you?"

Even if she wanted to answer, she couldn't. Her hands, on autopilot, dug and dug, raking fingernails across raw, exposed muscle below. Anything to get it out. With the next breath she was able to snag—it felt as if her ribs were thorny on the inside—the air had a pungent muddy taste. Like a river, stirred up into a muddy froth after rain . . .

"You'll beg me for this bullet while that water fills your lungs over and over just like it did his."

Chest convulsing, tasting river, she held Raziel's mismatched gaze, stubborn to the last.

"When are the Odium going to attack Geyser? Tell me."

She wanted to answer, if only to not feel this anymore, but she couldn't, wouldn't. "No."

Raziel sighed. "Fine. We'll just have to take you along and continue this conversation at a new location." He spoke into his walkie-talkie. "Get up here, Tym. We're jumping ship. Karl, get the Bullet Eater ready."

From his coat pocket, he produced a small black sphere and tossed it into the center of the dining area. Producing twiggy legs, the tripod righted itself. It flashed, and when her eyes adjusted, she saw the Dapper Tom, the Odium's winking cartoon cat face, burned onto the wall.

"The Odium want our city?" Raziel said. "Then they'll

have to deal with Adeshka's reaction to them shooting down one of their frigates first. Peace doesn't occur naturally. It's what results, never what comes first. It has to be sought to be had. And sometimes, using equations some may not think of as very nice."

The ball rolled, stood, and flashed Clyde's picture onto the next wall. Do Not Trust, it read. The ball rolled on, alternating the insignia and the libel about her fiancé— flash, flash.

"And he can have some bad press too while we're at it."

Nevele couldn't stand, let alone walk, and Raziel dragged her along by her hood. They passed through the kitchen into the crew quarters. She continued to paw at her chest, convinced that if she could spit right now, it'd be bloody.

The dagger happened upon something—a boarded-off room in her mind holding a memory that, if she accidentally bumped into in her day-to-day, would make her want to busy her hands with something, frantic for distraction.

But now the planks were coming loose, the dagger's edge working under each nail head, prying . . .

Nevele had gone to a crossroads a few miles outside Exalcrodt, the marshlands. A handwritten letter signed by Zoya Kesbanya had brought her.

Zoya wanted someone to help her. She was a weaver. Her gift: she could adjust gravity in little pockets of space. Make things levitate regardless of how heavy. The cost, the flip side, as there always is with fabrick: some bleeding from the ears whenever she overexerted herself.

Stumbling upon her elevating the backyard swing set

over her head, her father pulled Zoya from school so she could help save his floundering shipbuilding business. She worked like a dog, being tasked with moving the super-structures for fishing vessels. She was so tired it took her three days to write the letter.

Nevele went at once.

She arrived and was not warmly welcomed by the girl's father, a bone-thin man with a sheen to his eyes that suggested a crippling chemical dependency. She asked to see Zoya. He refused. After he pushed her away from the door, Nevele noticed his hand had left a red smudge on her cloak.

Seeing it too, he tried to lie. He'd cut himself working.

Nevele ignored his demands for her to leave then.

"She just gets worked up, and she bleeds from her ears when she does. It's no big deal," the girl's father said, following Nevele into the muddy shipyard.

"Where is she?"

Zoya's father sighed and pointed with that same bloody hand.

She was being kept behind the shipyard in a pen, hidden so that nonweaver employees wouldn't be alarmed. Not that it was a reasonable concern. The place was empty, evidence enough that Zoya's father had fired his entire staff and had Zoya assemble the ships alone, no need of costly help anymore.

The moment she saw Nevele, Zoya cried. Scream-bawling, animal-like, but from relief. As if she didn't know, or had forgotten, how to make happy sounds.

After freeing her, Nevele noticed the girl's hair and shoulders were crusty with blood.

Seemed she'd been doing a lot of overexerting herself . . .

The girl was eleven, gangly in that preteen stage but more so because of malnutrition—sunken cheeks and eyes. She held Nevele, pressing in and clutching hard.

Zoya's father was quiet when he saw Nevele coming back around from behind the rusty blue building.

He didn't say anything, nor did Nevele.

She couldn't even look at him. Afraid of what she'd do if she did. Even a peek.

But she knew she—unlike Zoya—would be seeing him again.

And maybe he, too, knew that.

So good-byes weren't necessary.

Nevele and Zoya stayed in a hotel in D'loon. When Nevele said she could order anything she wanted from the room service menu, Zoya was overwhelmed. Took her half an hour to decide on a hot fudge sundae, Nevele never rushing. They watched telly.

In the morning, at first glance, Nevele thought she'd left. She found Zoya curled up sleeping under the bed. They had cake for breakfast.

After a spin through the shops in D'loon, in a new set of clothes—and with a few additional outfits in a new suitcase—Nevele took Zoya to a school. From then until graduation, Nevele paid the bill. She didn't do this for every weaver who needed her, because none had needed help quite like this.

At Srebrna Academy, a red-haired woman with the curious name of Nimbelle Winter smiled as she greeted them. Nimbelle explained she doubled as the etymology professor—specializing in Platyhelminthes—as well as a fill-in at admissions. Taking the girl's hand, she promised

Nevele that Zoya would be safe and loved and get a good education and a good life.

Nevele told Zoya to keep her chin up and, curiously, Zoya told Nevele to do the same.

Nimbelle Winter thanked Nevele for bringing Zoya, and the moment the front doors closed behind them, the smile faded from Nevele's face.

Straining to keep from shaking, she turned away and boarded her starship. The faster-than-light drive got a lot of use that day.

She returned to the shipyard.

The girl's father waited for her. Not by choice. He couldn't have gone anywhere, packed into his daughter's metal cage as he was.

Nevele released the brake on the crane. The cage hit the water, its sinking slowed by trapped air. His hands turned white-knuckled on the bars as he pointlessly tried to climb. The hatch on top she'd secured herself, beating its lock with a hammer so it'd keep fast.

"This is murder," he said just before the water reached his chin, the top of his head crushed against the roof of the cage, final precious inches abandoning him. He seemed no longer angry but restated it in disbelief, seemingly wanting nothing more than for his words to catch Nevele's hidden heart: "This is murder."

Mud up to her knees, Nevele raised her voice to be heard as the brown water filled Zoya's father's ears. "You invited this. Which makes it more like suicide."

"Wait, wait, wait, wait, wait, wait—"

The cage slipped under.

Bubbled a while.

Then didn't.

Raziel giggled. "Well, now. Can't say I expected that." The pain dagger seemed intrigued by this brambly corner of her soul and roundly carried on, scouring for similar secrets to taste. "Good choice of schools, though. My alma mater."

Sliding along the floor, twisting and moaning, Nevele was too sick to speak.

A man stepped into the hallway, and Raziel let her slump to the floor. When her eyes cooperated enough to actually look at him and not roll back in her head, she saw the second, taller man was also wearing a black suit like Raziel's, and he was similarly slathered in almost-flesh-tone makeup. She could see a resemblance to Clyde, as she had in Raziel: pronounced cheekbones, sharp chin, big eyes.

"What happened?" the man said, noticing Nevele on the floor. "And what's that smell?"

Raziel, still dripping with broken glass and spirits, stepped over her. "She won't tell us when."

"But they are planning on attacking?" said the second man, whom Nevele assumed was Tym.

"They are. Confirmed now."

Tym worried something in his hand, a small plastic remote. Raziel nodded at it. "Are we primed?"

"Yes," he said. "Is the Bullet Eater ready?"

"Outside." Raziel cocked a thumb over his shoulder.

Nevele let her head loll back and clunk against the floor. Upside down, she could see the emergency hatch. The air lock? *But we're still moving.*

"Blow it?" Tym said, reluctance in his voice.

"Blow it," Raziel ordered. He snatched up Nevele by

her hood and dragged her into the air-lock room.

Tym stepped up behind, glancing down at her as she was pulled along ahead of him. His gaze didn't remain connected to hers for long. He looked over her, to his brother ahead.

"Now?"

"Yes, Tym, now." Raziel snapped.

"I . . . don't really understand why we have to do it at all."

"We've covered this. Chidester will have no choice but to move hunting the Odium to the top of his kingly honey-do list. We can't stop the pirates on our own. We need to paint a crosshair on them."

"But isn't there some other way . . . without hurting people?" Tym had a terribly young voice.

"Give it, then, if you haven't the spine."

Tym looked at the remote in his hands, agonized, and then held it out for Raziel to take.

Holding it under his younger brother's nose, Raziel made a show of pressing the button. With the hard click, Tym's painted face fell. He glanced in Nevele's direction briefly, then looked away.

The frigate trembled. The vibration on the floor shot through Nevele's back, almost to the point that the pain eating away at her was nothing but a faint itch. Maybe Raziel needed to focus to keep her wrapped in pain.

She took the opportunity to flop over and deliver a punch to Raziel's available knee—the heavy shroud of returned agony leaping from her instantly.

"Raz!" Tym, gangly, all arms and legs, lurched to assist.

Nevele flung out a backhand swing and lashed Tym across the face.

Both momentarily down for the count, she sprang to

her feet—just as the frigate began to list, the entire thing canting as if attempting an impossibly hard turn for a vessel its size.

But it kept leaning.

And leaning.

She spotted the gear rack on the wall of the air-lock room: fire extinguishers, inflatable slides for quick unloading of passengers—and parachutes. She snatched one up, kicked away Raziel's reaching hand as he tried to use the rolling of the room to propel him toward it, and went to the hatch, pulling the chute pack on.

As the room turned, the black-suited brothers slid away from the hatch, fighting to keep stable footing. Just before the wall with the hatch became the ceiling, Nevele leaped up and grabbed on. Her weight wasn't sufficient in pulling the release lever, so she kicked down, trying to bounce it open, all while struggling to get the parachute the rest the of the way on with her free hand.

Below, Raziel and Tym hit the wall, which was now the floor of the white-and-red-checkered room. Raziel clutched his leg, and Tym pressed his bleeding face. A smear of blood and makeup came away each time he rubbed at his eyes, moaning and sputtering.

Each bounce moved the lever a bit, but the outside pressure kept the hatch snug. Parachute now on, Nevele used both hands, swinging and tugging with nothing to use for leverage. Dangling helpless, she watched below as Raziel got to his feet, limped to his brother.

She watched as Raziel gently pulled his brother's hands away to see—and Nevele paused in her escape, struck by the horror she'd made of Tym's face. He'd never see again.

Raziel snarled, gaze shooting upward. He raised a hand, and Nevele felt all of Tym's agony. It was as if she'd mistaken a wood chipper for a pair of binoculars. Her hand sprang off the hatch handle, and she fell the length of the room, crashing next to Tym.

But while his suffering would last, hers cut away a moment later when Raziel's attention was swept elsewhere.

Directly above, the hatch flew off, suns pouring light in. A starship just outside kept time with the crashing frigate, and at the second hatch stood a man with a bloody shirt, tie fluttering about his face.

"You have to throw us something," Raziel shouted at him. He pointed to Tym on the floor. "We've a man down, thanks to this one." Nevele's ribs received a mirthless kick.

She coiled around the blow, coughing. As she struggled up into a sitting position, her elbow brushed something soft. She still had the parachute on.

Watching Raziel bark at the Bullet Eater, hissing at the new pain in her side, she looked skyward, her hand finding the rip cord. But if she deployed in here, she'd be pulled out of the frigate, banging all the way up through the room and probably along the outside of the frigate as it continued to crash, likely getting tangled in her own lines. She'd have to wait until they were moving across from one ship to another and then deploy in the open air between . . .

The man with the eye patch reappeared at the far ship's hatch and dropped a weighted rope. Grabbing it, Raziel shoved it toward Nevele: she was to go first. She began to climb.

She felt the rope go taut and saw Raziel, below, guide

his blinded brother on. She looked back up, climbed a little more, and was out in the open space between the ships. The eye-patch man was at the hatch's edge above, reaching for her.

Not taking his hand, she saw they were at an altitude where if she deployed, she'd likely be fine. Touching boots to the desert would be a grand thing. She freed one hand from the rope with exactly that in mind when the man above latched onto her wrist. She looked into his face, the one eye that had been staring down at her in a curious way. Apologetic, almost. He shook his head and, of all things to do right then, popped a bullet into his mouth. *The hell?*

Raziel shouted something stolen by the wind. Below, Tym swung around on the rope, holding on for dear life, lids closed over ruined eyes.

"Pull us up," Raziel screamed.

But the man above didn't. Instead, he leaned out of his craft, near Nevele, their faces nearly touching. He opened his winking eye, and a bronze shaft telescoped out. She didn't have time to ask him what it was—its function was made apparent with a blast, loud even amid the rushing wind.

Tym, never knowing the shot was coming, was winged across the forearm and tumbled free of the rope, sailed past Raziel, hit the edge of the hatch, and fell into the frigate.

Raziel glanced down, then back up, hate in his mismatched eyes. He started to coil his arm in the rope to free up a hand. Nevele let herself slide down. Her boots crashed into one of Raziel's hands, and he fumbled with his other, turning and screaming as he followed his brother, even hitting the edge of the hatch before dropping back in.

"Hold on!" came from above, but Nevele scarcely

needed the recommendation.

While they rose, she watched the frigate make a slow, awkward, twisting plummet. When it was completely up-side down, she could see the massive rip in its underside. It bled fire and something else that, when ablaze, burned with a syrupy green that curled and stretched like reaching tentacles.

The frigate hit the desert floor, a ringing shockwave leaping out from around it. The hulking craft continued to push, digging a long trench behind. It came to rest intact but still aflame. She hoped some kind of call managed to sneak out, some distress beacon for those surviving.

The Bullet Eater helped Nevele the rest of the way up and closed the hatch, inducing enormous silence as if a mountainous schoolmarm had just boxed her ears.

The man said nothing else, merely walked back to the cockpit and collapsed into the seat. He didn't reach for the controls. Just sat there, slumped, looking browbeaten, watching the autopilot work.

Stepping in after him, she noticed Coog McPhearson dead on the floor, wedged between the copilot seat and the bulkhead.

"Why'd you do it?"

The man twitched as if he hadn't heard her clunk up beside him. "He shot at me first."

"I meant about the other two."

He continued staring at the vidscreens, silent for nearly a minute. "Don't know," he said at last. Then, startling Nevele, he began shouting to someone not present. "Shut up, Karl. I'm changing sides, okay? Doing what we should've done months ago."

She didn't take a seat in the cockpit with him but instead folded down one of the jumpsuits just outside. She surveyed the contents of the starship. Lots of junk and chark bars scattered everywhere. "Is this Coog's ship?"

"Yeah. And to explain my outburst a minute ago, I was speaking to my ex-coworker. He works for Raziel and Tym. They're Clyde Pyne's younger brothers."

"I know."

"Oh. Then I guess you probably know what they were up to, what they wanted with you."

"Yes."

"So . . . you're probably wondering if you can trust me, then, right?"

Nevele, minding her aching side, took off the parachute. "You just told Karl—was it?—that you've quit, changed sides. And if you're no longer on Raziel's side, I don't really care what side you're on. Not that he's in any position to have anyone on his side anymore." The parachute thumped to the floor. She made note of where she dropped it just in case she'd need it again. "Either way, thank you is what I meant."

He shrugged. "I'm Aksel, by the way." He said the name as if giving an unfavorable diagnosis. "You're Margaret Mallencroix, right?"

"Nevele, but yes."

She noticed the rearview vidscreens. The frigate, as it shrank behind them, continued to not detonate. She asked Aksel to alert Adeshka. He said he'd already done so, even before turning on the brothers.

"So," Aksel said, "since we should probably make ourselves scarce lest we get blamed for that, where would you like to go?"

"Home." She withdrew her radio from her pocket. "That is, if you don't mind we check in on a friend first."

CHAPTER 8

Dusty Walk

Clyde felt cooked on the spot, each step heavier than the one before. Without need to eat or drink or sleep, all he knew of sustenance was taking confessions. It seemed to fill him up somehow, the same way, he imagined, that food nourished people unlike him.

He considered asking Bandit Boy if he had anything he wanted to confess but refrained, knowing it'd put the boy in even more danger. While the boy suffered an open wound that still hadn't been cleaned, jinxing him might not be such a good idea.

"What's your name?" Clyde said. He wouldn't be surprised if Bandit Boy's name was actually Bandit Boy.

"Emer. Well, Emer Junior."

"I don't expect you'll be forgiving Emer Senior anytime soon," Clyde said, "but after we get you patched up, do you have somewhere to stay? A mother or—?"

"Momma's dead."

"Oh. I'm sorry, I . . ."

"It's fine. Happened a while back."

But, Clyde thought, *you're only eleven*. You *barely happened a while back*.

Emer continued, "And yer damn right, I *don't* believe I'll be forgivin' Daddy anytime soon. He's done some stupid crap, but shootin' me was the last straw on *this* here camel's back, tell you what. I'll be my own man now, with nothin' or nobody holdin' me back."

Clyde nodded, glad to hear it.

"What's yers?"

"My name?"

"Yeah."

"Clyde."

Emer nodded. "I remember that now, from them signs." He carefully spelled Clyde's name and asked if he'd been accurate.

"Yes, well done."

Emer tried it out again. "*Clyde*. Not bad. Gotta good sound to it."

"Thanks. Emer's not bad either."

"This Emer," he said, poking a thumb toward himself, "sure as hell ain't." He took a second to pause and rub his leg. If the gunshot wound itself hurt, then having the rest of the limb starved for blood probably wasn't feeling so wonderful either.

"We'll get you some care soon," Clyde said.

"I know. We got only 'bout thirty-five, forty miles yet."

"Uh, *what*?" said Rohm.

They walked on.

When Emer spoke again, Clyde gave a start, his mind's deep drifting aided by the isolation of this place. He thought about Nevele mostly. Flam too.

"Ya was born in November," Emer said. "Am I right?"

Clyde tugged his bandanna down to speak. "You might be. I don't know."

"You don't know when yer own *birthday* is?"

"I don't, actually."

"Huh. I'd put you at . . . twenny years old. And November? Pretty sure on that too."

All Clyde knew of how old he was had been based on his history as told to him by Nigel Wigglesby. That fateful day, when the old miner gave him the royal revolver and with it, just as heavy, the truth about who he was—and who he had to be from that day forward.

"Didya hear me?" Emer said. "Said I bet yer twenny years old."

"I heard you," Clyde said agreeably, still lost in thought. The heat brought on daydreaming like a possession. He'd stared at the few photographs of Pitka Gorett he'd found in the palace's archives, memorizing every detail of the man's face. He wanted to see it in the flesh, albeit firmly behind dungeon cell bars. Was this what his mind made manifest, his mirage of what he desired to find waiting over the next hill, above all else?

"Even if ya can't confirm it, I'm going to say yer . . . twenny years an' two hunnert days, give or take few hours."

"And how can you be so certain of a thing like that?" Clyde said, welcoming the distraction. Thinking about Pitka Gorett too long made his stomach hurt.

"To me, folks wear it pretty plain, their age. Ya could be older, though. Got what mah granny used to call a worldliness to them weird eyes of yers. Ya been through some rough stuff, I reckon."

"It's been a challenging time for my city recently, yes."

"You too, seems like."

Clyde nodded.

"Got a thowzant-mile gaze on you like a man twice, maybe even three times, yer years."

"If your estimation of my age is correct," Clyde said with a smile.

Marching with his new, uneven gait, Emer looked over at Clyde. "Sheeit. No estimatin' to it. Ask anyone. I always get them birthdays right. Magic. Like a daggone weaver, I am. No 'fense."

"None taken."

When they took a break, Emer staked his walking stick into the ground and carefully snapped open a cactus for some water for him and Rohm. Clyde busied himself by trying Nevele on his radio again. Still no response. He turned south for a moment, toward where he approximated Geyser to be, somewhere past the Jagged Mountains, an indistinct serrated row of black peaks. Did she make it back okay? He wished, then, he could trade his fabrick for one that'd allow him flight.

After a few more cactus pods were drained, Emer wiped his mouth with his sleeve. "So if ya ain't out here to eht nobody's soul, what *is* ya out here fer?"

"We were on our way to Nessapolis, actually."

Emer goggled. "Whutcha wantin' to go *there* fer?"

"I'm looking for someone."

"Who? Ain't nobody livin' there, 'cept ghosts."

"Well, we'll have to take our chances—ghosts or no."

"Why?"

"It's kind of a secret." He winked, trying to end the conversation in a friendly way.

"If it's a secret, why'd you bring it up?"

Clyde rewound the conversation a bit. "I didn't. You

did. Are you feeling all right?"

The asynchronous crunch of Emer's boots and the chunk of his spear continued for a moment, two. "I *am* a little light-headed, and I mean, thankee for the cheese an' all—"

"You're *welcome*," Rohm muttered.

"But I usually eht more than that for dinner. Was gonna have somethin' *good* tonight, too, so I think mah stomach's still thinkin' we're havin' sky whale. That's what we were doin', actually, when Uncle Lou spotted your fancy buggy. Damn easier catchin' city folk than whale, he said."

Clyde said nothing.

"Caint blame us none; everybody's gotta eht."

"What about the rocky crawlers?"

"Poison blood."

"Oh."

"People say we eht each other up, but that's a damn lie," Emer said, head turned partly away to avoid the sinking suns' rays. "Plum *nasty* that is. But I reckon y'all from Geyser think that's the damn truth, though, don't ya?"

"No," Clyde said. "I don't think that."

"We should start bein' quiet now. Rocky crawlers hunt by listenin'. Be kind of stupid if we done got eht because we were *talkin'* about ehtin'."

Clyde agreed, and just then something not quiet at all happened behind them. A dull boom that reverberated over the arid landscape, shaking the air. Faint here, perhaps, but undoubtedly riotous near its source.

Rohm was perched on Clyde's shoulder in a second, whiskers flicking.

"What was that?" Emer said, afraid.

Far to the southwest, a bright emerald pinprick winked in the twilight like a dying candle, neither snuffing nor growing. "What burns like that?" Clyde said.

"Plasma, if it's caught a flame," Emer said.

"He's right," Rohm said.

Clyde's heart sank. Nevele was due to return to Geyser tonight on a commercial frigate. And if that was burning plasma, in the southwest, right where she would be passing over the Lakebed . . .

On Clyde's hip, his radio crackled. He snatched it free of his belt so fast the clip broke. "Nevele?"

Static.

"Who's Nevele?" Emer said.

Clyde didn't hear him. He collapsed to the sand, gear clattering. He kept staring at that sharp green dot as it faded and flared, shrinking only to blossom bright again. *Please, no. Please, please, please.*

Rohm scurried down onto Clyde's knee to stare into the radio's grille as if Nevele's fate played out behind the plastic grating.

Then, indistinct: "Clyde?"

Clyde stared toward the green dot as if it were his fiancée, glowing alive on the horizon. "Nevele! Are you okay?"

"Yeah, mostly. Where are you?"

Clyde turned to Emer. "Where are we?"

Emer, without aid of any device or map, rattled off coordinates.

Clyde repeated them to Nevele. She apparently pressed the Talk button too early and Clyde heard her conferring with someone else, relaying the coordinates. "Yeah, that's where we need to go," she was saying.

"Who are you with?" Clyde said. "Are you okay?"

"I'm fine. Listen, stay where you are. We're coming to you. Actually"—her voice grew faint again as she asked someone to flash lights—"can you see us?"

Clyde watched the sky. "No . . . yes!" Blinking white rays, far away, pierced the bruise-colored clouds. It was about the best thing he'd ever seen. "I can see you!"

Relief flooded both Rohm and Emer's features. But while Rohm's smile never faded, Emer's quickly did. He quickly looked to the side, zeroing in on something behind them.

Clyde got up, his hands snapping to meet upon Commencement, ready to draw. "What is it?"

"We got heard," Emer whispered.

Behind them stood a slight hill. The pod tines of a cactus patch rustled, scratchily dragging across something hard. Pushing under bristling limbs: long, bulky shapes, submerged in shadow. Each pulse of Nevele's starship lights caught otherwise unseen eyes, throwing back an eerie yellow. Six. Staring, unblinking.

Never looking from the glowing eyes, Clyde bent to blindly fetch the radio from the sand. "Nevele? Could I possibly trouble you to step on it?"

CHAPTER 9

A Guardsman's Job Is Never Done

With the first toll of the clock tower, Nula sprang out of her chair and buckled on her sword belt. "Evening rounds, then off the clock we go."

"And not a minute too soon," Flam said, not bothering to push in his chair. Mouflon custom dictated you did that only in a place you respected.

They joined the other guardsmen making their way out the back of the station to the large garage at the rear of the building.

"You and me? Fourth Circle?" Nula said.

"Sure." He flung his keys to her. "You drive."

After boarding the armored vehicle, Nula plunked down a helm and flipped up the visor. Flam donned his own, custom-made to accommodate his horns.

"Looks like you could benefit from a holiday too." Nula started the vehicle. "Maybe I should bring you, hide you in my carry-on."

"Holiday?"

Nula moved them in line behind the other Patrol vehicles. He knew it wouldn't matter much because she was only kidding; she wouldn't drag him along on any vacation. She was young, probably wanted to party with friends, lounge around on Crescent Coast's beaches, play holo-boxing until their thumbs were calloused, sing themselves hoarse at karaoke.

"Oh, nowhere special. Just the weekend." She leaned over and gave a buddy-buddy pat-pat-pat to his knee. "I wouldn't want *somebody* to be all lonesome at his desk, no one to pass the time with."

Flam snorted. "Thanks."

Their vehicle turned out of the garage and onto the cobblestone drive, swinging nimbly for such a large auto.

Flam furtively peeked to his right. Behind the wheel, holding the twin sticks of the eighty-ton machine with the evening suns hitting her face, Nula looked *beautiful*—nearly agleam, incandescent. Before his thoughts could move any further in that direction, he made himself look past her, directly into the orange luster, in hopes it'd char his crush on her. All he got were spots in his eyes.

"You're to leave tonight?" he said, blinking and shaking his head.

"Yeah." She added inwardly, "Hopefully they're punctual."

"You really want out of here, don't you?" Flam teased.

"I believe I'll miss it, actually," Nula said with a sigh. "Dealing with some family stuff right now."

"Everything okay?"

"Eh, yeah."

He let it drop.

At the intersection, the row of Patrol vehicles split off, each to its own route. Nula stopped for the Gwork traffic director, waiting for the whistle and wave of a webbed hand. As they passed, he pinched the bill of his flat cap in greeting, a fellow officer. Flam returned the gesture.

They continued on to Armand Avenue, which terminated at Fourth Circle Street, like all the spoke streets that fanned out from the town square. From there, Flam and Nula began their rounds in earnest—each watching out opposite sides of the vehicle.

Like every other time, they didn't see anything. Flam wondered if nefarious activity in Geyser was really that rare or if the ones doing it just knew the Patrol schedule that well. He imagined them watching the clock, closing up shop a few minutes before nightly patrols, and reopening again at ten after.

Well, he *knew* that's how it worked. As a transporter and accumulator of stock, he'd liberated gently used items from their owners to give them new homes in exchange for his fee. He'd never had a stand, but he knew a couple of guys who ran carts in the square. Aksel and Ricky were two of the better-known traveling salesmen. Flam often wondered what came of those two, who hadn't returned from the refugee camp with the others.

Nula drove them past the elevator station in the residential district across the street from the haberdashery. It immediately brought to mind when he and Pasty, newly acquainted, were on the run. Felt longer than just over a year ago. If fun made time fly, boredom made it crash.

"Tell me more about that," Nula said.

Flam raised his chin off his fist. "Tell you more . . . about what?"

"Oh, sorry. I just meant about how you and Clyde and Nevele saved the city."

"Aren't you sick of those stories yet?"

"Not at all. Wish I could've been there. I'd like even

more to be working with him now on whatever's going on at the palace," Nula said, focused on the road. "Give any more thought to what I said?"

"Some. But it's not that easy." He didn't want to talk about that anymore. If Pasty wanted his help, he would've asked. Flam thought aloud, "I think how I screwed things up made him think I was unstable, even though it wasn't my fault."

"What do you mean?"

They were just about ready to go into the mines. Their road lay ahead. Rag Doll, Pasty, the Chatty Mouse Consortium, and Flam. It already would've been a tough climb, certainly—up through the city's stone stem, into the mines with the Blatta—but then it had to go and get harder. Vidurkis hit him with that Meech-damned fabrick of his, that gray light. It seeped into him, little by little, like a poison of the mind, trickling and pooling drip by drip. For all that it enveloped him, it allowed Flam little snaps of clarity. Like when he belted Pasty across the face. Oh, the look on his face—such shock and betrayal—as he lay there on the ground, touching his hand to his lip and seeing it bloody. The blood Flam—and no one else—had drawn.

"I hurt him."

"But if it's like you said, then that wasn't your fault. I'm sure if you just asked, Clyde would let you work with him in the palace. And maybe you could recommend me as your partner."

"Okay, maybe I will." Flam felt himself clamming up. Realizing he was actually having this conversation and not just imagining it, he shook his head, dizzy a moment.

He looked at Nula's profile. Through the narrow

opening at the front of the helmet, he could see only the tip of her nose.

Apparently able to feel him looking, she glanced his way, did a double-take. "What?"

"Did we really just . . . ?"

"Just what?"

"Say all that."

Nula swung her gaze between the road and him. "What are you talking about?"

"Just now."

"About my trip?"

"No, about Clyde. And me working in the palace with him."

Nula laughed a Nula laugh. "I think *someone's* in need of a nap."

Flam tipped his helmet back off his quilled brow. "Maybe you're right." In his lingering loopiness, he decided to use it as a way to be bold. *Be bold* was, after all, tenet two of the Guardsman's Code.

"Think I could see you off, when you leave?" he said.

"Uh, actually, I'm not sure that's such a—" Gasping, she crushed the brake pedal.

If it hadn't been for his harness, Flam's horns would've bonked the dashboard. "Meech's sake, Nula. You could've just said no."

She pointed ahead.

A Mouflon in a tatty loincloth in the middle of Fourth Circle Street shouted at scared passersby. His fur was matted and caked with dirt, and even though he was brandishing no weapon, people gave him a wide berth.

"Had to be right at quitting time, didn't it?" Nula

reached down to make sure her sword belt was securely fastened before getting out.

"Don't. I know him."

The ancient Mouflon shook his fists over his overgrown bramble of horns, spewing his ravings at the top of his weathered voice. Flam and Nula slowly approached Greenspire.

"Uncle? It's me. Could you turn around for us?"

"He's your uncle?" Nula whispered.

Greenspire, shifting about a few degrees at a time, leading with his left ear closed in on the voices' sources, flaring his considerable nostrils again and again. He faced his nephew finally, rheumy eyes in a silver-streaked face. "Well? What is it? I'm busy."

"Uncle, it's me."

"I'm aware. I can smell it's you, even with you still wearing those man clothes. Leave me."

"Maybe after we get you out of the road, huh?"

Greenspire and the Lulomba and their trained Blatta had gone from squatting in the palace's long-unused stables to occupying a section on the edge of the residential ward. The expulsion from the palace hadn't been Clyde's call but Flam's. The Blatta were territorial creatures, and whenever any of the palace's staff so much as walked past, they'd nearly relieve them of a limb. Their keepers and wranglers, the Lulomba, weren't much more welcoming.

So an old auto-body garage, where the owner had gotten behind on paying the lease, became the palace's property. Not an idyllic cottage in the woods, by any stretch, but home enough. Even though it wasn't official—nothing had been signed by Greenspire or the Lulomba—Flam had seen to it that they'd be safe there, close to his own apartment so he could check in easily and near enough to the elevators so if they wished to return to the Kobbal Mines, they could at their leisure. Flam often hoped they would, especially since Greenspire tended to cause a scene like this at least every few weeks.

"He's insane," Nula said.

Flam turned to her. For a moment any crush he may've had evaporated in a misty pink puff. "He's my family. My *only* family."

"Sorry," she said, looking surprised at his sudden sternness.

They toed up to Greenspire as the old Mouflon continued to verbally accost someone else he detected nearby.

"You there! Spoiled, bloated sack of avarice! U'chanae. Heed my warning. The crusher of men will come and create disharmony in your life—a much-*needed* disharmony. You will be spared but only if you change your craven ways! U'chanae, u'chanae, bzzt!"

"What's the crusher of men?" Nula said out of the corner of her mouth.

"It's . . . a long story. One that probably shouldn't be common knowledge. Might make people nervous."

That thing. Half-bug, half-human baby. A year old now but already scuttling about on its own. Green and purple as a Blatta but with unsettling compound eyes. Unlike the Blatta, the crusher of men could mimic human speech well beyond the shrill, painfully human-sounding screams of its genetic cousins. Sometimes Flam thought it wasn't just parroting but actually knew what it was saying, learning Common piecemeal from Greenspire and from Flam himself when he dared speak to it, despite the creeps the critter gave him.

"Uncle? Let's go home, yeah? People are trying to get somewhere."

"Leave me alone," Greenspire huffed. "*I* was getting somewhere. Bzzt." He was still combining Common with the Lulomba language, Flam couldn't help but notice. *Bzzt,* he'd learned, was spoken punctuation, a combination exclamation point and footnote of *I adamantly stand behind the preceding statement.*

From his left, Flam heard a shop door open followed by the thump of rubber wheels coming down off the curb. Without looking their way, Flam said, "If you could, at your convenience, please leave the area—we're in the middle of something right now. Sorry for the trouble."

In his peripheral vision, Flam saw a man. "No trouble, lad, other than yer addressin' me like I'm a stupid arse."

Flam recognized the voice and the speaker's way with words.

Nigel Wigglesby.

His long, ropey arms were corded with muscle and festooned with tattoos, and his molting parrot perched on his shoulder. Crystal teeth flashed beneath his finely oiled moustache. His wheelchair hummed directly toward the chanting Mouflon, and without hesitation, he backhanded his flank. "Oy. Making another hubbub, are we?"

Greenspire spun about, walking stick hoisted and ready to bludgeon. But after he took a sniff, tension melted from him.

The two old friends exchanged some hushed words, too far away for Flam to make them out. Chin down, the old Mouflon nodded as Nigel spoke, appearing almost embarrassed, and before long they were moving out of the road together.

Some jerk applauded. Traffic resumed.

As they moved on, Nigel waved over his shoulder, a cue to Flam he had it under control and would see Greenspire home. Flam watched the ex-miner guide his stooped uncle down the sidewalk. Just as Flam got back into the vehicle and Nula started the engine, the eight thirty bell tolled.

"Sorry about that," Flam said.

"Not your fault." Nula dropped the vehicle into gear. "Happens. That was Nigel, though, right? Nigel Wigglesby?"

"One and only."

When they passed Nigel and Greenspire, Flam watched the idling pair from the vehicle's side mirror until the bend of Fourth Circle Street pulled them from view. They were laughing, like the old chums they were. The sight made Flam miss Clyde all the more.

"So that was the last bell," Nula said, snapping Flam back to the present, "and that means it's not only Friday; it's Friday at *quittin' time*."

While stopped at the next intersection, she took off her helmet, shook out her hair, and made a show of tossing the "brain bucket" into the backseat.

Flam's smile matched hers.

But as she returned her gaze to the road, Flam noticed something. She had this little white swipe on her cheek. Like someone at the station had played a prank on her by putting foot powder in her helmet—which wouldn't have been surprising. Lighthearted hazing of the greenhorns was routine.

"You've got something . . ." Flam reached over to clear

the smudge with his finger.

She recoiled, crushing herself against the driver's side door. He'd never seen her look so repulsed.

"It's okay. You've just got something here." He pointed at his own face approximately where the blotch was on hers.

Behind them a horn blared, joining the annoyed traffic director's whistle peals. After moving them forward, she took a hand from the wheel and delicately touched the spot on her cheek. When she brought her finger away, the spot hadn't left—but had grown. On her fingertip: a tiny pink mesa. Rendering it to a comma on her uniform trouser leg, she threw the blinker with a frustrated swat and swung them down Armand Avenue.

"Where're we going?" Flam said. "This isn't the way back. Nula, I'm sorry if I offended you somehow, but what sort of gentleman would I be if I let you walk around unaware you had something on her face?"

That white dash on her cheek. Connections began surfacing for Flam but were slowed by his disbelief.

Turning in behind the tannery, Nula parked them out of view of the road. She cut the engine, undid her harness, and turned to face him, her expression giving away nothing.

"I tried my best to avoid this," she said.

"What do you mean? I don't care if you're really that pale. Clyde's pale as can be. Plummets, I even call him *Pasty* he's so—" Sudden cold doused him, his heart's fifteen valves chugging.

A car turned on the road in the distance, its lights sweeping the inside of their vehicle. As the blue-white glare struck Nula's face, her gold-flecked hazel eyes cast a weird reflective shine. Like those of a taxidermy animal. Like glass.

"Who are you?"

Before she could answer, the dispatch on the radio blared, startling him. "Guardsmen, full alert. The Odium have attacked a commercial frigate. Please return to the station for orders. All hands. This is not a drill." When the call began to cycle, Nula turned the radio down until it was only a faint, panicked hum.

"You're Moira Pyne."

A small nod.

"What're you doing going by a different name, pretending to be a guardswoman? Clyde's been looking all over for you and your brothers—"

"And we've been looking for him."

"I don't think I understand. It's not like he's made it particularly hard."

"No? Then how can you, his *best friend*, not know where he is? He's not in the city. Nor does anyone know when he's due to return. So where is he?"

"I told you. I don't know. They don't tell me anything—"

She drew her side sword, the metallic scrape loud in such tight confines.

Eyes he'd once dreamed about staring into beachside grew apologetic.

Hands he'd wanted to hold on a long walk anywhere, everywhere, rested a blade across her lap, patient and capable.

With a voice he wanted to hear greet him in the morning, not in the office but from the other side of his bed, a voice he wanted to hear saying the Promise under the eyes of Meech, she said instead, "Flam, tell me where Clyde is and I'll let you leave this vehicle with your life."

CHAPTER 10

Indecision Kills

G ive me my weapon, mister," Emer whispered. He focused on the hill, a palm opening and closing toward Clyde.

One crawler tasted the air with its forked tongue, its slit pupils estimating them.

"We can handle this," Clyde said, drawing Commencement slowly, quietly. "We don't need to use guns for this."

"Ya thick? We're gonna die unless I can chase the others off by puttin' down the buck—but only if you *let me*." If he'd been more mobile, the boy likely would've taken the gun back by force.

"Use the harpoon."

"Seriously?" He shook the sky-whale-killing tool at Clyde. "This thing against *them*?"

Clyde swallowed. "We need to live by example."

"Perhaps you should listen to the bumpkin, Mr. Clyde," Rohm said. "I'd sooner trust his skills with a gun than yours with a sword."

"I've had lessons."

"From a man who admitted he knew how to merely *make* swords, not *use* them, and accepted only pub tokens as payment. You're not likely to dazzle a hungry lizard into submission with your sense of honor, Mr. Clyde. The only thing you'll get—as Emer would put it—is *eht*."

He hated doing it, but right then it seemed a necessary thing. Clyde freed the clunky antique from his belt and tossed it over.

Catching it, keeping one hand on the harpoon for stability, one eye closed and tongue poking out for added accuracy, Emer fired.

The lizard, presumably the buck, was struck between the eyes. But by some remarkable bit of evolution, not even a bullet could penetrate its scaly flesh. Clyde could see the flash of sparks of bullet connecting with organic armor, the *spack* startling the other crawlers into fleeing.

The crawler issued a menacing hiss and pitched itself down the hill. Thick arms ending in long claws spun, throwing sand as it drew an angry streak in the sand right toward them.

Emer shot again.

It kept coming, roaring.

Then, when it was scarcely a stride off, another. And another and another.

The crawler, gurgling, finally succumbed to its wounds at Emer's feet.

On the hill, the cactus patch rustled, shadows shifted, and the Lakebed's silence returned.

Emer lowered the gun and wheeled toward Clyde. "That was dumb as hell, mister. Ya think ya was gonna stand a chance 'gainst that thing with a sword?" Shaking his head, Emer sighed, his visible breath in the cool air mingling with the acrid gun smoke. He took a step back from the dead lizard. "That was too damn close."

"I'm sorry, okay?" Clyde sheathed Commencement. "I

misjudged the situation."

"I'll say."

Rohm pointed. "There's Nevele."

The whoosh of sand swallowed them. Clyde dropped his goggles over his eyes. Despite the grit stinging his face and fear still racing, he couldn't suppress a smile. The starship was a welcome sight.

The moment the two coordinates matched, Aksel cut the *Praise to Her*'s engines, lowered the landing gear, and set them down.

Nevele was at the hatch and tugging it open before the ship had completed its postflight venting. "Hold on a second," Aksel shouted, going unheard as she, apparently deaf with excitement, hopped down. Turning back to the console, Aksel watched the vidscreens as one geometric estimation of a human mapped by the nav systems raced toward a second and both collided in an embrace.

I helped that happen. Retiring from working for his most recent employers was already showing its benefits.

But then he noticed there was a third shape outside, shorter than the other two. *I thought we were picking up one.*

After detangling himself from his harness, he exited the starship too, dropping into the choking syrup of hot fumes gathered around the ship's landing gear. Waving a hand in front of his face, he marched toward the group under the nose-cone lights. The softness of sand felt strange after so much time on Adeshka's solid pavement.

Nevele had her arms wrapped around her friend,

peppering his face with kisses, hiding him from Aksel's view.

But as soon as she moved aside to introduce him, Aksel's DeadEye shot out of its socket, his eyelid momentarily caught on the barrel's tip.

Clyde looked just like them.

In a surprising display, Nevele put herself between Clyde and Aksel's DeadEye. Still, as dismayed as Clyde may have been, Aksel noticed he'd gone to draw his sword.

"Sorry," Aksel said, using his palm to coax the barrel to collapse into his head. "For a moment there, I thought . . ." *Did they really put that much fear in me?*

"It's okay," Clyde said. He moved around Nevele, released his hand from his sword to extend it toward Aksel. His handshake was firm.

Aksel was still unsettled by how much this Pyne looked like an amalgamation of the other three.

"Thank you for helping Nevele," Clyde said. "But who did you think I was? I don't believe there's many people I could easily be mistaken for." He smiled uncomfortably.

Aksel looked to Nevele. *Doesn't he know any of this?* he tried to make his face read.

Nevele took Clyde's arm. "Uh, well, we have some things to catch you up on."

"What is it? Have you found my siblings? Are they okay?"

Aksel said, "Actually, the thing is—"

A voice called out with the thickest Lakebed drawl Aksel had ever heard. "Might *also* wanna learn him that trustin' those familiar with the local fauna wouldn't be such a bad idear." A dirty-faced young man, using a harpoon as a crutch, stepped into the ship's lights.

Nevele looked at Clyde askance.

"This is Emer," Clyde said, bringing the boy into the group. "He has been an invaluable help to Rohm and me."

"Rohm?" Aksel said, not seeing anyone else present.

A white frisk mouse popped up from under the flap of Clyde's jacket pocket. "I'm Rohm. Pleased to make your acquaintance."

Aksel nodded. "Okay, then. Sure. A talking mouse. I probably shouldn't think it's all that strange, but somehow right now I do." A bubbly titter escaped his lips.

Maybe it'd come on a delay, the day's events catching up to him now. "You mind if I sit? I think I need to sit."

CHAPTER 11

White Lies, White Sand

So you really *don't* know anything, do you?"

Flam shook his head. "No. I've told you I don't."

And as soon as he was done speaking, Nula eased off. Relief came as his thoughts were relinquished into his control. He'd felt a similar sensation before, that invasiveness that would crack a whip and make his mind jump to Clyde or Nevele whenever Nula would ruffle his fur or pat his shoulder, the stories tumbling out on their own. This time it was as if she had his skull open and was snapping a pointer to the bits she found interesting, demanding his immediate explanations of what they meant.

Before, he'd thought it was only the butterflies you'd feel whenever your crush touched you, even accidentally. Not so. And apparently she could hear *that* thought as well.

She sighed. "Believe me, I didn't want to do it this way, but gaining your trust was just easier. Takes less when it's voluntary. Doing it by force, *making* you speak, would've invited unwanted attention, considering who you are. If you suddenly disappeared . . ." She peered down at her hands, crestfallen. "I didn't want to do that."

"Why do you want Clyde dead, anyway? What did he ever do that was so wrong?"

Nula swallowed. "It's not really mine, wanting it."

"Then who?"

"Raziel, my brother."

"Can't you say no?"

She closed her eyes tight, shook her head. "It's always been the three of us. Our father said Clyde was dead and . . . and he *was*, as far as we knew, for years. He came back and took the throne after we'd already lost it to Gorett—who we suspect had our continent passes blacklisted so we couldn't leave Embaclawe when our father was said to have died. Raziel was furious. We only managed to leave by stealing a starship from the academy—with some help from our small arms instructor's assistant, Karl—but by the time we'd decided to go after Gorett, we heard Clyde wasn't really dead. It filled Tym's and my hearts with joy, but Raziel took it differently. Much differently. And . . . I guess Raziel's anger was the communicable kind."

"Clyde *did* try to find you, though. It's just that he had to do something. With so many people coming back from the refugee camps, they needed someone to send their questions up to, someone to listen to them. He *had* to take the stewardship. I mean, it's not like the minute we got topside he plunked down in the throne and declared, 'This is henceforth all mine.' He hasn't taken the throne from anybody, because he hasn't taken the throne *at all*. He wants Gorett to pay for what he did—the man who had your father killed, for Meech's sake. But you act like Clyde was the one who stuck the sword in the man's—"

Nula raised a hand. "I don't . . . want to talk about that."

"Oh, I'm *sorry*. Would that sort of talk make you uncomfortable? Silly me. Because here you sit, grilling me to know where your own brother, my friend, is so you can go *kill him.*"

They'd been in the Patrol vehicle a while. It was starting to get stuffy. The tip of Flam's nose was always dewy, but now it was practically dripping.

"Well?" he said in her long silence.

"Yes. Yes, that's what we have to do. It's the right thing. Raziel belongs on the throne, not Clyde."

"Nula—"

"Please, Flam, that's not my . . . I know that you grew awfully attached to her and really liked her, but she was never real. And I don't blame you for not knowing anything about what Clyde and Nevele are up to. They've been thorough in keeping their plans secret."

"But why me?"

"Because you were his only friend still in Geyser."

"Okay, this time, why *really?*"

She finally met his gaze. "You were nice."

For a moment, they shared the dark quiet of the armored auto. Traffic passed by on Armand, passengers never seeing them parked behind the tanner's building. The dispatch continued to summon any straggling guardsmen from their beds or pub tables to the station.

They repeatedly called for auto twenty-one, theirs, but Flam never bothered to reach for the receiver, suspecting what Nula might do if he tried.

Instead, Flam listened to the death toll rise and watched, absently, as the headlights streaked the wall ahead of them. His mind ran on and on with shock. *The world is coming apart.*

"So what now?" he finally said, too disgusted to look at her.

"I'm waiting for my brothers to call." She withdrew a small device from a hip pocket and tapped the screen to wake it up. She stared at it, her face lit blue. "I don't know what's keeping them."

"Your weekend holiday?" He scoffed.

"Flam . . ."

His eyes went wide, more things clicking into place. "The frigate. Did *they* . . . ?"

Her face remained set. Flam watched her for any indication, *any* tell in her painted face. And there it was. The tiniest twitch wrinkling her left eyelid. Telling enough.

"Meech on his throne. You're not just Clyde's younger siblings all bellyaching you don't get to sit in the big, important chair. You're no better than the Odium. People *died* on that frigate, Nula. A *lot* of people. And it was heading here, which meant there may've been some people I know on that thing. My friends, *our* coworkers maybe."

"I *know*." Nula moaned, putting her face in her hands. "I know." When she lifted her head again, more of her makeup was gone—fingers leaving ten white dots on her cheeks and temples. "I'm sorry, but it was the only way to get help in protecting Geyser."

He moved to knock the blade away, to try and grab her, get cuffs on her.

But she was quicker. A small gesture: one shoulder shifting. At first he thought she had kicked him, feeling something knock against his breastplate.

But when he looked down, jutting between the panels of armor was Nula's side sword.

She actually just stabbed me. The thought passed fluidly, processed clearly. He looked up as she withdrew her hand from her end, leaving the blade stuck where she'd put it.

Tears created dual pale rivers down her face.

The pain came, delayed. He groaned, his back straightening on its own. The sword's bite seemed to spread.

He heard her door clunk open and managed to steer his glance—with pain dotting stars in his vision—in her general direction.

She stood there, her makeup mask mostly gone, a peerless white like that of the dead. But her face now was anything but dead. It wore a bouquet of things: regret, confusion . . .

"I'm sorry," she said again, barely a whisper. "I had to. He'd read me, and if he sees I didn't hurt you in some way, he'll think I may've started to . . ."

"Nula," he managed.

"It's Moira." She closed the door between them.

Flam reached. It hurt to move. He felt like he'd been pinned in place. "Wait!"

Her boot heels clicked on the asphalt as she tore away. From the side mirror, Flam glimpsed her bringing her device to her ear as she ran. He caught one final snippet of her small voice before she fell from view: "Karl, my cover's blown. I need extraction."

Nevele let Emer squeeze her hand as the *Praise to Her*'s on board mechanical medic dug the bullet from his leg and patched him up, the stitch work commendable, for a bot's. Then, flighty on painkillers, the boy was able to be a boy again. Under the moon, he made a constant circuit of the starship as if it were his to protect. Gun tucked into the belt cinching his threadbare jacket, he marched around and around. Even though he didn't need the harpoon anymore, he continued to march with it like a knight proudly flying with his kingdom's banner.

Wa-roooo, deep and melancholy, sounded out of the night. The first time they'd heard it, all but Emer had nearly jumped out of their skin. He, instead, clambered on top of the *Praise to Her* and pointed into the distance. There, among the wisps of clouds, was a pod of sky whales. Their long bodies lit up ethereally. Big tails slowly swept, propelling them in a patient tour of the Lakebed by indigo moonlight. *Wa-roooo.*

Emer suggested their song was a form of echolocation. It made Nevele think of Tym, who might require a similar method to navigate by since she'd struck him sightless. She wondered when she'd tell Clyde about what she'd done to not only Tym and Raziel but also to Zoya Kesbanya's father.

Still, honest with herself about what she'd done, she realized how often she wondered about Zoya. Where life had taken her, what kind of person she'd turned out to be. Nevele could dodge the memories of bubbles on a muddy river's surface easily enough, because the golden goodness of having saved Zoya's life outshone what she'd done to facilitate it. Or maybe that was how sociopaths thought, developing selective memories, cherry-picking what story fit their fancy best. Nevele cringed at the thought of being more nuts than even *she* was aware of and focused on imagining Zoya as she was now, safe and well.

How old would she be now? Nevele did the math, counting against her own twenty-two years. *Wherever Zoya was, she was sixteen now. Wow. Sixteen.*

But as hard as she tried, thinking about Zoya stirred up thoughts of bubbles. *Those* bubbles. Maybe Nevele did share a dark streak with her brother, after all. One that was hidden, as if drawn in ink that would remain undetectable until dragged under the right type of light.

She turned. Clyde. He was talking to Aksel, sitting in the holds as Aksel brought him up to speed on his family, hanging on the Bullet Eater's every word. Sometimes he'd turn, apparently able to feel her gaze, and loose a little smile her way. He loved her so much but knew so little about her. She returned the smile and turned away, unable to look him in the eye for much longer. She watched Emer pass yet again, patrolling, chin high.

"My mother was in the Fifty-Eighth militia with you?" Clyde was saying.

Nevele's ears pricked up.

Aksel nodded his greasy mop. "Yeah, she was. Practically the den mother to us brutes. And one of the strongest people I ever knew, weaver or not. And when I use that word, I mean, you know"—he shook a fist over his heart—"*strength.*"

"She was woven? But I thought . . ." He looked to Nevele.

She made a face that read, *News to me.* Susanne had passed long before Nevele had been given the title of Royal Stitcher. She'd been in school when it happened.

"You have to remember we were in a unit together only a handful of years," Aksel said. "I was eighteen by the time it disbanded, so it's been a while. A few times we came to Geyser to restock supplies and food and whatnot. She'd excuse herself to go off somewhere, and we didn't think she was . . . you know, exchanging sweet nothings with a prince."

"My father."

"And after I went my way and Nigel went his, I strolled into town one day and saw this procession going on, big fancy deal. And there was Susanne on the float right alongside Francois. A breeze could've knocked me over."

"I apologize," Clyde said, "but you didn't answer my question."

"Sorry," Aksel said. "But, yes, she was woven. She could make you feel good." He smiled, obviously remembering. "And I don't mean any sort of encouraging words or compliments or any faff like that. She could just *look* at you. Got me through a lot of rough spots, those looks. 'Diamond winks,' Nigel used to call them."

Clyde formed a faint, sad smile.

Nevele knew him well enough to realize he was thinking he would've liked to meet her, and Nevele had hated being the one to tell him about how a few months before his father fell ill, she'd passed away quietly one night after something had gone wrong delivering his little sister, Moira. Not even forty years old, Susanne was gone. Geyser had wept along with their king.

"Did you ever tell any of my siblings about this? That you knew their mother?"

Aksel shook his head. "Didn't think it would win me any favors, so I kept it to myself. Not like it was hard, forgetting they were your mother's children. Nothing like her. You, on the other hand, I can see some Susanne in you. Around here mostly," Aksel circled his lips and chin with a finger. "She was a good one, Susanne."

"When you knew her, did she ever say anything about—?"

"Perhaps we should think about moving," Aksel said, taking a sudden deep breath and slapping his knees before standing. "We don't have long to find Höwerglaz before the Odium does, if he exists." He gave Clyde a hand up and clapped him on the back. "Chin up, yeah?"

"Yeah, chin up," Clyde said with less heart.

Aksel stepped to the open hatch, leaning out to watch Emer make yet another pass around the ship. He turned back to Clyde and Nevele, thumbing over his shoulder. "We bringing him along?"

"He has nowhere to go," Clyde said.

"Fine by me. Oy, you there, get your arse on board. We're leaving." Aksel hauled Emer inside and told him to find a seat and strap in. Then Aksel turned back to Clyde and Nevele. "I don't understand something here. Why are you two looking for a man who may be make-believe, when people very much *not* make-believe are planning the destruction of your city? I have the Odium's home base coordinates. Could go straight up there right now and—"

"Here, awright?" Emer, in the cockpit, was pointing at the pilot's seat, currently under his bum, with a hopeful smile.

Aksel waved him off. "Yeah, sure, fine. Just don't touch anything."

"Y'all know thar's a dead feller in here?"

"Yes. Don't touch him either." Aksel grunted. To Clyde and Nevele, he said, "Funny, I don't recall drawing straws on who's going to babysit."

Nevele hid a smirk with her hand, playing it off as an itchy nose.

"So," Aksel began again, closing the hatch behind him, "why *not* go after the Odium directly? The FTL's tachyon generator seems to be in working order. Once it's charged, getting to them would be no problem."

Neither Clyde nor Nevele replied. Both wore hesitant, almost bashful looks.

"What?"

"I decided that when I became steward," said Clyde, "we wouldn't respond to any attack straightforwardly."

Aksel waited for the punch line. "So if someone comes guns a-packing, you just smile politely, let them do as they will? As neighborly as that might be, progressive and all, if you like Geyser *not* as a smoking crater, you might want to reconsider taking the offensive a *smidge*." He pinched the air and squinted.

"That's not to say we'd do nothing," Clyde said. "We'd use our brains, find a way to impede them. Locate their weak spots and employ subterfuge and sabotage. Anything we can to minimize instigating all-out war. Retaliation only leads to more retaliation."

That sounded rather prepared, but okay. "Just so we're clear," Aksel said, eye closed, hands out, "you've been at this for a whole year, and *all* you know is you have three days to sabotage their warhead and find Father Time—and Father Time is the one you decide to pursue? Because I saw that warhead myself. And *it* is certainly no myth."

"We've been working on this for a year," Nevele said. "And while we received the news late, at least it wasn't *too late*."

"And I volunteered to find Ernest Höwerglaz," Clyde said.

"You're wastin' your time," Emer called from up front.

"He ain't gon' get it."

"Shut it," Aksel said over his shoulder. He stepped closer to Clyde. "I think things worked out pretty well here. Your dodgy siblings don't want Geyser to fall any more than you do. While they kept me in the dark on a lot of stuff and, true, their *main* goal wasn't exactly cuddly, I think as far as Geyser is concerned, you have nothing to worry about. At least until you return home after all this." He spun a finger overhead.

"Did they survive the frigate crash?" Clyde said mildly.

Aksel exchanged a look with Nevele.

"I don't know," she said. "We didn't see any bodies. I can only assume."

Clyde took a moment. "If they did survive, we'll deal with them when it comes to it." He swallowed before continuing. It couldn't have been easy to know your own family hated you to the point of wanting you dead. "They are a secondary matter that concerns only my well-being. The city's is primary. Like you said, Nevele, if Raziel wanted it protected for his own ends, we could've relied on him—regardless of his feelings toward me. But without knowing for sure, we can't count on him to help protect Geyser. We have to act as if this is entirely up to us, as it always has been."

"Want to know what I think?" Aksel said. "I say we use what time we've got left intelligently. Do it your way: go hunt a myth. Give that a day. After that, do it my way: use the coordinates and go after the Odium directly. Without Höwerglaz, they've got nothing. And I imagine while the stone *is* important, they won't risk such an attack without having all of their pieces in place to break ground on this weaver factory they have in mind. We go in, guns blazing, take as many of the wankers out as we can. Surprise attack. Suicide missions, when they *do* work once in a great while, work *spectacularly*."

Clyde's gaze shifted to Nevele.

She raised her hands and took a full step back. "Your call, love."

Clyde faced Aksel. "All right. One day of searching, and then we'll *talk* about doing it your way."

Aksel nodded and ducked into the cockpit. "You're the boss." After ordering Emer to move it, he dropped into the seat and buckled himself in.

They lifted off.

Clyde, next to Nevele, stared straight ahead, cautiously confident. Perhaps naively so.

Nevele scolded herself for thinking such a thing of him. But, really, how do you define bravery? Is it by the circumstances? Popular opinion? Nevele considered maybe bravery was decided according to the beholder, individually, a subjective thing. Of course, that meant one individual's hero, seen by another set of eyes, could be just your garden variety psychotic with a death wish. Nevele wondered what Zoya thought of her, how she remembered her.

Turning away, watching the sandy emptiness of the Lakebed fall, she caught her own reflection in the porthole glass. For most of Nevele's life, she'd avoided anything with a reflective surface, even a glance of herself upside down in a spoon. Over time, she'd learned to not only accept what was there but embrace it, happy with her differentness.

She returned the fixed stare, the starry sky zipping by beyond her reflected eyes. In them, around them. She wondered who, underneath the patchwork, she really was.

Maybe I'm as torn inside.

When this was all over and she told Clyde everything she'd done, who would she be? The real her, or could she continue being the person Clyde believed her to be? Clyde's forgiveness was enormous but without a doubt, like all things, it had a breaking point.

If she told him, she'd risk destroying that make-believe her forever. Or, worse, she'd never get to pretend just for herself that her clean soul was really hers. Even calling herself Nevele was an attempt at distancing herself from Margaret. She'd adopted the name within minutes of meeting Clyde in that hospital basement, when he, Flam, and Rohm had rescued her. It was as if she knew they'd share a future in which the real her was not—and never would be—welcome.

When Clyde was being sweet and sincere and called her Margaret, it savaged her inside. Took every ounce of her to continue playing the part, never allowing a moment to sneak past that'd imply there was something unexpected beneath; she'd allow no corners for Clyde to find and pick at and peel back the veneer. No, she'd have to allow him to keep that one thing about her, her real name, and hear him use it with her and smile as if it warmed her heart. As if she were happy he knew who she really was. When he didn't. Not at all.

In the glass, stars moved behind her eyes, blinked when she blinked. *Close but not me.*

This is murder.

She hoped he could accept her. Almost as much as she hoped she could accept herself.

CHAPTER 12

Stalwart Companions

F inding Dreck's room empty, Gorett was free to approach the large window. With that stolen moment, he spied all there was to spy, allowed a small flight of fancy—a jump back in time to when he looked out a similar large window.

If he squinted, that ugly metal sculpture of the Mechanized Goddess could be the geyser. And the heap of junk at her feet could be the town square's fountains. He missed it. Home. He recalled a word he'd once stumbled across: *hiraeth*. Homesickness for a place that no longer exists.

Sure, Geyser was still there—for the time being—but it'd never be *his* home again. If he were ever spotted there, he'd probably be dragged off to the dungeon. Or simply killed on sight, slain at Clyde Pyne's feet.

The image snapped his focus back, fear rocketing him out of the dark daydream.

He spotted the *Magic Carpet* on the frosty plain. The rear ramp was down, and he could see the flicker and flash of welding being done. Dreck, steady at his work.

There'd been difficulties.

Not that anyone discussed them with Gorett, but he'd overheard how the warhead was giving them trouble. Something about incompatible engineering. The warhead, a leftover from the Territorial Skirmish, would require tinkering to get the *Magic Carpet* to effectively house it—and, with luck, *not* blow up while on board with them.

And just outside the starship, there it was, on its wheeled cart under a patina of snow, like an enormous bullet aching for its turn down the barrel. The reality of the whole plot sank in, a quiet panic seizing Gorett as he pictured Geyser in ruins.

Then do something about it, his mother said.

"Okay," he murmured to the woman who'd been dead nearly forty years, not fearing her voice anymore because it was at least some comfort. He left Dreck's room and went downstairs. He donned a parka, wrapped himself in scarves, pulled on three pairs of gloves, and pushed through the exit door.

Immediately the blue world outside jumped at him with morbid fervor. He felt the chill bleed in, as if sharp, icy hands scoured for any hidden warmth it could squeeze black.

Of all times, a terrible itch came. He tried scratching it, behind his left ear, but couldn't get at it with the gloves on. He tried to ignore it even as it became angry at his inattention.

He crunched on through the snow, each footfall making a pop when his heavy boots broke through the thin membrane of ice. As he turned the corner of the frost-smudged building, the wind became a little more tolerable.

Ahead, he watched a man lift a device in two hands, what looked like a portable cannon, sending a small sphere shooting. The endless sunlight danced off the sphere's surface as it blurred into the distance, silently propelled at a brisk clip. It seemed to hit an invisible wall, locked in the air. In a moment, a heap of metal jumped free of the snow below and became a thick coating of rusty scrap around the sphere, perhaps held with magnets. The pirate turned in place with the cannon, and the floating sphere carried its payload. He released the trigger, and the sphere shed its clanking brown armor onto an existing pile. Load delivered, he recalled the sphere and sent it in a new direction to do it again.

Gorett, in his fascination, had stopped walking. The Odium must have ransacked some fairly well-off locales if such a technological wonder was now in their possession. He moved on, shuffling through knee-high snow, remembering how cold he was.

Past the towering metal statue of the Odium's goddess, Gorett thumped up the ramp of the *Magic Carpet*. Here he could remove his hood since all around were space heaters, their buzzing coils throwing a lavalike hue across the ship's interior. Gorett warmed his nose near the coils, slapping circulation back into his cheeks.

A level below, in the ship's bowels, Dreck swore and something crashed.

Gorett stepped away from the glowing congregation of space heaters to take the ladder down, when something caught his eye. The doorway dividing where he was, in the holds, from the bunk area was made of retrofitted wood— a house's door. Carved with care, starting about three feet off the floor, was a series of notches.

—Nimbelle, 11

—Nimbelle, 8

—Nimbelle, 6

—Nimbelle, 5
—Nimbelle, 4.5

—Nimbelle, 3

Curious.

But then again, nothing of the Odium's was originally theirs. It was all *gently used*, as Dreck once said. Still, Gorett couldn't help but wonder who this Nimbelle was and what happened to her.

Mother was there, with him—he could feel her—but she had no opinion to give.

At the bottom of the ship, he found Dreck hammering a wide hole into the ship's belly. Gorett had to shout to be heard.

Dreck spun, hand halfway to his holster. Seeing it was only Gorett, he grunted, "What is it?" and gave him his back again, returning to work.

"How'd you come to own this vessel?" Gorett repeated.

Dreck set the sledgehammer aside and, without any

tools, disassembled another layer of the *Magic Carpet*'s shielding.

"Spoils of war." Dreck lovingly thumped the ship's hull, a ringing toll. "My first bird, what elevated me from a rule follower to the entrepreneur I am today." He paused, eyeing Gorett a moment, appearing caught. "But I assume that's not what you came out here to discuss. Out with it." Dreck lifted a cloud of metal dice from the new hole. Once free of the engine compartment, they rained into a messy heap, much like the process Gorett had watched outside, except more precise and without the aid of technology.

Gorett wrung his hands. "I'm wondering if we could discuss Geyser's future."

"What's left of it, you mean? Oh, about forty-eight hours?" When he laughed, the fog of his breath seeped through his scarves' material.

"Is its total destruction necessary?"

The pirate's shoulders drooped. "Pitka. I thought we covered this."

"There's no other way we can get the stone?"

"I don't know why you're so torn up over the place. Your reign's over. Done. Pyne's kid is in charge now. You should be happy. At least you're getting *something* out of this."

Gorett had no retort. Dreck was right.

"Now, if you've nothing else, leave me be." Again, he turned his back. When Gorett was king, the insult would've resulted in a thousand-spot ticket.

Something rose in him. Anger. It came simmering, frothy and red. Bubbling from it: *Take his gun. And shoot him with it.*

The boiling ended abruptly, cooled by cowardice. "I

can't do that." Aloud. *Blast*.

Dreck turned his head slightly. "I hope that was the wind I just heard."

Snowflakes swirled into the ship through the gaping hole, alighting on Gorett's eyelashes. Through them, Gorett studied Dreck's holster. The grip was within reach. *He's a devious man who knows he's a devious man. He's been waiting for someone with the gall to end him, wanting it. Be that man.*

"I can't . . ."

An annoyed sigh escaped Dreck as he tugged his arms free of the tangled mass of wires, slapped the heap to the floor, and turned around again.

Gorett remained where he was. He was shaking but wasn't certain if it was only because of the cold.

Dreck lifted his goggles, unbuttoned his hood. His bare face was pink. "You hearing things? Voices and the like?"

Don't tell him.

Gorett shook his head—but a little too late.

"What are they telling you?" Dreck pushed Gorett back. "To do *bad things*?"

"I'm not hearing anything. I check my eyes every morning, just as you said I should. Look. I'm not infected."

Dreck regarded Gorett, pushing his face toward him, eyes wide. He shoved him back again. "Doesn't always show in the eyes. They're getting wise. Learning to hide the symptoms."

"Learning?"

His gun, Pitka.

"Why do you keep eyeballing my shooter?" Dreck sounded almost amused. "Fancy taking it from me, popping me in the gut? Is that what it's telling you to—?"

"No, I just—"

Dreck grabbed him by the beard, wrenching his head to one side, then the other, and brought his jaw up so hard he thought his head might snap off. When Dreck looked behind Gorett's left ear, he stopped dragging his head about, let go of him, and took a long step back.

"Sure enough," Dreck said, wiping his hands off on his oil-stained trousers again and again, "you've got one all right."

"What?" Gorett slapped a hand over the spot Dreck had been prodding. It was where he'd been itchy all afternoon. There was certainly a bump, but he never thought to hold a finger to the pustule and wait to feel squiggly movement beneath. Now that he did and felt it, his hand leaped away from the spot.

"Fix me, then," Gorett blurted. "Do what you need to do. Use your fabrick, as you've done with the other men. Get in there and take that blasted thing *out*." He could feel the thing in his neck wiggling like a fly that'd fallen into a wound and somehow survived after the skin had healed over.

Dreck's lips curled. "Huh. Look what she's handed us, Gorett. The Goddess saw you were stagnant, a gear with stripped teeth."

Take his gun. Shoot him.

"The Goddess has put a knot in your life. Now it's your job to *unknot* it or let it become a noose. And I, always on the lookout for opportunities, see that you are in need of something. A remedy. One only I can supply."

"I'll gouge this thing out myself," Gorett threatened, eyeing Dreck's toolbox, the top tray heaped with many things that'd be suitable. "I'm not coming away from this deal with anything less than what we agreed on. That wouldn't be—"

"Fair?" Dreck chuckled.

Gorett's voice cracked. "Do you want to just leave me with nothing? This entire time you could've. You said so yourself. I have nothing over you. No leverage to make demands. I am completely at your mercy. But this is my *life* we're talking about."

"All right, then," Dreck said, crossing his arms, "let's talk numbers. How much is your life worth to you? Use a percentage."

"Percentage? Of what?"

"Of wendal stone you'd be willing to part with for me to save your life."

As Gorett considered, he competed with the noise whose origin he now knew, but now it had begun *screaming*. When he was about to throw out a number, Dreck raised a hand, the radio on his hip blaring his name.

"Dreck here. Go ahead."

"Sir, uh, you know how Proboscis took the *Praise to Her* to Adeshka?"

"Yeah, and has he found that fence for us? He's been gone long enough."

"Well, uh, actually, the *Praise* is showin' in western Lakebed now, sir."

Lips peeling back, Dreck closed his grip around the radio, its plastic cracking. "We already *have* men in Nessapolis. We need that ship here. Big day's not far off, might want to remind him."

"He's not answering, sir."

Dreck's glare cut to Gorett, who pushed on his neck

pustule, thinking he could suffocate the bone worm.

"Know anything about this, Gorett? Some kind of under-the-table goings-on with Proboscis? If you do, best speak up before I find out myself."

The radio in Dreck's hand droned. "If he shows up in Nessapolis, do you want me to have the men there send him back our way?"

Dreck steamed the radio grille with his breath. "How many more ships do we have in the fleet here at home?"

"Yours and twenty-five others in the hangar, sir."

"If Proboscis shows up in Nessapolis, have the men shoot him out of the sky. We can spare the *Praise to Her*. No mutiny or anyone showing symptoms of such"—he focused on Gorett—"will be tolerated. May the Goddess junk him. Out."

As much as it looked like he would've preferred smashing the radio, Dreck clicked it off and returned it to his belt. "Even if you're trying something—that thing digging around in your skull giving you ideas—it doesn't matter."

"I wasn't—"

"Ten you, ninety me. And that's generous." Dreck approached the ladder to leave the ship's oily guts.

Gorett tried reaching for him but fell onto his hands and knees in the dirty, melted snow pooling on the floor. "But the worm! Please, I'm begging you."

Dreck hesitated at the bottom rungs only long enough to say, "Think of it as a companion, a firm friend who's always with you, one that'll keep you honest."

"Proboscis and I had no deal, I'm telling you—"

With nothing further, Dreck clomped up the ladder and was gone.

Gorett's pants wicked up the puddles and froze his hands. Although he was technically alone now, he wasn't. The worm spoke, in his mother's voice, tsking him.

Now look at the mess you're in.

DAY
TWO

CHAPTER 13

Pilgrims and Pointless Pleas

All Flam remembered of the night before was the pain of drawing the sword out of his gut and the clunk the bloodied thing made hitting the floorboard.

After that, everything was flicks and flashes.

Getting the vehicle door open.

Hitting the parking lot on elbows and knees, the agony rioting his insides as he dragged himself along. He couldn't stand, could barely breathe. He halfway wondered if Nula—no, Moira, he remembered—had poisoned the blade.

He pushed with his hooves, dug his fingers into the striped parking lot wherever his fingers could find purchase.

Fading fast.

He had to get to the street, flag somebody down.

Hopefully someone would notice a crawling guardsman leaving a bloody smear on the ground. Flam wished Clyde or Nevele were here. He felt more alone now, dying on his belly just a scant few yards from the passing drivers' sight, than ever before. Another coarse scrape of his hooves, another foot painted red behind him.

He couldn't remember precisely when he stopped.

Then nothing for a while.

And then a face emerged from a wall of golden light, looking down. A Mouflon face, bearded, sagely, with glowing eyes, horns standing meters above his head, beautifully twisted and asymmetrical, as coral grows . . .

"Meech?" Flam said, both scared and excited.

A hand came down.

Flam thrilled at the idea of feeling the Great Mouflon's loving caress, here to welcome him to the Mountain.

Instead, Meech slapped him across the face.

"Stop smiling like that. You look like a fool. Bzzt."

The otherworldly glow behind Meech was a work light, and the Mouflon his uncle Greenspire.

"You're not dead," he grunted. "Good. Door's over there."

Sitting up, Flam looked around, confused as to where he was.

The corrugated steel walls reached high up to rafters. Taped sheets of oil-stained cardboard covered every window in the spacious place. He was in the auto-body garage, where he'd given Greenspire and the Lulomba a home.

At the edges of the single lamp's glow, Flam noticed only now the Lulomba and their saddled bugs. From hammocks made of old cargo nets and bright blue tarpaulins suspended from the ceiling, each of the bony, hunchbacked cave dwellers regarded him with rheumy eyes. Their heads were slightly turned, ears angled, seeing by listening.

"What happened?" Flam said. Next to him on the floor was his guardsman armor and surcoat. His midsection was banded with multiple layers of gauze. Flam put a hand over the hurt and got to his hooves, following his uncle into the next room.

It'd been a bay for fixing larger autos. The vehicle lift

was up, and a stained canvas drop cloth draped over it to create an indoor tent. Greenspire ducked through the opening.

Hissing at the pain in his belly, Flam stooped and stepped in.

Inside was a table piled with columns of scrawled-on parchment, a rickety bed, and several trash bags bulging to capacity.

Greenspire collapsed onto the bed with a huff, hands cupped over the handle of his cane, chin resting on his thumbs. He sniffed to confirm Flam had followed him in and, without even needing to see it, kicked a wheeled stool screeching Flam's way.

Flam caught the stool and eased down onto it, wincing. He nodded toward the overstuffed bin bags. "You can drop your trash at the chute down the street, you know. You don't have to hold on to it, Uncle."

Greenspire either couldn't hear him or chose not to. "You're living incorrectly."

Flam chuckled. "Well, howdy-do to you too."

"Wearing human clothes, driving their vehicles, insinuating yourself into their world of greed and so-called order. A Mouflon should never let his hooves leave the ground. Unnatural. *Bzzt.*"

Flam looked around the metal room. It was crowded with skinny, naked people, who were covered in green body paint, and their dog-sized insect pets. "Glass houses, Uncle."

Greenspire's face remained set. "I'm a pilgrim."

"Oh, well, that explains everything, then." The last night came back to him: the frigate crash in the desert, the call to arms. *Meech, what's going on?* Flam started to stand. "I appreciate you saving me and all, but I really need to be going." Flam ducked to go back through the tent opening.

"I didn't rescue you," Greenspire said. "I was out collecting cans when Nigel came and said he'd found my abomination of a nephew lying bleeding in a parking lot, unconscious."

"Hey now. *Abomination*? Seriously? They knighted me, you know."

Greenspire aimed his milky eyes Flam's way. "You should let it fall. Geyser's providence cannot be altered."

"Is this about your critter baby?" Flam peeked out to the garage surrounding the tent to look for it. They often kept it swaddled and hidden away in one of the auto-body's bathrooms they'd repurposed as a nursery. "Because I know *crusher of men* was a very popular baby name last year and all, but don't you think it's a little . . . blunt?"

"Don't mock. All around us is a great a coalescing, one thing leading to the next, which will culminate in him claiming his birthright."

"To crush men, yeah? Am I getting that right?"

"Disrespect after I save your life?"

"Apparently *Nigel* saved my life. You probably would've left me to die."

"I would, yes." Greenspire clicked his cane on the pitted cement floor. "But one of the Lulomba, our seer, seems to think you're going to wake up one day, so I let them waste some poultice for your wound. To save your life, so you'd have a chance to do the same."

"To save my own life?"

"Yes. By refocusing it."

"All right, so is that an apology, then?"

"Is that a thank-you?"

Flam sighed. "Yes, I'm sorry. Thank you, Uncle. I

mean it. Bzzt."

Greenspire said nothing, his lips working around deep inside his silver nest of a beard, as if he had an itchy tongue. He'd had that strange habit even before, back when Flam was just a pup, when working something out.

Flam stood at the tent flap, deciding whether to stay for a few seconds more, even if he couldn't really spare them. He hadn't visited much lately.

"Collecting cans, huh?" he said, nudging a nearby bag with his hoof. The tent was packed with them, piled into heaps along the canvas walls, some even peeking out from under Greenspire's bed.

"Yes."

"Changing them out for spots?"

"Geyser, collectively, drinks fifteen thousand cans of soda, beer, or juice per day. And all of them have to go somewhere. It's my task, and that of the Lulomba who have volunteered, to gather this potential that's been tossed away."

"Potential? Potential what?"

"This space doesn't suit us any longer."

Weird topic shift, but okay. "You could return to the mines," Flam suggested, trying to play along. "You guys were cozy down there, right?"

"We could, but we'd be safe only for a time. The seer has read it." His focus drifted to his table, which was covered with pages and pages of ink-filled parchment.

"The deposit, yeah, that's been pretty much the guess since the day Gorett took off with his new friends. But we're not going to let them do that, Uncle. Me, the Patrol, Clyde, Nevele, and Rohm—we're—"

"Pride won't keep you standing. It only makes the fall more surprising."

Since his uncle was blind, Flam felt comfortable rolling his eyes right in front of him. "Yes, yes, I'm awful. I get it. So are you going to explain the cans?"

"We bring it to Gonn Smithworks to have the tin melted down so we can repurpose it."

"Repurpose it? For what?"

Greenspire pushed the door open. In the dirt back lot of the auto-body garage, surrounded by a high fence and heaps of junk, was a starship, or at least three-quarters of one.

Only some of the hull had been patched over the skeleton framework, but one could easily discern the shape it'd have once the fuselage and wing sections were complete. Engines tucked under the wings looked plum and at least pointed in the right direction, the cockpit featuring a repurposed auto seat, and overall the welding wasn't too shabby.

Flam thought, *I really need to start paying attention when I visit. Here I thought he was putting together a jungle gym for the bug people.*

"You're more than welcome to join us, Tiddle." Greenspire fumbled a bit to find Flam's shoulder.

The Lulomba were busy on the wing, delicately adding pictograms with their fingers, which were coated in gritty organic paint. One was a simple representation of people boarding a winged craft. The next was a craft shooting off, leaving behind what looked like a tree stump—no, Geyser, cut off halfway up its stem.

Flam felt a chill in his heart.

He turned around, took his uncle's hand, and held it in his. "I really want to talk more later about . . . all this, but right now I have to go. My friends are in danger. Please, if I call Nigel and he comes here and tells you that you need to leave, will you listen?" He bobbed a horn over his shoulder, toward his uncle's backyard project. "It's obvious you've put a lot of work into this thing, but if people start heading to the docks to get out of town, will you *please* go with them?"

"There's no danger, Tiddle," Greenspire said, the morning sunlight drawing out the pearlescent quality of his eyes. "The enormity in achieving our mission protects, shoots back through time to shield me. This will happen. It has to happen."

The seven o'clock bell tolled. Flam wanted to smack some sense into his uncle, drag him kicking and screaming away from all this, but right now he had to get back to the station and find a radio powerful enough to contact Clyde and Nevele, wherever they were. That, for Flam, was all that *had to happen*.

After giving his uncle a quick hug, Flam cut back through the garage, sidestepping the scampering startled bugs, and out the front. He ran the streets, clutching his middle, groaning with every few steps, but never let his hooves stop.

When Flam burst through the Patrol station's front doors, not one desk was occupied. He found every green-coated man and woman in the break room, focused on the wall-mounted telly.

A suited man holding a sheet of paper was about to say something. Given his expression, something bad.

CHAPTER 14

Like Wildfire

On the *Praise to Her* as it hurtled above mile after mile of unoccupied desert, Clyde, Nevele, Aksel, and Emer listened. The bandit boy sat crossed-legged on the floor—Rohm on his shoulder, ears raised. Together they remained silent as the broadcast began.

"Adeshka forces, emergency crews, and volunteers attempted to breach the frigate's hull to get to those trapped inside, but many had either died from smoke inhalation or fires that spread through the passenger compartments . . ."

At the back of the break room of the Geyser Patrol station, Flam stood, hollow-chested, ears twitching in the curl of his horns.

". . . the intelligence branch of Adeshka security force is currently pooling all efforts into the matter, reviewing security tapes from both the frigate launch and any during the short journey it made over the Lakebed. Evidence points to this being the work of the Odium, with the dining hall of the frigate bearing their Dapper Tom insignia, their calling card . . ."

In the mess hall, Gorett found the entire group sitting at the old console radio in the corner. At first, hearing the newscaster's voice, Gorett thought it was a new droning only he could hear, before he noticed the radio's dial glowing alive.

While everyone sat before untouched plates, meals going cold, he remained at the back of the room, itchy and squirmy but still rapt.

Directly before it, Dreck stood, his tri-cornered hat in his hands. Not out of respect, Gorett suspected, but removed mindlessly out of pure shock. His gaze remained fixed on the radio's glowing dial, never missing a single word of the staticky broadcast.

". . . King of Adeshka and surrounding providences, Seddalin Chidester, has vowed to exact swift justice on the whole of the Odium and specifically on the one thought to be their leader, who goes by the alias Dreck Javelin . . . "

Barely above a whisper, Dreck breathed, "I'm being *framed?*"

"The starship the men used, authorities say, bore the name *Praise to Her*, furthering speculation that they were in fact members of the Odium. This just in—authorities reviewing the security feeds at the Adeshka sky port have identified the two men thought to be responsible or at least involved in the attack in some way."

"Oh, this oughta be good." Dreck folded his arms.

"The first man is Coog 'Proboscis' McPhearson, wanted in every city-state on Gleese for murder, kidnapping, extortion, robbery, and blackmail. Distinguishing marks: a prosthetic nose. The second, authorities have identified as Aksel Browne, once a member of the Adeshka Fifty-Eighth militia and—"

"What?" Dreck screamed. "I killed him. I threw him out with my own hands."

He whipped around to scan the pirates, seeking one face in particular. He found it: Pitka Gorett. "You saw it. How the hell did he live?"

"I . . . I don't know. It doesn't seem possible."

". . . he is rumored to carry an outlawed piece of technology known as the DeadEye and is considered extremely dangerous."

"And completely unkillable, apparently!"

". . . if you believe you have seen either of these men, do not approach them. Contact your local Patrol station immediately. A message for the trained professionals, though: King Chidester has put a bounty forward of one million Adeshkan spots, to be rewarded to whoever can apprehend either man and return them to Adeshka—dead or alive. In addition, during his public address he added the statement, quote, Up until now, the Odium have been written off as a nuisance we believed would take care of itself. And I will not even address the rumors that certain individuals of political standing have sided with these awful men. But this latest example of evil has proven that the Odium is a true threat to the whole of Gleese, unquote."

Aksel leaned forward and switched off the *Praise to Her*'s console radio. For a few minutes, it was quiet. Nevele,

Clyde, Emer, and Rohm said nothing. Just the hum of the starship's engines, the soft rumble of speedy flight, and the occasional creak of warming metal.

Aksel tore off his tie—*swip*. He wrapped the black spider silk band around one hand, then the other, his gaze absently on a metal wall.

"The truth will out," Clyde said.

"Stuff it, okay?" Aksel ripped the tie in two. "They didn't just announce a price on your head to the entire bloody planet, did they? One million spots, mate. Think any bounty hunter's going to concern himself with truth? One million spots, dead or alive—like they'd even bother considering. Dead bloke's easier to transport. Prime for overhead compartments."

Nevele offered, "Bright side: at least now Adeshka's taking the Odium seriously. They'll do something. Geyser's all but saved."

Aksel snorted. "Really? Did you actually listen to that quote? He never said they were actually going to do anything. That was king speak for yes, it's a problem and, sure, I'm upset but since it doesn't directly threaten my life, I can't be arsed to do anything about it."

"Maybe we can explain to King Chidester you weren't really involved," Clyde tried.

"Yeah, Mr. Aksel, think about that," Rohm piped up. "Your name will be cleared in due time."

Aksel's eye burned with rage. "Doesn't matter if it gets called off or not. That sort of news travels nothing short of glacial on Gleese. Most likely the minute that hunter hears the bounty's been called off will be the same moment he's sawing the last bits of connective tissue between my head and shoulders. I'm dead."

"Maybe you should stop thinking about yourself and make use of what time you have left, then," Clyde said.

Aksel, shocked, looked his way.

"Do something dignified with it instead of worrying about when it'll be over. You're not gone yet, are you?"

Everyone turned to Clyde, who was now standing.

Aksel eyed him. Even though the pale man had a point, something about the way he'd said it had jabbed him in a way he didn't appreciate. Self-righteousness, maybe, or perhaps Clyde just reminded Aksel of the other Pynes too much right then. Either way, his DeadEye came unfolding from his head. Something in him at that moment apparently wanted Clyde dead as much as the entire world probably wanted Aksel dead.

Clyde drew Commencement.

"Clyde," Nevele shouted.

Aksel made his DeadEye retract, but his anger remained unfurled. "It was an accident, mate. Nothing more."

"Do it, Bullet Eater. You'd be saving us the trip," chimed a voice in Aksel's head then. Not Karl.

"What is it?" Nevele said, apparently noticing the shift in his expression.

Despite Clyde still having his sword out, Aksel turned his back to him and padded out of the cockpit, down toward the heaps of cargo spilled everywhere. He braced himself against the bulkhead, back toward everyone as they followed and asked him what was wrong.

His mind spun.

He can't still be alive.

"You piece of shite," Aksel said through his teeth to

the voice in his head. His hands throttled the hanging cargo straps. "They'll likely attack early now. If Adeshka can't stop them, you've made yourself lose Geyser. I hope you know that."

Around him, a riot of noise, an overwhelming hornet's nest: the roar of the engines, shaking through the steel paneling where he was pressing his forehead, the *Praise to Her* announcing they were only a few miles out from Nessapolis now. And Nevele and Clyde were still demanding to know who Aksel was talking to.

Ignoring it all, he listened to Raziel's laugh ring as if he were a relentless demon immune to all exorcisms, impossible to ignore though he didn't want to believe he was there. "Early? So you know when the attack will be, I take it?"

"All of those people on that frigate," Aksel murmured.

"I'm saving Geyser. Though I have little trust in Adeshka's security checkpoints, I have all the faith in the world in their servicemen and women. I provided Adeshka with not just a reason to join the fight but a personal one, a vendetta.

"Of course you know that already, if you were listening to the news like the rest of the planet. You're public enemy number one now, and after Adeshka's through with their dustup with the pirates, they'll come for you next. Maybe even put a certain flophouse hotel manager under arrest because she recently rented room six to the man in question—"

"I'll kill you."

"It's not me you have to worry about. But I can have Karl block her from the citizen registry and have her remain unfound by Chidester's secret police if you tell me what I want to know."

"I swear if you go anywhere near Vee—"

"If I wanted your sister dead, I could just go down-stairs and shoot her in the head. I'll continue not doing that if you tell me what you know. You escaped with my brother's fiancée, and I can't imagine she was anything but ungrateful. Maybe she mentioned what she knows about the attack? Specifically, when it'll take place? Also, if you would, tell her I owe her for blinding Tym. Maybe I'll kill Clyde first, have her watch, making her wish she was just as blind."

Aksel looked over his shoulder. Nevele and Clyde. They trusted him now. He'd proven himself to them. And now, to save his sister's life, he'd have to dash that newly built confidence.

"The day after tomorrow."

"Lying?"

"No."

"We'll go early just in case you are. Maybe Clyde would like to meet us there? Is he with you?"

"Yes."

"Wonderful. Say hello for me. But before I go, some advice. Grow some eyes in the back of your head, Bullet Eater. The entire planet's eager for you now."

Aksel waited for more creative threats, but Raziel's whispering intrusion was silenced with a small burst of static as the transmission went dead.

"Who was that?" Clyde sounded unsure if he actually wanted to know.

"Your brother."

Nevele's face twisted. "He survived?"

"Apparently. Both he and Tym, somehow." Aksel's

shoulders slumped, his hands slapping against his legs. "It was all a plan. The frigate crash, framing me for it right alongside the Odium, everything. And I had to tell him. I didn't want to, but he threatened my sister and me—"

"I understand," Clyde said. "I don't think I'll ever be able to look my brother in the face knowing what he's done, but if he can do something we can't to save the city, it might be best to just let him. You're innocent in all this, remember. You had to do what you did."

Aksel nodded. *Innocent in downing the frigate, maybe. But everything else? All the other odd jobs Raziel sent me on? Knife tips under fingernails, wrenches that never cranked a single bolt but instead a whole lot of teeth. Every item in that lost bag of mine got plenty of use, every stain upon those implements I—and I alone— am responsible for adding. If these new friends of mine only knew, or Vee, they'd probably volunteer me to Chidester's men. Innocent? In the tableau of my life, innocence only accounts for a few microscopic flecks, maybe—*

A series of hard slams rocked the *Praise to Her*, gunfire pelting the underside of the ship, the vibration almost painful on the bottoms of his feet.

Emer shouted back. "Doesn't look like Nessapolis is as abandoned as everyone said it is."

"—we'll return at noon for another update."

Dreck drew his scattergun. Everyone in the room leaped away, overturning chairs and spilling plates to the floor, afraid to get in the crossfire as their captain emptied the magazine into the radio's grille.

It lay there, silenced, shooting sparks as Dreck holstered, seething.

Gorett and the pirates waited for Dreck's next word. He remained glaring at the dead radio. After what felt like an eternity, he drew a deep breath, turned, and said to all waiting, "We hit them early."

CHAPTER 15

A Kingdom Too Far

In the Patrol station break room, as soon as telly programming returned to normal morning broadcasts, the group of guardsmen turned to Sir Flam, a wall of eyes.

Flam's hand moved down from his heart, back toward his stomach, a red dot blossoming on his bandage. He tried to find something reassuring to say, but when he touched his wound, there came a sound that matched his pain exactly: from every window, alarms blared a whoop that started low and came to an earsplitting crescendo. The sound wasn't uncommon in Geyser. It typically signaled fires and severe weather, but this time it seemed to have a particular pitch heralding something worse.

Cheerfully contributing to the cacophony, almost buried under the enveloping racket, Flam's desk phone rang from across the room. Momentarily forgetting his position, he exchanged looks with the guardsmen, hoping it'd be— even if just this one time—someone else's responsibility.

"That's your phone, sir."

"Yes, thank you, George." Flam lumbered over and picked up the receiver.

"Hello?"

"This is the office of Lord Seddalin Chidester, King of

Adeshka and surrounding provinces, to speak to the head of security of the Geyser Patrol."

"Uh, speaking."

"Please hold for line decryption." The line went quiet a moment. When audio returned with a hard click, Flam felt his ears prick up and his back straighten, pain piercing his gut.

"Are you there?" a gravelly voice said. Flam had heard Chidester speak plenty of times, but it was odd hearing him pose a question directly to *him*.

"Hello, sir. This is head of security, Tiddle Flam—*Sir* Tiddle Flam, I mean."

"Sir Flam. We tried contacting the palace there a moment ago, but it seems your steward is somehow indisposed?"

"Uh, yes, he's . . . away at the moment."

"You're next in the chain of command."

"I understand." *Where the plummets are you when I need you, Pasty?*

"As I'm sure you're aware, many innocent lives were lost late last night during what I am considering a declaration of war."

"Yes, I just saw the news report, sir, and I'm very sorry for your city's loss."

"Not just an Adeshkan loss, Sir Flam. The good people of Gleese as a whole suffered a loss. Which is why I'm calling to ask Geyser's assistance. Last year during a troubling time for your city, mine was happy to provide assistance. Now I request your consideration in answering the call for us in kind."

"Actually, sir, I meant to call you earlier about something, but . . ."

"Yes? Yes? Speak, man. Time is of the essence."

"Well, thing is, I've recently learned some information regarding the true culprits who crashed the frigate. Raziel, Tym . . ." He hesitated, then closed his mouth before Moira's name could escape. "Pyne."

Behind Flam, a hushed rabble began to brew among his guardsmen. A backhanded swat of his arm silenced them.

The alarms continued to scream, making it hard to hear King Chidester, but his bewilderment cut through the wailing just fine. "Francois Pyne's sons? Preposterous."

"Preposterous or not, it's the truth. I suggest you call off your attack on the Odium—and have it announced on the radio, a *public* address. Because while they might be to blame for a lot of nasty things, that frigate crash was not the Odium's work. And by poking the sleeping bearcat like that, you open us up for a whole slew of retribution, just like any bigmouthed dumb arse tends to find himself in when tossing accusations around willy-nilly. Your Majesty."

Chidester harrumphed. "I beg your pardon!"

"Forgive me, but they won't attack you directly. No, *we'll* receive the brunt of it. Geyser's always been an easy target. And we have the deposit—wendal stone."

"Yes, I remember hearing about that." Chidester sounded jealous, as if he wanted a deposit under *his* city just to say he had one.

"So we need to strategize here. We have to go on the defensive, not the offensive."

King Chidester was quiet a moment. "I'm sorry," he began, and as soon as he'd said it, Flam closed his eyes, "but I'm afraid I cannot reroute anything your way. We're deploying now, everything we have to scour the ice caps.

But I assure you, we'll do our utmost to stop them in the event they choose to attack Geyser in response to any *supposedly* false accusations I may have made. And even if they are false, Sir Flam, consider this: having the Odium finally conquered—something that's been put off far too long—will not cause too many sleepless nights. Innocent or not for this particular attack, they are guilty of many others. Having them gone will be a boon for Gleese—a disease finally meeting its cure."

"Is this because they've been talking about giving you the boot these past few years? Happy to take up some crusade against the bad guys to make yourself look a hero?"

"Sir Flam, this is war. It has nothing to do with my appearance as king. It's an obligation, as all wars are, and it isn't *taken up* without scrupulous consideration."

"Sure."

"We'll try our best to contain the threat and be systematic in our counterattack, but your choice to remain idle may lead to collateral damage. It's true: war may still find your city, making your involvement beyond your control. Better to join now, while it's still a choice."

"We're not *choosing* to be idle here. We *can't* do anything else."

"Well, it may not appear so to you, but cowardice has many faces—"

"Cowardice? Let me tell you something, Chidester. Here in Geyser, we're *anything* but—"

Chidester rattled off without conviction, "May Lord Aurorin keep you and your city in his protective light, Sir Flam. Next time your people are in need, I might suggest calling out west upon the city-states of Embaclawe. Or farther, to Rammelstaad. The Territorial Skirmish was, after all, quite some time ago. Maybe one of those fine nations would be willing to help a former enemy now that you've found yourself with nothing but new ones." The line went dead.

Flam remained holding the receiver, listening to the droning dial tone, trying to think of what he'd say when he turned around.

The alarms wailed on.

The phone shook his hand, the disconnected line humming out an ominous, dead note.

The whispering behind him started up again. "What are we going to do?" one guardsman managed, his panic spilling free. Another asked the same, stepping toward Flam. Fear. So much fear, and so fast. It spread amongst them like wildfire. *Say something to them, you twit.*

He couldn't turn. Not yet. He fought hard to keep his knees from quaking. His throat stripped itself of moisture. His pulse beat faster, faster. Alone. Four hundred against *however* many the Odium might have—dedicated cutthroats all, probably now boarding up, snapping magazines to rifles, dragging whetstones down the lengths of thirsty blades.

Back when he was a solitary treasure hunter, any sort of alarm going off meant one thing: beat feet. But this was something he couldn't run from. Clyde had asked him, as a friend, someone he trusted, to occupy this position. Sure, maybe not right alongside him and Nevele, but to be here, at home, watching over things. Pasty hadn't touched Commencement on Flam's shoulders and dubbed him Sir Flam for nothing. He must've seen *something* in him.

Flam finally set down the phone, drew a breath he hoped would steel him and keep his voice from shaking in the presence of his guardsmen.

"Get to your posts. We're going to be on our own."

Gorett stood before the mirror, the sound of the pirates racing up and down the hall like thunder just outside his door. He watched the shiny, pale entity coil and uncoil inside the semitranslucent yellow hill on his neck. It moved in time with its words: *You know what I'm implying, Pitka. You're by no means a stupid man, despite how much you sometimes feign.*

What do I need to do?

It went still, perhaps contemplating. Then it gave a quick, snapping wriggle: *Go do what we're already both thinking. We need to stop him before takeoff if we want Geyser to remain standing.*

Okay, Gorett thought in reply, dragging the collar up around his neck. He gave it a reassuring pat and made for the door. *Thank you.*

Just go. Before it's too late.

Almost immediately upon leaving his room, Gorett was tugged aside from the swell of pirates all rushing to the elevators. The length of Dreck's arm pinned Gorett's frail, wrinkled throat to the wall. The worm thrashed under the threat of being squished.

Unable to speak, Gorett pleaded with his eyes, banishing any trace of sabotage from his mind—as if Dreck could suddenly be like the worm and hear what he was thinking.

The Odium flowed around them like two stubborn rocks in a river, all packing into the station's freight elevators twenty at a time to the hangars below. Once they were in position, the ceiling would split apart and spray life into the sky like a pregnant spider crushed underfoot.

"And where do you think *you're* going?" Dreck said over the clattering of boots and armor and the pirates' shouting and slapping one another, getting themselves bolstered, shaking off dust that'd gathered on their bloodlust.

"I," Gorett choked out, "I was going to make sure the *Magic Carpet* was fueled."

"Of *course* you were."

When the elevator doors shimmied aside with a grating creak, Dreck dragged Gorett in with him to share the ride down. "I think today you're going to be my copilot. That way if you feel the temptation to do anything silly, it'll be where I can keep an eye on you."

The elevator jerked down the shaft in starts and stops. The entire ride, even though Gorett had nowhere to escape, Dreck kept a firm hand on the ex-king. Once down in the hangar, he pushed Gorett out ahead first, to move of his own volition only a moment before Dreck snagged him like a hooked fish and dragged him along again.

Gorett's feet fought to keep him standing. In the hangar—and inside his head—it was hot and noisy.

Up the back ramp of the *Magic Carpet*, they passed the Nimbelle height chart and entered the cramped cockpit, a glass bubble making up the nose cone.

Dreck shoved Gorett into the copilot's pit, removed his own lime-green hat, jammed it onto the headrest of his seat, and pulled on a leather flight cap. He threw various switches, and in a few seconds, the rear compartment of the *Magic Carpet* filled with tagalong pirates, all brandishing weapons, loading, reloading, checking breaches, whooping and cheering.

Pitka Gorett felt the main engines kick on, shaking his back, despite the seat's dense padding.

A widening wedge of the suns' blue light fell in as the ceiling of the hangar split. Chunks of ice rained down, shattering on the hard floor. Gorett flinched as one particularly large piece fell, growing as it descended toward the glass above his head. But something prevented it—a quick zap, lightning springing from nowhere—shattered the tumbling boulder.

"At least we know the shields are working. May the Goddess bless Everlasting Guide Tesla, aye?" Dreck laughed and flipped more switches. He donned a pair of headphones over the flight cap, angling a microphone down in front of his bearded face. "Is Bessie onboard, all tucked in?"

"Aye," came the reply from somewhere within the station, or perhaps in the *Magic Carpet* herself; Gorett didn't know.

Gorett peeked over. He knew which trigger on Dreck's flight stick would launch it and which would detonate it once it had dug a satisfactory depth into the city's stem. He'd been watching for months.

When the time comes, said the voice inside Gorett he'd almost involuntarily come to refer to as Mother Worm, *you still have a chance to stop them. It will undoubtedly cost your life, but remember how much Geyser meant to you. To us.*

I miss you, Mother.

And I miss you too, Pitka. But you'll see me again soon.

Dreck's hands expertly fell onto the controls. He was smiling, downright electric. When he pulled a cord overhead to sound a horn, an ear-splitting wail, twenty-six ships all threw their main thrusters.

Gorett spilled side to side, the *Magic Carpet* ascended, the engines straining to punch the starship up through the slate skies, barreling through the protective blizzard.

The world past the cockpit glass became awash with blaring sunlight, unfiltered and undiluted. It'd been the first time in a while Gorett had seen the suns as something more than just hazy disks.

Once at a satisfactory altitude, Dreck leveled out the *Magic Carpet*, a moment of weightlessness stirring Gorett's guts. The artificial gravity was flipped, and various equipment and weaponry clanked back snug in nets.

Gorett pressed his forehead against the window's cool glass, hoping it'd subdue his mounting nausea. "Twelve o'clock, sir."

Dreck didn't reply, merely jammed a thumb on his flight stick. To either side of the cockpit, gun barrels slid out and locked into position.

From the blue expanse, vague shapes came straight at them. The distant starships opened fire: white, silent flashes.

A second later, the shots streaking toward the *Magic Carpet* were torn off course by the shield. Gorett covered his face and screamed, but his fingers had become too narrow to hide much.

Forgoing evasive maneuvers, Dreck drove the *Magic Carpet* on, the tempo of oncoming bullets increasing, their shields slapping each thunderbolt away.

Nearly upon them.

Neither group diverted.

Dreck made an inhuman shriek, his war cry.

Mere yards from impact, the Adeshkans broke formation. The *Magic Carpet* charged through.

"They're circling around, sir."

"Let them," Dreck shouted.

Below his feet and through the cockpit bubble, Gorett could see the ground far, far below. It was snow-covered, as always this far north, but slowly faded into rougher terrain: black rock, the occasional grove of spindly conifers, the glassy surface of a pond. The Odium fleet tore over its surface in reflection: a mass of indistinct triangular shapes, white contrails pointing unerringly south.

More shots rang out, aft.

The manmade lightning cracked, slapping at the bullets. A few slipped through and thumped into the hull. Gorett held his breath, waiting for the telltale whoosh of depressurization, but thankfully the Odium had thoroughly armored their crafts.

"Still on us, sir. Might I recommend the sizzler?"

Dreck waved a hand over his shoulder. "Sure, but be sparing. This isn't all of what Chidester has for us."

"Ready, sir."

"Fire."

A breathy *fump*. Gorett watched out the top of the cockpit's glass bubble as a rod striped like a candy cane streaked high into the sky, quickly reducing itself to a pinprick among the blue vault of the sky. When it burst, Gorett felt its concussive detonation in the core of his chest.

From the snap of light came countless tiny rockets—zipping around in spirals and drunken twists. The knot of insane rockets went after anything, friend or foe, carrying a heat signature. A few even banged down against the *Magic Carpet*.

But apparently the swarm was still effective. From behind came a detonation that made Gorett's teeth snap together. Then a second and a third. Clutching his harness to keep himself in the seat, Gorett watched between his knobby knees as Adeshkan fighters tumbled, oily black smoke chasing them down, bursting into flames upon crashing.

"How many did that sort?" Dreck called back, eyes forward.

"All three, sir. Radar shows zero pursuers."

"I'd reckon that was only a drop in the bucket of what Adeshka's got. Can't blame Chidester, really. Wouldn't want to blow all the fun right at the start. A gentleman *eases* into a scuffle." He retracted the ship's guns to reduce drag.

He doesn't care anything about the stone, only the fear he can create. He dangles reward only to retain his men's assistance.

I disagree, Gorett replied. *He wants the stone so he won't be alone anymore. He's the only weaver in the Odium, and I think he's ashamed, seldom using his power in their presence. He wants more like him.*

And what do you suppose he'll use more weavers for? Mother Worm posed. *The companionship? He'll continue this reign of terror, even more with the aid of those like him. If it works, that is, and if Father Time agrees to do it. Speaking of which, Dreck hasn't even confirmed he's anything more than legend. Shows how much he believes in this plan, how besotted he is in following his Goddess. And even if he does find Höwerglaz, a powerful one such as he would not likely side with such sentient filth as Dreck Javelin. But—hypothetically—if he does exist and does work with Dreck, there will be* no force whatsoever *capable of stopping the Odium then. Think of that, Pitka. Not Adeshka, not Embaclawe if they deign to do something. If he can manufacture weavers, Dreck might as well begin calling himself King of Gleese.*

That's terrifying.

But you know I'm right. Your mother is always right.

Something in that moment told Gorett to look out the side of the cockpit, to the west. Not Mother Worm, no flash of starship fire pulling his focus that way—but *some* force made his focus swivel.

Outside he saw nothing but blank sky, the occasional stippling of the brown world. All the same, he felt something out there looking.

CHAPTER 16

A Warm Welcome

Clyde didn't know why, but he found himself gazing out the left side of the *Praise to Her*. But as bullets pattered against the floor beneath his feet and Aksel's shouting continued, Clyde snapped to. He stood, clutched the wall as the starship quaked beneath him, and stumbled into the cockpit.

Nevele was already there, gripping the back of Emer's seat at the copilot controls. The boy looked over his shoulder as Clyde stepped in. Clyde expected him to appear terrified—seeing as how they were nigh shot down—but instead Emer bore an eerie calmness.

Nessapolis was mapped in with geometric shapes, all cubelike, but every building looked halfway submerged in something. The nav computer had a hard time discerning this, but Clyde assumed it was sand. Nessapolis had been the victim of a cataclysmic sandstorm. Only the tallest buildings spiked the landscape.

"They're all over us," Aksel said. "Four at least."

Another salvo peppered their starboard flank, a dotted line of dents appearing inside, each glowing orange a moment.

"Land somewhere," Nevele shouted. "If the Odium are still here, it means they haven't found Höwerglaz yet."

"Probably because he isn't here *to be found*," Aksel put in, shifting the sticks.

The *Praise to Her* ducked and dodged, slipping between buildings. Clyde was tossed around, one hand on a grab bar, the other pressing Commencement's sheath to the bulkhead so he wouldn't get slammed with the next sharp bank.

The ship's condition reading went from an *I'm sort of hurt* yellow to a flash-flashing *Now might be a good time to worry* red.

"If there are any parachutes back there," Aksel said, pausing to concentrate as he passed them through a beige cubicle farm *inside* a building, "might want to consider strapping up."

Clyde took a crooked hop back, into the holds. He swung from handhold to handhold, kicking things aside, scanning for parachutes among the tossing cargo.

Only one chute pack, marked with a commercial frigate company logo, slid by. Clyde snatched it by its belt.

"Here," he said, presenting it to the group.

"There's only *one*?" Aksel and Nevele said in unison.

"I got that off the frigate," Nevele said, breathless. "There must be others."

"No. I looked."

Without warning, Aksel wrenched back the sticks. The floor slipped out from under Clyde. Nevele snatched his wrist. If she hadn't, it would've been a fall down the empty tube of the ship with nothing soft to land on.

The ship's frame groaned and rattled. Clyde was certain at any moment the *Praise to Her* would disintegrate.

Nevele's threads unlaced from one arm to snare Clyde's, cementing the hold she had on him.

Aksel leveled them out, and the floor became the floor again.

Clyde stumbled into the cockpit. He pushed the parachute at Nevele. "Take it and go."

"No." She pushed it back. "You take it."

"Very sweet, you two," Aksel barked, "but if you wouldn't mind, can it."

They were going back through the building again. In their wake, a concussion—one pursuer hadn't been so deftly piloted.

"There's one down," Aksel noted joylessly. And again over his shoulder, "Which one of you is it going to be? I'm taking another swing across that roof. That'll be time to hop."

Nevele and Clyde held the parachute, locked in a stalemate.

"Sheeit, *I'll* volunteer." Emer unlatched himself from the seat, snatched the parachute pack, and shoved his way past them. Without hesitation, he flung open the hatch and jumped, Rohm screaming from the boy's pocket.

"Well, that settles that, I guess," Nevele said.

"He's down," Aksel said, still weaving through the dead city. "Now it's just a matter of us doing the same— *without* dying, preferably."

Something hit the ship. Not a bullet. Heavier, as if a man-sized cannonball had just dropped onto their wing. Aksel began rolling them, apparently trying to break the grip of whatever had landed.

Nevele sprang forth a net around her and Clyde and their surroundings, twining around every available bit of exposed frame to suspend them in the middle—just as the thing detonated, blasting their wing entirely off.

The ship went into a floppy, end-over-end spin.

Even though his feet were no longer touching the floor, Clyde could feel gravity taking back control. Smoke poured into the cabin. Things popped and pinged, bolts flying, alarms bawling.

"Look at me," Nevele said through the chaos. "Clyde. Look at me."

Even with their faces an inch apart, smoke blurred her. He held her tight. She squeezed him in return.

He loved her and believed she knew it, but holding her was the only way he could express it—now and ever. If he told her, she'd be ripped from his mind, replaced by a bleached spot, a stranger again.

And in spite of death charging in, he refused to tell her. He wanted to remember her, even if that was all he'd have after this.

"I love you," Nevele said. A loose panel of her cheek slid off. "I love you, and I'm sorry."

You're sorry? For what? is what he *would've* said if his lips hadn't been stilled: over her shoulder, the cockpit vidscreens displayed a widening, flat square, growing. The ground.

Clyde looked into her eyes.

Blackness swallowed them.

Coughs swelled in her chest and fought free of her lips, bringing Nevele back to consciousness.

A fire crackled. She could feel its heat lapping but, unnervingly enough, couldn't see its glow. Smoke. So much smoke.

"Clyde? Aksel?"

She reached into the darkness, fumbling. A narrow

shaft of light peeped through a bullet hole.

She pushed herself up, groaning. Everything hurt. Reallocating some threads, she bit her lip and cinched closed a slice crossing her shin.

"Clyde?" The darkness ate her words.

A soft moan—somewhere near. Cautiously, keeping low to avoid the denser smoke collecting near the ceiling, Nevele scuttled on.

The moan came again.

As she crawled, she realized she wasn't feeling the rubberized floor of the ship under her palms. Now it was a carpet of warm, granular texture. Nessapolis's burying sand.

Her fingers brushed a hand, which was weakly reaching.

He was damp and tacky, as if he'd been dipped in paint. Through the smoke, she recognized the smell—that coppery tang she was unfortunately well acquainted with.

"Clyde?" Cough, cough. "I can't see. Where are you hurt?"

A drowsy "Ugh."

Something near them buckled, and a load of fresh smoke and fire-warmed sand dumped in, hissing as it rained. "Can you move? We need to get out of here."

"It . . . hurts."

"What hurts?"

More delicate than her hands could be, her threads explored him. Up his sleeves, down the collar of his poncho, traveling her fiancé's form.

He'd been punctured by something.

She followed the rivers coursing down him, soaking his clothes, to where it was the warmest, the blood's source, the injury.

Something solid and cold. She swallowed and carefully

traced its shape. Embossed metal, flamboyant and intricately hewn. Familiar. Commencement.

Like everything else in the ship during the crash, it too had gone through the cement mixer that the *Praise to Her* had become but had somehow managed to abandon its sheath and find a new one: its owner, just below the ribs.

"*Nevele . . .*"

"I know, sweetheart. I know it hurts. But just lie still, okay?" A cough swelled in her chest, demanded out. She was lightheaded.

She felt along the floor, gently squeezing fingers under his back. The sword was *through* him, the blade tip buried into the ship's floor, Clyde a pinned entomology specimen.

"Aksel," she shouted into the darkness, "Clyde needs help. Aksel?"

Her answer came in a report of gunfire. She yelped and ducked, throwing herself across Clyde. She must've bumped the sword because he screamed as if he'd been run through a second time. "I'm sorry," she whispered, covered his mouth. "I'm so sorry."

Past the crackle of small fires and Clyde's hot wheezing under her palm came voices—outside the wreck. Footsteps too. Close by, plodding across sand, crunch, crunch.

If he dies, she thought, *I will tear all of you apart.*

Nevele forced herself to leave Clyde for a moment to feel around for any of the guns Coog had stored on the ship. She cut her hands several times, felt bits of steel dig under her fingernails as she blindly swept hands around, but kept on as quietly as possible.

A supernova burst inside the ship. Her eyes focused for the half second it took the figure to push aside the hatch door and throw himself out into the white-yellow world beyond. The door slammed behind him and gunfire followed—haphazard and surprised. It trailed off, shouts following it.

Aksel had just saved their lives.

She crawled back to Clyde, bumping her head twice.

Outside, far away now, the shouting and gunfire continued. Good. If they were still firing, they hadn't caught him. She hoped Aksel was actually trying to draw them away and wasn't just running for his life . . .

Either way, it had bought her time. She found Clyde's hand in the dark, entwined her fingers with his. They snapped together easily, slickened as they were. She held tight . . . while the other wrapped around Commencement's handle. She paused, readying herself: settling threads near where Clyde's flesh and the sword met. The moment she pulled the sword free, she'd try to rush in and patch him quick as possible.

The tempo of his breathing increased. Apparently she didn't need to explain what she was about to do.

Forgoing any sort of countdown, she tugged on the sword. And for the first time ever, she heard Clyde swear.

But it hadn't come all the way free.

She felt—delicately as she could—along the damp blade. Another ten inches of the metal remained inside him. She echoed his pain with a scream of her own, one she couldn't help but make. She hated this more than anything—hurting her love to save him—but it had to be done.

"Please," he said, weakly clutching her arm. "Please stop."

"I can't. I'm sorry, but I can't. We need this thing out."

"Please . . . Margaret, please."

She felt just as impaled, hearing that name. "Just a little more. Hold on to me."

As soon as he'd returned his hand round her wrist, she didn't give him or herself time to catch a breath. She wrenched again, her fiancé's body reluctant to relinquish the sword.

Another pull, more screams, both his and hers.

The sword popped free, and the blood leaped out in a sloppy gush. She dove her threads in, working fast. She got the wound—front and back—closed, pulled tight, the flow damming off.

She used Commencement to cut herself free of him. Not letting him suffer another second there on the floor, she tossed aside the sword. For right now, the heirloom didn't mean anything. On hands and knees, she dragged Clyde in the general direction she'd seen Aksel escape.

She was blinded again when they broke free of the wreckage. Falling out onto the dusty floor of the city, she pulled Clyde out and knelt beside him. Blocking him from any danger that might be waiting, she took a squinting scan of their surroundings.

Nessapolis, the Necropolis as it was more commonly known now. Fitting. Among the widely scattered skyscraper tips that still showed of the sandboxed city, a few raised roadways rose and dipped like a cement sea monster. Everything was so still. She looked down the hill they'd crashed upon, the littered trail of starship pieces— some still smoking, others stabbed deep into the sand. From the direction of what was probably once downtown, she could hear gunshots echoing, bouncing around in the man-made valley of drowned high-rises.

She turned back to Clyde. His wound was still pushing blood up around the brown-and-black laces she'd sewn into him, painting his snowy skin as well as the sand beneath him. She pulled the poncho from around his shoulders, tore off a long strip, and tied it around his middle.

Doing so got sand in his face, collecting in the corners of eyes that floated loosely in his head. Most people had a hard time telling which way he was looking precisely, because his eyes were entirely black, but she knew, just by the way the shine on them shifted. She'd had practice watching them, more than just where he was looking but how he used them: whether he steered his gaze away before telling her bad news or because he was growing shy, as he sometimes still became, even after a year together. She could tell he was looking at her now. And that he was scared.

"It's going to be okay."

Nodding faintly, he said nothing. She didn't like how cold his hand was.

She pulled her focus from him to try to orient herself, looking for the office building they'd dropped Emer onto. There. It was a ways down the block, a plain glass slab topped by a wind-twisted communication tower. She shielded her eyes, peering to see if the boy was still up there.

A distant double pop of gunfire echoed past. Then another. Aksel. She didn't want to leave Clyde here alone, but . . .

His hand squeezing hers brought her attention back. "Tell me something," Clyde whispered weakly.

More gunfire repeated throughout the dead city, echoed.

"Stay here, okay? Just stay here." Before he could argue, she gave him a quick kiss and raced down the hill, the wind hot in her face, the coppery taste of blood on her lips.

CHAPTER 17

Signed in Blood

Geyser was in chaos.

Flam hadn't been here when Gorett ordered the town evacuated last year, but he assumed it was similar. Everywhere he raced through the streets, trying to get back to the auto-body shop, people were shouting at him, saying they were promised that they'd never have to leave their city again, that they'd be kept *safe*. Flam didn't have time to explain but insisted they stay inside their homes, there was no mass evacuation planned, and they were not to answer their doors regardless of who came knocking.

He charged on through the crowded streets. Despite the orders to stay put, people were voluntarily evacuating. A line stretched for blocks to the elevators in the citizens' ward. Honking autos added the horn section to the ugly city-wide symphony already playing: ringing alert bells and the loudspeakers' redundant "Stay calm, stay calm, stay calm" reprise.

Finally reaching the garage, lugging the rifle he'd picked from the armory after the guardsmen and women had chosen their own, Flam stepped inside. He saw nothing but hammocks dangling empty, every tent and Blatta hive pocket abandoned. Flam grimaced and pushed through the door leading to the back lot. The ship was still there, and from within, he could hear muffled chatter—that weird Lulomba language.

Some of the paneling wasn't on all the way, and one of the engines was shoddily tacked on.

The engines were on now, warming, emitting a low hum.

"Uncle?" Flam approached the cockpit, rapped on the tinted glass.

It slid aside. Instead of Greenspire Flam framed there in the window, it was Nigel, staring at Flam as if his head were aflame. "What're ye doing here?"

"I'm looking for Greenspire. Is he in there with you?" Past Nigel, Flam could see only the tangled mass of Lulomba people and the serrated legs and shiny carapaces of the Blatta, all stuffed in together. He could also hear the flapping of wings—Scooter, Nigel's parrot.

"I thought he was with ye."

"Did he say anything?"

"No, he just took off. Not even a minute ago. I figured he was looking for ye, to say good-bye. Look, lad, I might suggest coming with us. Not exactly a lot of room back there but space enough for ye and Greenspire, when he gets back."

"You have no idea how tempting that sounds right now, but I can't. Also, I think I might have to ask you to stick around as well."

Nigel's substantial brows crushed together. "Haven't ye been listening to the news? Gleese is at war, son."

"But Geyser needs you."

"I'm in a wheelchair, mate. Fighting landed me in it, and I doubt more's gonna get me out of it—unless we're speaking in the mortal sense." Nigel stared at Flam a moment. "But I must say, talk like that coming from ye surprises me. Didn't think the uniform would fit a lad such as yerself too well, but now"—he tweaked Flam's badge straight—"can't say ye'd look quite right *without* it."

"*Without it*," Scooter contributed.

"Thanks," Flam said quickly, grateful for the genuinely kind remark, "but I really need the help. We can't do this with the men we have. We need fighters. Whether you're in the chair or not, it doesn't matter to me."

Nigel nodded. "Aye, aye. Listen, I put some shooters on this bucket in the event we're not too welcome in the next orbit yer uncle's pilgrimage takes us to. Tell ye what, until I spot Greenspire, I'll make a circuit around the island a few times, keep an eye out. But the minute I see yer uncle, I'm only touching down long enough to pick him up. After that, we're gone."

"Thank you." Flam backed away as the engines screeched their first and second rounds of ignition.

As they ascended for the first pass around the city, Flam turned and bolted back through the garage. He slapped aside canvas tents and pushed through the door leading onto Fourth Circle Street.

He stepped out just as Nigel rocketed past overhead. He stole a moment to watch the starship streak the sky— and saw a second coming in toward it. The two nearly collided. The second ship swooped low, spun about, and dove over the edge of the platter, out of sight. Nigel's ship stopped in midair, hovered a moment, turned, and shot after it.

But in that second when the other ship—a compact, sleek

vessel—had slowed, Flam could've sworn he saw a handful of figures drop out from the bomb compartment doors.

He estimated where they landed in the city, a few blocks over, and moved that way, readying his rifle. Turning down alleyways, he saw storefront shutters rattle down, windows close, and locks click. *Good. At least some of them are listening.*

Most of them, anyway. Next to him, from the mouth of an alley, he heard a rustle of feet. "Get to your home!" he shouted to remind whoever was down there.

An auto horn drew his attention away.

When he turned back to see if the alley stragglers had done as he'd ordered, his snout nearly bumped the barrel of a gun.

The individual holding it wore a body suit with a featureless, smooth mask. Behind, another person dressed the same also brandished a pistol. Their suits were black, but viewed from a particular angle, parts of them became invisible, the edges shimmering like oil on water.

Flam tried to very slowly shift around with his rifle, but apparently, even though the masks hid their eyes, they never missed a thing. With deft fluidity, they snatched the gun from Flam's grasp and sent it clattering onto the flagstones.

"Where's the steward?" The voice was creaky, robotic through breather filters.

"He's not at the palace?" Flam said, hands up now.

"No. He's not."

"Well, you might want to go look again," Flam said. "Place *is* awfully big, and last I checked, the steward's just a bitty fella." *Play dumb. Frustrate them. Let them give you an opening.*

The gun's hammer ratcheted. "Stop stalling."

It'd taken Flam a moment to realize they weren't in suits for scouting but for sport—specifically speed-skull fencing, a game that involved hopping around invisible in a cube arena, scoring on your opponent by bopping them on the head with a twenty-pound mallet. Weird, rich-people fun. And when the closest one moved again to angle away his compact shooter, Flam saw the emblem on his suit's chest. The upside down black triangle with the white albatross leaping up, wings spread, a spear in its chomp. Srebrna Academy.

"Listen, if you kids are here as wannabe looters, I'd suggest swinging by another day. Kind of a bad time."

The figure reached a shimmering hand up and flipped a switch behind the jaw. The helmet face peeled away like a flower blooming, its panels retracting into the high collar.

Flam reeled.

He looked just like Clyde.

Flam's gaze moved to the second speed-skull suit. *Nula? Er—Moira?*

Although he couldn't be sure, with her still wearing her mask, Flam gave them a withering glare. The semi-invisible figures shifted, apparently able to feel the glare's heat—or read his thoughts, if it was Moira. Right then, anyone could've picked up on his feelings, screaming in his head as they were.

"Yes, it's her," the one Flam assumed was Raziel said. "Go ahead. Let him see you."

After a slight hesitation, the helmet opened: Moira's true face. Pale, ashen skin, black eyes, lips the faintest of pinks.

The wound in Flam's trunk ached again.

"We want to save Geyser as much as you do," she said, small.

"So you can steal it out from under Clyde." Flam grunted.

Moira seemed unable or unwilling to say anything more.

Raziel watched their exchange, smirking. Just as Flam was about to address him, ask him why he wanted Clyde dead so badly, or just punch him in the face—whichever— a burst of static interrupted him.

"Flam?" came from the radio clipped to his belt. It was Nigel, distorted by engine noise on his end. "I saw that thing take off like the dickens, but I can't get a steady bead on her. Any of yer men good with hittin' moving targets? Could use a hand with this one."

"Our pilot," Raziel supplied, gesturing to the cloudless sky as the shiny pellet of a starship streaked past again, performing evasive maneuvers always just slightly ahead of Nigel's pattering shots. "And if he gets taken down, that's less help against the Odium."

Flam took the radio off his belt. "Stand down, Nigel."

"Aye?"

"Yeah, leave that one alone." He lowered the radio. "You're going to help us?"

"Yes." Raziel holstered. Hand now empty, he leveled it toward Flam, the half-invisible fingers spread. "You've hurt a lot of people," he estimated plainly.

"Part of being a guardsman sometimes, unfortunately."

"No." Raziel smiled. "Before that. Civility is new to you. Stains of a ruffian's life still mark you. Many of them were cheats, I see, people you punished for daring to pull a fast one on you. Understandable. But maybe, if you like, I could install some empathy in that big, dumb Mouflon head of yours . . ."

Moira stepped forward. "Raz, stop."

Raziel glared at the small, pale girl beside him. "Really? Him? I thought you took reconnaissance and subterfuge at the academy. I did. And I remember one bullet point on the syllabus being *Don't fall in love with your marks*."

She took a step back.

Raziel, smugly satisfied, swung back to Flam. "Look. You need us. If we help, what will you give us to serve as a suitable reward?"

Flam's gaze drifted to Moira.

"Don't look at her," Raziel snapped. "Look at me and name something of value you'd be willing to give. Because we can just call our man to pick us up and leave you with this mess, if you'd prefer. How about my brother? Where's he, during all this?"

"I don't know."

"Then you have nothing of interest to me. Nothing of value at all except what currently stands in your boots. Mouflon custom dictates that if you promise something, you have to stick to it, right? So how about you deposit yourself in the kitty? Your big, smelly Mouflon self that's bursting at the seams with infatuation for my demure little sister."

Flam's jaw tightened.

"I'm not stupid. She cares about you too." He added inwardly, "Can't imagine how you'd feel about her after seeing her do some thorough interviewing with someone, but there it is, the blindfold we don for love."

"What are you saying, then?" Flam said. "You want me to give up any feelings I had for her? Because hate to break it to you, but those pretty much went out the window when she stabbed me."

In his peripheral vision, Flam could see Moira stand up straight. Flam would've liked to think what he'd just said was true, that he felt absolutely nothing for her still, but he did. The affection was stuck in there deep, wedged between the bones, more painful than even her sword's bite.

Raziel smiled, looking at Flam and then Moira. "So go on. Name it."

"I don't know what you want me to say here," Flam shouted.

A few people in the surrounding buildings were now watching from their windows, peeking out from between shutter slats.

"You're the speck in my sister's vision that refuses to blink free—ever since she was planted here. Even after she ran you through and we collected her, she's had this silly lovesick look to her. Sighing constantly, requiring me to say her name two or three times to get her attention. It's annoying. And since she can skim a mind like a Mouflon would a dessert menu, she knows you felt the same way. Which is even harder for her, I'm sure. Isn't that right, Moira?"

Moira said nothing, dark eyes downcast. Flam wanted nothing more than to pull her toward him right now, forget everything she'd ever done to him or anyone else and rocket off someplace where Raziel could never find them. But his hooves remained planted on the cobblestone. "Fine."

"You do understand what we're agreeing to here? I know Mouflons aren't exactly the sharpest bunch."

"If you help save Geyser, my life is yours."

"Okay, okay, let's not get ahead of ourselves here. I want to make this deal a little more interesting than that.

I don't want to be the one to kill you, Sir Flam. I want her to do it." He gestured to Moira. "Because apparently one thing she missed at the academy was the importance of finishing one's assignments. I'd like to play the tutor, like a good big brother, and help her with that."

CHAPTER 18

Right on Time

I t was almost comical, Aksel leading the pirates around the dead city in a serpentine circuit—running through abandoned buildings, hopping through broken windows, weaving aisles of forsaken shopping centers. He ate bullets and fired them over his shoulder when he could, but every pause he took would yield a barrage of gunfire. He opted to just keep sprinting, trying to draw them far from Clyde and Nevele.

Out on the street, a silhouette raced his way. He trained his DeadEye on it, backlit into near invisibility by the suns' glare bouncing off the vacant buildings' windows. It stopped, raised hands, gasping, "It's me. It's Nevele!"

He retracted the bronze shaft into his skull. "Go!"

She didn't need to be told twice. Together they bolted, retracing her fresh footsteps in the sand.

Sweat stung his eye. He shot over his shoulder at the men in dogged pursuit.

Return fire whizzed over their heads, nearly parting Aksel's hair. He followed Nevele as she dodged around the corner of a sand-drowned building, nearing the crashed *Praise to Her*.

"What do we do?" Nevele said, dropping next to Clyde.

Aksel couldn't help but feel a cold finger on his spine at

the sight. The pale man's mouth hung slack, head drooping to one side.

"Clyde," Nevele shouted into his face, "open your eyes. Come on. Clyde! Open your eyes!"

One slow inhale, another. Bright red striped Clyde's face, sand sparkling where it'd stuck. He had a half-foot gash on his side. Blood squeezed through the network of sutures, working only to slow his inevitable bleed out. Nevele pressed her hands onto it, and still it pushed through her bloodstained digits.

Aksel positioned another bullet between his lips and bit down to load his jaw hopper. The taste of brass and lead was bitter, commingling with a realization.

If Clyde was anything like his siblings, he didn't eat or drink or sleep but got nourishment using his fabrick. Nevele seemed to already understand this before Aksel did, and even though her fiancé's life was in the balance, she was hesitating, lips open but not saying *something*. Whatever it was, whatever she had to say to him, it was clearly ready. She made half a dozen half starts, stammering, the words trying to force themselves free, but she kept biting them back before they could escape.

Aksel turned to face the bottom of the hill, DeadEye ready. Instead of men's footsteps, a distant rolling rumble of starship engines kicked up. Dancing out into the sandy street came little yellow tornadoes. "Whatever he needs, you'd better give it to him quick. They're going to be on us in a minute."

"I . . ." Nevele stammered. "I don't know how."

"Figure it out. We need him mobile."

"Clyde," Nevele began, "I have a confession to make."

The Odium starship rumbled into view, low, horrible, shaking what few panels of glass remained in the surrounding buildings' frames. The pirates behind their flying hunk of armor, the cheaters, were probably smiling. Guns sprouted from its nose cone and slanted wings. It swept forward, nearly overhead so the gunfire would be economical.

Nevele talked over the plasma-scented gales of exhaust. As she did, Clyde continued to fade. His fluttering eyelids seemed determined to close. She held his hand in both of hers. The stitched lines crossing her face caught her tears, steering them toward her chin.

". . . and I came back to the shipyard, and Zoya's dad was in the cage . . ."

A screech preceded overamplified words from the starship's loudspeaker: "Hungry, Bullet Eater? How's about a nibble? Tuck in."

A patter of gunfire, deliberately off mark. Aksel knew—from experience, sadly—this was just them playing the cat. Dangle death, then steal it away. The three-round burst, inches from Aksel's feet, threw a spray of sand ten feet in the air, the sharp grains raining down a moment after.

"Like that?" The voice cackled brokenly, overloading the speaker. "How about another?"

The ground was pelted at Aksel's feet again. He didn't move.

Knowing it'd be pointless, Aksel still focused on the ship's nose cone and fired his DeadEye. The shot smacked the ship's armor and ricocheted away. A tiny scuff, not even a noticeable ding among the myriad badges of other fights the ship already bore.

"That's it?"

Aksel reached into his pocket for another bullet to eat and felt only his slacks' cotton lining. *Great.*

Behind him, Nevele said, "And there were some bubbles. I had time to pull him back up. I could've, if I wanted to, but I didn't."

Aksel expected this to be it, their end, but the next burst pounded the *Praise to Her*'s blackened hull instead, inches from Nevele, who was bent over Clyde. She didn't even seem to notice.

It was pointless. Even if they did get him to his feet, they'd be gunned down the minute they tried to run.

Aksel, spreading his arms, shouted at the starship. "Get it over with!"

Just laughter, blasting down from tinny speakers.

But as Aksel whispered an apology to his sister, Vee, for being such a lifelong headache, the scuff he'd put into the nose of the starship began to . . . fade. The one he'd put there disappeared, then the few surrounding it. Dents popped back out, long scratches courtesy of poor piloting reversed, unmarred steel restored.

Was Clyde doing this? Aksel watched as more damage erased until the starship looked factory new. And then it began to shed even more of its wear. Then components of the ship itself, the nonfactory stuff, vanished—poof, gone.

A panel of the hull disappeared.

One of the engines winked away without a trace, leaving only weld lines where it'd been tacked on. And, soon following, those too vamoosed, gray wobbly lines slipping, undrawing themselves.

Apparently the occupants had become aware something very strange was going on. They tried to turn and tear off at full thrust, but as they did, the ship was wholly unmade.

Steel leaped away, crumpled up, and became lumpy, misshapen hunks of raw ore. One by one they fell to the sand as the starship, piece by piece, quicker now, disassembled. Soon so much was stolen away that the men inside were visible. They appeared appropriately frightened and confused, guns drawn, looking around for the cause of this impossible thing, barking for answers and aid from their goddess.

The ship—now just the simple frame and some seats— slammed to the ground, one man crushed as it rolled. The two surviving the fall got to their feet and zeroed in on Aksel, Clyde, and Nevele on the hill. Small-arms fire came.

Aksel was ready to carry Clyde if need be but saw he was already up. Moments ago he'd been limp as a dead fish, but now he looked about as fresh as a daisy. The blood-spattered wound on his narrow trunk, a gaping mouth in his abdomen seconds ago, had healed to a wrinkly line.

Next to him, though, Nevele looked about as grave as she did when she'd been suspended between the frigate and the *Praise to Her* by a thin rope. She gave Clyde a motion indicating that his sword was still inside the crashed starship behind them and moved forward to assist Aksel with the oncoming pirates.

Once her betrothed had ducked inside, she turned to face their attackers, expression shifting into a hard sneer as she began unspooling herself to gather small heaps of thread into her waiting, open hands.

The two beleaguered pirates emerged from the boxy mass of metal bars that'd been their ship, but the stinging snaps of her tendrils drove them back into cover. She plodded forward, fully free from cover and apparently not caring, recalled the threads, and brought them thunderously back down again.

One pirate took the strike to the hand and dropped his gun. His partner dragged him down behind a sand mound.

Nevele didn't hesitate, stepping headlong toward the fray.

Head still spinning, Aksel chased along behind her with nothing but his bare hands to protect himself or her. Some part of him said she wouldn't need the help anyway.

One of her arms flew up, and the trailing mass of coiled thread arced high. With it still swinging, she stepped directly into their sand cover with them. Answering their alarmed cries, she brought her arms down, panels of flesh popping free, and rendered one man into a screaming pinwheel, launching him several yards. Nevele ignored the other one's pleas, slamming him flat into the sand with the return swipe, etching a deep slash down his face.

The man tried to get up, shielding his face but unable to hide the twisted terror.

With wild eyes in an otherwise bland expression, Nevele raised her other arm, more of her face falling away, a long stretch of her threads craning back . . . and back . . .

"Nevele," Clyde said, stumbling free of the *Praise to Her*, seeing what she was about to do. He sounded more confused than anything, as if unsure he even knew this woman.

The pirate, profusely bleeding from a half-flayed face, cowered on his knees before her.

Her cheek fell away. A part of her chin. Red underneath.

Blood dribbled through the pirate's fingers, diluted pink by tears.

"They almost killed you, Clyde," she said.

Aksel watched, heart in his throat.

Clyde seemed, in that moment, scared to approach.

The pirate begged unintelligibly.

Her threads crawled along the sand, zigzagging a path to him as if ushered along of their own accord. They slithered up the pirate's legs, waist, and torso and found his neck—and began to wrap around and around and around.

"Nevele," Clyde shouted, moving in with Commencement.

Her lips and a portion of the other cheek fell, flopping to the sand. Under her blank countenance as more fell away, bare teeth smiled broadly. Absently, she watched the threads work.

"Nevele, stop."

Rushing in, Clyde cut through the lines with a downward sweep, dropping the pirate, gasping and clutching at both a split face and a purpled neck, to the ground.

"What are you doing?"

Remaining still, Nevele's threads retreated to her. With a shaking hand, she bent and picked up one, then another piece of her face, pressing them to where they belonged until the threads could take over holding. When her bottom lip reattached, it trembled immediately.

"Now you know what I am," she said, sputtering. "Might as well own it, be just like my brother." She looked at him finally, eyes wet. "I don't need to pretend anymore."

"You're my Nevele," Clyde said, voice raw. He took her by the shoulders. "You're not a killer."

She looked down, hair hanging in her restored face. "I am, though."

The pirate, on hands and knees, freed a hand from his shredded cheek to pick up his fallen sidearm.

"Watch out," Aksel shouted, reaching with one hand as one does when something bad is about to happen—as if some sudden ability would hopefully rise in him, a dormant fabrick of his own, to make the bad thing stop.

Clyde and Nevele turned.

The pirate took unsteady aim at Nevele.

And with a finger on the trigger, the pirate kept steady . . . ready to fire . . . then did nothing. Just stood there, aiming, not blinking, staring at them, ready but not doing anything.

At his temples, the hair began to gray.

Wrinkles pressed themselves into his face, sliding in around his wound that now began to knit shut and scar over.

The gun in his hand developed a rash of brown rust and crumbled in his frozen, outstretched hand.

His clothes faded, faded, became threadbare rags.

The pirate's flesh became saggy, gray. His hair blew from the top of his head, leaving a silver horseshoe, and even that soon fell away. A soft tremor in the next desert breeze whooshed away in a knotty cloud, leaving only unlaced boots to mark his last stand.

Aksel swallowed. Had he really just seen that?

Clyde and Nevele turned, blanching at having noticed something behind Aksel. Just as the Bullet Eater turned around, throat locked, mind reeling from seeing a man turn to dust, a voice came—accented heavily by a Lakebed drawl.

"What were ya doin' standin' there like that? He was gonna shoot y'all. You know that, right?"

An old man stood on the sooty wing of the *Praise to Her*, clothed in battered leather and rough industrial-grade rubber. A long beard hung to his belt, and his eyes were blue and wet and not unkindly, squinting down at them. Aksel recognized something within that wrinkled mug, and those clothes . . .

The old man jumped down. Trailing from an exploded satchel on his back, nigh-invisible cords ended at scraps of white silk. A shredded parachute.

As if also under some kind of frozen-in-place spell, Aksel, Clyde, and Nevele watched as the old man carefully picked his way down the hill to them, chuckling softly to himself.

When he approached the dumbfounded trio, a frisk mouse popped up in his breast pocket—who appeared absolutely petrified, whiskers flicking about wildly before saucer eyes.

"Rohm?" Clyde said, breathless. Then, to the old man, "Emer? You're . . . ?"

The old man tipped an imaginary ten-gallon hat. "Ernest Höwerglaz, yes, indeedy. Pleasure to meet ya, truthfully this time."

The man reached up to scratch Rohm's ear, and Aksel noticed the number eight tattooed on the back of his hand. But when he lowered it to his side, Aksel realized it wasn't an eight but a lemniscate, the infinity symbol.

On unsteady legs, Clyde approached Höwerglaz. "You were with us the entire time? But how is that possible? If you're Höwerglaz and he's who knows how old, how was it the man who shot you was your father?"

Höwerglaz cocked his head. "You really that gullible? Ever notice that poacher never addressed me as Son, nor did I ever call him Daddy?" He chuckled. "Buncha crap, all of it. Shoot, mah daddy's been dead for goin' on sixty thousand years now."

"But why . . . why were you even with them? I . . . I don't understand. Why didn't you . . . ? Did you know I was looking for you?"

"Sure did."

"Why didn't you say something earlier, then? We're running out of time."

"Well, way I see it, when ya been 'round long as me, ya start to get bored. Antsy-like. I been with every group that Gleese has to offer, every club and outfit under the suns. Some made up of nice fellers, others not so much. Heard ya were lookin' fer me. Decided I'd arrange a meet—juss one you weren't privy to, heh. To see what ya were made of. Just so happened the poachers were recruitin', lookin' fer strappin' young men willin' to do a lot of work and not bellyache too much about skinny pay. Knew ya'd be comin' 'long soon enough, so I suggested to my new fellow poacher men we try lookin' for sky whales in that particular area, have us cross paths, accidental-like."

"But how did you know?"

Höwerglaz looked into Clyde's face, growing serious. Then he laughed, a rascally he-he. "Don't worry yerself too much on that. I juss knew."

"But—" Clyde started.

"Worked out pretty dern good too, dinnit? Feller shootin' me down and leavin' me for dead like that. Otherwise I woulda had to find some other way to join up with ya. Kill 'em, I guess." He shrugged. "But I reckon that probably would've been off-puttin', you bein' the squeamish sort an' all."

Aksel watched Clyde run his gaze over the disassembled

starship, the pirate's boots brimming with powdered pirate. "Why didn't you help us earlier? If you could do that"—he waved at the time-sponged starship—"or that"—the boots—"was it really necessary to wait so long?"

"Had to see if ya were interestin'. I ain't gonna help nobody if they caint liven things up 'round here. And if ya weren't willin' to down somebody—or somethin', like a rocky crawler, by way of example—well, I wasn't gonna assist. Still, I freed ya from havin' to go through with it since none of these fellers were worth the privilege of tastin' that particular blade of yours. Better to save that for someone more deservin'."

"Like Pitka Gorett and Dreck Javelin?"

"Sure. Why not? Still, now that I know ya got it in ya, that potential, consider me considerin'." Wink. "Yer name, top of the short list, by gum."

"So you'll help . . . if you find I'm interesting enough?"

"Yep."

Clyde palmed his face. "We had you with us the entire time," he repeated, exhausted. "And although we've finally found you and gotten your agreement to help us—I think—our ship's been shot down and the Odium's on the way to Geyser and . . ."

"Hang on there one minnit, feller," Höwerglaz said, finger raised, "You misunderstand me. I dinnit say nothin' about helpin'. Ain't never been accused of bein' that hospitable. I said I'm considerin'. There's a difference."

"But Geyser—"

"Is just a spot on the map. To me, nothin' more. Ya call it home? Whoopie. Don't mean it's gotta concern me none. Like I said: Ya let me see ya's interestin', worth mah time,

I'll consider helpin'. That's what I been doin' this past day an' some: seein'."

"We wasted so much time," Aksel said.

"Pfft, naw." Höwerglaz waved him off. "It'll work out."

The wind moved the hair hanging in Nevele's face. "And you know this for certain?" Her voice was hoarse. She still held a portion of her forehead until the stitches could secure it back in place.

Höwerglaz laughed. "Sorry, no, not really. Well, maybe. No, just kidding. I don't. Well . . ." He eyed them a moment, cheeks puffing, and subjected them to another gap-toothed he-he.

Clyde sighed. "Will you at least help us get home?" He pointed at the dismantled starship nearby. "Put one of these back together for us?"

"Sure. How about this one? I liked this one." He started back up the hill, trailing ribbons of his parachute. He approached the *Praise to Her*, which smoldered at its summit. "Intriguin', tell ya what: a feller willin' to bury bad men that don't deserve to be nothin' but carrion, helpin' young pups cross the desert even though they meant to kill ya, comin' after the likes of me in the hopes of recruitin' me, not even knowin' whether I was real or not while back home yer city's 'bout that daggone close to bein' smashed to bits. And even prevent your lady friend here from killin' a man who'd sooner eat your heart with a spoon—while you watch—than say good mornin'." His beard waggled over his shoulder like a windsock. "Truly a complex one, Clyde Pyne. Interestin'."

"Does that mean you'll help us?"

Höwerglaz stopped short of the starship wreck. "I

suppose."

He held a lemniscate-tattooed hand toward the *Praise to Her*, a lazy motion.

With a blink, the ship was new, pristine as the day she rolled off the assembly line, nary a dent—while Höwerglaz, in turn, became a young man.

The sprightly clean-shaven teenager, possibly Emer's older brother, Höwerglaz rolled aside the port hatch, that new starship smell wafting out. Before either could step aboard, Höwerglaz swept Aksel and Clyde aside with his arm and waved Nevele forward. "Ladies first."

CHAPTER 19

Brotherly Love

With Raziel breathing down his neck, Flam kept his radio turned up loud, chatter coming in fits and starts.

Adeshka's military pilots had engaged the Odium a few miles into the ice caps, and the fight had slowly moved south over the mountains dividing the Great Woods from the Lakebed's northern fringes. A few Odium ships had slipped past, but it was suspected they were the ones accompanying the missile. The Adeshkan vessels' electronic sniffers had picked up something that bore the signature of charged plasma, but they couldn't pinpoint which ship.

The Odium had shot down their pursuers with startling ease. Adeshka, in turn, was forced to dip into their military reserves and deploy a second salvo of fighter ships, which would take time.

All that was fine and good, except that particular ship, the one with the missile, they'd *lost track of.* Those three little words stirred more fear in Flam than any before. Leading Raziel and Moira through town, when they passed the citizens' elevator, he could confirm with one glance he hadn't been alone in hearing that report. People were fleeing by the dozens now, pushing onto the elevator, no longer patiently taking turns.

Flam was about to shout for them to be orderly about it for their own safety, when Raziel stepped near his side. "Not your concern right now. Lead on, Muffie."

Suffering the pejorative silently, Flam did as told.

He guided the Pynes past the geyser's jutting tip and fountains to the other line of buildings across. Sometimes Flam forgot how beautiful the city was, such a mixture of the new and old. Shapely, asymmetrical architecture courtesy of the Cynoscions' crooked eye. The squared-off brick and mortar of humans' work. The rough, squat domes of Mouflon design. Seemed everyone had put their stamp on Geyser.

"Somewhere high," Raziel said. "With a clear view."

"This way." They ascended marble steps. At the stately front doors, heavy wood with wrought-iron bracings, Raziel tapped his toe as Flam used his guardsman skeleton key.

Inside, they were met by the unmistakable smell of books. Geyser was proud of its library, boasting tomes printed not only in Geyser but some from sol systems as distant as PBW-441. Near the entrance, the library had a display especially for local authors. One title in particular jumped out at Flam as they passed the glass case: *The Royal Stitcher's Guide to Patches and Other Small Garment Fixes*. If only he could use it to contact its writer to tell her to keep her fiancé away.

Flam led Raziel and Moira through the main stacks to the stairs leading to the second floor, the nonfiction and reference sections. Farther on, using his skeleton key again, he led them into the attic: a repository of folding chairs, pianos, and easels. Leaving footprints in the dust, they passed through a small hatch and onto the roof.

Jagged Bay lay ahead in magnificent view, with clear

sight of the southernmost lip of the mainland, Scoona Port straight north and Talon Peninsula to the west. The skies were clear, no starships besides their two ringing the island like stir-crazy junkyard dogs. The silvery flying fish, the *Gareista,* leaped about with a ballerina's grace, while Nigel's slapdash junker swooped and patrolled with a more determined, focused trajectory.

"My man Karl won't hesitate to shoot him down if he gets in the way," Raziel said.

"It's fine," Flam replied. "Nigel's a sound pilot." He had no real way of knowing that, but the man had been in the Fifty-Eighth, so he probably knew how to fly somewhat.

Moira and Raziel began readying rifles. Customized to excess, the weapons implied style over function, making Flam consider Raziel liked guns, the idea of the bottled carnage they possessed, but knew precious little about using them.

Between the invisibility suits bearing the mark for the Srebrna Academy—when he could see it—and the artillery, Flam didn't really know what to make of them. He wondered if their inclination toward destruction was born when Gorett stole the throne and, in their minds, Clyde stole it after him, or if a dormant wrathfulness had always occupied their hearts, twiddling its thumbs.

Raziel squinted behind his rifle scope, calibrating it to zero in on the Aurorinean church spire across town.

"He spent months looking for you," Flam told them.

Moira, who'd been feeding bullets into her own rifle, paused.

Raziel cradled his weapon as if it were a steel infant. "You're to help us, not concern yourself with my family.

Remember you gave your word, Muffie."

Moira gave Flam a look of worry as her brother spoke, but she quickly returned her focus to her work.

"And what about you? Is this what you want?" Flam asked her.

Raziel, baring teeth, stepped in to block Flam's view of her. "Do I need to repeat myself? It doesn't matter what she thinks—about anything. We're helping you save the city, and you're paying for our aid with your life. That should be all that's of concern to you."

As soon as it was clear Flam had gotten his point, Raziel returned to his preparations, stepping near the roof's edge to take aim below. People, autos with families in them, the old man guarding his bakery armed with a coal shovel. Behind the scope, Raziel smiled. The Executioner's twin axes wouldn't have looked out of character piercing his lapel, Flam decided.

Flam peeked over at Moira, hoping she'd read his thoughts right then. *Help me stop him.*

When Raziel caught Moira returning the glance, look-ing pained, apologetic, she suddenly found her feet very interesting.

"Oh? Did I interrupt something?"

"No."

"Because it looked to me like you were making eyes with the Muffie." Raziel turned to Flam. "Trying to pass *notes* without me knowing?" Eyes on Flam, he bent to whis-per in Moira's ear. "He's not of our caste. He's beneath us. He's not even a *he*; he's an *it*. Mouflons, for eons, were no more than beasts of burden, boulder pullers. They're free now only because we have robots to do that sort of thing. Would you really want to sully our royal blood with a packhorse?"

Bumping him aside with her shoulder, Moira wrenched away, wordless, arms crossed.

Raziel smiled at her, then at Flam.

To keep himself from caving Raziel's head in, Flam turned toward the north skies. Feeling someone's gaze, he scanned below. On all other roofs and every available bridge that allowed a clear view north, the guardsmen were ready. A good number were looking his way, raised visors revealing faces composed of worry but determination: they were ready to see their duty through.

Flam saluted. Every one, every brother and sister of the Patrol, returned the gesture: a fist presented at chest height, as one would hold up a shield. He held his salute as they did the same, the sinking suns' warmth on his balled hand, galvanizing it like a kiln, hardening it to nigh invincibility. Flam squinted toward the north just as the first black dots on the horizon appeared.

"Got the pricks' coordinates," Aksel shouted from up front. "So if we choose, we can always take the fight to them, make them host the shindig instead of the other way around."

"Hopefully it won't come to that," Clyde said, no longer needing to shout. He was surprised at how cleanly the *Praise to Her* now ran, being factory new once more, humming instead of grumbling.

"Well," Aksel said, "still good to have it in the ol' back pocket just in case." He tapped at the control panel. "Looks like we're going to be late. I'm seeing a fleet ahead, nearing the bay right now."

Clyde stepped into the cockpit. Aksel nodded toward the radar. Watching the little red dot that was so small on a vidscreen but represented something so enormously catastrophic, Clyde felt his heart turn to lead. "Get us there. Now."

"Aye-aye." Aksel glared back at Höwerglaz. "I just wished that if I *had* to get roughed up—it'd been for something other than a shite-headed weaver's prank."

Höwerglaz gifted Aksel with a look of indifference, held it, then winked, laughing boyishly, snorts and all.

Aksel shook his head and faced forward.

Clyde kept Commencement across his lap, staring at Höwerglaz until he looked his way. "Why?"

Höwerglaz's smile faded. "Why what?" He raised his tattooed hand, the lemniscate nearly faded to nothing. "Oh, this? Had it put on a while back. Comes in darker when I'm edgin' close to millennial. Alarm clock of sorts."

"Not that. Why not side with us completely? Why *wouldn't* you want to help? The Odium's nothing but—"

Höwerglaz watched the landscape speed past. His small smirk never leaving, one that suggested humbleness and curiosity.

The way he moved his eyes over things made him seem less like a fellow organism and more like a fish looking through its bowl. Clyde could imagine Höwerglaz perched on an underwater castle's mossy crenellations, smiling, observing.

"Can you see the future?" Clyde said, wondering if that wasn't what Höwerglaz was actually doing, looking out the window like that.

"See enough stuff happen, yer likely to pick up on patterns. I mean, it's not like I have *visions*"—he wiggled all his fingers—"or consort with the spirits or a damn crystal ball or nothin', but, yeah, to a degree, I can see how things'll shake out.

"But to answer it plain, I knew ya was comin', true. And another thing: I don't know *why* everybody thinks I live in Nessapolis. Ya saw it. Ain't sheeit there. Somebody ol' as me needs activity or mah brain gets to driftin'."

Clearly. "And what did you determine?"

"Look. I had to see with mah own peepers ya'd do *what* was necessary *when* it was necessary. Get me?"

Clyde flashed back on the rocky crawlers and the argument about returning the pistol to Emer—Höwerglaz. Or allowing Nevele to strangle that pirate to death. "Killing is not the answer. I've never killed anyone. You said you weren't going to help us if I wasn't interesting, yet here you are. You're breaking your own rules."

Höwerglaz stroked a beard that'd shrunk to a dark thistle from the great gray banner that earlier had hung to his belt. "Yer right. Ya dinnit kill nobody. But that's not the point I was tryin' to get at. *You* came up with that all on yer own. I never said nothin' about killin'. Speaks pretty loudly of ya, if ya ask me, jumpin' the gun to that mighty big conclusion."

"I—"

Nevele put her hand on Clyde's knee. "I think he means that killing *isn't* the answer, you're right, but it's more about the willingness to accept the burden that comes with an act, any act."

Höwerglaz tapped the end of his nose. "One smart gal

right thar. That's what makes a hero, son."

Clyde nearly missed what Höwerglaz said, recalling Nevele's confession about Zoya Kesbanya's father. He'd always adored Nevele for how she'd helped weavers in need, but he'd always felt she was giving edited versions of those stories. But he never expected something quite like *that* was left on the cutting room floor.

And as much as he wanted to remove her hand from his knee and scoot away, he couldn't. What she'd done had been cleansed from her conscience by his fabrick. The weighty badness of her confession had healed him when he'd needed it most. But for it to have healed such a wound, it must've been something that bothered her immensely, threatened to crush her under its weight. If she'd felt that bad, she must still be the woman he knew—good at heart.

Still, it was a big revelation. And as much as he hated to think it, he couldn't help but feel he didn't really know her anymore.

He looked at Höwerglaz, who gave Clyde a knowing stare, as if he could parse the exact cause of Clyde and Nevele's sudden discomfort. Reading body language was probably one of those things that sharpened as you grew older. If that was the case, then for Höwerglaz, speaking aloud was probably all but superfluous.

Höwerglaz cleared his throat, sat forward. "I've lived long enough to see—from a distance, up till now—an entire line of Pyne men and women learn things the hard way. Don't know what it is with y'all. Each of ya's had trouble with this. 'Specially after fabrick got introduced into yer bloodline. Probably more so, since it takes a certain kind to not let power shoot straight to yer head."

Clyde looked at Commencement balanced across his legs, the ornate sheath depicting the twin souls twisting about the sword in the middle of the embossed tableau. Grigori Gonn had copied the pictures from archival photos of Clyde's father holding the sword and had taken molds from the gun barrel's imagery before melting it down. Clyde felt better holding it as a sword. He never liked Commencement as a gun, the royal revolver. He was scared even wearing it, afraid it would go off by accident each time he sat down. But as a sword, it felt . . .

"A sword's still a single-purpose thing," Höwerglaz said, "regardless of how much nobility you pin on it. Weapons are tools, nothing more. Like a paintbrush. The painting itself, the product of a tool's use, is equally likely to be a nice one as a crappy one. A weapon—sword, gun, doesn't matter—ain't no different. Good and bad: mutually possible. Ya never can tell which'll pop up in somebody. And keeping yerself as blank as that fresh canvas ain't the way to go about it. Ya gotta put a few licks on to see what colors stick."

"So, given enough time, eventually I'll give up on my beliefs? It's just a fact, an inevitability? I will have to end someone's life?"

Höwerglaz drew a deep breath. "If you want to continue to believe in somethin', anythin' at all, *fightin'* is an inevitability, yes. Not killin'. *Fightin'*, understand? Defendin', protectin', savin' folks through action, not words or finger-waggin' while soapboxin' your beliefs. There's a difference. But . . . I think, deep down, some part of ya already knows that. Otherwise, why keep luggin' that thing 'round? Looks heavy."

"It is." *In more ways than one.*

Aksel called back from the cockpit. "Charging up the FTL. Five minutes."

"Do you know what'll happen with us, then?" Nevele said.

Höwerglaz ignored her question, asked his own. "Either of y'all keep up with astrology much?"

Clyde and Nevele shook their heads.

"I do," Rohm piped up.

"Well, at least we got one of ya. But for the others' benefit, let's start with astronomy. Y'all know in our particular galaxy we got the two suns, I hope. Aurorin, named after the light lord. And Teanna, the light lord's lady. And Gleese, unlike any other planet in the *entire known universe*, moves in a shape like, well, this." He held up a hand, the faded infinity symbol. "We move around the suns in turns, from one to the other. Once every five hunnert years, the suns get close enough for the handoff: Gleese shiftin' from goin' 'round Aurorin, to Teanna. Y'all knew that, right?"

Clyde and Nevele nodded. "Mucks up the weather," Nevele added. "Half the planet won't see the suns for over a year."

"Gold star for the lady. Now the astrology. In a week's time, Gleese will be movin' out of Teanna's orbit, where we've been, and into her husband's care. And they say that while we're in Aurorin's orbit, only war and destruction follow. Backwards, I'm sure it seems, being that Aurorineans believe the Light Lord to be a more benevolent and understandin' god. Still, that's how it'll be."

"You've been here that long—to have seen this happen before?" said Nevele.

"Well, the memory's vault gets some rust on the hinges

sometimes, so . . ."

Never a straight answer.

"But I will say, again, patterns. It's not mah intent to be a downer, but let's be honest: nothin' bad ever happens just once. Sad, 'specially with how everythin' has been pretty nice this past trip 'round Teanna."

"Wait. You call these past five hundred years *nice?*" Nevele said. "How about the three million who died in the Territorial Skirmish? Or everyone who was in Nessapolis when that freak sandstorm hit? And let's not even consider the frigate crash *yesterday*."

"By *comparison*. Ya see, the door that lets bad things mosey in an' make themselves at home is *always* open, girlie. Things always go bad before they go good—nature's law. It's the easy route, and nature'll always take the easy route. Ain't no river goin' *up* a mountain. And let me tell y'all one thing: last time we were orbitin' Aurorin beats *these* past five hunnert years by a damn *sight*." He developed a faraway look. "Mercy," he finished quietly.

Talking to Father Time made Clyde feel as insignificant as he did when looking at a star map. Like nothing he could ever say or do would have a lasting effect on anything.

"How old are you exactly, anyway?" Clyde accidentally thought aloud. And remembering his manners, "That is, if you don't mind . . ."

Höwerglaz chuckled. "Old. Old enough to remember Earth." He gazed out the porthole again, as though if the clouds moved just right he'd see this Earth again.

"Will you help us?" Clyde said, desperate.

Höwerglaz shrugged. "That's entirely up to y'all. You need to surprise me. Make me clutch my chest and proclaim, 'Golly dern, would you just look at *that*?'"

From the cockpit, Aksel said, "All right, mates, here we go. From three hundred miles per hour to about nine million. Next stop: Geyser."

"Are you sure you know what you're doing?" Rohm said with a shudder.

"It'll work," Aksel said brusquely, accidentally illustrating his uncertainty. Thumb poised over the flashing green button, Aksel twisted in his seat to shout back, "In five . . ."

Nevele's hand on Clyde's knee tightened, her fingers making a stone claw. Clyde put his hand on top of hers. She was shaking, keeping her focus on the floor. He gave her hand squeezes until she returned one. He loved her more than anything, even if he could never say it. He hoped she knew that.

"Four . . ."

"I'm sorry," she said, her voice a peep. "I should've told you."

"Three . . ."

"It's okay," Clyde said. "We all make mistakes."

"Everyone but you." If she was attempting levity, it came off slightly accusatory instead. "I'm just scared that nothing has happened yet. I mean, I'm supposed to be jinxed now, right? Because of what I told you?"

Clyde hadn't thought of that. He kept his expression calm. "It'll be okay," he said, late.

"Two, one. Firing the FTL drive now."

The view out the window became still, as if the starship had suddenly stopped. There was no tremor under Clyde's seat. Nothing jostled them anymore.

But, no, it wasn't stopped. They were just moving

entirely too fast for anything to be observed in detail, the world outside a snapshot to Clyde's optic nerves.

For a moment, it felt peaceful in the starship, silent except for the soft trilling of the FTL tachyon generator. Clyde closed his onyx eyes, knowing the tranquility would be brief. What they were barreling toward would be the complete opposite.

Clyde wondered if Höwerglaz really could see his thoughts, predict them just from experience after having seen people—apparently some who had been his forebears—go through similar events. He questioned if Father Time really knew how scared he was and if he cared.

CHAPTER 20

Homecoming

Gorett, lost in black thoughts, flinched when Dreck spoke. The pirate captain asked over his shoulder, "Colin, 'Eve of Destruction,' if you'd be so kind."

The *Magic Carpet* was on autopilot as they tore along over the great unchanging field of sand, Lakebed. Dreck put his feet on the control panel, legs crossed at the ankle, hands behind his leather-helmeted head. Colin found the cassette tape and jammed it in. From bare speakers tacked all over the ship's interior came a slow drumbeat.

Strumming.

A gravelly-voiced man began singing—about violence, war, and the general unmaking of a world and how, apparently, he'd been told by someone unnamed that they didn't believe this was the end times and he reassured them it indeed was. Because of the archaic recording style, the singer's voice came only from the right set of speakers—basically shouting into the side of Gorett's head.

The sudden, sharp harmonica blat made Gorett twitch.

He felt almost as if the singer were addressing him directly, naming places he'd never heard of—*Jordan River? Red China? Selma, Alabama?*—the song went on. He could do nothing to stop it. The song's general vitriolic nature grew as it continued, building and building, made all the more haunting by the choral backup.

Apparently familiar with the song, Dreck mouthed the words, eyes closed.

Look at him, Pitka. He believes he's a champion for the little, stepped-on man, Mother Worm whispered, almost sounding as if she was stepping forward from the chorus to lay out some spoken-word lyricism. *But even he sees dirt and filth has hidden potential, like modeling clay cut from the ground that can be shaped into something beautiful. And having walked away from so many fights, he's only hardened his resolve that he's doing the right thing, that he's divinely shielded by his goddess. No one has ever discouraged him, Pitka. Until you. You will stop him.*

Leave me alone. I . . . I'm just one man. What can I do? I've accepted what's to happen, and you—whatever you are—should do the same.

Tsk. I'm your heart's mouthpiece, Little Pitka.

A sharp beep tore Gorett away from Mother Worm. Next to him, Dreck sat up, slapped his leather cap up from his eyes, dragged his feet off the controls, and took the joysticks. "What've we got, boys?" he said, clicking off the autopilot. "And turn the music down—can't hear myself think."

Gorett watched the Lakebed drift by far under the glass floor. They were nearing its southern edge, the terrain becoming a series of rash-like bumps, the foothills of the South Razor Mountains. In the occasional pond and lake, he saw the reflection of both the *Magic Carpet* and the fleet behind her—and now, two new starships trailing, keeping a cautious distance.

"Adeshkan pursuer classes, both attempting missile lock, sir," the pirate manning the radar answered.

"Ready flares, and get another sizzler ready," Dreck said. "They know we're close. Maybe Geyser and Adeshka hammered out a deal." To himself, he added, "Chidester's lending a hand to someone? Ha. That'd be the day."

"Flares ready, sir. On your mark."

Another pirate said, "Dead south, two ships in Geyser airspace, sir."

"Repeat that," Dreck said. "At Geyser?"

"That's what the readout's showing, sir. Two ships, running patterns around the island."

"We'll deal with them when we get there. What of the shites tailing us?"

"Still trying to lock."

"Hold the sizzler, but as soon as they loose on us, give 'em the flares."

"Aye, sir."

Dreck's thumb moved to the joystick that'd launch the missile, stroking the waiting red button.

Dreck was clearly mulling it over, considering launching it prematurely and trying to steer it to its destination from here. It'd likely not make it, run its fuel to E before even halfway there. Losing that much velocity, it'd likely just bounce off the city's stem instead of piercing it, a complete waste.

Mother Worm was right about Dreck, Gorett decided, watching his thumb reluctantly draw away from the trigger. He wanted to live to see the destruction as it happened. Bear active witness. Not merely throw a last-ditch effort while they got robbed of the sight by getting shot down. The stone waited, and his eyes were hungry, his fingers rapped out individual beats on the flight sticks—giddy with anticipation, so ready to see his prize, and hold it to his chest, well won.

Pitka knew that feeling well. He used to lose entire weeks of sleep waiting to hear from the miners that they'd finally gotten access to the stone. Pacing, imagining how it'd feel under his hands—if it'd be cool or permanently warm like some volcanic rock. He used to imagine kissing it, laying his cheek against it as if it were his mother's shoulder, telling it how much he'd dreamed of this day.

An attempt by the Adeshkan fighters to raise the *Magic Carpet* snapped Gorett and Dreck back into their seats. Dreck dragged his goggles back over his eyes, straps dangling like a dog's floppy ears, and keyed his mic. "Please stop following us. It's rude."

And immediately from behind: "Missile lock, sir."

"Flares!"

Tiff-tiff-tiff-tiff. Over the cockpit, bright white dots and smoke trails punched the smeary purple-gray sky.

Every Adeshkan heat-seeking rocket sought the flares instead of the *Magic Carpet,* veering in different directions. Still, each harmless detonation shook Gorett's teeth.

Then, in prompt retaliation, the sizzler. It repeated the show: sailing high and then unleashing its barrage of stinger missiles.

"One down, sir."

"Good."

"Last one's still with us. Taken two—er, three—of ours, sir."

After switching channels, Dreck addressed the squadron. "Do what you need to, boys. May the Goddess guide your hands to cut their cords and smash their inner workings beyond repair."

From Dreck's headphones, Gorett could hear the other pilots shouting similar prayers for their captain. Dreck smiled, swerved his focus from one side to the other, the shadows on the clouds around them drawing a vague picture of what was going on behind them.

One sleek shape darted in and around, banking nimbly. Gorett watched this agile shadow move directly below the *Magic Carpet*, mere yards beneath his feet.

"Running a scan on us, sir."

"Oh, no, you don't." Dreck wrenched the sticks back, bringing the ship high, and then jammed them forward.

Gorett watched the ship below—the helmeted Adeshkan pilots visible in their cockpit, looking up at him. They fell away, then leaped near again. The *Magic Carpet* slammed its underside directly upon the second ship. The brunt of the impact hit its bulbous cockpit, spiderwebbing its glass. The pilots inside flailed as their oxygen bled free. The ship dropped, spinning out a dark smoky corkscrew. A yellow flower soundlessly bloomed on the landscape, flaring the clouds for a moment.

It'd been a reckless move, but Dreck seemed unable to stop laughing. His men joined in a moment later but with markedly less gusto.

He wants martyrdom, Mother Worm said. *But only on his terms.*

Right then Gorett couldn't really disagree.

"We're close enough now. Break formation," Dreck ordered. "Remember, boys, when we get to Geyser: men, women, children, full purge. Patrol uniform or not: zilch them all. And take out those two ships they apparently have. I need a clean shot for Bessie, and you lot need to be my backers. On my mark." He cupped the mic with his grease-darkened hand. "Chin up, Pitka. It's payday."

But the pirate captain's winning smile was snatched away when the *Magic Carpet* suffered a violent bout of turbulence. Dreck cursed, fighting the sticks to keep level.

Gorett watched, wide-eyed. An unerringly straight white line went true south.

"Bloody hell was that? I didn't give the go-ahead yet," Dreck shrieked, pointing a grubby finger at the craft that'd overtaken them, the soft crackle of FTL travel coming a beat later, audible even through thick cockpit glass.

"One of ours," the communication officer replied unsteadily.

"Who?" Dreck roared, watching the faint blue-white line dissipate.

"The *Praise to Her*, sir."

Dreck tugged the microphone back up. "Full on to Geyser." Spit flying, he screeched, "Unload *everything*. Drop men on the streets. Shoot *anything* that moves from above, below, wherever—just kill *everyone*! Everyone! Everyone! Now! Now!"

Look ahead, Pitka, Mother Worm suggested warmly.

Pushing through the clouds ahead of them, Geyser came into view.

Towering over the island was what could've easily been mistaken for an incredibly tall tree by unlearned eyes. Clearer and clearer by the second, it became solid, real to Gorett again as the ship drew closer, closer, slowly.

A puff of steam set free from the city's namesake just as he looked upon it. It was as if it were cheering, a trumpeting portending his return with delighted shock. He wished it were so.

Gorett and Mother Worm thought in harmony: *Home.*

Raziel and Moira opened fire. And upon hearing those initial shots coming from the library roof, every waiting guardsman and woman joined them. Geyser erupted into disharmonious bangs and pops. Flam, pressing the stock of the antique rifle to his shoulder, contributed to the bedlam.

Nigel in his slapdash moon jumper and Karl in the *Gareista* took after the ship that'd shot past overhead, chasing it down as it shed its impossible speed, became visible—its details accumulating, its pockmarked hull catching up—and banked around. It didn't fire on anyone below, Flam noticed. He lowered his rifle as it came in low right alongside the library roof, to land in the square, presumably.

Framed in the porthole was quite possibly the most heartening thing he'd ever seen: Clyde and Nevele's faces. He immediately got on the radio to order Nigel to stop firing, telling him who it was in that ship.

As soon as Raziel heard Flam say his brother's name, with zero hesitation, he turned his rifle from the Odium onslaught and fired. The bullet struck true, dead center toward Clyde's forehead, but was stopped short by the glass. Immediately, Clyde dodged out of view. Raziel continued to fire at the starship as it tried to land. One engine began smoking.

Flam charged toward Raziel, ready to swing his own rifle like a club.

Raziel leveled his rifle at Flam. "You gave your word. No reneging."

Flam let the barrel poke his chest. "To fight the Odium," Flam shouted, pointing at the ships that were nearly at the island's shores now—and getting closer. "Clyde's not going to do a damn thing against Geyser. You want to try and kill him afterward, I . . . can't do much to keep you from that, but if you want to keep the city from falling, concentrate on the real enemy here."

Moira cracked another shot at the Odium, placing it expertly. The ship went into a wild spin and collided with the geyser, bounced off, leaving only a minor scuff in the sediment stone, and erupted upon impact with the street.

Moira paused to drop the scope from her eye, looking at her brother and Flam.

"Call your pilot off," Flam ordered her. "We need them to help us fight."

As she reached to press a finger behind her ear to do so, Raziel snagged her wrist. "Tell Karl to keep an eye on it, though. We don't want the little prince sneaking off before we get to have a word."

Flam grunted and turned back around, raised his rifle, and took another shot as more ships passed over the city while they rained fire along the town square, crisscrossing trails, demolishing autos and striking down guardsmen. Thankfully, those fleeing had packed into the elevators and gone. Many people had abandoned autos but made it to the island below with their lives. Some, most likely, unwilling to wait for the overloaded ferries, were swimming all the way to the mainland. Good—anything to get them away.

The ship with Clyde and Nevele in it leveled out and

squeaked down upon its landing gear, getting pelted like everything else. The back hatch hissed open, and a few people Flam didn't recognize charged down, weapons at the ready.

Over his shoulder, Flam saw Raziel inch back to the door leading down through the library attic, his black eyes zeroed in on the ship's rear hatch. As soon as Clyde exited, Raziel's expression became animalistic.

Flam rushed forward before Raziel could run, crunching roof rocks under his hooves. "You stay right here with me." He aimed at him.

Raziel's hand remained on the doorknob. "What luck. Two birds with one stone, Moira," Raziel said, glare locked on Flam. "Our brother *and* the man who cheated us, that useless Bullet Eater *you* thought would make a good spy. Come, let's remind him of the penalty for cheating the Pynes."

Moira remained where she was, hair dancing as another Odium ship screamed overhead.

"Moira, come," Raziel said, scolding in singsong. He turned the knob some more . . .

Flam stepped forward, finger on the trigger. "Don't." He looked away for barely a second to glance below.

As if aware he was being observed, Clyde stopped and looked up at the library roof, probably searching for where he'd last seen Flam.

Flam shouted down, "Go!"

Raziel had started down the stairwell. Flam fired, but it hit the door behind him. He charged past a frozen Moira and took the stairs two at a time.

Raziel was much faster than Flam. He'd already made it to the library's first floor. Deciding it'd be useless to try and give chase, Flam took aim, the shimmery back of Raziel's bodysuit in his sights. Just as he was about to squeeze the trigger, a shot rang out—from right beside him.

Raziel, below, stumbled and spun, colliding with a row of study tables. Green glass lamp shades smashed to the floor. Clutching his side, he struggled to his feet, coming up with his handgun, aim wavering on Flam on the balcony above.

Moira threw herself over the railing, turned midair, landed on the marble floor, and charged forward. Her movements were fluid, precise, quick, as they had been while she'd dodged puddles in the town square. Except now she was using them to kick her brother's arm. His gun fired harmlessly toward the poetry section. She loosed him a second to pitch him onto his back.

He fell heavily. Before he could stand or retrieve his sidearm, she rested the barrel of her own upon his ashen forehead.

"What do you think you're *doing*?" Raziel spat.

"You weren't planning on killing just Clyde. You made a new plan on the way here." She spoke in a low, even tone—but Flam could hear her anger, tightly coiled inside. "I was there, when you had it."

Raziel groaned, clutching the side of his suit. Checking his palm and seeing it bloody, he sneered up at his sister. "Suppose I should take this as a lesson. Never try to work on a plan B in the presence of a mind reader."

"That might be advisable, yes."

Flam came down the rest of the steps, his aim steady on Raziel.

Raziel regarded him, then his fallen handgun on the

floor nearby, then Moira.

"I wouldn't," Moira said, her own gun still on him.

"So when it came to *your* life being at risk, that's when you decided to have pity on our older brother?" Raziel said, having to pause for breath. Groaning at the pain, he continued. "*Some* part of you wanted it, the original plan, the three of us in the palace, the Pynes ruling Geyser. As it should be. Otherwise, why go along with Tym and me this long?"

"Tym didn't want Clyde dead," Moira said. "He's been working up the nerve to ask why we couldn't just reintroduce ourselves to Clyde, be satisfied that we have a Pyne on the throne at all, that it's anyone but Pitka Gorett. We're his *family*, Raziel—"

"Did he tell you this?"

"No. But he certainly thought it. Often."

"Clyde doesn't deserve it. He doesn't know anything of us." Raziel's voice free of acidity now, he sounded heartbroken. "We're nothing to him, forgotten people."

"But we never tried," Moira said. "And hard as I avoided hearing your thoughts, sometimes you think *so loud* . . . and awful."

Raziel seemed suddenly afraid. "What did you hear?"

"You don't really blame Clyde. You blame Dad. Even if not to take over in Dad's place but just to be here, *with him*, not sent off to school, kept around, a presence in the city—even if just a small one, as his children. Involved in any way we could be. In his life. And I already know what you're going to say. I *know* he sent us away because he was growing mistrustful, he'd changed, and you didn't like how he was becoming scared . . . with things getting worse, the Executioner getting out of hand, and how Dad thought he was losing control . . . and the rumors about Prime Minister Gorett's plan to usurp him . . ." Her voice, already small, ebbed off to a whisper.

Raziel tried sitting up, winced, and lay back. His voice was just as quiet, just as calm. "When he came back, Clyde never even asked if I wanted to take over, as Father had said I'd have to. He just *took* it. He was always the favorite. That's all Dad ever talked about, how much he missed him. When he had us, right there, all along. It was like we were nothing, like attempted replacements that weren't up to snuff, mistakes and failures. Sent off to Srebrna because he didn't want us reminding him of his precious son he led us to believe was dead."

A rumble passed overhead. Flam instinctually ducked as dust fell from the library ceiling in chalky rivulets. The gunfire and screams outside persisted, the city was at war, but neither Raziel nor Moira seemed to notice.

Moira leaned in. "I believed you were right for a very long time. That we had to outdo our older brother, beat expectations. When Gorett took the throne and we weren't allowed to leave school to even attend Dad's funeral—which I'm sure Gorett had something to do with—I was angry too. And I stayed angry. I wanted to be angry. But it was killing us. Making us into people Dad would've been ashamed of. I hurt people for you."

"Moira. You really could've quit at any time. If you'd just *talked* to me."

"No, I couldn't have. And you know that. I could see it in you, hear it, that if Tym or I ever dared leave, you'd kill us. You thought Clyde had abandoned us by dying, and then Mom, then Dad. It's not that you feel cheated out of your destiny. You're scared of being alone. Even as a boy, you always had to have Tym and me at your side, everywhere you went—and once you discovered your fabrick, you found a way to *keep* us from—"

"Please, I . . . Moira, I'd never hurt you. Or Tym. I just think things sometimes. Everyone does. They just pop in. They don't *mean* anything. I'd . . . I'd *never* hurt you."

"But you did."

"Okay, Moira, okay. Please. You've shown me what I need to do." He reached for her hand, ignoring the gun pressed hard against his forehead. "I was upset. But—but you've helped me. I remember how I wanted to lead now, *alongside* Clyde. Let's go out there, reintroduce ourselves, fight together. Let's start over, be a family, do this right."

Moira remained quiet.

Flam, not liking the pregnant pause, thought as loudly as he could, bellowing in his mind: *If you can hear me thinking this, Moira, don't do it.*

If she heard it, she didn't let on. "You had a family."

Raziel's expression changed. Shoving Moira back, lips curled away from his bloodstained teeth, he threw out his hand toward Flam and Moira.

Flam felt an insatiable thing feasting on him at once, chasing and clawing deep into his core.

"She was doing *so well* before you, Muffie," Raziel said.

Moira dropped the gun, crumpling to the floor, clawing at her suit, reflective scales snapping off with each drag of her fingernails. She was digging at her side, the same spot she'd shot Raziel.

"You can suffer my pain right along with me, the pain you caused all on your own this time," Raziel said. A red bubble popped on the edges of his teeth as he smiled. Slumped in the heap of a broken study table, he reached one hand, tearing both Moira and Flam apart from the inside, breaths slowing while his red smile grew and grew.

Moira's trembling fingers inched for her fallen pistol, weak. With most of his focus on Flam, Raziel didn't notice. Flam was fine suffering Raziel's fabrick if it meant he was providing distraction. With a final push, Moira scooted along the floor on her belly, snatched the gun up, and took aim.

Awestruck, Raziel shifted his open hand, that fire hose of agony, back to her . . .

A sharp pop spiraled through the statuary and the dusty old volumes of Geyser's library. Outside, it was still loud; the attack persisted. But in here, sheltered in all the marble and stonework, it was starkly quiet, that breathless time following any violent act. The torturous chewing left Flam instantly, like fanned smoke.

Using the bookcase to stand, Moira gazed down at her brother on his side, one arm over his face. She lingered, one hand bracing a shelf, her breathing small whimpers, smoking gun shaking in the other hand. She watched, as though her brother would spring back to life.

Flam reached for her, and when she lifted her arm, he thought she'd take his hand. Instead she triggered her collar, the helmet raising its panels out and up, enveloping her head in wide, flat petals. Only once masked did she face him.

He didn't know what to say.

The only evidence anyone was actually inside the suit was the rubbery wheeze of her oxygen scrubbers. She was unreadable behind the black visor. Flam could see only his own face reflected there.

She turned away and headed back up the stairs.

"Moira, wait. You were forced to do all that—by him. If any of you is like Nula at all, then I know you're a good person. That sense of humor . . . your . . ."

She didn't stop, her suit shedding more scales with each step, sprinkling the floor behind her.

Defeat solidifying in his chest, Flam remained where he was.

She reached the top, but before moving on toward the attic door, she paused on the balcony. Resting a hand on the varnished railing, she gave him her mask's profile. "The three months sitting next to you were . . ." She sighed. "I wish I could be her all the time."

Flam's eyes burned. "You *can*."

She turned away.

"Moira . . ." Flam remained where he was, listening to her footsteps.

Distantly, as she pushed back out: "Karl, if you've found your father, I'll be on the library roof. Let's go."

CHAPTER 21

Knee-Deep Pandemonium

G eyser's streets were too narrow for flying vehicles. Each time a ship would carefully lower
to the cobblestones, Nevele would wait for the
pirates to drop out and open fire. She hated the carnage,
the ending of life, almost as much as knowing Clyde was in
the vicinity, seeing her commit it.

Ducking behind the square's fountain rim to reload,
she watched Clyde assist Aksel. Often staying one step behind as the one-eyed man downed a pirate, Clyde would
then charge up to collect what was of use: ammunition or
a gun, Rohm aiding him in pointing out fallen armaments.
While they handed the bounty to Aksel, it was plain Clyde
wanted to rid himself of the weapons as soon as possible.
Aksel, thanking them, accepted each and made immediate
use of them. They worked well together.

But they weren't bringing the same enthusiasm to the
task as Höwerglaz was. When two pirates ran up and took
aim at him, Höwerglaz didn't run for cover but merely put
out his hands, his hair whitening. The two stumbled forward, suddenly finding themselves gawky teenagers in their
too-big clothes, tripping over trouser legs. They looked at
each other, terrified as they became kids, toddlers, new-
borns—shrinking where they stood—until they appeared

half-formed, bulbous pink things, until—pop—erased.

Nevele's hands, which had been busily reloading, stilled.

Höwerglaz thrust his hands toward a ship's undercarriage as it shot over. The entire thing became a brown, fuzzy lump of rust and dropped out of the sky, crumbling. Liver spots left the back of his hands, and his hair returned full and dark, once again Emer-like. Noticing Nevele had been watching, Höwerglaz winked. All she could do in return was stare.

Once the current barrage of pirates had been dealt with, they regrouped.

"How're you doing?" she asked Clyde, taking his hand. It was cold. No answer came from his lips. She asked him again, and still he wouldn't look at her but would only nod.

It was empty in the square for the moment, quiet, even if around them the rest of Geyser was in anarchy. Smoke rose in dark columns, fires spreading like rashes up and down streets. Explosions that set their ears to ringing, constant gunfire here and there, far and close . . .

Her mind raced. It felt unreal, this happening. Here. In Geyser. She couldn't help but feel she may have somehow contributed to inviting home this awfulness. She doubted their efforts would do much. That doubt was an easy thing, coming on swift and settling hard in her heart. This wasn't going to end well. How could it? Even if the Odium were stopped *right now*, Geyser was already lost. But they had to do something. They had to keep trying. Something might be shaken from the ash after. They could rebuild. But still, that thought: she hadn't done enough to prevent this. Here it was. The end of Geyser, her home.

Keeping low, using newspaper stands and peddler carts

for cover, Aksel showed Nevele a radio Clyde had claimed from one of the pirates. From it poured manic barking, barely comprehensible.

"Who is that?" Nevele said.

"Dreck Javelin," Aksel answered gravely.

"What's he going on about?" She gave up on deciphering the thick-accented ravings.

Aksel listened, translating the butchered Common. "'Thin them. I can't come in any closer with this thing. Remember what I'm carrying here.'"

"So that one ship that's hanging back over the bay," Clyde said, "is the one with Dreck in it, the one with the missile?"

"Sounds like it," Aksel said.

A small group of beleaguered guardsmen ran into the square, pursuing pirates as they spooked them from alleyways and hiding spots. Another starship streaked overhead, gunning them down, killing guardsmen and their own men alike before moving on to rain destruction elsewhere.

"This is horrible," Clyde said.

"It's war. It's always horrible." Höwerglaz brought up a tattooed fist and yawned.

Nevele nodded at the radio in Aksel's hand. "Dreck doesn't want us to focus on him. All these men he's dropped off here are just a distraction." She made a circular gesture—the town square was a panopticon and from there, up every street, the four of them could see all that was going on, none of it good. "It's busywork."

They all readied weapons as a silvery shape blew past overhead. It sidled up to the roof of the library they'd seen Flam atop when they'd come in. From the roof a single masked figure leaped off and in. As soon as they were aboard, the expensive-looking starship turned and took off. Barely clear of the city's platter, it engaged its FTL, a ghostly trace plunging into the distance. East. Adeshka, maybe.

Clyde asked exactly what Nevele had been thinking. "That was my siblings, wasn't it?"

Gaze down, Aksel nodded. "Yeah." He stood, grabbed his most recent firearm, a flimsy-looking scattergun. "But I'll go out on a limb and say if *they're* running away—it doesn't bode well for us."

"Mr. Flam." Rohm pointed a tiny pink finger.

Clyde drew Flam's attention with a broad wave.

Nevele had wondered what was keeping the Mouflon from coming down sooner. She remembered briefly seeing two others up there with them—she hadn't gotten a good look—but when he emerged, limping down the library steps, he was alone.

"Did they leave?" Aksel asked as he joined them in cover.

Clyde leaped at him and threw his arms around the big lug.

The Mouflon clapped Clyde on the back, nearly smothering him in his arms. "Good to see you, too, Pasty." And to Aksel: "Yeah, they're gone. Well, one left of their own accord and the other . . . Listen, Pasty, when this is all over, I have a few tales you need to hear. It's been quite the time in Geyser while you were away."

"Likewise everywhere else on this cursed rock," Aksel put in, leaning out to peek up the street.

"Aksel Browne, right?" Flam said to the Bullet Eater.

Aksel swung round, sizing up the Mouflon. "We know each other?"

"I bought some parts for my auto off you, few years back, in the cart market." Flam indicated a corner of the town square, which was now piled with something on fire. "How is that skinny bloke of yours, anyway? Ricky, wasn't it?"

"Dead."

"Oh," Flam said, eyelids fluttering. "Okay, then. Sorry. So, um, what's the plan?"

"Stop them," Aksel said. From the moment this Ricky person had been mentioned, Nevele noticed how Aksel's face became creased—his brow crumpling down around his eye patch. He stared off for a moment, two, then drew a deep breath and shook his head, and only then spoke again, noticing everyone was staring his way. "Sufficient?"

"Works for me," Flam said. "Who's this?"

Höwerglaz stuck out his tattooed hand. "Ernest."

They shook, but Flam's face went through a series of shifts. "Ernest what?"

"Höwerglaz."

"Ernest Höwerglaz? Father Time?"

"Don't break out the autograph book just yet," Nevele cut in. "He's only helping if we keep things *interesting* for him."

Höwerglaz shrugged.

"Well, long as he's not shooting at us," Flam said, "I like him."

"Fantastic," Aksel said. "Now that we all know each other, let's move." He stepped out onto Armand Avenue where it split off from the square. The rest followed. Nevele scuttled up to Aksel in the nearest patch of temporary shelter, a shattered bus station.

"Hold up," she said. "Mind sharing your plan with the rest of us?"

The one-eyed man was about to move on down the next street, ignoring her, when she caught him by the arm.

"My *plan* is to go to the southern edge of town and shoot at Dreck, the man angling to blow up your city. Anyone with better ideas, I'll be all ears."

Since no one had any alternatives, Nevele gave him a permissive wave. "Fine. Lead on."

Even before turning the next corner, Nevele could smell blood. The street ahead was like a butcher's floor. Pirates, townsfolk, and guardsmen, none moving. Spent shell casings and whatever implements the townspeople had tried to defend their homes with: pitchforks, sharpened broom handles, croquet mallets.

"Heavens," Rohm murmured.

A solitary Lulomba came into view, perched high on a building. The pale naked man with his hair hanging in his face inclined his head, tracking an Odium ship. He pointed, and a flurry of Blatta took to the air, diving headlong at the ship. The dog-sized bugs banged carapaces against the ship, voluntarily squeezing themselves into the air intake scoops. Engine suffocated, the starship went dead, crashed to the street, skidded for a block, and ended its slide with a fiery blast. After, a man scurried off, bounding across rooftops on all fours. The remaining Blatta troops scuttled behind him, awaiting orders.

"Y'all *see* that?" Höwerglaz said. "Such dedication. And all that without sight!"

"Yeah . . ." Aksel remarked. "Real *interesting.*"

It grew impossibly quiet on the street, where dreadfulness had dragged its hand through. As much as it made Nevele's guts ache to do it, she plucked a machine gun from a dead pirate's hands. Its grips were still warm, but it had a nearly full clip.

"We keep moving," Aksel said, "get him within range of our meager artillery." He raised a finger. "Try for just below the nose of the ship. That's where the aiming systems will be for the missile. After that—"

An Odium ship circled around the square and, on its second pass, dropped open its bomb bay doors. Instead of a rain of explosions, a fine mist dribbled out, coating everything as they raced up the street.

One of Geyser's familiar sea breezes pushed the smell, and Nevele realized what it was. "We need to move." She shot to her feet, grabbing Clyde and Aksel. "They're going to—"

The starship tipped itself back. The engines' glowing heat coils touched the stream. Ignition was immediate, rushing along the long trail the ship had slathered onto the street. A wall of heat pushed behind them as they ran up the remainder of Armand Avenue, passing through the empty intersection of Second Circle, then Third.

When Nevele dared a glance over her shoulder—the ship was dragging a long flaming serpent, keeping it sated by pouring more green syrup down its throat as it chased.

She could feel the heat on the backs of her legs and arms. On her neck, through her clothes—that first tingle preceding a bad burn.

They dodged through the strewn rubble of Smith's Grocer.

"Here," Aksel shouted, ducking into a bicycle repair shop. Nevele and the rest followed, nearly bottlenecking themselves in the doorway. She shoved Höwerglaz and Flam ahead, then Clyde, and moved inside just as the flames were a mere yard away—and roaring closer.

She pushed the door just as the reaching fingers of flame came crackling and pouring through the gap, trying to fling the door back open as they pushed against it. As one, they shoved and shoved until it finally slammed shut.

Aksel's hair was crispy. Clyde had to slap flames out of a sleeve. Flam's surcoat bore black smudges. They'd all been singed, but it was a far better than what could've happened.

The worst of the long tail of fire dragged by, making every window in the place rattle and even some of the bicycles on display click as the wheels were bumped into motion.

The starship, even though they couldn't see it, passed back and forth in front of where they'd gone, spraying down more and more fuel, probably dousing the roof of the building as well. They couldn't stay in here long. Already the air was growing hazy.

"I think we can pass through the alley, Ms. Nevele," Rohm said, "get to Fourth Circle by moving along Grass Street, then Ossa Drive."

Nevele nodded. Rohm knew Geyser's layout better than anyone.

Without further discussion, they moved to the back door, peeked to confirm it was safe, and pressed on. They zigzagged between the buildings, as the alleyway's wonky course demanded, and came out onto Grass Street. It was the agricultural ward, where seed sellers and flower shops and miller sheds lined the street.

The smell of burnt bread filled Nevele's nose. Elevated wheat platforms towered next to them, now with only blackened stalks in the wooden field derricks' burnt soil. The windmill's rice paper blades, alive with fire, turned, squeaking sorrowfully.

Flam's radio came to life.

"Where ye be, lad?"

Aksel stopped in his tracks. "Who is that?"

Before he could answer, Flam's finger paused over the radio's talk button. "Our friend."

"Yes, but who? What's his name?"

"Nigel."

"Nigel Wigglesby?"

"Yeah, why? You know him?"

Nevele recalled Aksel mentioning he'd been a serviceman for Adeshka's Fifty-Eighth militia. And that he'd made a bad call at some point. Nigel was in a wheelchair. Perhaps that's what had landed him in it.

Aksel cleared his throat, his blue eye flicking erratically. "Did, yeah. Just . . . answer the man, would you? Bloke's" — he flopped a hand around—"clearly worried."

Flam, snout wrinkled with confusion, looked to Nevele.

She shrugged.

He clicked a button. "Flam here. We're okay. On Grass Street, south end. How're you holding up?"

Aksel strode off a ways, then stopped to press a hand to the brick side of a building, leaning into it.

Clyde approached him.

Nevele couldn't hear what was being said except for Aksel barking at him, "I said I'm fine."

Clyde drifted back to the group, shrugging.

Aksel remained where he was, folding and unfolding his arms, shaking his head a lot.

Höwerglaz said, "What climbed up his ass?"

". . . about as well I as I can," Nigel was saying. "Any

sign of your uncle anywhere?"

"Sorry, no," Flam said. "Where are you?" He scanned the skies. Nothing resembling Nigel's craft passed by.

"Under the platter, hanging back for a minute to finish up some field repairs."

"Mind giving us some cover here in a minute? We're moving south, and it's pretty open."

"Certainly. Back your way shortly." Before Nigel cut off, a quick chitter of Lulomba-speak snuck through.

When Nevele asked why it sounded like Nigel had the Lulomba with him in his ship, Flam explained, rolling his eyes whenever the word *pilgrimage* came up.

She nodded, mostly understanding.

"Might be a tick," Nigel called out after a second. Starship fire sounded. "Rotters found us."

Preceded by streaking tracer rounds, Nigel's starship pushed over the city's platter. The overworked engines screeched, leaving a long black trail.

"Madman," Aksel breathed.

Behind Nigel's rickety moon hopper, chasing closely, were two Odium ships that weren't in much better condition. Some clever twisting and banking kept most of the fire from finding its mark. Nigel executed a textbook loop-the-loop, dropped behind the two Odium ships, and shot down both into the Margin. As he tore overhead again, he gave a thumbs-up out the window—but it was clear the old miner was a bit rattled.

"I'll scout ahead," came from Flam's radio. "Full speed ahead, team!"

Together they moved onto Wilkshire Lane.

CHAPTER 22

Whispers

Through the cockpit glass, Gorett could see much of the residential ward was in ruins. Beyond it, into central Geyser, were so many columns of dark smoke. His heart was breaking.

Below, some guardsmen fired from a broken window, each bullet smacked away by the *Magic Carpet*'s Tesla shields. Dreck grumped over his shoulder, "Blow that building. I want to be on our way home before the hour."

"Aye, sir," a pirate replied.

A moment later, the building buckled, bricks flying and spinning away with one well-placed mortar round. It held; then half of the building slipped and tumbled off the side of the platter, into the bay.

"Done, sir."

Why, do you suppose, is Dreck always so quick to remove the worms his men pick up? Contrary to the old wives' tales about how I soak away calcium, I don't. Nothing to the point of harm. I lay eggs, yes, but it's so my nesting dolls—my children inside my children, them and you respectively—can make more, spread enlightenment. We're no threat to your well-being whatsoever. So why do you think he butchers his men?

I don't know, Gorett thought in reply, assuming he was about to find out.

He fears growth. Any man who develops a mind of his own is a man who cannot be led. Happens enough times, Dreck, neck-deep in thinking men, will lose his hold.

Is that what you do: help the infected think?

I am a teacher, yes.

Who are you?

Perhaps it's still there. Look under your seat.

What?

Under your seat, Pitka.

Gorett bent forward, pushing a hand under. Amid the foam and cold metal springs, his fingers brushed an intricately folded piece of paper. Keeping it low between his knees so Dreck wouldn't see, he opened it. Within was a crayon drawing of a man and a woman in pilot attire: goggles and flight suits. Between them, a shorter figure with crazy red coils for hair. *Mommy, Daddy, and Nimbelle*, it read in a child's handwriting—still crooked despite how carefully scrawled the crayon appeared to have been wielded.

How did you know this was here? Things aligned. *This isn't about saving Geyser. This is revenge, isn't it? You were using me. You're using the worm to—*

Yes. But don't sound so hurt. Reverse psychology isn't new.

What?

Pushing you to stop Dreck—I knew full well it'd only harden your inaction. Just let your true nature take over, allow cowardice to speed bump you. You bleed weakness. But rest assured, as flimsy as your will is now, with my help, you won't have to be forever.

She must've heard him thinking.

You will do nothing to stop them. Dreck getting the wendal stone deposit and Ernest Höwerglaz is all part of the plan. My plan within Dreck's plan. Hidden as I am within you. Soon, we'll be even closer—fused together, king and queen, as one.

No. I will save Geyser.

You will do no such thing. Do you hear me? You will mind your mother.

Gorett turned in his seat. And with every ounce of courage Pitka Gorett had left, he unfastened the straps and threw himself across. He'd fire the missile but aim it so it went harmlessly askew—into space or into the sea.

"Gorett. The hell are you doing?" Dreck shouted. He drew his gun. "I won't warn you a second time."

Pitka! Mother Worm raged. *Stop! You can be a king again. Feared, worshipped, lauded in story and song.*

I'll be known as an awful man, he responded, still reaching, fumbling and scraping and stretching for the launch button, *but I refuse to die before doing one thing right.*

CHAPTER 23

Words and Steel

Clyde led the group up the walk to the front doors of the chateau, locking up once all were in. Despite everything going on outside, it felt good to be here. Since Mr. Wilkshire's funeral, Clyde and Nevele hadn't changed a thing. The tile in the entryway, the fireplaces, the illustrious paneling running throughout the first and second floors—none of it.

"Nice place," Höwerglaz said.

A brittle female voice called down from the second-floor staircase railing: "Know now, you dogs, I won't hesitate to put you down if required! I'm armed. Abundantly."

"It's us, Miss Selby," Clyde shouted.

With visible relief, Miss Selby came winding down the staircase's brass twist, wrinkled face rosy—evidence she'd been crying. "Oh, oh." She threw her arms around Clyde and Nevele, squeezing them tight. "Where have you two *been*? I've been so worried." The scolding ended upon her noticing how bloody, burned, and ragged they all were. "I thought for sure . . ." A fragile hand covered her lips. "Oh, my dears. You're all so . . ."

"We're all right," Clyde said, hands on her shoulders. "But why didn't you leave with the others?"

She straightened. "Dearie, I've been booted from this

house once, and I don't intend to ever suffer such again."
She'd been sent to the refugee camps. Her watery eyes lingered on Aksel. "You're familiar. Were you there, in the camp, last year?"

"I was."

She smiled. "You made it."

Aksel nodded weakly. "Mostly."

She turned to Flam. "Besides, our head security officer said to stay indoors, so I did."

Aksel paced into the music room. "Got a clean view here."

Everyone moved into the next room, peeking through the gauzy curtains past the gardens, toward the edge of the platter. There, hovering over the bay in the near distance, was the *Magic Carpet*.

The glass bubble at its front allowed sight of the two men piloting the thing. They were slapping and punching one another. It took a moment for Clyde to recognize the one in the copilot's seat, especially since, he now realized, he'd never seen Pitka Gorett in the flesh. Compared to his picture, he now wore a long beard and was remarkably thinner. He was reaching for something on Dreck's side, pawing wildly, seemingly not caring at all that the pirate captain was beating him, bloodying his nose.

"Did their partnership sour, you suppose?" Nevele snorted.

"They're distracted. That's the important thing," Flam said. "Let's use that." The Mouflon moved out of the music room, through the kitchen, to the back doors, and out into the gardens. He lifted his rifle, fired.

"Stay inside, Miss Selby," Clyde said over the gunfire.

She was as reluctant to let him go as always.

Flam, Aksel, and Nevele, in a row, fired together.

Dreck shoved Gorett away, took the controls in his hands. He turned the *Magic Carpet* and returned fire.

Clyde pulled Aksel back into cover as the hedges were mowed apart by the salvo.

The house behind them absorbed many of the shots, the pale stone cracking apart, the back windows of the kitchen and dining room shattering. Shredded plant stems and petals and seedpods rained on them. The smell of spent gunpowder mixed with that of freshly-manicured lawn in a heady, incongruous bouquet.

Flam moved out from his cover behind a raised cement planter, fired, and moved between Aksel and Nevele. He handed them some spare ammunition before kneeling to reload.

"That thing's shield"—Aksel panted, ducking in as Dreck opened fire again—"keeps knocking everything away."

While Dreck reduced a row of rose bushes to a flurry of petals, Nevele took the opportunity. Clyde saw it this time, a snaggle of lightning deadening her bullets' velocity.

Aksel's Odium radio crackled. "Clear off, boys. I'm taking it down." Then another voice: "No! You can't!"

"We've got to do something. He's going to fire the missile," Clyde shouted. Peeking over the planter, he saw Gorett again throwing himself onto Dreck.

The *Magic Carpet* made a sudden sideways leap through the air. This, for Dreck, was apparently the final straw. Using his scattergun stock, he cracked it over Gorett's head. Gorett immediately slumped unconscious in his seat, tongue lolling.

Dreck, free from distraction now, took the joysticks— thumb poised.

Clyde snatched the radio from Aksel's hand. "Dreck. Stop. Please. Let's talk about this."

Höwerglaz tried grabbing Clyde to drag him back down. "What're you *doin'*?"

Clyde spun free and walked the garden pavers, one arm raised in what could be read only as a request for a ceasefire.

Nevele rushed out to him. She paused when she realized not a single Odium ship was firing. It was silent as a Sunday morning.

She stayed beside him, facing the ship.

Dreck pulled up his goggles, shook his head, smiling.

Clyde tried again. "Please just come down. Send someone to talk face-to-face."

Dreck eyed them a moment, chewing his lip, then turned in his seat. Cupping a hand over his headset mic, he conferred with someone behind him, his voice not coming through the radio.

From behind Nevele and Clyde, Höwerglaz, crouching in cover, called, "Yer juss gonna try an' talk sense into them? After all they've done to your city? After what Gorett, their new buddy, did? He had your father killed; your friend Mr. Wilkshire. Ya juss gonna forgive all that?"

Clyde, hands staying up, answered Höwerglaz. "My revenge means nothing right now, compared to what the city will lose if we continue to fight. We've been bested, Ernest. I can admit that."

Dreck finished speaking to his men, faced forward, chewing his lip again. His shoulders rose, then fell. He unwrapped his fingers from around his mic. "You in cahoots with the queen?"

Clyde raised the radio. "What queen?"

Dreck, framed in his glass bubble, said, "Answers that, I suppose. All right, we'll land, have a chat. But one of your Patrol fires a shot, we'll let loose. Understand?"

"Okay." Clyde looked over his shoulder and shouted to Flam, "Tell the guardsmen to stand down. No one's to fire."

Flam repeated the request on his own radio.

Clyde faced the *Magic Carpet* again. "We'll meet you in the town square. This is a ceasefire for negotiations. We won't fire on you if you don't fire on us. You and I, alone."

Dreck issued a crisp, if entirely sarcastic, salute.

They picked their way back to the square, passing the hellish landscape Geyser had become in just a handful of hours. More than once, Miss Selby cried out as they passed a dead body or one of her friends' homes burning to its foundation. Clyde and Nevele walked on either side, arms around her, letting her cry. Right then, Clyde would've liked to do the same, really.

They entered through the back of Margaret's Mends. Miraculously, it appeared untouched by the attack. Not even a cracked windowpane.

Clyde drew aside the blinds, looking out on the ravaged town square. The *Praise to Her* had gone from a haggard bird to brand-new to what it was now, a blackened husk. Dreck stood beside it, as if lamenting the starship, tugging the rope he'd descended from the *Magic Carpet* so it'd be drawn back up. Sticking to his word, surprisingly, he was unaccompanied. Apparently the pirate had just as much doubt in Clyde, for his ships remained hovering nearby, bomb bay doors open and ready to bring him back up.

Dreck checked his watch, scanning the square.

"I'm going alone," Clyde said.

"What?" Nevele said. "No way."

"Please. Let me try. This is my job. He came out alone, and I should do the same. As a courtesy."

Höwerglaz had taken a seat behind the counter, where Nevele normally sat when waiting away slow days. He grunted a little laugh, chin resting on a tattooed fist. "Courtesy. That's hilarious. They're *pirates*."

Rohm, apparently having had enough, left the proximity of Höwerglaz on the shop countertop to scamper up Nevele's arm and sit on her shoulder.

Höwerglaz shrugged at the mouse's display of disdain. He thrust a finger Clyde's way. "Look here. This ain't what I wanted. I wanted a bang, not a whimper. Something *excitin'*. And here yer juss gonna raise the white flag? Which, come to think, ya'd actually stand in well for. Pale as surrender."

With balled fists, Flam stepped forward. "Say that again."

But Clyde moved in first. "What, doesn't this *interest* you, someone trying to save their city with words?"

"Yer absolutely right, it *doesn't* interest me," Höwerglaz said. Languidly, he reached toward one of Nevele's mannequins, and the plaster and papier mâché figure creaked, shriveled like a raisin. Höwerglaz went from thirtysomething to about Clyde's age, then younger, his voice doing the same as he continued, ratcheting incrementally in pitch, "But go on ahead, give it a whirl, see what good it gets ya. Juss know, when it blows up in yer face, don't come cryin'."

Grinding his teeth, Clyde turned to Nevele, Flam, and Aksel. "Keep him in here. They can't know we have him."

Before leaving, Clyde took Nevele in his arms, kissed

her on the lips. It took effort to look away from her, to turn toward the door, unable to say the words letting her know how much he cared for her.

He had to rely on his words now, just different ones. Clyde exited, closed the door behind him, the little bell jingling, and began his lonely march into the square.

Geyser by twilight. The scant remaining street lamps clicked on, blue-white halos in the hanging smoke.

Dreck Javelin noticed him and waved a greeting.

Clyde's heart hammered. His boots, still coated in Lakebed dust, impacted the cobblestones, making him feel as if he'd break apart at any time. Dreck remained where he was, under his hovering ships' careful watch. He was sweaty, still dressed for colder climes, in furs and leather.

Clyde stopped a few paces short. "Thank you for agreeing to this," he said, having to speak loudly to be heard over the idling ships.

"Not a problem." Dreck nodded toward Clyde's side. "Nice stabby stick, by the way. Is that Commencement? I thought your pop had it turned into a gun."

"I had it turned back into a sword."

Dreck squinted. "Funny thing to do, but whatever suits your fancy."

Above them, the *Magic Carpet*'s hatch was open. Clyde had easy view inside. There it was—the missile—big as an auto, hanging by clawlike clamps. They'd given it a paint job, a sharp-toothed maw, and burning red eyes.

Dreck must've noticing him looking. "And that'd be *my* stabby stick, aye, although it's got a wee bit more oomph than yours. Not to compare."

Clyde dropped his gaze from the terrifying sight of the missile to look Dreck in his merry, bloodshot eyes. "Is there any way we can work something out here? Can we allow you to take the wendal stone but leave the city standing?"

"What, with picks and shovels and all that?" Dreck guffawed. "It'd take years. And I'm sure within minutes of us headin' in, you'd collapse the whole thing behind us."

"I wouldn't," Clyde said sincerely. "If it meant saving Geyser, I'd let you take it. Even if your men had to live on the island, work right alongside our own miners, I'd let you have it." Clyde noticed a second ship had its bottom hatch open as well, and inside was an enormous spool of metal rope, like a giant squid's coiled tentacle, a waiting spearhead of a drill bristling with spikes and cutting implements, ready.

"Forgive my bluntness, but I'm not the patient sort. Unless you can give me the coordinates for an even bigger deposit somewhere, we're gonna have this one." Dreck stamped on the cobblestone, as if the city were nothing but a stubborn lock on a treasure chest. "And don't even try being all humble, telling me it's not that big."

"But have you seen the deposit with your own eyes? And did you consider the source of those stories?"

Dreck's eyelids went half-mast. "I know Gorett's a shite, but he wouldn't lie about something like this."

"Would you be willing to trade Gorett for the deposit?" Clyde said. *Please, anything.* Might even be a bonus, since it seemed Gorett and Dreck weren't getting along, given their squabble earlier. Nothing would please Clyde more than being able to appoint Gorett a cell in the palace's dungeon. Maybe even the one Gorett had caged Vidurkis

Mallencroix in for years like a caged attack dog. Or like Gorett had done to Nevele. It'd be fitting, if nothing else.

"Eh. No, thanks. I've something set aside for him," Dreck said.

"You can't make weavers," Clyde said.

Dreck tried to hide his shock. "Who spilled the beans? It was Proboscis, wasn't it? Where is he, anyway?"

"Dead."

"By your hand?" Dreck glanced at Commencement again. "You must've caught him off guard. For a man missing a nose, he could sniff out danger like nobody I ever knew."

"No, it wasn't me, but it doesn't matter. We know your plan. *How* isn't important. And even if it were possible to create new weavers, you still don't have Höwerglaz."

"And you'd know that *how,* exactly?" Dreck leaned forward, head cocked. "He could be right up there in my ship above our heads, taking a snooze alongside Gorett, for all you know. So the only way you can say *I* don't have Höwerglaz with such conviction is that *you do.*"

Splendid negotiating, really, Clyde scolded himself. "I—"

"Let's take a time-out here. I'm being a bad guest. So. When you suggested talking this over, you came out here carrying your little pick stick along. Were you going to talk, then if that didn't work, strike me down—or try to?"

"No, I brought it only because I'm Clyde Pyne, steward of Geyser, and Commencement is to remain with—"

Dreck waved a hand until Clyde shut up. "Stop. Drop the pomp and circumstance. No, you were doing just as I heard your father always did: waltz out onto the battlefield, try and pound some sense into people with a whole lot of talk and a daunting vocabulary, and if that didn't work, really *smash* sense into them in the traditional way. With that." He cocked an eyebrow toward the gaudy green blade. "But really, just doing so—coming out here armed *at all*, even with that letter opener, speaks more about you than anything. It shows you doubt. Doubt your negotiation skills, doubt me ever possibly being open-minded, but most of all doubt solving anything whatsoever with talk."

"You're armed." Clyde nodded at his holstered scattergun.

"We're not talking about me right now." Dreck cleared his throat. "Peril is a stage when we don't put masks on but instead take them off. And as much as you stand by being a traditionalist—clearly, since you're carrying a damn *sword*—you have that same niggling fear your father had, that remaining resolutely analog yourself can't make everything else revert that way. Eventually, you'll have to give in, get your hands dirty like the rest of us.

"Like me, in particular, during the Territorial Skirmish. When the Unified Kingdoms of Adeshka, Geyser, and Nessapolis took on big, bad Embaclawe. Pointed ourselves west, toward those who wanted to come here and claim this land as their own, dragging taxation and all that shite along with them. But, unlike us, they'd long ago adapted to the modern age: black powder, steam power, and eventually electricity and plasma—all that wizardry so mind-boggling to us cavemen. We squeaked by only because of numbers, not weaponry, mind you. But next time, they would win. We'd clash again. They'd adapt to us, and we would to them. Your pa, stubborn as he was, eventually came around to toting a gun instead of a blade. Sure tried to stick to the old ways, quaint as they were, but he *learned*. Once you get shite on your shoes, might as well stop watching where you're treading." Dreck's gaze drifted over Clyde's shoulder.

"All right, it's official, I'm bored out of my wits," a voice called out.

Spinning around, Clyde gaped.

Höwerglaz, shuffling up with hands raised, announced, "Go ahead. Take me. Maybe y'all can keep mah eyes open."

"What are you *doing*?" Clyde shouted.

Behind him, Nevele, Aksel, and Flam were reaching out from the front door of Margaret's Mends for Höwerglaz, but he was already too far out.

Dreck stepped around Clyde, training his scattergun on the boy boldly approaching. Finally, understanding crossed the pirate's face. "Are you—?"

"This is just Emer, a boy we found in the city," Clyde tried. "He's a bit strange, likes to make pranks. Why don't you go back with the others, Emer?"

"Because you bore the ever-lovin' crap out of me," Höwerglaz said, shoving Clyde away. "I told ya, didn't I? I wanted *action*, and this, far as I see, is about the only way to prod ya into doin' any."

Dreck pulled the ageless weaver to him, tucking the scattergun against Höwerglaz's chest. He smiled Clyde's way smugly. The boy looked wholly unbothered by being there, under Dreck's arm, or having a gun barrel pressed to his ribs. "Looks like I was right," Dreck said. "But apparently any speech you laid on him wasn't too convincing. Came out here on his own."

"Ernest. Why?" Clyde said.

"I done warned ya, didn't I?" Höwerglaz said. "You gonna have to act eventually."

"But there's . . . there's got to be another way." Clyde stepped forward, thumbing his blade.

And together, almost looking like father and son, Dreck and Höwerglaz laughed.

"Next thing," Dreck said, "you'll be whining, 'Why can't we all get along?' I swear, apple didn't roll far. You sound just like your old man."

Stern-faced, Höwerglaz regarded Clyde. "Really does."

The pirate captain waved a hand to the craft hovering above, and a rope came spiraling down. Dreck, busy feeding the rope through his harness, didn't see Clyde's hand move to his side, taking Commencement's hilt in his grasp.

While Dreck snapped a clip onto Höwerglaz's belt to fasten them together, Höwerglaz undid the top button of his shirt, then the next down, and let his shirt fall open. His gaze drifted to Commencement, then back to Clyde's eyes.

His lips moved. "Without me, they have nothing."

Clyde, understanding, drew up Commencement an inch, then another . . .

The rope snapped taut, and Dreck and Höwerglaz were reeled inside the *Magic Carpet*. Clyde rushed forward, swung, managed to only graze Dreck's boot heel. Too late.

The others rushed up next to him, Flam raising his rifle but hesitating. He couldn't risk hitting the missile. Nevele lashed, smashing out one of the *Magic Carpet*'s landing gear lights, nothing more.

Höwerglaz appeared at the bomb bay doors. Peering down at Clyde, lips tightly pursed, he put out balled fists and gave a hearty shake. *Act*. He shook again. *Act*.

The missile next to him angled around on the inverted gimbal. Dreck, from somewhere within, screamed, "Fire Bessie."

Flam yanked Clyde aside as the missile made the short journey from the *Magic Carpet* to pound into the town square, scattering cobblestones.

It remained wedged upright for a moment, looking like a butted cigar.

Clyde rushed forward, with every intention of slicing into its side, to strike whatever explosives it held within its metal skin, killing himself but saving the city—but when the missile's rockets fired, he was propelled back, Commencement clattering aside.

His face singed, Clyde lay sprawled out, watching helplessly as the missile burrowed into the ground, the propulsion rockets' flames shooting twenty feet high.

Struggling away from helping hands, Clyde sprinted to the hole's edge as the missile plunged in eagerly. He hoped beyond hope it'd get stuck and he could climb down and find some way to disarm it. But as he stared inside, all he could do was watch the white fireball descend, effortlessly piercing through layer after layer of sediment.

It grew dimmer and dimmer, and with one final flash, way down, the ground began to shake.

The *Magic Carpet* lifted to a safe distance.

A street lamp tipped, its glass bulb shattering in a bright flash. Distantly, an auto alarm whooped.

A second and third rumble struck Clyde's feet, each more powerful in succession.

A manhole clanged and shot heavenward like a coin flipped by a white finger of steam. Just as the Odium ships spiraled around the geyser, it let off one long blast, bigger than any Clyde had ever seen, raining down hunks of rock and snapped metal, the shattered steam works, instead of the typical innocuous mist.

"They actually did it," Clyde said absently, the steam and the fog mixing into a humid, choking fog around them, a sulfuric tinge to it, like eggs.

The library's columns broke free, rumbling away like giant rolling pins. The building where the *Gazette* was written and printed tipped, becoming a cloud of smoke as cinder blocks and glass shards splashed into the street.

"We've got to get off the platter," Nevele shouted. Clyde had heard her scared before, but not like this.

A black lightning bolt jumped up the palace's blond sediment stone and spread fingers up its towers. The entirety of the illustrious, asymmetrical castle split in two with a terrific snap as loud as cannon fire as the sparkly stone gave. In the rush of dust, Clyde raised his arm, momentarily losing the others.

Through the murk, he could see darting paths of cracks forming. Immediately they'd begin to spread as the weight of the platter pulled itself apart. Each widening mouth seemed to want to swallow him and everyone associated with the man who'd failed the city so completely.

"Clyde!" Miss Selby shouted.

He turned just as a split in the ground opened between them. "Jump," he yelled. A curtain of steam pushed up, obscuring her. "Ms. Selby, jump!" He screamed it again and again, reaching, even after the section of the town square fell away, into oblivion, steam consuming her.

She dropped, never making a peep.

Clyde stared, squinting into the hot air into which she'd vanished.

No.

Flam grabbed him. "She's gone."

Clyde couldn't move.

The Mouflon picked him up. As they charged off, Clyde watched the ground behind them give way. Flam jumped again, and the next piece fell out, and again.

"The station house," Flam choked out. "The elevator, we can get down to the island."

"But it won't be much safer down there. We need *off* the island," Nevele screamed back.

Aksel pulled her aside.

Below, a crack formed and more earth fell away.

Nevele followed Flam as he charged ahead, probably not making the best guess how to get away with their lives, but at least taking the lead.

Flam dropped Clyde back onto his feet. This next gap was bigger than the others, and Flam wouldn't make it across while carrying him. When the wall of steam dissipated, they jumped, then moved on to the next, less-turbulent segment.

A particularly violent quake came, and they all stumbled. Pausing, dumbfounded, they watched the geyser, the symbol of the city, and what it was named after and built around, blow apart. Each segment shot in a different direction, the whole of the mile-high stone tower erupting. Beneath, one detonation after another.

"Go," Aksel shouted.

The Mouflon took a running start to cross a gap. Nevele jumped next, then Clyde. The entire time Rohm, in Nevele's pocket, emitted one long peal.

Reaching the station house, they rushed up the front stairs.

Clyde wished the city's destruction could be like rain, avoided by merely going inside, but the Patrol station house interior wasn't a bit safer. The desks were sliding all over the place. The world tipped and shifted like a funhouse tunnel. Ahead was the basement where Flam said the emergency elevator was. A wall broke apart, the floor above it coming down.

"Move," Flam cried.

None of this was real. It couldn't be real. Charging down the stairs, Clyde felt as if he were in someone else's body. For Höwerglaz to deceive them like that, to lose Miss Selby . . . And now the city, his home, was coming down under their feet.

Clyde felt Flam drag him into the elevator car. The gate skidded closed. Flam mashed the down button. The five of them packed in.

The elevator began its jerking, slow descent. They passed through the platter. Outside the elevator, the underside of the city was an inverted mountain range of stalactites.

The elevator suddenly swung, all of its occupants pitching to one side, the cable twanging. Just outside the car the geyser below the platter, the trunk-like stem, was spreading with cracks. From each small fissure, a new geyser sprayed. Flam rushed in, spinning the elevator car, and took the brunt across his broad back before it could boil all of them alive. He snarled but held the position, fingers pressing either elevator wall, shaking, until they'd lowered through the worst of it.

When he stepped away, collapsing to one knee, Clyde saw a majority of the fur on his back had been sloughed off, the skin beneath already gathering colonies of bright blisters. He tried to help him to his hooves.

"I'm okay, Pasty," the Mouflon said, sounding anything but. "Really."

The cracks were increasing, allowing more places for the steam to escape. Aksel began hammering the down button, but their descent continued at a stubborn snail's pace.

A neighborhood-sized section of the platter broke off above. Whooshing past, it crashed to the island below. It continued to sink, pushing soft earth and trees down until its impetus finally bled dry and came to a stop.

Above, stalactites loosened, popping free of their millennia-old moorings to stake the island, making new, unnatural steppes.

The five remained suspended in the elevator, only halfway to the island. The stem began to fragmenting at the base, like an enormous tree chopped most of the way through, leaving gravity to do the rest.

Clyde felt like they were being lifted all of a sudden, as if the crank above had decided to bring them back up. Geyser was beginning to tip, falling away to the south, levering on the island.

"Not good, not good," Aksel shouted and closed his eye.

Nevele grabbed Clyde's hand.

Rohm vibrated in Clyde's pocket.

Flam stared out as Geyser leaned and leaned . . .

The elevator swung in toward the stem as it continued to buckle, the car bashing into the sediment stone. The occupants crashed to one side, and the angle of the tipping geyser became more and more severe, the elevator now nearly horizontal.

Flam aimed at the bolts holding the cable to the car.

No one had time to argue about what he was doing. He fired. The cable snapped, and the car began to skid down the inclined geyser stem, gaining momentum down the side of the smooth surface. A spray of sparks came into the car and shot out behind.

For four breathless seconds, the car turned and spun and careened.

Clyde attempted to steer it by leaning, but it was no use.

Nor was there any way to brake.

When they reached the end, the car was driven right to the ground. Not pointy enough to spear the soil, it bounced, spun into the air, everyone inside tumbling weightlessly against one another, and then another bounce, each giving them less airtime—thankfully. Finally they came to a stop on the damp, debris-strewn beach.

Clyde sat up amongst the heap of his groaning friends and looked back from where they'd slid.

Beside him, Nevele pulled up onto her hands and knees and went pale.

Rohm peeked from his pocket. A tiny gasp.

Aksel got up, and a tear rolled down his face.

Flam, forgetting his burns, put a hand over his chest.

The geyser lay in pieces.

Cut off less than two stories high.

It continued to blow, rushing a ceaseless blast of steam into the air as if crying in its defeat.

Amongst the pieces: buildings and homes, schools and churches, street signs, mailboxes, autos, clothes, furniture, and people.

Fires burned, sirens wailed from somewhere, possibly the coast guard sent by Adeshka, but right now it didn't matter. Clyde looked at the city, his home. Most of his memories of it had already been gone, and the ones he still had were crushed. The platter lay half-submerged in the bay, looking like a tombstone.

They'd lost.

And before the city's corpse could even cool, the carrion birds came. The Odium ships hovered down around the column of steam pouring up out of the earth. In coordination, they fired drill heads into the new, gaping hole. Behind each, cables and a complicated series of pulleys and tension lines trailed.

Clyde kicked open the elevator car, stumbled out through the wet sand, and ran up the hill toward the city, dodging crumpled buildings and homes and smashed, burning autos. The others followed, limping and favoring hurts.

The ground shook again, the stump of the geyser splitting wide.

The starships screamed as their engines flared bright, struggling to hoist aloft the buried treasure.

The deposit slid up foot by foot until it finally came free, soil and rock splintering off around it. Gleaming in the residual sunlight in the atmosphere, the wendal stone winked down at them. It shined blue, green, purple, black as the ships ascended.

Clyde spotted the *Magic Carpet*, which was not going to be one of the load-bearing crafts, it seemed, but merely an overseer of the process. The eight other ships began turning, the deposit suspended between them by thick cables. When the *Magic Carpet* crossed over Jagged Bay, the other ships and their retrieved burden tailed behind.

They didn't use their faster-than-light drives. Didn't

need to. They'd fought Adeshka's air force on the way here, bested them, and with Geyser in no shape to put up a fight anymore, the Odium had no predators. They had clawed and kicked and shot their way to the top. They had everything now. Everything. Clyde dropped to his knees. "Everything."

"Look. Someone's on that thing," Aksel said.

Clyde peered, seeing a tiny speck on the massive deposit's flank. Hanging on precariously from a small ledge. It was a man, a bulky man with something tucked under one arm, like a small bundle of clothes or . . . a baby.

"Uncle," Flam said, rushing forward to the water's edge. "Greenspire's on that thing! What the hell is he doing? Uncle! Oh, you stupid old . . ."

Somehow Clyde knew that was precisely where Greenspire wanted to be.

They watched Greenspire Flam and the pirates until they couldn't be seen anymore, weren't even dots on the horizon or glowing specks in the distance. They turned around, toward their city, their home, but it was just more hopelessness. How many had survived? It was so quiet. It seemed the five of them were alone on the island.

While in the Lakebed, Clyde had always kept Geyser, almost as much as Nevele, close to his heart. Something to keep his chin up.

And now, sitting among its rubble, Clyde felt as if a still-living part of him had been carved free. An oasis for him and many others, who'd depended on him to protect it, was in ruins.

From over the Jagged Bay, a starship limped along, trailing smoke, bobbing as crookedly as a starving fly.

Sparks crackled from an engine, and the starboard wing appeared partly bitten off.

"I'm sorry, lad," came Nigel's voice on Flam's radio. "I'm sorry."

CHAPTER 24

The Numbers

In the back of Nigel's wheezing, smoking starship, Flam, Aksel, Nevele, and Clyde sat cramped in among the few surviving Lulomba and their saddled Blatta, whose compound eyes surveyed the new passengers with detached interest. Unaware of the destruction of their home or simply disinterested—Flam couldn't determine which.

They crossed over Jagged Bay, engines crying out painfully, control panel flashing red, red, red. The landing gear dragged the water.

Aksel moved forward, ducking into the cockpit. "Is this thing gonna make it?"

"I'm putting her down in Scoona Port on the beach," Nigel said, struggling with the trembling joysticks. "We'll be lucky to even get that far. Hope ye all know how to swim, if it comes to that." He seemed to hesitate, studying Aksel over his shoulder. "Ye got old."

"And you got younger?" Aksel said—tried to smile but failed.

Smushed in between two Blatta, Flam recalled they'd been compatriots in the Fifty-Eighth, perhaps even friends. Some bad blood had passed between them, apparently, since they'd seen each other. The exchange was not unkindly but certainly uncomfortable.

Nigel settled the struggling starship down.

The beach was littered with charred pieces of what were once people's homes—and of some occupants as well, Flam couldn't help but notice. He turned away from the window.

Nigel unbuckled his wheels from the floor and turned his chair around, passing through the crowded holds. "We'll give chase, soon as we're able," he said to no one in particular, his voice arid. He threw a switch and lowered the rear ramp, rubber wheels rolling down to the moonlit sand below.

The port town of Scoona lay along the curving shoreline, a collection of ramshackle houses on a long boardwalk. Dockworkers, fishermen, and even the port saloon's wait staff were at the wharf railing, gazing toward Geyser. No one said anything. Hands were to mouths, clutched over chests; tears shined on cheeks. Flam looked the same, even though he'd been present for its destruction.

A column of smoke at the edge of the bay. That's all she was now.

Nigel pried open the flank of the starship. The engine sparked and hissed, blades grating broken and bent as it persistently tried to spin its turbines. Nigel shook his head, slumped in his wheelchair, and stared in at the ship's broken guts.

Flam didn't need to ask if it'd be a tough job to get them in the air again.

White light poured over them. Everyone with weapons drew, but after the other starship wheeled about overhead, making an elegant turnaround, it was clear to see it was an Adeshkan ship by its angular silhouette against the night sky. It began to ascend, harrier engines stirring the beach, making Scoona's windsocks snap and coil.

"Flam," Nevele tried. The rest of the group remained back while Flam marched forward, hooves crunching through the cold mainland sand. He waited at their hatch for the Adeshkan guardsmen to exit clad in thick armor of maroon, the city's color.

"Please step back, sir. We have evacuation teams coming shortly."

"I don't give a toss about evacuation teams. I want to know why the plummets you didn't do anything to help us." Flam poked the soldier's breastplate.

The few others that'd dropped out of the ship readied their weapons, safeties clicking off.

Flam stood his ground.

"We did what we could. We confirmed ten Odium ships neutralized, about half their fleet."

"Oh? Well, then, commendations all around! Good work, boys! Way to half-arse a job." Flam scoffed. "That's shite. Chidester was going to send everything after them. And I didn't see more than a handful of Adeshkan birds in the air in our neck of the woods—when we needed help most."

The guardsman pilot's boyish face, framed in the wraparound helmet bristling with antennae and various swivel-in eyepieces, held Flam's gaze, squinting. "Are you . . . head of Geyser's Patrol—?"

"Damn right I am. Sir Flam. So don't even bother with the need-to-know rigmarole. I spoke to that old cuss directly. And I thought maybe he was just trying to play the tough guy, saying he wouldn't do anything to help us. But lo and behold, just like he said, we were all on our own." Flam flung his arm toward Geyser, which was smoking on the horizon. "Even though you had *more* than enough fire-power to take the lot of them on, without difficulty. Well? Say something. Explain yourself."

"The remaining fleet had orders to stand down once the Odium got within Geyser airspace."

Flam had to resist shoving the guardsman. "Why?"

The guardsman broke eye contact, cleared his throat. "Because, per Lord Chidester's orders, that was where it stopped being Adeshka's fight, sir."

"Then what are you doing here now, after the damage is done?"

"We have an assignment." The guardsman's posture stiffened.

"And that is?"

Before he could answer, one of his fellow guardsmen pointed.

Flam turned toward his friends, who were helping Nigel with the repairs. Mindful of his various sores, he lumbered back to the group.

The guardsmen followed at a casual rate, rifles at the ready.

"What's going on?" Nevele said.

"They're here for somebody," Flam said.

At once, Aksel's face tightened. Clyde wore the same expression. It was as if they both had been watching the clock, dreading this moment.

Aksel turned to Nigel, having to tap him on the shoulder to draw his attention away.

The ex-miner sat back in his chair, arms coated in engine grease. "Aye?"

There it was again. Anytime Aksel and Nigel had an exchange, a chasm plunged between them.

"I'm sorry, mate," Aksel said.

Nigel's brow furrowed. "What for?" He turned, spotted the Adeshkans approaching. Then he gazed back up at Aksel, frowned.

Flam did too, remembering. The broadcast. There was a hefty price on Aksel Browne's head. He was a wanted man. One of the *most* wanted on Gleese, after Dreck Javelin. Flam hadn't gotten to know the blond one-eyed bloke all that well but suspected he'd been wrongfully accused. He'd fought alongside them, after all, helped greatly. How could he be working for the Odium? But Flam was coming to the realization just as everyone else probably already had. It didn't matter. If Chidester had his sights set on someone, he always got them eventually.

"You damn well know what for," Aksel said to Nigel. "Don't make me . . . spell it out. Hard enough as it is."

"The battlefield scout?" Nigel said, still confused.

"*Yes*," Aksel said, pained. "You wouldn't be in this damn thing"—he bumped the wheel of Nigel's chair with his boot—"if it weren't for me."

Nigel shook his head, laughing. "That was a mistake, lad. Nothing more."

"But you . . ."

"I'll agree, I was mad. For a long time. I blamed you. But it wasn't like ye did it on purpose. Ye didn't know that was going to happen. If ye did, I'm sure ye wouldn't've done it, right?"

"I wouldn't, no."

"Then ye don't need to carry that around anymore. I let it go. Ye should too." He wiped the grease off his hand and stuck it out for Aksel. They shook. Aksel drew in a deep breath, the sound quavering in his chest. Nigel played his own tears off as if muck from the engine compartment had gotten in his eye. They laughed, and you could almost see the weight lifting from Aksel's shoulders.

Clyde moved near the old friends. "We need to explain you weren't involved, Aksel. We need to explain you're innocent."

Aksel, oddly serene, turned to Clyde. "The Chrome Cricket in Adeshka. Front desk." He reached into his pocket and took out a small metal key with a dangling tag that read *Room 6*. "Give this to the lady who works in the pub and tell her I'm sorry, that I should've listened to her and Mum a little closer."

"What?" Clyde took the key but didn't seem to want to. "What're you—?"

Aksel interrupted, saying two numbers: "Negative nine-nine-one; positive one-two-one."

"I don't . . . What's—?"

"Coordinates," Nigel said.

"But that's clear up in the—"

"The ice caps," Aksel finished and turned to Clyde. "Go get 'em." He cuffed Clyde on the shoulder in a chummy way and shifted on one heel toward the approaching wall of marching maroon armor.

"Aksel, wait." Clyde grabbed his sleeve. "You didn't do anything wrong. We have witnesses, people who'll vouch for you. *I'll* vouch for you."

"Mate, my ticket's been punched for some time."

Clyde opened his mouth, then closed it and released Aksel's sleeve.

One of the guardsmen lifted his visor. "You Aksel Browne?"

"Aye."

Pasty darted forward, trying to get between their friend and the troops. Flam pulled him away, his dragging feet leaving dark stripes in the sand.

The guardsman fingered a holopanel floating above his wrist. There was Aksel's mugshot, from years back, and a sizeable block of text detailing his misadventures. "Been looking for you."

"I heard."

"Need the offenses read?" the guardsman said.

"Naw. I was with me."

Arching an eyebrow, the guardsman chuckled. "As you wish. We'll patch you in." He tweaked a knob on his wrist, and Aksel's rap sheet was replaced with another holo. Scribbled in at high resolution: King Seddalin Chidester, bent and robed, ruddy of face, jowly, and ginger-haired. His voice was a weathered, wheezing creak that implied long-term illness.

"Aksel Browne?"

Aksel sighed. "Again, *yes*, present."

Chidester grimaced at the bold disrespect. "How do you plead?"

"Hmm. Any recommendations?"

Chidester smacked his lips, savoring the word: "Guilty."

"Sure, okay, sounds good. I'll have that. All right, boys, you heard the man. Get on with it."

"I'll give the orders, thank you," Chidester said, paused, then gave a terse nod. "Arms."

Clyde, in Flam's grip, became a twisting flailing bundle of limbs, crying out. Nevele had to restrain him with her threads, although she too seemed to want to run to Aksel's defense. Flam didn't know him as well as they did, but he certainly didn't want to see this man die. But this was not their place. Interfering in royal machinations would only get bounties placed on all their heads. Aksel had accepted it, false accusations or not, but it was his choice, his alone. Flam told Clyde as much, but it didn't seem to comfort him any.

Under the watch of their king, projected much taller than he likely really was, the guardsmen shouldered their weapons.

Aksel thumbed his patch over so it covered his other eye and drew a deep breath, holding it. A whisper: "*Vee*—"

"Fire."

Ten shots, as one.

Flam was deafened by Clyde's scream.

Job done, the guardsmen lowered arms and turned to board their starship again, apparently intending to just leave the executed man lying on Scoona's beach, like litter.

Displaying sudden, secret strength, Clyde wrenched free of Flam.

"Chidester, where were you? Geyser needed assistance."

The holographic representation of the humpbacked king turned, surprise creasing his already rumpled, fleshy features. Then, amusement. "Clyde Pyne. Perhaps next time you might think it wise to be present when a call comes offering aid." His translucent eyes moved to Flam, behind Clyde. "Because your chief of security left something to be desired. But, I say *next time*"—his eyebrows arched—"when we both know there's not likely to be a next time, with your city so sufficiently failed. By you."

Clyde stabbed a finger toward the mountains. "The

Odium have barely left. You can get them. They can't be much more than a few miles into the Lakebed by now."

Chidester sneered. "We fulfilled our obligation. We got our man." A baggy sleeve gestured toward Aksel, dead in the sand. "What happened to your city was your responsibility. On your shoulders entirely."

"We have the Odium's coordinates," Clyde burst, nearly pleading. "We know where they're taking the deposit."

"Good for you. May the lord of light lay upon you fortunate rays." With a shallow bow, the king's holo winked out.

The Adeshkan guardsmen's ship closed up and lifted off. As it tore over the bay, its warm exhaust stirred Aksel's hair over his still face.

Flam hoisted the man up and carried him to the ramp of Nigel's ship. As he laid him down, the Bullet Eater seemed at peace. For as little as he knew him—from those days in the city square with his carts of likely stolen goods, to the fight across the city less than an hour ago—the man seemed to wear a scowl, as if he were weathering cold blasts of rain upon his shoulders only he could feel. Not now, though. To Flam, Aksel Browne looked serene.

The others congregated around him. Nigel kept a hand over his mouth, and for once the molting parrot on his shoulder had nothing to contribute. Nigel kept clearing his throat, lips under his oiled moustache tight. When Nevele tried patting his tattooed arm, he wrenched his chair's wheels about and returned to the cockpit in silence. No one followed him up there.

Flam turned to Clyde as the pale man took a seat in the holds across from Aksel. Coal-black eyes remained focused upon their friend's corpse, as if Clyde were listening to the man spin a long, harrowing story. And if he was, if Clyde's expression was any indication, it'd just reached its sad but ultimately fitting end.

"Clyde," Flam started.

"Negative nine-nine-one. Positive one-two-one," he said.

Nevele stepped close. "Clyde, we—"

"Nigel," Clyde shouted toward the cockpit, "can this thing make it to the ice caps?"

At the helm, with his back to them, Nigel wiped an eye and grunted, "We sure as hell can try." He punched in something on a keypad—the numbers.

DAY
THREE

CHAPTER 25

Sired by Stone

Pitka Gorett's eyes focused. He was in the back in the ice caps, in the hangar, starships all about him, engines still steaming. He sat up, feeling sick.

Then, refocusing, he saw he was in a circle of the pirates. In their dense winter coats, furred collars, they eyed him knowingly. Especially Dreck, who pointed at something behind Gorett. "Look."

Gorett turned. There it was. An enormous glistening blue-green rock, bigger than even he'd imagined. For so long he'd wanted this moment, to see the wendal stone with his own eyes, but now in its shadow he felt only afraid. At such a cost, they'd claimed it.

Even after he'd struggled to his feet, the deposit towered over him. They had the hangar doors open above, and the suns shined down—the stone bouncing their twin glare in green, purple, blue, shifting as he moved. Each snowflake landing upon it immediately collapsed to a drop of water.

Gorett laid a hand on the deposit. Warm.

"Don't you just want to kiss it?" Dreck said.

It'd been dragged through the sky all this way, within miles of the planet's pole, and yet it was still warm.

Heavy boots clunked up. "I know I've hardly been

kind, Pitka, but I'll allow you a final word."

Gorett turned. "Final word?"

"Nothing like this has been tried before. May not go well. Should be prepared."

"But I thought it was going to be Colin who . . ."

Colin, Dreck's right hand, grinned and shrugged.

Gorett sighed. Mother Worm had been right: this was the plan all along. He refused to be used by Dreck—or her. "I will not allow you to do this to me! Dreck? Do you hear me? We had a deal. And *no part* of it involved me being some . . . test subject for you." His rage dissolved. "You can have the whole damned deposit. I don't care. Just . . . let me go."

Dreck didn't speak until Gorett looked the pirate in the face. He squinted, disappointed. "You'd really want to leave us? Now?"

"Yes, I want to go. I know I cannot go home, since it's . . . gone"—he could scarcely believe it still—"but I want no more part of this."

"Afraid it's too late for that. You need a function, and best I can see it, this is how the goddess has assigned it. What's with the long face? If this goes well, just imagine what you might end as. Sky's the limit." His hands slipped from Gorett's shoulders, and he turned and merged back into the group of pirates. "Still, to get test results, there needs to be a test. Ernest?"

Out from the circle stepped a middle-aged man in ill-fitting clothes. He had a square face and kind, sky-blue eyes. In a thick Lakebed drawl, he said, "Hello, Pitka. If somethin' does happen to go bad, know now in advance that I apologize." Höwerglaz's focus shifted, contemplative a moment. Gorett felt the man's gaze within him, invasive. "Especially so close to yer birthday," he said finally. "Shame. Big six-oh, huh?"

"Maybe it's you I should be appealing to," Gorett said. He folded his hands and knelt at Höwerglaz's feet. "You. You can stop this. Why help them?"

As if not hearing him, Höwerglaz carried on. "Chin up. You'll get to be a kid again. A few times, actually. Rare thing." A wink. "I would know."

"What?" Gorett could only whisper, his throat dry.

Dreck nodded toward something. Gorett was afraid to look, afraid of how things could possibly get worse. It took four pirates to roll forward the glass tank filled with murky water. Affixed to the inside, apparently with waterproof tape, were fist-sized pieces of wendal stone.

"Shite's harder than cuss," Dreck contributed. "Burned out six laser picks getting even that much off."

Gorett turned back to Höwerglaz. "Please. I'm begging you. I've nothing to offer, no, but if you've any mercy . . ." Gorett sadly concluded. It was useless.

Father Time said nothing, and his face betrayed as much. Apparently he'd already come to this same summation.

And what of Mother Worm? Where was she now? If she was so powerful, couldn't she help? Gorett paced, silently calling out to her, the pirates tightening the circle to keep him from straying too far. *If you can, please, please help me.*

She answered. *It's this or death. If they're successful and you become woven, you'll already have more power than nearly everyone there with you. Imagine emerging stronger than Dreck or even Höwerglaz—the supposed most gifted of all weavers. Visualize being able to give new tinder to the anger that's been burning out the bottom of your soul.*

But I don't want to kill them, Gorett thought in reply. *I just want to—*

Go home? Your home is gone. The only thing you have now is the future or death. I promise you, I will see to it that you will have the upper hand. They destroyed your home, made your life hell for the last year. You survived, so now excel at surviving—and become the better man, in all definitions. Accept your fabrick, whatever may arise in you, and come to me, be with me, rule with me. We will own Gleese together. As it stands, those are your options.

Gorett looked at Dreck, then Höwerglaz. He could see them dead, and that possible future thrilled him. "Okay."

The water was shockingly cold. One of the pirates fed a writhing, burbling tube down to him. Gorett caught it and took a deep breath of plastic-flavored air.

He looked through the thick glass studded with taped-up hunks of wendal stone. Smeary, Dreck and Höwerglaz approached the tank. Dreck said something, talking with his hands in his usual way, put his tri-cornered hat back on, and slapped Höwerglaz's back. Höwerglaz's face pushed in close and became clear. He was mouthing something that Gorett thought looked like, "This is not for nothing," but he couldn't be certain. He motioned, trying to articulate he didn't know what Höwerglaz was saying, but the man stepped away without a second attempt.

He didn't have much time to think about it. Pain ripped through him, bolting him through from the bald crown of his head to the tips of his yellow, overgrown toenails. He bit down on the tube and was thankful it was there;

otherwise he may have crushed his few remaining teeth into powder. The pain came in waves. Gorett screamed out a torrent of bubbles. Reaching up, an inch above the waterline, he felt something hard. He saw a sheet of plywood fastened down tight. While he scrambled to push the lid off, another blast ripped through him—and he lost all strength. Agony mauled him.

Rebirth, of any kind, should never be an easy and painless process, Mother Worm intoned. *Anything worth having warrants suffering the path. A trophy shouldn't be accepted with anything but bloody hands.*

Gorett's hands drifted before his eyes. Miraculously, the liver spots one by one faded away. Deep creases shrank, the skin tautening. Fingers grew shorter and shorter, and he himself felt smaller and smaller, his legs pulling closer to his trunk. His beard, swaying like seaweed in the water, coiled up toward his chin, growing dark as it receded.

He was a boy again. A joy filled him, despite the circumstances. But much like the first time, it didn't last nearly long enough. Youth, again, was robbed from him. Returning in a blink: spotty, papery flesh. Bony fingers. Knobby, sore knees.

Then young again.

And old.

Young.

Old.

Old, young, old, young, old, young.

Then, soon, the switch was so fast he felt he was both simultaneously. Screaming, he lost the tube, fought to retrieve it. The tube, bursting bubbles into his face, grew impossible to reach as an arm became stunted—a chubby pink paw at the end of a wrist. Then, again, a gangly bony thing.

And as his eyes began to roll back in his head, he could feel it, a thundering in his chest that wasn't a heartbeat but something calling from within, deeper. Tolling from every bone, every vein, every cell . . .

The knots of wendal stone began to simmer like a stomach-soother tablet. Under their Xs of tape, they popped away with a golden flash to leave only an oily cloud that quickly dissolved to invisibility.

And when he brought his hands up again, fighting with his own writhing body, trying to block out the pain just so he could get a glimpse of what was happening to him now, to understand, they weren't an old man's hands or a baby's hands.

Höwerglaz, Dreck, and the pirates reeled—terror in every pair of eyes. Many ran.

His, now, were hands Gorett had never known. Not hands at all. No, not hands. Claws, bleeding liquid shadow.

Oh, look how beautiful we are, Pitka.

CHAPTER 26

Hero Maker's Folly

Nevele had hated FTL travel even as a child when going from planet to planet with her parents. The nausea was tolerable now, but anxiety had a stronger hold. Snapping the magazine free of her machine gun, she frowned at the six remaining bullets inside, hoping but knowing it wouldn't be enough.

The control panel beeped. Nigel pressed a button. A new holopanel manifested, shoving in among the others. In it was a vid feed of another starship cockpit. A face came into frame, and Nevele's blood immediately boiled.

Höwerglaz. Rosy-cheeked, young, but the deep exhaustion of a grizzled veteran clouded him. "Clyde? Is that y'all comin' this way?"

"What the plummets do you want?" Flam grunted.

Clyde leaned to be in clearer view of the vidscreen. His aversion was undisguised. "I think Flam here said it best, Ernest."

The ID for the starship Höwerglaz was piloting popped up in the corner of the holo. The *Magic Carpet?* Dragging a tattooed hand down his face, he glanced away from the camera to check his ship's controls—or perhaps not. Maybe he couldn't bear to look them in the eyes right now, even over ship-to-ship vid comm. "Well, even though

I said all that about takin' action, I might recommend you bench yerself for a while. It's not lookin' too good for the Odium. Might consider lettin' the problem take care of itself. Ask me, looks like it's well on its way."

"What did you do now? And why did you betray us?" Clyde snapped. "Why should we ever trust a word you say?"

Höwerglaz sighed, his blip on their radar now falling out of range and, with it, the connection between them growing fuzzy and pixilated, skipping frames. "It's like I said, son, I'm not on any one side."

"Yes, you claim you're firmly neutral. But neutrality, as I understand it, doesn't mean changing sides as you please; it means not taking one at all."

Beside Clyde, Flam nodded.

On the radar, a ship streaked past in the opposite direction. South by southwest. It's destination Nevele couldn't guess, but with so little left on the continent now except small crossroads in the desert, it stood to reason he'd seek refuge in the nation of Embaclawe. If so, the prospect terrified her. If Höwerglaz was afraid of something, anything . . . What had he done?

"Listen, we're about to lose the connection. I did what I did only because I know you can be great. I—"

"Stop," Clyde said. "Do you have any idea how many people died because you were trying to make things more interesting? Geyser fell, and we still have no idea how many people managed to get away with their lives beforehand."

"They would've sacked Geyser whether they had me or not."

Clyde sat back, mulling that.

"Mark me as one of the baddies if you need to. That's

fine. But me doin' this will align things. Trust me. Already is. This was for the best—truly—but this fight, the one yer headin' to now, isn't yers. Not yet. We let her have Dreck, and then we take her on—just, later. I am in control. I know what I'm doing." He paused, eyes fixed in a thousand-yard stare. "I knew Gorett had a worm. I just didn't think it'd end up making him into—" Frame freezing, his image became jerky.

"Wait, who are you talking about? Her who? And Gorett would become what?" Clyde leaned in. "Become *what*, Ernest?" Clyde's imagination was more than happy to provide possibilities.

Connection lost. The words replaced Höwerglaz's image on the vidscreen.

"Maybe he was actually being honest," Nevele said. "Should we just let whatever he made take care of the Odium for us? Perhaps he really does have a plan."

"If Höwerglaz was trying to make Gleese a more interesting place," Clyde said, an unsettling smirk forming, "why disappoint him?"

"Pasty. Weren't you listening?" Flam said. "*Father Time* is scared."

Nigel kept them moving north, but he eased back on the thrusters. "Ye say it, son, and I won't think ye're yellow bellied. Any fighter worth his salt knows ye need to pick yer battles."

"No. We go," Clyde said. "Trying to find a way around problems only led to Geyser being destroyed." He turned to look at Aksel under the sheet in the back. "We go."

"Aye-aye," Nigel said solemnly and triggered the FTL.

As soon as they dropped out of FTL travel, ice and snow pattered against the hull. The windows frosted over, and soon the chill bled inside the ship as well.

Nigel brought the ship about, lowering it incrementally. Trying to find a flat place to land was hard enough, but he was also fighting wind that seemed determined to fling them against sharp glacier walls.

Coming down through the blizzard, passing underneath the millennia-old storm where it was slightly less turbulent, they spotted a fissure in the ice. It was almost easy to miss with this place so uniformly white-blue. The coordinates were for the gap: inside it, apparently. Nigel pushed them on through the screaming blue mouth in the ground. The wind's howling silenced as soon as they were through, belowground.

An enormous cavern spread out beneath them, as if the glacier were an egg with a thin shell. It now made sense why no one could find this place. The Odium had discovered quite the secure hiding spot.

No gunfire drifted in. No alarms, no sounds at all. Everything was still: every piece of mining equipment, every docked starship. No one hid among the expansive field of stolen goods organized into heaped rows.

"Did they go somewhere else?" Flam suggested. "A second, double-secret base?"

Clyde went to the window. A few smaller buildings were arrayed around a larger, central one, connected by a network of glass tunnels that bounced the sunlight into incomplete dotted-line rainbows. The buildings' architecture fit this place, asymmetrical and frosty white. It was hard to tell where the man-made structures ended and the glacier began.

"Mr. Clyde, look at that," Rohm said, pointing out something portside.

Towering and watching over all was a giant metal sculpture: a woman, arms outstretched, glowing electric eyes making the flakes spiraling about her flare.

Flakes of not just snow but ash as well. The main building hemorrhaged fire from a long rip in the wall.

Nigel set the ship down at the edge of the loot field. The environment welcomed the starship with its frigid squeeze. As soon as Nigel shut off the main power, the entire ship creaked.

As Flam was about to open the rear hatch, Clyde stopped him, pointing out the control panel's reading of the exterior temperature. Sixty degrees below zero with a wind shear of negative one hundred two. "We can't go out there dressed as we are," Clyde said. He wore ripped trousers and a bloodstained jacket and poncho. Flam was in only his guardsman surcoat and trousers and no footwear. Nevele had her thin jacket, holey dungarees, and boiled-leather boots. Not a pair of gloves between them. "We'll freeze in a second."

"Nippy," Flam said humorlessly.

"At least you have fur," Nevele pointed out.

Flam moved to a window that was already nearly opaque with frost. "I wonder how long my daft old uncle managed to hold on . . ."

When Clyde sighed, his breath was a pocket-sized ghost. "We'll find him."

In what condition was left to be determined.

The six Lulomba seemed unnerved. Their Blatta had

made constant noise the entire flight. Now they were chittering and buzzing, keeping clear of the windows, congregating into a small phalanx, carapaces always touching their neighbors. Was it the cold they didn't like, so unlike the balmy climes of Geyser? Or were the insects and their keepers picking up on something the others weren't? Clyde certainly could feel the gloom of this place. Not entirely because of the cold. The tomblike silence didn't help. He stared out at the Odium base, so still, unable to imagine anything other than waiting traps within.

"I'll take 'er back up," Nigel said. "Maintain a bird's-eye view of things. Keep your radio on," he instructed Flam.

Clyde snapped to and reached for the starship's hatch handle. The moment it opened even an inch, Clyde's eyes felt frozen solid in their sockets. He winced, but there was nowhere to get away. The cold's invisible wrath gushed into the starship, lapping against them with a sharp-toothed ardor.

Together they dropped out of the ship and ran for the base's door. Clyde's lungs burned, bones ached, teeth felt as if they'd shatter if he spoke.

Nevele marched through the knee-deep snow, lugging her machine gun.

Flam, the least hindered by the snow, strode with his rifle.

Nigel took off a moment later, starship engines struggling. He passed overhead and sank out of sight around the bend of the building.

Clyde had read that Gleese's ice cap was under an endless blizzard. It was rumored to have begun with the planet's formation. He'd never expected it to be like this—so sadistic. It was as if the place itself took joy in finding people who dared to set foot there, wanted nothing but to transform the interlopers into blue-skinned statues, permanent additions.

And not even three days ago, he'd been in the desert, cursing the heat . . .

The door opened like a ship or a bank vault, with a big round wheel that had to be turned. The seal snapped, and the door came free, swept open by the wind. They rushed inside the base, and Flam pulled it closed behind them. Pirates potentially waiting for them be damned for a moment. They all fought to catch their breath and rub frozen knees and hands, summoning blood that'd retreated from fingers and ears.

Not that it was much warmer in here, but being out of the wind certainly helped.

They were alone in this small anteroom. Moving on into the first hall, Flam took the lead. They treaded softly, cautiously. A majority of the lights were out, their path lit by the white rays that managed to sneak through frosted skylights and the occasional glass tunnel. The wind continued to tear about outside as if wanting to follow them in, ice smacking and crashing as it raged. Still, it was the only sound.

"I thought the Odium was like a thousand strong," Nevele whispered. "We put a good number of them down during the attack, but it couldn't have been that many."

Clyde couldn't say for sure, but he knew he was thinking on Höwerglaz's warning again: the word *monster*, specifically. He was beginning to think maybe Flam's earlier suggestion might've been right. Maybe the Odium had abandoned this base in favor of a second, even more secret, aerie. That is, until he saw a figure at the far end of the hall turn the corner.

The person, barely discernible from the shadows surrounding, moved as if full of broken bones, movements twitchy and uncoordinated. But he didn't moan or shout in pain. Merely lumbered about, aimless, silent. Apparently the figure, a pirate, spotted them too—and at once approached in an unbalanced lope. When he passed a row of windows, a blue glare shot in on the side of his face. The man's eyes were vacant, rolled so far back they only showed whites. His mouth was slack, something black dribbling down his chin and onto his chest, leaving a splattered trail.

"What's wrong with him?" Flam said, voice hitching.

Trying to draw Commencement, Clyde found the sword was frozen into its sheath. He yanked on the handle. The blade wouldn't come free.

Nearer now, the man drew a ragged breath and exhaled a peal of anguish or anger.

Nevele opened fire, the machine gun's pops deafening in this tight hall.

All three shots struck into the pirate's chest but only made him temporarily lose his balance. He advanced, gray hands reaching—screaming, nearly as loud as the gunfire, like a wailing alarm.

Bringing his rifle overhead, Flam rushed forward and crashed the stock across the man's face. He spun, trembling palms slapping to the filthy floor, cries cutting off abruptly. He paused, then sat on his haunches, looking dazed. With the aid of the wall, fingertips blackened with frostbite, he pushed up to his feet as if drunk. Just as crookedly, he turned, blank eyes scanning, somehow perceived where his attackers were again—and reached out, screaming anew.

"Let's try that again," the Mouflon said and rewarded the man's dogged, dead-eyed efforts with a second smack. Like a fist colliding with an overripe melon, the blow sank in half of his head. He lay on the floor, feet still shuffling and fingers squirming, but then he curled into a tight ball, clutching his stomach, coughing and gagging.

As he retched violently—sending Clyde, Flam, and Nevele leaping back—a brown-black typhoon was freed from the man, settling in a broad, steaming puddle. A puddle that . . . squirmed. The man went still, but within the muck, a handful of snake-sized worms, wriggling atop each other in a loose mound, sprang awake. They raced free of the puddle in all directions.

Flam shrieked, danced his hooves back.

Nevele was about as pale as Clyde.

Rohm shivered in Clyde's protective pocket.

Clyde . . . didn't know what to think.

The worms crawled off, up and down the hall, sticking to the edges, as rats trying to remain stealthy would travel.

"What in the plummets was that?" Flam kept his distance from the dead man. "You don't suppose that's what Höwerglaz was talking about?"

"Those looked like bone worms, but I've never heard of them getting so big," Nevele said, glancing around as if sure one of the gray worms was crawling its ribbed, slimy, three-foot body up her pant leg. Her whole body shivered. With tremulous hands—either from cold or fear, Clyde couldn't tell—she checked her machine gun's magazine, frowned. "Three rounds left." She turned to Flam. "You?"

"Two."

"Fantastic," Nevele said and sighed, a white plume exiting her lips.

"So this is what happens when someone tries to make a weaver, then?" Clyde asked no one in particular, stepping closer to the worm-vacated heap on the floor with the mushed-in noggin. His eyes—Clyde only glimpsed them a second before averting his gaze—remained inflexibly wide, as if even in death he was surprised at the twisted thing he'd become.

When Flam spoke, Clyde flinched. "Let's find Dreck and Gorett and get the plummets out of here." Flam paused to work the rifle bolt. "I don't think we should spend any more time than absolutely necessary in this place."

"No argument here," Nevele said.

The ice cementing sheath and hilt together finally gave, and Commencement sang free, grating with a long *shhhing* as it tasted the stale air. Clyde held the blade in two hands, and as much as his chilled-numb legs were telling him to run the other way, he stepped on, around the dead pirate, following the worms' oily trails.

CHAPTER 27

Cannot Be Unmade

The base was enormous, and they covered the first and second story, following the worms' trail. As it lost more of its syrupy blackness, the trail began to fade. But soon auditory cues told them which way to go. A rolling murmur, like a group of people speaking under their breath, intercut with the occasional blast of a gun.

"I swear," Flam said, watching the others' backs, "if we ever see Höwerglaz again, I don't care if he's in the middle of a sit on the porcelain throne, I'll . . . I'll do something that defies words. Something *so* bad you two will probably never be able to look me in the eyes again without cringing. Something *so* bad that the primordial crone that shited him into this world won't even recognize his ugly—"

Turning the next corner, Flam fell silent.

The group stopped short.

No fewer than twenty of the plagued pirates were piled against a door. As one, they beat upon it, gathered up into a tight group, working together to try and shove themselves through the door's steel, like a living battering ram. It was metal, but they had made one dent, a triangle of open space. From within, someone was shouting.

In the gap the muzzle of a scattergun appeared, angling about blindly. The gun cracked, and one of the pirates fell away. When his back met the floor, he fell into spasms that increased in severity until, at its climax, a brown-black volcano erupted free, sending more worms raining about. The corpse deflated as it noisily emptied. The worms then gathered around the remaining diseased mob, contributing another inch to the ankle-deep mass that also aided in pushing against the door, like an ocean's waves eroding a coastline.

"And here I brought each and every one of you aboard," someone beyond the beleaguered door shouted, "giving you a home, a job—and *this* is what you do?" The scatter-gun fired again, dropping another pirate to flail and un-load his inhabitants like the one before.

The group remained at the corner, peeking around.

"That sounds like Dreck," Nevele said, hushed.

Flam grunted. "And who says the universe is unjust?"

They remained for a while, watching the diseased men crowd against their captain's chambers one slam after an-other. Every once in a while another one would join, com-ing from farther up the hall, drawn to this place by the noise. Clyde listened in between Dreck's shots, hearing footsteps above them. They were all over the place but were slowly being drawn here. If any of the plagued pirates noticed Clyde and the others, they gave no sign. They were being willed on, congregating for a purpose, for a single ob-jective: Dreck. Clyde considered how Rohm, when he was whole and one frisk mouse was separate from the others, could still see what all the members were seeing even while separated by miles. Could these parasitic worms work the same way? They certainly didn't seem to be communicat-ing by any other discernible, outward means.

"Where do you suppose Gorett's run off to?" Flam said. "In there with Dreck or somewhere else? Because if we want them alive, we might need to intervene after all . . . as much fun as it might be to let them get what's coming to them."

Nevele peeked around the corner, then pulled back. "If that's what we want to do, we'll need to act soon. That door of his won't hold forever."

Clyde ran his gaze about their surroundings.

The base was a bent horseshoe shape. Directly across the hall from their hiding place, Clyde could see out a set of frost-smudged windows: not only the sprawling icy wasteland but the room in which Dreck was hiding across the small gap. In the well-lit room, set with a giant pane of glass at his back, the bloodied pirate captain was using his flipped-up bed as a barricade in case the diseased pirates managed to break in. Kneeling behind the makeshift shelter, his hands shook as he fed shells to his scattergun. He didn't see Clyde watching him, and the moment he had his gun reloaded, he marched to the door, sweat-slicked face scowling. Clyde looked farther out, to the blowing white past the windows, seeing a glass tunnel connecting another hallway with the room Dreck was in. He wondered if the plague-ridden men had gathered at only the one door or both. He couldn't see into the glass tunnel, with it wearing a dense sleeve of ice end to end.

"Come on," Clyde said, and together they moved out into the hall, carefully plodding up the other direction. They turned a corner and went up to where the tunnel would lead them to the second door of Dreck's chambers.

Down the tunnel, it was blindingly bright with the

suns cutting in through the ice, causing refractions and brilliant little warped rainbows to puddle the floor. None of the plagued attempted to siege this entrance.

Carrying Commencement low at his side, Clyde tried shielding the midday suns with his arm, but the brightness was all around, bouncing into his eyes from the crystalline formations sleeved around the glass tube. Eyes stinging from the suns' rays, he banged on the door, beating rhythmically to let Dreck know the person outside was in fact human, still capable of more than animalistic thumps.

The reply came at once: a gunshot to the door.

Clyde leaped away. None of the scattershot had broken through, but a cluster of small dents goose pimpled their side. Keeping clear in case Dreck repeated his greeting, Clyde shouted, "You've lost, Dreck. There's nowhere to run. It's either them or us, so choose."

"Who is it?" Dreck said in a cheery falsetto.

"Clyde Pyne. Steward of—"

"Fancy this. I've got the Sequestered Son, undoubtedly accompanied by his merry band of thumb suckers, at one door and this unholy accident at the other. Gee, decisions, decisions!" Another blast rang out. "Go find the abomination Gorett turned out to be, see if you can talk any pity into him. I may have painted myself into a corner, but I'll find a way out. Always do."

Clyde turned back to the others, whispering, "Abomination?"

Flam drew a deep breath and stared vacantly.

Nevele swept a hand through her hair, gathering a handful of it and squeezing, as if to push the notion out of her head.

Höwerglaz's warning haunted them all. He'd done something to Gorett. And now Gorett was something else. What, though, was still a mystery they were all hesitant to crack.

Clyde shouted through to Dreck, "Is that what you did? Have Höwerglaz use the wendal stone on *Gorett*?"

"How many times do I have to say it? Piss." *Blam*. "Off." *Blam*. Through the clatter of reloading: "You can tell Queen Disease that she may think she's being all secretive and shite, hiding behind that cult of ninnies of hers, but I got little birdies too. I know *right* where Miss Nimbelle Winter is, and she's on my to-do list. Matter-of-fact, when I get out of this, she's going to be bumped up to priority one."

"I say we go back and join forces with the uglies," Flam said. "Help them break down the door and just let them *have* the arsehole."

"Nimbelle Winter," Nevele was saying, saucer-eyed, barely audible with a hand crushing over her mouth. "She's Queen Disease?"

"Do you know that name?" Clyde said.

Nevele's focus moved back to Clyde, as if she were surprised she'd been heard, that she'd spoken aloud. "I do, and if he's telling the truth, then . . ."

Over her shoulder, Clyde caught a glimpse of a figure at the far end of the glass tunnel. Nevele turned and raised her gun in time with Flam. Clyde stepped forward, Commencement at the ready.

A man, alone, in shadow, remained at the far end, where the sunlight didn't reach.

Tall, lithe. The illumination from the tunnel seemed to not fall upon it but pass right through it. He was blurry at the edges but with a core that seemed to pulse—solidify and drift apart, solidify and drift apart—like the disturbed floor of a muddy creek. He had an emaciated face and chest, exposed ribs, seemingly no legs, as if the torso hovered, in an armor of wispy darkness. Within the chest, something chalk white throbbed, like tree roots or some wraithlike tumor.

When Flam fired, the bullet passed through, sparking off the wall behind. The entity didn't react whatsoever, as if it weren't even aware it was being observed. Black vortexes in its gray skull stood in for eyes, mesmerizing in their ceaseless, pulling swirl.

Daring a single step forward, Clyde said, "Pitka Gorett?"

It remained still, saying nothing. It bore no features resembling him, but Clyde couldn't help but feel this was Gorett. He'd been pursuing this man for so long. He'd seen his picture plenty of times, crumpled a few copies, but he'd never actually laid eyes on him. And, really, if this thing before him now was Gorett, he never would see him alive—for this thing seemed not of blood and bone, just living smoke.

When it spoke, its voice was so low-pitched it was nearly incoherent. "The Pyne boy." It had an almost effeminate lilt to it, unlike the recordings of Gorett's speeches. Not his voice—*if* it was him—but another's.

"You need to call off the men you've . . . possessed," Clyde said, unable to find a better term, "and come with us to Adeshka. You're guilty of usurping the crown from Francois Pyne, hiring an assassin to kill both him and Albert Wilkshire, and most of all aiding in the destruction of Geyser." With one hand still blocking out the blinding rays, Clyde used the other to present Commencement as authoritatively as he could. "There's nowhere left to run."

Ignoring the threat, the entity moved into the tunnel with them but immediately shirked back, a scrap of its darkness fizzling away. Its eyes of eddying pitch studied the ice, the glass, and the light passing through—and didn't dare a second attempt.

"Come out, Dreck," it murmured at length, apparently not needing to move its jaw to speak. "Accept your quietus."

Behind them, Clyde heard Dreck rustling about. "Is that him? Is that you, Gorett? How are you liking it, being a weaver? I bet you regret all that shite you said about us before, don't you? Not so easy, is it? Think you and her pulled a fast one on me, working together? You're twice a traitor, I hope you know. The Goddess has a particularly deep place in the junk heap for tossers like you—nothing but beds of barbed wire and battery acid rivers."

The swirling gray on the entity's left shifted, like wind cutting through ash. For an instant Clyde could see a word glowing, as if it'd been written upon the being's soul. *Trayter?*

"Assist us, Pyne," it said. "He is the true threat here."

"Go ahead. Bark all you want," Dreck shouted, "but you showed your hand a bit prematurely, jumping back like that when I blew the armory. Explosion didn't do anything, so I knew you couldn't be harmed that way, but the hole it made sure had an effect. It's the light you don't like. Your fabrick's flip side, your curse. And if it's one thing any weaver knows, it's to never let anyone know your flip side if you can help it."

Clyde took stock of where his feet were. He was four paces from the edge of the tunnel, where the sunlight made a vague line Gorett didn't dare pass, if it was Gorett. He still wasn't sure why he was referring to himself as *us*.

Its whirlpool eyes settled on Clyde again. "David Joplin—or Dreck, as you know him—took from me just as Gorett took from you," the entity said. "Aid us."

It made a soft choking sound. Skeletal, long fingers clutched at its gray rib cage. It tipped its head as if in a great deal of pain. The ashy mass within, where a heart should have been, gave great heaving pulses—then slowed again. The entity stood upright and looked about, as if surprised to find itself here. When it noticed Clyde, its voice changed— even deeper than before, more like the Gorett whose voice Clyde knew from his archived speech recordings.

"Clyde Pyne?" Again, the entity coughed, its edges going wild for a moment, a riot of sharp edges, then smoothing back to a cloak of ever-shifting dark whorls. The female voice again: "Break open the door, boy. Bring him to us, and we'll allow you the pleasure of watching him die."

It was as if it had two minds.

Nevele stepped forward. "Are you Nimbelle Winter? The teacher, at Srebrna Academy?"

The entity's gaze icily slid to Nevele. "How . . . do you . . . ?"

Nevele sank back.

Clyde flashed upon her story, the one that'd saved his life in Nessapolis. Nevele raised the machine gun, training it upon the shadow creature. "I trusted you to take care of her."

It stared at Nevele with eyes that didn't blink, unreadable. "Zoya. You brought me Zoya, didn't you?" It sounded pleased. "I should thank you for her."

"What'd you do with her?" Nevele demanded.

"She's still a student. Doing well, I might add. High marks all around." If it was going to expand upon that, the entity never had a chance.

The door opened behind them, and Dreck stepped into view in the hall.

The Nimbelle/Gorett creature's edges went into a frenzy of darting spikes, eyes growing into enormous gray-black storms, nearly overtaking the entirety of its bony face. "I'll kill you," it screamed.

Dreck, almost heedlessly, brandished his scattergun. "Down." He aimed at Nevele, who reluctantly raised her hands after tossing down her machine gun.

Flam slowly turned in place with his rifle held at waist height.

Unfortunately, Dreck noticed. "Nope. Drop it, Mouflon. On the floor." Dreck pulled back the hammer of his scattergun. "Your sort might be tough, but not this tough—not at this range."

Flam grumbled something and clunked his rifle onto the glass floor.

"Good boy." Finally, Dreck came up to Clyde, standing before the swirling thing trapped where it was. The pirate captain smiled. His lip was split, and he bled from a gash on his neck. He was so close Clyde could smell him: sweat, grease, and gunpowder. He slung his arm over Clyde's shoulder as if they were old friends, peering indifferently at the entity as it raged back and forth just outside its invisible barrier. Just sunlight—that's all that was keeping it back.

Now's your chance, Clyde thought. *Act. Do something.*

"See that, boy?" Dreck said. "Gorett-slash-Queen-

Disease here doesn't like the light. Not one little b—"

Clyde brought Commencement around, intending to drive its point into Dreck's ribs.

The pirate was quick. He threw his free hand in front of the slashing green blade.

The sword stopped as if hitting a tree trunk. Dreck held it locked where it was in space, his open palm spread before it, not even touching. Eyeing Clyde, Dreck flexed his index finger, just a twitch really, and Commencement broke apart, raining down in green metal mulch, leaving Clyde only the hilt.

"Nice try."

The double-voiced entity continued shrieking, "I'll kill you, I'll kill you," until it blended into a single sound: "Ki-lyukilyukilyukilyu." Sometimes, apparently, they thought as one in this shared body—and at other moments, they clicked in and out of the smoke-ghost shell independently. Detached some moments, unified others.

Out of the room Dreck had emerged from came a loud bang. The plagued pirates rushed their way.

With a toss of his hand, Dreck reassembled Commencement. "Just remember who's full of ick and who isn't."

Accepting the sword, Clyde almost bolted ahead, passing over the line of light on the floor, into the shadow creature's waiting hands. He turned to Dreck, who wheeled on his heel and fired past Nevele and Flam into the flood of black-dribbling pirates.

"Trapped, trapped, trapped," Nimbelle/Gorett cheered.

Dreck threw the scattergun down and raised an empty hand.

The first pirate nearly reaching Nevele splattered

apart, meat cubes rolling between her feet. Nevele kicked away the ones that settled on her boots.

Flam snatched up his rifle and, with his final shot, took out one of the nightmares before it could grab him—and used the gun like a club on the next.

Nevele sent out one lash of threads after another, cutting deep bloody swaths into the sea of oncoming bodies, distributing plague-blackened viscera onto the glass walls, floor, and ceiling.

The four were pushed back by the ceaseless onslaught, until they all had their heels on the edge behind them. The entity reached as far as it dared before the sunlight seared its hands. They were slowly being pushed back, with more and more of the plagued pirates coming in. Behind him, past Nimbelle/Gorett stirring at the tunnel's edge, the sound of pirates came around from the other side. They, unlike their maker, suffered no ill effects from Aurorin and Teanna's light.

Dreck and Clyde were killing them as fast as they were coming, but each one that fell sprang a dozen or more black worms. Several of them attempted to climb Clyde's leg, forcing him to stop worrying about the pirates for a moment to peel another slimy thing off. Each was hard to grab, and once in his clutch it writhed and twisted about. One even tried looping itself around his arm to continue ascending him. He threw it to the floor and stabbed Commencement into the end he assumed was its head.

The carnage raged on, their small pocket of space in the hallway reducing as more plagued pirates rushed in. Dreck turned and fired through Nimbelle/Gorett to kill those now coming from that direction. Nevele and Flam took care of those flooding in through Dreck's chamber from the opposite end. Clyde killed the worms that came their way, those his friends—and Dreck—hadn't noticed while they fought off the larger, bipedal enemies.

Nimbelle/Gorett spoke to him, his back nearly within its reach. He could feel its radiating coldness on his spine, the smell wafting off it like sour sickness, contagious hopelessness. It spoke in its own voice alone now, the stronger of the two that could apparently shove Gorett aside when it wished. "Ernest is using you, Pyne," she whispered. "Tells you not to come to a place and you do, because he knew you would. Tells you that you need to act and you don't, because he knows you won't. You're obstinate; I'll give you that much. But in reality, you're not much harder to steer than a horse with a carrot."

The pirates kept coming in a constant wash as if being freed from a faucet. Clyde kept stabbing and slicing the worms, unable to ignore Nimbelle Winter as she whispered behind him, inches away.

"Why do we build sand castles? To kick them over. And what do you think life is to someone as old as he? We're all his playthings, his amusements. And when he's done with you, he'll find someone else to fix with puppet strings. But since you came here even though he said not to, I can assist. I can be your true friend here. Turn around, give David—Dreck—there a shove so I can end him, and I'll let you and your friends live. The pirate deserves it, Pyne. You'll be doing Gleese a favor. And I assure you, if Höwerglaz had found himself in my position, he'd sooner let you die. I, however, am being most kind."

Clyde turned to Dreck, who was busy putting down a

pirate—smashing its head in with his gun's spiked pommel. He was distracted. He'd never even know it was coming. Two hands to his side, one shove toward Nimbelle/Gorett, and Clyde could avenge Geyser. And maybe she'd keep her word, call off the plagued. Or maybe not. But was justice worth the act? Dreck cared nothing for his own life. He'd welcome death. But living out the last of his years in Adeshka's underground prison? That'd be a fitting end for the likes of him, one that didn't involve ending any life.

"Do we have a deal?"

One of the plagued ran at Flam, who was already busy dispensing another. Frustrated, Flam grabbed the oncoming pirate, hoisted him over his head, and slammed him headlong into the floor. The pirate, like the others, shed its worms upon its carcass, but as the worms spread away, cracks splintered the glass floor as well. The ice was all that was holding the tunnel together for a moment, before everyone began to slide on the leaning, breaking panels—right toward the hole in the floor as it sprang apart, shattering under them.

Clyde fought to find Commencement among the blocks of ice and glass and the swallowing snow. While the entity that'd spawned them couldn't chase any farther, the pirates could. They streamed out of the hole Flam had made, raining down all around them, just as one pirate sprang out next to him. Nevele snatched its head off its shoulders with her threads before it could bite into Clyde. Together they pulled themselves from the snow, then got Flam. Dreck had already pulled himself free and was running away, leaving the others to their fate. More pirates flooded from the hole in the glass tunnel, Nimbelle/

Gorett roaring with dissatisfaction from above, trapped where they were, in the shadows.

Clyde, Nevele, and Flam charged away, lungs burning and eyes tearing up from the cold and brightness, to the clearing behind the base.

"This way," Dreck shouted. They reached where he'd fled, at the feet of the Mechanized Goddess. They put their backs to one another, as from every door, window, and blasted hole in the surrounding buildings came more and more of the plagued Odium.

They came stumbling and dragging broken limbs, eyes uniformly rolled back into heads, hands reaching, drooling blackness staining the snow at their feet. Clyde felt something bump into him, realized it was Dreck who was backing away too. The pirate captain must've, for all his power, still had a zero point to his gift—and it'd been reached. Each swing toward one of his former peons was fruitless. None scattered into bloody cubes as before, only shed the snow gathered on their faces or shaved away a scrap of beard or tatty clothing. They marched inward, from all sides, unhindered, moaning, seemingly wanting nothing more than to infect.

Looking back from where they'd run, Clyde could see through the crystalline covering of the tunnel as the figure stood watching from afar. Clyde held Commencement in two hands. He was not yet willing to think they were safe from it. He could almost feel its eyes on him, in him. He imagined it dropping out into the sunshine that allegedly pained it, willing to cope if it meant finally reaching them.

The pirates continued to close the circle, droning, tripping in the deep snow, swelling from their mouths papillae-like fingers, the worms ready for new hosts . . .

From Flam's radio: "Get down!"

Sweeping overhead, Nigel swung low, raking gunfire through the plagued—downing them ten at a pass. Nevele pulled Clyde aside as another line of erupting snow passed, scattering the encroaching pirates into black mist.

The moment a line was broken in the circle, Dreck stole through, bolting across the sparkling snow. From its dark perch, Nimbelle/Gorett let out a screech, tracing the pirate captain's escape, reaching but unable to chase— held where it was by the sunlight. Apparently deciding the fight was over, it began breaking down from the edges, the darkness collecting in its middle. It lowered its hands, the staring gray rictus fading. The tight black sphere it became shrank and shrank until it was a pinprick, then nothing. A soundless pop signaled its departure.

Nigel hammered down gunfire. When the next sweep passed, Clyde ran after Dreck, feet and hands numb, his throat raw from the cold. The suns' rays bounced off the ice and made it almost impossible to see. Most likely, Dreck had run this direction for this very advantage.

Fighting to get even one breath in without choking on it, Clyde chased on, only able to discern the vague shapes of his friends as they leaped over the ring of corpses of the collapsed pirates. Dreck was leading them into the piles of snow-buried junk heaps, small metal mountains dotting the base's backyard. He dodged past tanklike earth-moving equipment, bounding through the piles of junk and stolen goods only he knew the best way through and across. It was clear he had home field advantage here. They were unquestionably on his turf.

Nevele fired out her threads after him, hoping to catch him around the ankle. The first shot slapped the scatter-gun from Dreck's hand, sending it spiraling into a mound of junk out of reach.

Dreck was ready for it, and he moved aside to let the barreling multicolored column of cotton, leather, and wool stream past him.

Nevele's barrage collided with the arm of a power shovel and knocked it away. The small mountain of jewelry it was keeping chocked up crumbled.

Clyde dashed past before it could avalanche over him. So did Nevele, but Flam was caught by the glinting, golden flow, buried under a billion spots' worth of pilfered pretties—probably how most treasure hunters wanted to leave this world, but Clyde raced back to help him.

Nevele was already flinging aside handfuls of the flashing jewelry and heirlooms to get at the Mouflon below. "Just go," she shouted to Clyde. "I'll get Flam. Stop Dreck before he can get away."

He didn't want to leave his friends behind. He sheathed Commencement to aid Nevele, discerning by the Mouflon's grunts where he was under the bauble heap.

Nevele took his wrist. "Clyde. Get Dreck."

CHAPTER 28

Showdown under Ceaseless Suns

Clyde had to take two strides for every one of the large man's. He followed the dotted line of deep footsteps in the snow, having to cup his hand against the suns to see where they led. Finding the trail again, he carried on, weaving between the heaps of rusty refuse, trash, an entire pile of nothing but not-yet-cracked safes.

Ahead, in the shadow of one of the larger piles of pilfered things, something slowly accumulated substance in a puff of dark that swirled and grew into a human figure. Clyde brought Commencement up.

"Killing David Joplin," it rumbled, coalescing complete, "would be doing me a favor, I'll admit, but it'd also cause you problems, Pyne. My revenge outweighs yours." It coughed, its edges going spiky for a moment, then softening again. "We haven't much to offer, except for you and yours to be spared, overlooked when the time comes."

"What are you talking about?"

With a bony hand, it made a noncommittal sweep traced by an arch of black steam. "What Drcck's men became—more of that. We can turn a blind eye to you, spare your friends and family from servitude, if you agree to a different role."

"What? Willingly become one of those things?"

"No," it said. Was that a smile? "Not that. Sully those fair features of yours? Banish the thought. No, keep David alive for us, keep him prisoner here long enough that we can dispatch someone to collect him. Consider your re-imbursement no servitude—being overlooked during the coming blight."

"If any of Gorett is in there with you," Clyde said, "I'd never side with you. Nor will I allow Dreck to escape now that we've finally cornered him."

What am I going to do now? He didn't know, but allowing anyone Gorett had sided with to win didn't interest him. How many times was he going to change sides? How long could he run? Where would he go next when this new pact inevitably failed too?

The entity stared, its fleshless face betraying nothing. "Fine," it said at last, "Kill the pirate, but consider the offer rescinded. He was ours, and you, in taking his life, will simply replace him. You'll be swept in with every other one on Gleese. But remember, Pyne, when it takes you and everyone around you, we offered a pass."

It curled up on itself, folding into a black dot, and disappeared.

Clyde lowered his sword, staring at the now-unoccupied space. Had he just made a terrible mistake? Could Gorett and whoever was copiloting that monster really do what it'd done to the pirates elsewhere, to others?

"Maybe we should've listened to her," Rohm said, muffled within Clyde's pocket.

"Maybe," Clyde said after a couple of false starts. His teeth chattered. Tucking his chin into the collar of his jacket and bringing up his hood, they pushed on deeper into the rows of tall loot mounds.

They'd cross that bridge when they came to it. Shielding his eyes again, he continued searching for Dreck—or David Joplin, his real name, supposedly.

Snow fell upon a clearing amongst the high loot piles, a meadow of undisturbed white.

Ahead was a shallow indentation in the ground, a round metal pit. It had a split up the middle, closed fast, striped in cautionary black and yellow. The door to the belowground hangar, Clyde assumed, walking its edge, keeping his eyes peeled for the slightest bit of motion. He scanned the surrounding piles, the crane towers, and their stretching rusty booms. No sign of Dreck anywhere. He'd lost the footprint trail. The pirate must've doubled back somewhere.

"See anything?" he asked Rohm.

"No." His voice was small. He was freezing. They had to get this over with now and get back in, where it was warm. "I'm feeling very tired, Mr. Clyde. And I think that's probably a sign of hypothermia setting in."

"I know. I'm sorry . . . We need to find Dreck before he gets away, though."

"I agree. I wasn't suggesting otherwise. I'll hold on for as long as I can." Rohm's small quivers in Clyde's pocket, right over his chest, were slowing. No longer a constant quaking but an infrequent thrum, dulling with each pulse.

They pressed on.

The cold was making his knees creak like rusty hinges. He tried to catch his breath, but everything deeper than a slow, small inhale would make him cough raggedly. Commencement felt like it'd be permanently affixed to the palm of his hand. He turned around. Everything looked the same. He couldn't even see the base anymore through the drifting curtains of continuous snowfall. He decided to follow the loot field's edge and start making lefts to hook back around.

Upon reaching the far corner, Clyde came to a pile of swords. Varying types and sizes, mostly rusted to uselessness.

The heap rustled. Clyde raised his own steel, which was entirely unlike any in the snow-dappled pile. From the other side, Dreck climbed to the top, frost in his beard that crackled away when he smiled. He turned a heavy device at hip level toward him, what looked like a portable cannon with a small sphere affixed to its end. The reflective orb slowly spun free of the cannon's muzzle.

For a moment, neither man—the one above or the one below—said anything.

"Who is she?" Clyde shouted up. He hated having to pose anything but blows to the pirate, but he was afraid he wouldn't learn any other way.

"Nimbelle? Her parents oh so generously gave me my first ship. All that you see around you is thanks to her folks' contribution."

"Who is she now? You called her—"

"Queen Disease. Made something of herself, it seems. Which, I guess I'm partly responsible for. No shortage of trying, certainly, plaguing my men like she'd been . . . of course, that was a lot less vile than the new breed she's got now." He paused. "Surely you've heard of her and all her . . . followers, zealots. No? Never heard of that outfit of hers, the Sign of the Wyrm? Or what their goal is?"

"No."

"The bone worms are *wyrms*, as in dragons. Not as romantic as springing out from volcanoes like in the stories, no, but from an equally fiery place—men. And with each mutation the worms go through, each host they take and then spread to the next, they're one step closer to that of their ancestors—*before* the Great Snuffing, of course. And maybe I knew Gorett still had a worm in him when I had Höwerglaz do what he did. Maybe I *wanted* to see if she could succeed. Shite, *I* barely know what I'm after half the time." He paused to grin. "But I'm going to assume by the look on your face that all this about worms, wyrms, and dragons is news to you."

"Yes."

The pirate shrugged. "Damn shame you won't get to see any of it, should it happen." Dreck fired the ball, sending it darting toward Clyde, making a harmless pop as it was sent flying.

Jumping aside, Clyde watched as it bounced across the landscape behind him, hitting the snow once and bounding high. In the middle of its arc, it suddenly struck still in the air as if it'd hit an invisible wall of glue.

A low hum—and a portion of the sword pile leaped away from under Dreck's feet in a dizzying, clattering sweep. The mass raucously collected around the ball, armoring it in a dense, bristling coating—thicker and thicker.

With one pull on the cannon, the bristling boulder began rolling—following the dragging gesture orders of its commander, jangling as it raced toward Clyde over the frosty ground, leaving a gouged trail in its wake.

Dodging free of its trajectory, Clyde felt he hadn't been fast enough when the enormous wad of forsaken weaponry scraped along his side, a dozen blades dragging dull edges across his flank, arm, and waist. Hissing at the pain, Clyde flung himself away before the sword sphere could roll over him on its next pass.

It rumbled off, bounced with a clang when it hit the rim of the hangar door, stopped in its terrible trek, and began rolling back. Gaining momentum with terrifying speed, it tossed sparks as it ricocheted off metallic debris, pinballing among the loot piles.

Feinting to the left, then the right, Clyde dove aside, and felt the ground shake as it trundled past.

While it raced off to a safe distance, Clyde stole the moment to pick up a sword from the fringe of the pile, craned back, and flung it up toward Dreck. The rusty short sword floppily flew, and Dreck only had a second to react. He brought the cannon up in front of his face, and the sword bounced off with a clang. The sword boulder crumbled, the fist-sized ball inside shedding its dense, rotten-metal skin.

Charging down the heap, kicking blades out ahead of him, Dreck leaped the last few yards, bringing down a sword retrieved from the pile.

Commencement up, the blades connected, crashing.

Dreck, a head taller than Clyde, continued to press down with his own blade, pushing Clyde to his knees. Over the nicked blade, Dreck snarled, weighing himself behind his. Clyde pulled Commencement, the blades sparked apart, and he rolled aside.

Dreck charged in again at once, swinging a diagonal swipe. Clyde deflected, leaped back again, spun, and attempted a riposte. Blocking the jab, Dreck quickly replied with a swing of his own.

The blades met.

Both men pushed away, scrambled back, and circled one another, breathing hard, drawing a ring of footprints in the muddy frost, passes eclipsing each other.

"You kill me, you'll lose an ally," Dreck said between foggy puffs of haggard breath. "I'm the only one who can help you find her. You want to spare everyone on this rock from becoming like my boys, it'd be wise to keep me around."

Clyde moved in, feigned high and came in low for a swipe at Dreck's middle.

The pirate jumped back and deflected by adding a smack behind Commencement's momentum—nearly throwing the blade out of Clyde's numb hands. Dreck allowed Clyde a small window to recover, continuing to circle him, sword low in one hand, body turned partly away: a fencer's stance.

With his free hand, he worked the cold-pinked digits open and closed. When he thrust an open hand toward Clyde, he dodged, a portion of the junk heap behind him dissolving into portioned cubes.

Dreck attempted one throw of his fabrick again and again, Clyde narrowly moving aside each time—except for one, when his leg was winged by the Fractioner's effect. He stumbled, the pain waking up his frozen limb, a shallow square divot stolen from his calf. Blood dribbled, leaving rubies in the snow and ice—but he continued to circle, trying to coax the pain away so he could move in for a plunging attack. He charged, throwing Commencement's blade in high, angling for Dreck's throat.

The pirate swatted the attack away with his free hand

and brought his own blade down, dragging it the length of Clyde's back. Agony. But—without hesitation—Clyde turned, stabbing low.

Dreck deflected again. Clang. And again and again. Clang, clang.

A blade came down onto Dreck's right, slicing into his bicep. The pirate yelped and wheeled away, swinging back at whoever had just dared to do that. It hadn't been Clyde.

Not willing to let Dreck out of his sight for even a moment, Clyde glanced—and saw Greenspire emerging from behind the sword pile. The ancient Mouflon wielded a claymore in one hand as if it weighed nothing, his other bulky arm pulling a swaddled bundle tight to his chest. Head tipped, he tracked Dreck by his crunchy footfalls and exhausted breathing.

Dreck was equally bewildered. "Where the hell did you come from?"

Stealing the chance, Clyde issued a backhanded swing. This time he connected, catching Dreck across the chest. The blade cut open his coat, the long slit spilling bloodied clots of goose down. Dreck hissed but still managed to move when Greenspire brought down a high, powerful swing.

Dreck deflected the strike, but the force of impact knocked him back, breaking his stance.

Stealing this opening as well, Clyde plunged Commencement forward, Dreck narrowly dodging with a sideways hop.

Together Clyde and Greenspire, with the swaddled hybrid infant clutched to his chest, continued to push Dreck back. They kept the pirate busy deflecting right, left, left, right, left, a rapid, broken beat of steel on steel, skidding apart, meeting again.

The crusher of men, with compound eyes, humanlike features intermingled with pincers and a platelike organic armor, could be seen when the infant's swaddling fell away as his elder charged at Dreck. It seemed wholly indifferent to the fight, possibly even asleep.

"He will mend the whole of Gleese, even if you kill me," Greenspire said, nodding horns at the infant in his arm. "Your blood will fuel the start of this planet's recovery."

"Ha, a horrid little bug baby drink my blood? I think not!" Dreck swung, and when an opportunity arose, he planted a boot into Greenspire's middle, shoving him back.

Clyde saw it coming as Dreck drew his hand in close to his side—and then thrust it forward—but he could do nothing to stop it.

The pirate's fabrick tore into the old Mouflon, barreling into his broad, furry abdomen. At once, Greenspire's belly was broken down into cubes, deeper and deeper. Clyde could see the other side of him as soon as the hole broke him down from front to back. Greenspire let out not a sound, a shout, nothing—merely dropped to the snow, the crusher of men tumbling from his hands, rolling away.

Dreck barreled forward, his sights on the squirming, now bawling infant, his sword high.

Clyde rushed, met him, putting himself between them. He came in swinging low, catching Dreck across the knee with a panicking swipe. He could feel the gritty scratch in the handle as his blade dragged bone. Dreck shouted out; the sword he'd intended to chop the child to pieces with fell as he dropped to all fours.

Clyde readied Commencement—and himself—to

bring the blade down on the back of Dreck's waiting, exposed neck. *Act*, he heard in his mind, considering it, even if it was advice from a man as deceitful as Höwerglaz. *I have to do this . . .*

But even if he was ready, he hesitated and it was long enough. Bolting up with a backhanded swing of a fist, Dreck caught Clyde across the jaw. Losing Commencement, the emerald-green blade sinking into the snow, Clyde fell in beside it on his back, tasting blood.

Dreck fell atop him, pinning his knees into Clyde's shoulders. Blood and melted snow dripped onto Clyde's face as Dreck squeezed his hands around his throat. Dreck's lips peeled away as he stared down at Clyde, the pirate's head backlit into shadow by the suns above. Framed in the glacier's fissure, it looked like an eye with two pale irises. Watching, apathetic.

The darkness swallowing Dreck's face spread as Clyde fought for breath, feeling the heat swell in his cheeks as the trapped blood battled to get back to his brain, hands slapping around uselessly at his sides.

With a screeching war cry, Rohm pushed out from Clyde's pocket, raced up Dreck's arm, neck, and across his cheek—and buried teeth into Dreck's eye. It made a sound like a bursting grape as Rohm continued to push his head in, snapping and tearing and nearly entering Dreck's skull entirely as if chasing the blood in.

Clyde fought to find Commencement while Dreck was preoccupied, but amongst all the churned snow and earth, he couldn't.

Dreck caught Rohm in one hand, his ruined eye painting a red river down his face. His remaining peeper was full of rage as his hand squeezed around Rohm tighter and tighter.

The frisk mouse cried out . . .

Clyde spotted something flashing in the suns amongst the broken snow and ice. Grabbing it up, hoping it was a sword, he struggled when he found whatever it was to be much heavier. The magnet cannon. The chrome sphere darted out of the sword heap and slapped to the end of the barrel, ready.

He turned, trained its end on Dreck.

Dreck saw what Clyde had in his hands.

A blood-soaked Rohm, stealing the opportunity with the pirate captain's distraction, wriggled free and leaped aside.

Clyde pulled the trigger. The cannon lurched in his hands, the ball careening toward its target.

Dreck threw out a hand to cube the magnet ball as it raced toward him. He wasn't fast enough. The shining metal sphere smacked into his palm with a fleshy crack. Peering down at it in his pink-fingered clutch, dripping melted snow, Dreck sighed.

"May the Goddess junk me—"

A whirlwind of swords broke free of the nearby pile. A slithering, jangling river of steel plunged toward him, the magnet's holder. The blades turned and wheeled about the others that'd reached him before, crushing inward tightly. Quickly covered, Dreck let out a scream from somewhere within as the mass clenched and clenched, every rusty blade fighting to get closer to the magnet ball than its fellows, crushing themselves in their determination.

The round heap of swords gave a small tremor, blades clinking, then went still. A few of the bent steel bristles dropped red into the snow.

The magnet cannon clattered at Clyde's feet. He took one step forward, then another, the forgotten cold racing back in around him, harsher than before. His various cuts sang out, each breeze across them excruciating. Nausea flooded him, and he fought to keep himself standing. He picked Rohm up from the snow, finding the white frisk mouse easily by how much red he was covered with. They exchanged a look—pure exhaustion—and after thanking him, voice weak, Clyde returned him to his pocket.

He looked away from the end he'd delivered upon Dreck Javelin, noticing the insect baby had rolled from Greenspire's clutch that now wasn't so snug.

It ran its barbed hands over the Mouflon, ruffling the fur about his neck and face. It made small chattering coos, poking and prodding but eliciting no reaction. It managed to get him halfway rolled over in an impressive display of strength before the ancient Mouflon flumped back again. It picked up the red dice scattered about, trying to arrange them back as they had been connected. It dropped them into the gaping cavity.

Clyde approached, and before he was even three strides within Greenspire's inert form, the crusher of men turned on him, hissing. Pincers spread, flashing several rows of small, sharp teeth.

"He was a friend," Clyde attempted.

Whether or not it understood, it gave no indication. It dropped itself onto Greenspire, squeezing its keeper, softly weeping, still not quite ready to give up.

"Clyde?" came blaring through the icy wind. Flam. Clyde met him in the middle, hands out to keep his friend from seeing.

Nevele followed.

Flam's gaze was locked on the sight ahead.

There was no way to hide what had happened. Clyde dropped his hands to his sides.

Flam stopped short, staring past Clyde.

"Is . . . is that . . . ?"

"He—"

Flam looked down at Clyde, lips quivering. "Is he . . . ?"

Clyde swallowed.

Flam moved around Clyde and went plodding toward Greenspire.

The hybrid child screeched at Flam when he got too close to Greenspire.

Flam grabbed the baby roughly, pinning its six arms to its side, holding it in the air and shaking it. "This is all your doing, you little shite."

The hybrid child screamed out, writhing and twisting, half its wings still trapped.

Clyde and Nevele rushed up. "Flam!"

"You and the Lulomba—you turned him crazy down there, down in the Meech-damned depths, making him believe all this garbage about prophecies and pilgrimages and equilibrium and—"

"Flam, stop," Clyde shouted. "He didn't do anything."

The green infant broke free, flitting over the junk heaps. Clyde couldn't be sure if he heard bawling or if it was just the wind as the hybrid child crookedly fluttered away.

Crunching down beside his uncle, Flam pulled the slumping Mouflon to his chest. Flam howled, pawing over him as if it'd all be okay if he could just get him to sit up. Flam continued just as the hybrid child had done a moment ago. The cubes that'd been dropped back into him tumbled out, and Flam did the same in attempting to collect them, scooping the half-frozen dice and pushing them back into the perfectly square, no-longer-bleeding wound.

"Flam, I'm sorry," Nevele tried, "but we need to get out of this cold."

"Give him a moment," Clyde said, guiding her aside. He was unsure what to do to comfort Flam—if anything could be done.

One of Greenspire's belt pouches had come free, some pieces of rough parchment growing dark wicking up melted snow. Each held what was obviously writing in a blind man's hand. Clyde said nothing of them for the time being, merely stuck them inside his jacket to dry.

CHAPTER 29

Good-byes Are Hard

They laid Greenspire on the floor inside the Odium's silent base. Clyde took off his cloak and draped it over Greenspire, covering him to the neck. While unclasping it from himself, he heard the pages crunch in his pocket. He delicately handed them to Flam. "These fell out of his pocket."

Flam quickly skimmed the pages. He frowned at some lines, smiled a little at others, and brought a hand to his mouth when he crossed a particular passage.

"What'd he say?" Clyde said.

Flam lowered the parchment. "Usually, when a Mouflon meets the morning suns and writes to someone, it's to a deceased family member. But these are all to me. But, really, when you read Meech's book of ways, it says any family member you've lost touch with, not necessarily dead, as most folks assume . . . I never thought he cared we'd lost touch or didn't see eye to eye on his whole pilgrim thing or . . ."

Nevele put a hand on Flam's wrist.

"I'm okay. It's just . . . surprising is all. Especially this one, with the ink still wet. He must've written it only a couple of hours ago, while hitching a ride up here." He chuckled at the insanity of Greenspire's bold move.

While searching the remainder of the base, they came across more of the dead pirates lying in groups, black blood splattering the floor about them, the worms that'd managed to break free of their hosts scattered in inert black ropes about them. Clyde and the others gave the bodies a wide berth when passing.

Reaching a large open gate in one of the lower levels, since there were few other places remaining to explore, they took the elevator down.

The underground hangar had only a few lights on, and the deposit was partly illuminated, making it seem much larger than it probably was. Standing six of Flam high and what Clyde estimated to easily be an entire city block wide and deep, the deposit was impossible to miss. It took up so much of the hangar's floor space that all the remaining parked starships nearly touched the distant walls to allow it space. The hybrid child, who'd apparently found his way back in, sat atop it, not looking their way even as they walked up. He just continued staring off into space, his small sobs echoing. Losing Greenspire must've inspired it to find the next closest thing resembling home—the wendal deposit.

"How are you, little guy?" Flam asked, the corners of his lips tightening with visible regret.

While Flam stood below the hybrid child, talking up to it in soothing tones, Clyde took a look about the area surrounding the deposit. There'd been a glass tank of some kind, now reduced to shards and puddles of water going glassy with creeping ice. Next to it, on the side of the deposit, one section looked shinier than the others, the surface less craggy. It'd been chipped at, as evidenced by the broken set of jackhammers cast aside on the floor, the chiseling tips of both crushed to useless nubs.

Circling to the other side, he found Nevele eyeing another section that looked similar but chipped deeper into the deposit. Apparently not with efficient digging tools but what looked like one patient scrape after another with rudimentary handmade implements. It formed a sort of shallow hole, where inside was a makeshift tent fitted snugly with a wooden frame and canvas walls, padded with fur blankets. Comforts one would never need in the warmth of the Geyser tunnels' depths but would if, say, the deposit were hauled somewhere like one of the planet's ice caps.

"He knew what they were going to do," Nevele said, backing her head out of the small hiding place. "But how? *We* barely knew before it was too late."

As Clyde was about to shrug, Flam came around the far end of the deposit. The hybrid baby tottered behind at a cautious but curious distance. "Greenspire said the Lulomba had a seer," Flam said. "Thought it was a bunch of crap, myself, *but* . . ." He reached one hand to his belt pouches and delicately removed the still-wet parchment pages. "Some of these go back a few years, but I'll be damned if he wasn't nearly on the nose each time."

"On the nose with what?" Clyde said.

Flam flipped open the pages with care. "The Hidden Pale One will return." He eyed Clyde. "Wonder who he means there, huh?"

Clyde swallowed. "What else?"

Flam read on, "The spout city will get sacked. The corrupt king will flee and become corrupted further. The cyclopean man will give a sacrifice."

"Aksel," Rohm said.

"The queen will breathe new life into the sleeping things."

Nevele took one of the pages and skimmed it. "Might've been good to have seen these earlier."

Flam said, "Greenspire wrote here, in one, that he tried telling people, but no one would listen. And here he says he considered bringing the prophecies to us but doubted we'd believe him."

Clyde sighed. "Sadly, that's probably accurate."

"Anything about what comes next, Mr. Flam?" Rohm said.

"Pretty much ends with that, about Geyser."

From the irising door high above, Nigel brought the starship into the hangar, carefully setting it down alongside the deposit; a tight fit among the remaining Odium ships.

"Anything about you in there?" Nevele asked Flam over the engine noise.

"Actually, yeah," Flam said and noticed the crusher of men peeking around the deposit at them. "Come here, little fella."

Wringing his hands, compound eyes uncertain, he slowly approached. Flam took a knee and apologized for earlier. Whether or not the green child understood, Clyde couldn't say, but it seemed he comprehended Flam's sincere tone.

"Well, cut the suspense, then," Nevele said. "What'd Greenspire say?"

"The unbeliever nephew," Flam said, adopting the tone of a sage, "is to take over for the patron pilgrim, whereupon he will become the *believer* nephew, the new patron pilgrim."

Nigel rolled down the ramp of his ship and scooted their

way, followed by the Lulomba and Blatta—who crawled atop the deposit, running their hands over the familiar granular drawings, exchanging smiles and reassuring hugs. They seemed comforted to have this piece of home—even if it was thousands of miles away from where it used to be. A small thing.

"I suppose," Flam continued, "it means Greenspire knew he was going to . . . well, not make it." After a moment of him grinding his teeth, he stiffened his lip. "And he wanted me to take over." Unable to accurately paraphrase any further, Flam flapped the stack of papers open again with a flick of his wrist, making the coiled page snap open.

"Dear Flam, I know you probably think I've lost my mind. Most people do when someone takes on a rather new way of life that doesn't really agree with the person they used to be or the normal trend of things—believing odd things. And if you don't wish to take this burden upon yourself, I'd understand. But I do wish, since I know my end is coming, that you will find someone to take your place. Hand off the divinations, give them to someone who will follow them. I'm sure by now you've read a few and seen how accurate the seer has been. The Odium will take the wendal stone somewhere, and you must guard it once it's safe. Undoubtedly, where it's brought will be more secure than below Geyser. And if any of your friends has perished in the city's razing, I'm sorry. I know I will be lost, and I hope you forgive me for that. I hope to rewrite my destiny, if such a thing is possible, and if so you will never read this, so it won't matter.

"But I believe things will work as the seer has said, and I've already come to accept the divinations as they detail my life, the echoes whispered from ahead to our seer. I feel confident that when this deposit sets down wherever the Odium mean to take it, I will get to fight by your side. The child, prophesied as the crusher of men, will live on. He has much more to do in this grand scheme yet, and I hope you take care of Rogeff. Yes, I named him Rogeff. After my brother, your father. Do not take offense. I named him that only because your father Rogeff Flam was a great Mouflon. Anyone named after him takes him on as an example to live by, someone who was loving, understanding, and caring. And hopefully you, if you agree to be the new patron pilgrim and guardian of the stone, will be the source by which little Rogeff will receive his lessons on how to be a great man. I love you, Tiddle. Take care."

Tears in his eyes, Flam lowered the sheet.

Clyde said, "That's quite the charge he's put upon you."

After clearing the shimmer in his eyes with a thumb, Flam said, "Guys, I think I'm going to do it. I mean, in a backwards sort of way, Greenspire made me give my word. And you know what that means to Mouflons."

Clyde nodded.

"So," Flam said, hiking in a deep breath and letting it out, "I think I'm going to stay here. Maybe tidy it up a bit, carry out some of the dead bodies, find a place to put Uncle . . . you know, in a final resting place . . . and . . . well, start along with my new job. No one knows about this place. Where better to hide the deposit?" Flam put a weighty, warm palm on Clyde's shoulder. "I'm sorry, Pasty."

"Why?"

"Because it feels like I'm giving up, not coming with you guys to find this Nimbelle Winter person."

"Flam, you're doing *anything* but giving up. You're needed here."

Nigel cuffed Flam on the side. "It's not like ye'll be alone. Can't be expected to keep yer eyes open all hours." The Lulomba, atop their Blatta, came around, gathering among the stone's new guardians as they turned to Nevele and Clyde. He had to admit, they made an intimidating sight.

"It's not the end, Pasty. You can visit anytime, and we'll certainly help when we can."

"Aye," Nigel said. He saluted, adding, "Consider us your reserves."

After gathering the pirates and gray bone worms into heaps and setting them ablaze—no one was sure whether or not burying them would be a swell idea—they laid Greenspire and Aksel to rest.

In the fields of ice, a quiet patch past the statue of the Mechanized Goddess—which Flam said would be the first thing he'd remodel—the icy ground gave their shovels difficulty. The work warmed them, aided by the suns filtering from the fissure above. It was still horribly cold, but no one complained. This was for their friends.

They used his cane, a slender fang of sediment stone, as a marker for Greenspire.

A spike of crooked steel for Aksel, his name impressively etched in by Nigel's deft laser pick. Onto it, Clyde hooked Aksel's eye patch, the elastic hoop and black plastic dish tossing in the cold wind. Another for Miss Petunia Selby, for whom they needn't dig a grave, but the marker stood alongside their other friends just as proud.

Flam said some words from the teachings of Meech,

and for the first time Clyde heard Flam use the Mouflon tongue, a language composed of mostly hacking and snarling.

With Rogeff on his shoulder, Flam sang two songs. The first was upbeat, a rousing ululating that built and built, something befitting warriors. The second was a dirge. Clyde's eyes burned, his throat knotting. Nevele took Clyde's hand, their fingers warming, so tightly clenched.

The final few notes were sent ringing up through the hollow glacier, out over the white plains, the first chorus in Mouflonian, the second in Common.

"With us always, with us always."

While Nigel programmed the autopilot for Clyde, Nevele, and Rohm with a course set for Adeshka, Flam—mostly kidding—tried to ask them to stay. Whoever this Nimbelle Winter person was, like all bad folk, she would eventually make herself known.

Clyde, as hard as it was to do, politely declined Flam's invitation. Producing it from his pocket, Clyde showed him the hotel room key, room six, saying he, too, had made a promise. They'd set up a base of operations in Adeshka and begin looking for Nimbelle Winter there.

Nevele was quiet, Flam easily seeing she was working something through. She buckled herself in and stared out the window, looking lost.

Clyde extended a hand. Flam took it.

"I made for a rather shite knight."

Clyde stepped forward, turning the handshake into a hug. "Anything but. You fought for your city, Sir Flam. That's all I ever asked."

The starship, piloting itself, lifted off through the hangar doors above and through the split in the glacier, vanishing into the blizzard. Flam turned back to Nigel, the Lulomba, and Rogeff, surrounding the deposit. When he was a treasure hunter, he would've done just about anything to say this thing was his. And now he would do just about anything to keep it from falling into the wrong hands.

Maybe Moira, when she was playing Nula, had spoken something true. Maybe he did deserve better out of life.

Right here, watching over this, seemed like the ideal challenge. And he couldn't really beat a job with no dress code.

CHAPTER 30

Separation, Reunion

A deshka came into view. The entire flight in, Nevele's heart ached. She didn't want to be back there. Not because she detested the city but because she had to tell Clyde something before reaching it. She'd put it off the entire flight, unable to find the words.

The starship began descending in gentle dips. The ship swung over Déashune River and up into a repurposed cavern, finding a docking divot.

Clyde undid his harness, stood.

"Clyde, I have to say something."

She was interrupted as the depressurization process began, making her ears pop.

He paused at the hatch. "Something wrong?"

"No, but . . . when I told you what I did, in Nessapolis . . ."

"It's all right." He smiled, always the optimist.

"It's *not*, though." She made herself look him in the eyes, hold his hand. "I never told you about the things I'd done, during that period of my life. And I consider that the same as lying. Maybe I am more like my brother than I care to admit. If I could just bury those wretched things, I thought I could just ignore the fact I'd done them. But because I *did* do them and never told you, the person you *think* is me isn't really real. I wanted to be her, and for a while I thought I really was, but it was like a costume. And now that you know what's underneath, I—"

"Nevele, I don't care about any of that. I know you, the you *now*. That's all that matters."

"I hurt people. I thought since those people had abused their weaver children that they deserved the same, but . . . that's not how healing is done, and *you've* taught me that, but . . ." Uncurling one finger at a time, she let his hand go. "It shouldn't have taken you being in such a dire situation for me to tell you those things. I should've been honest from the start, maybe told you before . . ."

"I still want to marry you. I asked you to because I . . ." He faltered, always coming just *that close* to actually saying it.

"Say it," she said. "Tell me you love me."

"I won't. You know what'll happen."

"Say it."

The moment he left her sight, the next time he saw her, if he ever did, she'd be a total stranger. She wondered if he'd recoil at the sight of such a woman: stitches and cuts that would never heal, never mend, never close.

"I do . . . *do that*"—he took her hand—"with all my heart, but . . . I won't say it. I *will* say that I accept you, everything, good and bad."

Depressurization finished, the hatch finally slid open. The din of the city, even from this distance in the docks far below, plunged in, accompanied by the oppressive, humid heat—and that god-awful *stink*.

Nevele took her hand from Clyde, even as he reached for it, and stepped away. Pausing at the open hatch, she bit her lip to keep it from trembling. "I'll be in the city," she managed. "Do you still have your radio? Good. Keep it on. Give my condolences to Aksel's sister, if you would."

"Nevele. Wait, *please*."

She dropped out of the ship, and as soon as her boot heels struck the catwalk connecting the various suspended docks, she took off at a run, sobs choking her.

Up outside, through the front doors, people openly gawked at this strange, stitched-up woman crying as she ran.

She couldn't even summon a sneer right then for a one of them.

She heard Clyde calling her name but kept on. She pushed into what she once hated—the crowds and their staring eyes—but was thankful now for their camouflage. She brought up her hood and walked on, Clyde's calls fading behind her. Across one street, then another, not looking back. Forcing herself not to.

The ring in her pocket, she carried with her, ran a fingertip around its rim as she walked but didn't dare let it slide on. *She was engaged. I am not.*

Margaret Mallencroix reached into her bag, put on her mask so she could once again breathe easily, and then put on her respirator.

The city, without even going a few strides into it, seemed to engulf him. So many people, of every species, size, shape. He scanned every figure for anyone resembling Nevele. It was as though she'd disappeared, just as easily leaving his life as she had come into it.

"You still have me, Mr. Clyde," Rohm said in his

pocket, barely audible over the honking autos and trams screeching along their tracks. He patted the pocket to let Rohm know he'd heard him since he knew he wouldn't be able to answer, having a hitch in his voice.

He'd asked a few people for directions to the Chrome Cricket, but either he was entirely ignored or they'd just sigh, "Tourists." After hours of wandering, Rohm's natural sense of direction all but useless in this glass-and-steel labyrinth, they finally arrived at the tall narrow brick building on Delmark Avenue.

The sign above the door was also of holo; scan lines ran down the image of a robotic cricket bearing a fiddle and a corncob pipe and sitting on an overturned washbasin. Before stepping in, Clyde was nearly bowled over by a mob of people in long red robes rushing into the street. None spoke, but they were clearly trying to get somewhere—or away from something. Adeshka was a weird place, Clyde decided. A different world from Geyser. His heart sank. He might have to get used to the city. He had nowhere else now.

Entering, Clyde found himself in a cool, dimly lit corridor. Ahead was the check-in kiosk. Electric candelabras were set to either side of the heavily varnished counter where a lectern and sign-in book waited. Seated behind was a blonde woman, whom Clyde didn't need to be told was Aksel's sister.

She gave a somber hello once Clyde had stepped into the candelabras' undulating glow. "A room? A drink? Pub'll be open in a minute, just got a fresh cask of potato wine in if it's been that kind of morning," she offered with genuineness, warmth, and welcome, but clearly she had something else on her mind. Had she heard the news report? That Aksel was a wanted man? Had they announced it when he'd been executed?

Her forced smile eased away slightly "Aren't you . . . ?"

"Clyde Pyne."

"My *gods*, I just heard it on the news." She indicated an old radio on her side of the desk. She paused, turned her face, brow clouding. She turned back, slow, as if afraid to look him full-on. "They said a while ago that they got one of the men they think did that to that frigate. They didn't say which, though. I feel wretched asking since your city just . . . but do you happen to know if it was the one man or . . . ?" Her hand met reddening lips, balled into a fist in time with her eyes clenching.

Clyde didn't know how to say what he came here to say. He took out the key to room six and laid it on the counter—the heavy brass thing clinking on the varnished wood.

Vee Browne drew in a sudden, powerful breath, a choked gasp. Her gaze locked on the key as if it were her brother's bullet-riddled body. She collapsed back into the chair, out of the reach of the candelabra's electric light. Tears shined in the dark, and she shook and shook her head. "No. *No.* It must've been a mistake. He wouldn't've *done* something like that. Aksel was a good man. Don't tell me he's—"

"I'm sorry."

She sniffed, face hardening. "Was it *them*? Did they . . . frame him, set him up for that?"

"Who?"

She stared at the key on the counter between them. "Those three upstairs." Her hand moved under the ledger, fishing around for something. "They had something over him. I just thought it was, you know, having him rough people up, loan shark stuff, I didn't think they were bleeding *terrorists*."

Clyde recalled what Aksel last said to him. *Go get 'em.* He hadn't meant just the Odium when handing over the room key and the base's coordinates. Clyde asked Vee, "Did they look like I do? Are they still here?"

"I don't know. Never saw them." Vee freed what she'd been digging around for—a small revolver. She snapped it open, then closed, and came around the counter. Her eyes, framed with runny black eyeliner, were trained on the stairs ahead. "But I damn sure intend to go up and introduce myself."

"No," Clyde said, blocking her way. "I'll take care of it."

Up the creaky stairs into more dimly lit brick hallways, Clyde kept as quiet as he could. He approached the door at the end of the hall, silently unsheathed Commencement.

He leaned near the door.

"Mr. Clyde, I think I hear someone," Rohm whispered.

Clyde didn't hear anything but trusted the frisk mouse's ears over his own.

But then, a raspy cough. A man, older. Steady footfalls and the hiss of a faucet running.

"What should we do?" Rohm said timidly.

Not answering, Clyde wrapped his hand around the doorknob and, with his heart in his throat, turned it and pushed it aside.

The room had one bed, a figure asleep on one side, not stirring. He continued pushing the door, allowing him to scan the room as it swept wider, wider.

A woman stood before a dresser in the far corner, her back to him. Long, raven hair hung past her shoulders. She was dressed in a long-sleeved black tunic and leather trousers, heavy boots. She was sweeping her hair back in one drag of her gloved hand after another, gathering it for a ponytail—until her hands fell away.

Clyde's gaze switched to the mirror before her and realized she was staring right back at him—with a face not so unlike his own.

Remaining where he was, hunched in the doorway, sword ready, Clyde said nothing either but listened for others in the room with her. The faucet shut off, dropping the room into silence.

An older man emerged, flinched when he noticed Moira holding the gun and then again when seeing Clyde standing in the doorway. Facing him now, Clyde glimpsed toward him and recognized the man as Geyser's resident blacksmith, Grigori Gonn.

Clyde was about to ask what he, of all people, was doing here, when Moira spoke. A soft, efficient voice.

"What are you doing here?" She posed the question plainly, no fright in her voice whatsoever. Coolly, evenly, as if she'd been expecting him but merely asked the question as a formality.

"I could ask you the same thing," Clyde said.

The man in bed sat up. His face mirrored Clyde's own—except his eyes were covered in thick gauze, tied in a loose bandanna about his head. "Is that . . . Clyde?"

Stepping over to the man Clyde could only assume was Tym, Moira said, "We're packing up, preparing to leave."

Clyde let his gaze drift for a split second to survey the room some more. At the foot of the unmade double bed, a load of bulging luggage was neatly arranged. In a smaller, second room past Moira, what apparently could be used as a sort of office for the temporary residents, a third person—large, dark caramel skin, shirtless—sat before a set of holoscreens, eyes wide, hands raised. He looked like a younger Grigori.

"Karl," Moira explained, reading Clyde's confusion.

"My son," Grigori put in. He stepped near his own belongings, what looked like a hastily grabbed supply of toolboxes and portable gas-powered kilns.

"You were working for Raziel against your will, yes?" Clyde asked them, all of them. "That's what Flam said." He hoped he was right.

Upon hearing Flam's name, Moira visibly tensed. "Yes. *Raziel* wanted you dead. How . . . is Flam, by the way? Is he okay? We heard it on the radio, what happened to Geyser. And your fiancée?"

"They're fine," Clyde said, wanting off that subject. "We could've used your help."

Tym shifted in the bed, his bandaged eyes looking away from Clyde's general direction to Moira. Grigori, Karl, and Moira averted their gazes from Clyde. They were ashamed. Appropriately so, in Clyde's opinion. Still, he muttered an apology. What was done was done. There was no changing that. He'd failed as much as they had. Maybe more so.

"The Odium are through," Clyde went on. "Now we're looking for Nimbelle Winter. She, we've learned, is planning something."

Tym sat up. "Nimbelle Winter? Moira, isn't that . . . ?"

Moira frowned, stepped nearer. "There must be some mistake. She was a teacher at the academy. She'd never . . ." Her coal-black eyes looked away. Maybe she was remembering something—small tells she'd seen in Nimbelle Winter that, now, revealed her as a possible leader of a cult.

"Either way, she, whoever she is or was, has aligned with Gorett," Clyde said.

"Where are they?" Karl said, returning to his small room packed with computers, dropping into a chair, big hands hovering over holo-keyboards, poised.

"I don't know." Clyde recalled the rolled-up eyes and blackness-bleeding mouths of the afflicted pirates. Incubating inside each—if Dreck was to be believed—weren't just parasites, but wyrms. What if more of that were to happen elsewhere? In a densely populated place, like here, the affliction could spread quickly. His pulse raced as he remembered the promise—that he and his friends would not be spared.

Moira approached. Her hand landed on his arm, softly. For a flash, Clyde felt accompanied in his thoughts— something else was in his mind, tapping in carefully, not at all intrusive.

"If you'll have us, we can help."

Tym got up, navigating by touch. "As a family."

These people were strangers to him, but Clyde could sense they remembered him. Lots of years together had been expelled from his mind because he'd said three simple words to each, by their father's order. Why, Clyde still wasn't certain.

The same words Nevele had wanted him to say to her.

He wished he could take it back, remember his child-hood with his siblings. The gap echoed in its vastness, a struck-over portion of his life he felt would never be known. He'd just have to make new memories with them, from this point forward. That's all that could be done. The future was all they had.

"Karl and his father are quite skilled," Moira said.

"That we are," Grigori put in, with a grin and a tip of his ashy hat.

Moira smiled weakly. "Clyde, I'm sorry we—"

An ear-splitting alarm started up outside.

Rohm scampered onto Clyde's head, leaning over his forehead and out, whiskers flicking.

The five of them crowded at the windows, Tym asking Moira, panicked, what was happening.

Outside, barriers were being raised at the intersec-tions, blocking traffic with steel pillars lifting out of the asphalt. From the open window, the general din of a bus-tling metropolis shifted into a sharpness that illustrated fear spreading. On every holosign up and down the street, advertisements dropped away and were replaced: Quaran-tine Now in Effect.

Storming robotically past the Chrome Cricket below, guardsmen in full armor—adopting gas masks—formed a line straddling the street. Waving batons, they scraped foot traffic along, barking them off to their homes. A man leaped out from an alley, Clyde gasping. He had the papil-lae sprouting from his mouth, eyes rolled back, black slime draining from his nose.

It's already here.

The guardsmen halted, raised arms. The afflicted man

wheeled, screaming. A barrage of gunfire flung him to the ground. He lay still. The line of guardsmen moved on, parting around the corpse, on the search for more.

From their position above at their window, Clyde and Moira watched. Clyde's hand was still on her shoulder—and now, his fear wasn't isolated. She was letting him hear hers too. If it was meant to calm him, let him know he wasn't alone, it wasn't quite working.

"Moira, please, I can't see. What's going on?" Tym repeated.

"The coming blight," Clyde answered, echoing Nimbelle Winter. But Clyde didn't expect she meant *so soon*.

Tym moved back to the center of the bed, as if it were a shoddily crafted raft on tumultuous waters. Kneeling there, he turned his bandaged face from one corner of the mattress to the others, as if the arising awfulness were about to drag him down. "The blight? What blight? Moira? Clyde? Please, tell me what's going on."

Moira sat beside him, and Tym threw his arms around her, squeezing tight. She looked at Clyde—worry in her eyes.

Clyde turned to Grigori and his son, their faces lit by the yellow lights pulsing in through the room's windows all around. "Mr. Gonn," he said, having to say it twice to gain his attention, "do you have your tools with you?"

"Aye, right there." Grigori steered Clyde's gaze to the heaped stove, sooty billows, and the bundle of tongs held together with twine. "What do you need?" His voice was shaking, and he was clearly confused. Why would Clyde want something smithed right now?

With sirens wailing, Clyde had to speak up. He held

Commencement for the old, perplexed smithy to take. "I apologize asking you to undo your work, but will you turn this back into a gun?"

S rebrna Academy stood on the cliff, a frozen wave of azure stones—leaning, cresting, but not crashing. Once a daunting fastness, as far as Ernest Höwerglaz could recall, the lookout had been bought after the Skirmish and put to a new use.

It certainly looked like a fastness now. On the arch of its front gates, bodies hung by their necks. Teachers with multilayered robes turned in the breeze alongside uniformed students. Birds pecked at them, taking them back to nature. Ernest passed under their dangling feet, entirely indifferent. Specks of sand, just like those of the beach below the cliff, where he'd parked the *Magic Carpet*.

Figures in red, seeing him approach, all sprang to their feet—throwing aside cups of tea and smoldering mold pipes—and drawing guns. Like the professors they'd killed when taking this place, they too were robed—in uniform red. Red as the hair of the lady who emerged from the front doors of the school, a small smile playing upon her lips as she stepped onto the bloodied grass courtyard.

"Calm," she said, voice soft, to her underlings. They heeded at once, putting their weapons away.

She stepped toward Ernest in bare feet. A face of small, soft features. Wise eyes, a smattering of freckles, a narrow neck. Thirty, if a day.

She, too, wore a red robe. More illustrious than those of her followers.

She wasn't unaccompanied. Moving in her shadow, keeping time with her steps, a swirling gray plodded behind like an obedient dog. Ernest knew his own work well enough to know what—or who—the second shadow really was.

"I brought your ship," Ernest said. He had no fear of this woman.

Pale blue eyes traced the architecture of his face. He was old now, having dropped some of his years into the *Magic Carpet* to ensure it'd make it across the Margin, to here, Eastern Embaclawe. "Thank you, Ernest. Have some time for tea and cards?"

"I've always got time for a game."

"Good," Nimbelle said. She looked over a shoulder. "Zoya, dear? You're in charge."

A girl with brown curls—robed as the rest—nodded. When she turned to bark orders at the idle Sign of the Wyrm followers, Ernest noticed the girl's ears were packed with red-stained cotton balls. She met Ernest's gaze a moment, apparently feeling him looking. Despite her beautiful face, a trace of something sinister bled from her steely gaze. A shame, another spoiled talent courtesy of Nimbelle Winter.

"Shall we?" Nimbelle asked, hooking her arm in his.

Together Ernest and Nimbelle wound their way down the cliff to the shore. Upon approaching the *Magic Carpet*, Nimbelle's smile bloomed. She ran a hand down the flank of the starship lovingly.

Inside, caressing every counter and every inch of bulkhead as they moved into the crew quarters, she paused at a doorway. Upon the jamb, there were some notches starting two feet up off the floor. Her name next to each and her age. With a fingertip, she traced her father's handiwork with the knife from long ago.

When the kettle screeched, Ernest got up to take it off the burner, filling two cups. The smell of cardamom filled the air. He listened to her hands gracefully shuffling the cards, a rapid flicking sound as she scattered them into organized chaos again and again. Ernest set the cups down for her and himself and had a seat again. She began dealing, able to speak and count at the same time—something Ernest, even at his age, couldn't often successfully do.

"I've missed this rust bucket," she said, savoring the old smells. Sapping some years from it had undone some of the Odium's graffiti and wear and tear but not all. She didn't seem to mind what lingered.

"Glad to return it to ya. Rightful owner, after all." He picked up his cards once she'd tossed down ten to him and arranged them by suit. The game was Usurp, as always. "I hear y'all are already moving on to Adeshka," he said over his cards. "Quarantine got called about an hour back, I heard on the way over."

"Why postpone something if you're ready today?" she said mildly.

"You know the Skirmish is long over."

"Yes." She sounded amused. "Who's to say when a war truly ends? When the battlefield falls quiet or when all affected are dead and forgotten?" She smiled at her cards.

"I'm still around. I still remember. To me, it's still going—echoing around and around and around."

Ernest didn't feel much like philosophizing. "Ya get David Joplin?"

"No, the Pyne boy beat me to it." She repositioned a card within her hand, fingers graceful. Something just below the collar of her blouse shifted, swelling the material. She patted it, soothing its quaking. Her eyes returned to Ernest over her close-held cards. "But Chidester remains."

"Fancy yerself some kinda do-gooder, huh? Settler of scores? Ha. Then what're y'all doin' decoratin' the school with dead bodies? What about *their* families, *their* kids?" Some of the hanging corpses were children—a good number of them. "Their parents?"

Nimbelle eyed him coldly, same as the entity hovering just over her shoulder.

Ernest sighed. "Fine. We gonna play this game or what?"

"Go. I dealt."

He showed his cards. The mage, two princes, and a princess.

Nimbelle Winter snapped down hers. The queen, a prince, and a maiden knight.

Total stalemate.

The shade—darker than its surrounding shadow—shifted behind her, slate-gray eyes always watching, a second head. Breathing in slow rasps, it never contributed to the exchange, only watched—ambivalent, or simply not feeling that this was its place to say anything?

The thing in her blouse throbbed under the crimson fabric, illustrating its owner's excitement like an exterior heart. Her tell? Or evidence of a thrill in a game well won—or was it well cheated?

Ernest sat back. "Be honest now. Did ya stack this here deck?"

Nimbelle Winter grinned. "I don't know, Ernest. Did you?"

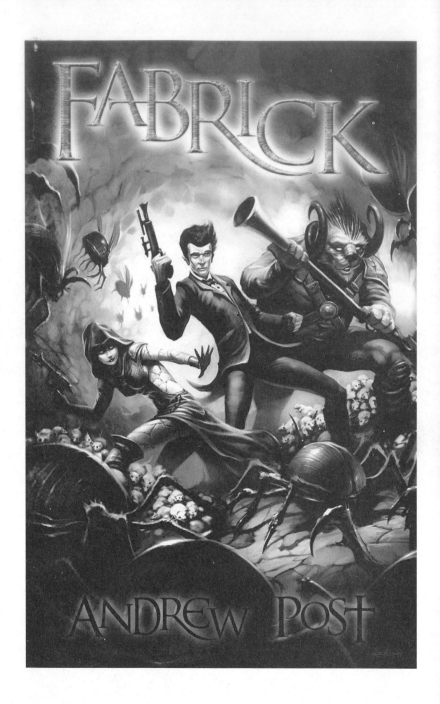

Book 1 in the Fabrick Weavers Series

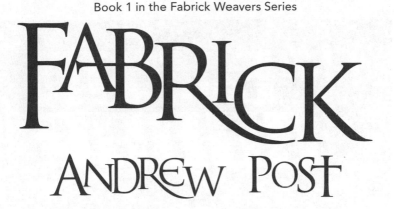

FABRICK

ANDREW POST

Clyde has worked for Mr. Wilkshire for a very long time. Life is comfortable in his keeper's chateau—until Mr. Wilkshire is attacked. Clyde reluctantly goes into hiding and emerges to find his only friend dead.

Brokenhearted and clueless how to bring Mr. Wilkshire's killer to justice, Clyde accepts the help of a unique group of friends, including Flam the Mouflon treasure hunter and Nevele the royal stitcher. Throughout their adventure, Clyde learns he isn't alone in this world with his magical ability: there are others like him called fabrick weavers, and for all it is both a special gift and a curse. His gift is to ease the conscience of anyone who makes a confession to him, but the curse is that the person's luck will be reduced in proportion to the severity of the offense.

Having left his pampered life behind to set things right, Clyde joins his new friends traveling into the razed city of Geyser, into the labyrinthine world beneath, and to the palace beyond. Along the way, the group deals with an unrelenting maniac pursuer, a corrupt king, a band of pirates, a small army of guardsmen, and just a few million dog-sized bugs—all while hopefully managing to avoid jinxing their own members.

Yeah, no problem.

$9.99 US/CDN
Young Adult | Trade
ISBN#9781605425016
Available Now

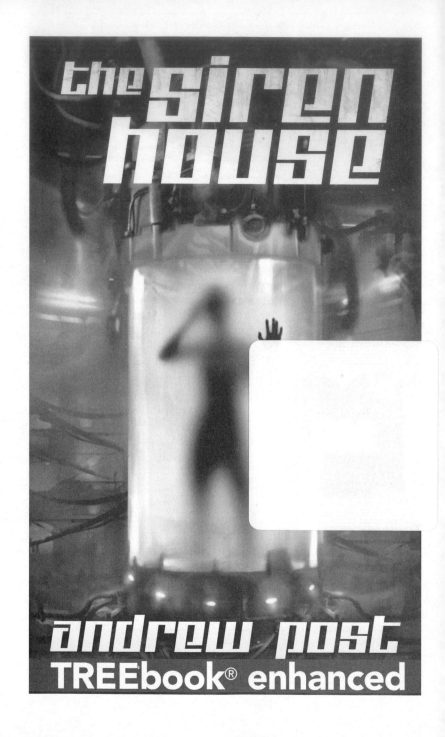

the siren house

andrew post
TREEbook® enhanced

Once upon a time, the world ended. Or maybe not.

As a kid, Cassetera Robuck has it hard enough, suffering from a nerve disorder that makes her legs useless. Then the apocalypse happens. To survive, Cassetera and her family make a new home of an abandoned oil rig on Lake Superior. There, she and her father discover a machine: one that can take things apart, molecule by molecule, and reassemble them.

Ten years later, her family all but lost, Cassetera heads into an apocalypse-torn Duluth, Minnesota, to find a man who calls himself the Fabulous Thadius Thumb, head writer and ringleader of the Thickskulled Thespians. He's also a resistance leader and, most importantly, knows how to use the machine.

Meanwhile, the Regulators work from a few dimensions over, escalating catastrophes with machines all too similar to Cassetera's. When she becomes their target, Cassetera finds herself in a web of betrayal, murder, and the mystery of her own multidimensional existence.

Can she uncover the truth behind the apocalypse before life on this universe ends?

ISBN# 9781605427263
$12.99
Cyberpunk/Sci-Fi
TREEbook® Enhanced
Coming Soon

TREEbook

thetreebook.com